ABOUT FACE

Also by Fern Michaels . . .

KENTUCY RICH

KENTUCKY HEAT

KENTUCKY SUNRISE

PLAIN JANE

CHARMING LILY

WHAT YOU WISH FOR

THE GUEST LIST

LISTEN TO YOUR HEART

CELEBRATION

YESTERDAY

FINDERS KEEPERS

ANNIE'S RAINBOW

SARA'S SONG

VEGAS SUNRISE

VEGAS HEAT

VEGAS RICH

WHITEFIRE

WISH LIST

DEAR EMILY

FERN MICHAELS

ABOUT FACE

Doubleday Large Print Home Library Edition

ZEBRA BOOKS
KENSINGTON PUBLISHING CORP.
www.kensingtonbooks.com

ZEBRA BOOKS are published by

Kensington Publishing Corp.
850 Third Avenue
New York, NY 10022

ISBN 0-7394-3413-6

Zebra and the Z logo Reg. U.S. Pat. & TM Off.

Printed in the United States of America

**This Large Print Book carries the
Seal of Approval of N.A.V.H.**

Chapter One

Dust covered the out-of-date eyewear displayed on the rotating rack, and the scent of stale smoke hung heavy in the air. Casey Edwards sneaked a look in the mirror on the sunglasses rack. Long-forgotten ads for Creomoltion cough syrup and Miss Clairol decorated the pea green walls of Reed's Drugs. Tom Clarence and Howard Lynch sat at the snack bar in the back of the store, mugs of coffee in front of them, cigarettes hanging loosely from their mouths. Casey knew they would be telling the story of the Great War the way they did every day of their lives. Howard and Tom were institutions. Each man would tell how he almost didn't make it home. Casey had overheard the story so many times, she knew it by heart. She knew when they would pause, look at one another, then shake their graying heads and continue on. They were as much a part of Sweetwater as the land. Both men raised a hand to her as she walked to the cosmetics counter. She smiled and waved back. She was in no mood for conversation today. She found the cream she needed and hurried to the register.

Today she wanted to be ignored.

It was the last time she'd buy concealer. Covering the bruise from the latest fight had been the clincher. For the second time in three weeks, she'd had to sneak to Reed's Drugs to purchase another tube of heavy-duty cover cream to disguise her latest black eye.

Sheldon Reed, Sweetwater's only pharmacist, had looked at her with suspicion. Laurie Phelphs-Parker—with a hyphen, mind you—who'd never lower her high standards (well, maybe temporarily as she liked to put it) to cashier for Sheldon since Mrs. Reed had died, clucked her tongue as Casey walked to the register. Casey wondered if Laurie remembered how her daddy left her momma high and dry. Took everything with him, too. Ran off with a girl younger than Laurie. Now, she *had* to work.

Everyone in town knew *that.* Laurie went to work at Reed's about the same time her snooty momma went to work as a teller at Sweetwater Savings and Loan. It was that or starve.

Casey adjusted her sunglasses and placed the tube of concealer on the counter.

"Hmm," Laurie muttered as she punched in the price, her bright red nails clicking on the register's buttons. "Seems like you been buyin' lots a cov-a-cream lately." She looked at Casey with an all-knowing smirk.

"I suppose Kyle wants a feisty woman now. You know when he and I . . ." Casey threw the correct change on the counter and grabbed the cover cream. As she opened the door, she heard Laurie's "Well, I nev-*uh*. . . ." followed by the flat slam of the screen as she made her escape.

If Laurie only knew, Casey thought. If she could only tell someone about the horror that had become her life.

The eight short years she lived with Mamaw were perfect. Her father's mother had been her protector and treated her like a daughter. Life was good then. She'd had hopes, dreams, and expectations. As she got older, she learned not to have expectations. That way she knew she'd never be disappointed.

She put the cream in her purse as she hurried along Sweetwater's Main Street. She had to be home before Momma returned from getting her hair done at Ida Lou's, or there would be hell to pay.

Safe in her room, she remembered why she'd risked a trip to town.

Kyle. She couldn't let him see her black eye. He would be shocked, and his parents would look down on her more than they already did. Kyle kept telling her they never meant to make her feel bad, it was just the way they were. She'd only been to Kyle's a few times, and always felt ignorant after leaving their house. Fiona, Kyle's holier-than-thou mother had done her best to make her feel anything but welcome. Kyle had coaxed her into each visit, telling her his parents insisted.

On her first visit Kyle led her to the dining room, where a lady with caramel-colored skin, snow-white hair, and a toothy smile served her a glass of milk along with a plate of fresh-baked chocolate chip cookies.

She'd told Casey her name was Myrtus, the hired help. Speaking over her shoulder as she stood by the door waiting for further instructions, she told Casey her friends called her Myrty and flashed a toothy smile. Kyle laughed as they'd seated themselves at the long, dark table.

"My, Lawd, Myrty, you'd think we was still elementary-school children, serving us cookies an' all." Kyle's words were laced with sarcasm, his Southern drawl dragging the words out. Casey recalled the look Myrtus gave him. Hard and cold as steel.

"If the shoe fits, Mr. Wallace." She'd looked at Casey and winked as she left the room.

"Don't mind that old bitch. She's been tryin' to boss me around for years. I don't understand why Momma keeps her on."

Casey bit into the cookie and thought that reason enough. She'd never had cookies so good, not even her grandma's.

"Excuse me, Kyle," a high-pitched voice shrieked from the hall. Casey looked up from her plate into the flat brown gaze of Fiona Wallace.

Wiping the crumbs from her mouth with her napkin, Casey stood and held her hand out to Mrs. Wallace. Her hand hung there, limp as a hothouse daisy while Mrs. Wallace turned to Kyle. Embarrassed, she jammed her hands in her skirt pocket.

"My goodness, son. I thought we'd agreed you wouldn't bring"—the tall, thin woman whispered and pointed her conelike head toward Casey—"her kind into this house."

Casey felt the heat rise from her neck to her face. She stumbled away from the table. Her awkward movement caused her chair to tilt and fall to the floor. As she ran for the front door, she could hear Kyle shout at his mother. The rest was a blur. And she'd wanted it to remain that way.

She'd stood on the porch taking gulps of fresh air as the screen squeaked, then banged against the wall. Kyle eased next to her, crowding her breathing space. She took a step back and glared at him.

"Casey, I'm sorry, and so is Momma. She thought you were someone else. I know that sounds feeble, but please, sweetheart, come back inside. Give Momma another chance."

Casey stared at him. He was sinfully handsome, with his blond hair, chiseled features, and bright blue eyes. A bit on the thin side like his momma, but still, she thought she was the luckiest girl in Sweetwater to have Kyle as her boyfriend. She wondered how his momma could mistake her for someone else. She had to remember to ask later.

Maybe his momma really thought I was someone else, truly. Kyle had dated a lot of girls. Maybe it was Brenda. Brenda always went for the best-looking guys in school.

"I suppose I should, that being the polite thing to do, but Kyle . . ." She'd let the words die as he put an arm around her and led her back inside.

"Momma says to tell you she's sorry. She doesn't see how she could have . . ." He never finished the sentence as he led her inside. He immediately excused himself, forgetting he'd invited her to stay. Mrs. Wallace didn't return to apologize, either. Casey knew she wasn't going to apologize when she heard her talking on the hall phone.

"That was some tramp Kyle brought home. Sewing his oats, you know." Fiona laughed. The rest was a blur, and Casey wanted it to remain that way.

Ashamed of herself, she'd walked home.

A slow rage burned deep in the pit of her stomach, and each step she took ignited the flame brighter. By the time she'd reached home, she'd calmed down, reminding herself what she stood to lose if she let Kyle get away from her.

Kyle had called the next day to apologize and invite her to dinner. Lately, things had been a little better.

Tonight she'd managed to convince Momma she was ill and had gone to bed early. After half an hour, she climbed out the window, her book bag filled with the only decent dress she owned. She'd stop at her best friend's house to change.

"Dammit, Casey, why do ya put up with that shit? You're almost eighteen, and still you have to sneak out." Darlene's drawl was thick like honey, her words flowing slow and sweet.

Casey looked at her best friend as if she'd lost her mind. "You know why. I don't want to go over this again. Just give me your curling iron, the one that crimps." Casey seated herself at the vanity while Darlene plugged in the cord.

Darlene stood behind Casey and took her time pulling Casey's thick tresses through the crimping iron.

"I can't believe you're still doin' what that mean ol' bitch demands. And that perverted stepbrother of yours. He makes my skin crawl." Darlene gave a mock shiver, the curling iron in her hand positioned like a weapon.

"As soon as Kyle and I get married, it'll be over." Casey told her friend about the beatings, the constant threats.

Darlene tilted Casey's chin and forced her to stare at her reflection.

"Look in that mirror. My Gawd! Why that bastard's hit you again. Why don't you kill him, Casey? Daddy's an attorney. I promise he'd have you outta jail in a minute flat. I'm about ready to go over there and kick his ass myself." Casey smiled at her friend's words.

Darlene was a true Southern belle, blond and barely five feet tall, with just a bit of northern bitchiness. Casey had learned early on never to underestimate her. What Darlene lacked in size, she made up for in opinion.

The day after they graduated, Darlene always said, she was going north to start a new life and she was never, ever, coming back to Sweetwater.

As her best friend brushed her hair, Casey closed her eyes and wondered what her teen life would have been like if she'd had a mother who cared about her as much as Darlene's did. Darlene's room, done in pink, white, and gold, was a young girl's delight. Casey remembered almost to the day when Darlene's mother had redecorated it because she'd been so jealous. She'd confessed her jealousy to Darlene. Then Darlene had promised her that whatever she had, she would share with Casey. After all, weren't they best friends?

"How do I look?" She danced around Darlene's room, the white, gauzy dress billowing around her.

"You look perfect. Go on. Knock 'em dead!"

Darlene gave her a final hug before shoving her out the door. "Git!" Darlene's laughter dimmed as Casey walked along Sweetwater's streets. Dinnertime, all was quiet. She prayed that none of her mother's friends would see her. Not that they'd ever venture to this end of the island, but you never knew.

Stately homes with long, sweeping lawns perched back from the street, their presence commanding respect for all they housed, whether they deserved it or not. Casey passed the gatehouse to the Worthington mansion. Mrs. Worthington used to be president of the Married Ladies Club before she died a while back. Casey despised the club. They seemed so petty to her. The *Sweetwater Sentinel* reported the meetings as if they were of national importance. Like who wore white gloves, who had a spot on her best white linen tablecloth, who had what to eat, who ate too much, and who wore last year's dress. Pathetic.

Casey didn't resent the privileged women their socializing, she just dreaded it when her mother ranted and raved about the secret meetings that went on. Casey knew her mother longed to be part of the monthly dalliances, but marriage to a man of wealth was required. And, unfortunately for Casey, her momma wasn't remarried, yet, only engaged. To John Worthington, no less.

Her mother used to complain about how they thought they were royalty and thought nothing of snubbin' those who slaved in their carpet mills. "Just remember your father," she'd said, "and remember what it cost him to work for the bastards. A pathetic excuse for a man," Momma had said. "In the end all he could do was die for the bastards."

Casey paused when she reached Kyle's house. It couldn't compare to the Worthingtons', but it wasn't a shabby dump, either. White brick, it was two stories high. A wraparound porch decorated with white wicker furniture and ferns placed along the porch in huge pots made it look comfortable and yet charming at the same time. Casey thought the place more than adequate, but she wouldn't admit to Kyle that she was the least bit envious of where he lived. She'd keep that thought to herself and maybe someday she, too, would have a home of her own. One that she could be proud of. One that she didn't have to be afraid in.

She rang the doorbell and waited. She hoped Kyle's parents weren't going to lecture her on the ways of polite society. It was 1987, for God's sake, and they were still acting like they were living in the days of Margaret Mitchell.

Kyle opened the door. When he pulled her close for a quick hug, Casey shuddered. This was something she'd get used to. She had to, if she was going to marry Kyle. She'd just close her eyes and pretend. . . .

"Casey, are you listening to me?" Kyle's deep voice silenced her thoughts.

She looked up at the man she was engaged to. Tall and fair, with slate blue eyes, Kyle was a dream. He'd turned many heads before settling on Casey, something he reminded her of quite often lately. Especially when they were parked at Lover's Cove. A part of her wanted to tell him to go after all those girls and leave her alone. The other part of her remembered where she came from. If Kyle wanted to boast now and then, so be it.

"How could I not listen to the best-lookin' man around? I missed you." Casey freed herself from Kyle's embrace and smiled. She knew he approved of her when his eyes sparkled, and his gaze traveled the length of her.

"Good Lord, Casey, where *did* you get that dress?" Kyle took a step back and continued his appraisal.

"It's my best. Do you like it?" Casey whirled around, giving him a glimpse of well-defined, tanned calves.

"You know I do. It's gorgeous on you, babe. It's just that . . . my parents . . ."

Casey felt as if she'd been doused with a bucket of cold water. Somehow, Kyle always managed to bring his parents into their private moments.

For a moment he seemed to be deep in thought.

"What, Kyle?" Casey stood under the soft glow of the porch light, unaware of how attractive she looked in the subdued light.

"Never mind. You're beautiful. Have I told you that lately?" Kyle took her elbow like the Southern gentleman he was and led her inside.

Casey was so nervous she felt like she could jump right out of her skin. What did Kyle's parents want? They knew about their engagement. They knew they wanted to wait until her graduation before they married. Maybe they were going to try to convince Kyle to wait until he finished college.

The evening passed slowly. Casey caught herself stifling a yawn more than once. After two hours of small talk, she finally got up the nerve to say her momma would be worried if she was late. She smiled her apologies and moved quickly to the front hall, Kyle following her.

"I'll drive you home, sweet," Kyle said.

She wished she could just blurt out that her mother would kill her if she found out she wasn't in her room.

"No, really, I prefer the walk. It gives me time to think about us. And other things." In the end she knew he would relent and let her have her way.

"Casey, you're not leaving, are you?" Fiona Wallace called to her as she opened the door to the front porch.

"I'm sorry, Mrs. Wallace. I have to get home." A chill ran down her arms when she saw the look that passed between mother and son.

"I wanted to talk to you earlier, Casey, but wasn't quite sure how to approach the subject."

Tall as Kyle and thin as a stick, Fiona Wallace was an unattractive woman, just short of being downright ugly, and with a disposition to match. She reminded Casey of Olive Oyl, except she lacked the friendly personality of the cartoon character. Fiona never bothered with makeup or an updated hairstyle. She wore dowdy clothes and shoes with the heels run-down. Casey was glad Kyle had taken after his father in the looks department.

Steeling herself for what she thought was about to be bad news, Casey was shocked when she heard Mrs. Wallace's words pour out of her thin pursed lips.

"Mr. Wallace and I have decided that you and Kyle might like to have a small wedding. Here at our home."

Casey reached for the doorknob to steady herself. "I don't know what to say," she said miserably. She looked at Kyle, who was leaning against the wall with a cat-that-ate-the-canary look. It was obvious to her that he'd known all about his mother's little surprise.

"I just found out myself this afternoon. I thought it would be best if Mother told you." Kyle looked at his mother, whose thin nose was almost at a ninety-degree angle.

Why is Fiona Wallace doing this? Casey wondered if she looked like an idiot. She certainly felt like one. Were they waiting for her to shout with joy, to throw her arms around them? Did they expect her to thank them from the bottom of her heart? Not in this lifetime. It was Kyle's idea to elope and save all the fuss and bother. Where was this wedding nonsense coming from? She felt a chill wash up and down her arms.

"Casey, aren't you going to say anything?" Kyle reached for her arm and pulled her away from the door.

"I'm too shocked. I don't know what to say," Casey repeated.

"See, Mother. I told you. You don't have to do a thing honey. Let Mother take care of all the details, and we'll be the talk of Sweetwater."

"But, Kyle, I thought we . . ." Casey could feel her heart pound. Just the thought of her momma and Fiona Wallace in the same room was going to kill her. They wouldn't need to plan a wedding, they'd be attending her funeral.

"Don't tax that pretty little head of yours about anything. You leave that to Mother. All you need to think about is the color of the icing on the cake."

Kyle turned to his mother. "If we could have a minute, then I'll be in and we can have a nightcap together."

Fiona nodded. "Of course, sweetheart. I'll need to talk to your mother, Casey. I'll call her at some point." Casey nodded. She didn't know what else to do. Fiona and her mother in the same room. A disaster waiting to happen.

"What do you think? Are you surprised? You'll be the talk of the town. Don't worry about a thing, Mother will handle it all. She's good at that sort of thing. That'll give you more time to think about ways you and I can . . ."

"For God's sake, Kyle! Is that all you can think about?" Suddenly all of her previous doubts surfaced. Could she really go through with this? Maybe she should tell Kyle the truth. Would he still want to marry her?

He whisked her to the side of the porch, away from the front door.

Drawing her close to him, he cupped her buttocks and squeezed, pulling her to his groin. Casey felt the swollen length of him and cringed.

"Seems that way when I'm around you." He continued to grind himself against her, all the while nipping at her neck.

"Stop it!" She tried to push him away, but he held her arms to her sides trapping her.

"Just relax, you don't know what you're missing." His words were slurred with all the wine he'd had during and after dinner. Releasing one arm, he traced the swell of her breasts through the thin gauze.

Casey froze. If she closed her eyes, she could pretend.

As fast as he'd pulled her to him, he thrust her away. "Goddamn it, Casey, you act like a fucking virgin. I know you're not, so let's just stop that bullshit right now. My parents are willing to pay plenty for you, the least you can do is give some kind of deposit on what I'm gettin'." He pushed her, making her stumble. She clutched at the porch railing for support.

Numb, she stared at Kyle. He'd plopped down in the wicker rocking chair, a smirk on his handsome face.

"What's gotten into you, Kyle? Why are you acting this way?"

"It isn't what's 'got into me' as you say, babe, it's what ain't coming out." He snickered.

Casey felt sick to her stomach. She'd thought he was different, her chance at a normal life.

"I'm going home. I'm going to forget this ever happened." Casey walked down the steps into the darkness. All she had to do was put this little incident behind her and not think about it again. Kyle was only a man. She knew he had desires and urges, all men did. She just thought he'd be a bit more gentle with her. She told him she wanted to wait until they were married. Until now, he'd respected her decision. Maybe he *did* think she owed him something. She would never have asked his parents for anything, let alone ask them to pay for their wedding.

Casey heard Kyle calling her name, but she ignored him. She wanted to go home and hide. Hide in her miserable skin and ponder what she was to do with her life. At eighteen she felt old and worn. Kyle was her chance to feel young, and carefree, but that's not the way she was feeling at the moment.

"Casey, dammit, I'm sorry." She heard Kyle's footsteps behind her and stopped. She felt the heat from his body as he slammed into her. They toppled to the ground, Kyle landing on top of her.

"I said I was sorry, what more do you want?" She could feel the swell of him come to life again as he thrust his groin against her.

Raising her knees between Kyle's sprawled legs, Casey dug her heels into the soft grass and scooted away from him. He was left grinding the lawn. If she weren't so frightened, she might have laughed. But she knew what could happen. And she wasn't willing to take that chance.

Kyle pushed himself up from the ground, giving her room to back farther away. Casey rose, brushing red dirt and grass from her best dress. It was ruined.

Freshly dug earth and mowed grass scented the night air as she stood trembling in the warm darkness. Kyle stared at her, yet said nothing. Knowing this was a turning point, Casey was afraid to say the words that would be the final cut. Let him say them.

Kyle took a step toward her, his hands held out before him. "My God, I don't know what's got into me tonight. I'm sorry, Casey."

Casey could only stare at him. She could feel her insides trembling, and her hands were visibly shaking. She squeezed the material of her dress to hide her tremors.

"Can we forget this happened, Casey? I love you." He looked like the twenty-year-old that he was. The hardened glint in his eyes softened. His posture, usually so ramrod straight, was now relaxed, casual, as if he were striking a pose for *Southern Gentlemen.*

He held out a hand as if wanting to call a truce. Against her better judgment, Casey held her arms out to him. He pulled her to him in a gentle embrace, placing her head on his chest. This was right. He was comforting her. The rest would come later, she just needed time. She lifted her head and looked at Kyle. He cupped her chin with both hands and slammed his groin into her. Hard.

"Stop!" Casey pushed at his chest while he clenched her face between his hands. She struggled and stepped back.

"You teasin' bitch. You just wait." Releasing her chin, he laced his fingers around the neck of her dress and pulled. The white, gauzy material shredded like paper.

Casey stood still. She knew better.

Her ragged bra went next. He pulled the straps down from her shoulders and ripped the cups apart, tossing them to the ground.

She covered her breasts with trembling hands and prayed that he wasn't going to rape her.

My God, this is Kyle, the man I'm going to marry.

The night air was cool, causing her nipples to harden. Kyle's hands grazed the pebbled nubs. Taking each nipple between thumb and forefinger, he pinched her, then laughed.

Casey couldn't move. She was on fire, each tug sending jolts of pain throughout her body.

"I knew you'd have big breasts."

Casey heard the clack of metal as he un-hooked his belt. Then the zipper.

"Dammit, don't just stand there. You want this as much as I do."

Casey looked past Kyle to the sidewalk in front of his house. When she'd left only moments ago, she ran into the darkness provided by the trees at the end of the lawn. There was no chance they'd be spotted by Kyle's parents. There was no one to come to her aid unless she screamed.

Kyle's blond head was at her chest. He licked her nipples, then bit her tender flesh.

Tears blurred her vision as Kyle continued his journey downward.

In one swift movement her panties were a white dot on the dark lawn. Kyle's breathing was heavy and coming fast. Casey went limp, knowing that if she put up a fight, she'd lose.

Kyle pushed her to the ground and pulled

his pants to his knees. With only one hand holding her down, Casey gave a mighty shove and rolled away. A second later, the torn dress clutched to her body, she ran through backyards, across garden hoses and lawn chairs, until she was out of breath. When she found a thicket of oleander, she wiggled behind it and crouched. She waited, hardly daring to breathe, until she was certain she could move and try to wrap her dress around her. She ran home as fast as her feet would take her.

Their house was one of the oldest on the block. Her grandmother had given it to her father when she moved to the new condo ten years earlier. Casey still hated the place, even though Grandma had lived there. Nothing but bad things happened to her in that house. She couldn't wait to leave.

Two stories high, with peeling yellow paint, the house could have been nice if her momma had spent some money on repairs. Momma said it didn't matter what the outside looked like. It was the inside they all ought to be worrying about because that was where the people looked. They liked to look at fine things, lace curtains and thin china.

At her window, Casey quietly lifted her screen out, shoving it through the open window. The scent of honeysuckle and confederate jasmine lingered in the night air as a cat's screech startled her. She drew in a deep breath as she hiked one leg over the windowsill, then the other.

Inside, Casey's glance darted around to make sure no one was in her room. The chain lock that on occasion provided her with a bit of safety was still in place. Her room was secure. It only took a second to put the screen back in place.

Leaning against the window frame, Casey viewed her room through the eyes of a stranger. What would a stranger think of the twin bed with its thin mattress? The white chenille spread worn with age? The oak night table covered with nicks and water rings? Her chest of drawers was a pale blue; she'd painted it herself. Many times. Posters, curled at the edges with age, hung lifelessly on the faded walls. The ballerina lamp, the one Grandma Gracie had given her, was the only girlish decoration in the room. It wasn't a room like Darlene's.

She knew she should soak her stained dress in cold water but that meant she would have to leave her room, and she had no intention of unlocking the door. She should also call Kyle and tell him to go drop dead. No matter how desperate she was to leave this house, she knew now she could never marry him. She would call him first thing in the morning, and, if he was still sleeping, she'd leave a message on his answering machine. She placed the dress in the back of her closet, along with her shoes. Tomorrow would be time enough to soak it in cold water. Maybe it wasn't worth it since Kyle had ripped the entire bodice. She eyed the chain lock. She'd better unlock it. Momma would raise nine kinds of hell if she tried to open the door and couldn't get in. So much for privacy. Once she'd asked Momma why she couldn't keep the lock in place. Her answer had been a slap to the face. Her momma had said if she weren't such a slut, she could lock the door. Momma said she didn't want no surprise guest greetin' her when she went to wake Casey up for school. Casey knew that wasn't the reason. And Momma knew it, too.

Gently, Casey slid the chain from its lock and let it dangle against the door. She lay on the bed, hoping for sleep. Praying to be left alone. Tonight of all nights. Tonight, when she felt her future slip through her fingers, she wanted to be left alone.

Chapter Two

Casey woke to the sound of the front door slamming. She shoved the thin spread aside and prayed it was Ronnie who'd left.

She squeezed her thighs together. Still tender from the night before, she winced as she remembered how Kyle had gone off the deep end. She bolted from the bed and quickly slipped the chain lock back in place. What mattered just then was getting out of there. She wasn't going to wait around for Kyle to apologize. Last night was beyond her wildest imaginings. She tried to conjure up a mental picture of marriage to Kyle. It was an impossibility. When something was over, it was over.

Where Kyle was concerned, all she had to do was tell Momma they had a fight and wanted to stay apart for a while. Her mother would rag on her, but she was used to it.

In the back of her closet, inside the Folger's can, rested her life savings. Four hundred seventy-three dollars and sixty-seven cents. How she'd managed to hang on to that much money astounded her. Momma kept track of every penny she'd earned baby-sitting. On occasion, unbeknown to her mother, Casey would help Flora, who was the Worthington's housekeeper, with a housekeeping job. She tried to keep these small jobs secret from her momma because she always knew the day would come when she'd have to run.

That day had arrived.

The white dress stuffed in a ball reminded her of her shattered dreams. She'd often dreamed of what her life with Kyle would be like once they were married. A small house, not too big, but with a yard filled with trees. And she'd plant a garden. Kyle would have fresh vegetables served at every meal. After the dishes were finished, they'd hang a damp, flowered dish towel over the edge of the sink, announcing the evening as theirs. After a pot of coffee, they'd remember the dog. Hand in hand they would stroll along

Sweetwater's serene streets, with their Labrador leading the way.

It was a pipe dream. Even she knew that. She couldn't believe she'd harbored such juvenile dreams. With her life as it was, she would've been lucky to nab a weekend drunk from Paw's, the newest club in Brunswick. People like her didn't snare the richest, most eligible guy in town. People used people like her to slake their lusts and serve their families.

Casey grabbed the red can and held it close to her. Her future was in that can. Picking her book bag up from the closet floor, Casey ran her fingers along the wire hangers that held her pitiful wardrobe. A pink, cashmere imitation went first, followed by several loose shirts. Forget the clingy fashions of late. She preferred the full, shapeless style of the sweatshirts and baggy jeans.

Grabbing an old denim purse from the top shelf, Casey dumped the contents of the can into it. She tucked the purse inside the book bag. A picture of her and Kyle, along with Darlene and a boy named Henry, stood on her dresser. She grabbed the photograph, frame and all, and stuffed it in the book bag, too. Fleetingly, she thought it might be her only reminder of where she came from when she left the godforsaken island.

Having no idea where she was going intrigued her. She would travel north; maybe she'd end up in New York, then again, maybe she would go to Atlanta first. She'd decide later. When she had time. To think and plan. That day, however, she had to leave school early and stop by Doc Hunter's office. She'd called yesterday for an appointment, so it was all set.

"Casey, get up!" Her mother's gruff voice sent a quiver of alarm through her.

She had to act normal.

"Comin', Momma. I'm almost dressed." At least that much was true.

She prayed that Ronnie wouldn't pop back in as he was sometimes known to do. With him there, she'd never get a chance to leave.

Placing the stuffed bag under the bed, Casey looked at her image in the mirror. She didn't look any different. She was still the same person. The same dark hair fell to her waist. The same shadows lurked beneath her pale green eyes. The familiar fear rested in the pit of her stomach. That hadn't changed either. She kept staring, waiting to see if somehow she would change. Nothing happened. She still looked the same, still felt the same. How strange. Nothing different.

"Casey." Her mother's harsh tone bellowed down the hall.

Peering over her shoulder one last time, Casey was assured her mother wouldn't know what had happened to her.

Casey suddenly realized there *was* a difference after all. She would think about it later.

Casey entered the smoke-filled kitchen and hurried to the refrigerator, where she grabbed eggs, butter, and bacon. For as long as she could remember, she had made breakfast for Momma. If Ronnie was home, she made breakfast for him, too. All the while Momma would sit in silence, sipping a cup of coffee as Ronnie poked fun at Casey. Sometimes Momma egged him on.

Thank God Ronnie was working the early shift at the mill. He'd know something was up. His eyes wouldn't be glazed with alcohol at this time of the morning the way her momma's were. His brain wouldn't be as slow as Momma's either. One thing about Ronnie, Casey couldn't put anything over on him. He had his way of getting things out of her.

"Damn, girl! Hurry it up. I'm hungry, and you'd better not be late for school."

Casey quickly placed the iron skillet on the electric burner and laid several strips of bacon in the pan. Within moments, the kitchen was filled with the aromatic sizzle of bacon frying and brewing coffee. The whirl of the whisk beat against the sides of the bowl as Casey whipped eggs into a froth.

"I don't know what's up with you, girl. You been laggin' behind. You shoulda been up for Ron. He's got a hard day to put in at the mill, he needed to be fed," her mother said between puffs of cigarette smoke.

"Sorry, Momma, I didn't know." Casey hunched her shoulders in anticipation of a blow. When she didn't receive one, she turned to observe her mother, who sat at the table chain-smoking.

Evie Edwards was a beautiful woman. Alcohol and anger had roughened her features, but Casey knew it only took a few nights away from the alcohol to ease the lines and soften the expressions so commonly etched in her mother's face. Yes, her mother could be beautiful on the outside. Inside, Casey knew, she was filled with rage. Rage at her lot in life. Casey didn't know all the details of her mother's childhood, but knew something tragic must have happened to turn her into a mean, bitter woman. It would probably all change now that she was "seeing" John Worthington.

Her mother crushed the cigarette in the ashtray and lit another. Casey saw her hands shake as she held the match. A wave of pity washed over her. Pity that she couldn't have the kind of mother she'd always wanted. Pity that her mother had lived as she had, never allowing anything but harsh, cruel words to exist between them. She vowed right then and there that if she was ever fortunate enough to have a family, she'd never allow a day to pass without telling her children she loved them. And when she said the words, she would mean them.

Taking the bacon from the skillet, Casey poured the egg mixture into the hot grease, the smell gagging her. How her mother could eat like this first thing in the morning was beyond her comprehension. She could barely manage to force lunch down her throat. She knew she had to eat something or her mother would notice she had lost weight and all hell would break loose.

"More coffee, Momma?" Casey knew the routine. She hoped this would be her last performance.

Evie slid the cup to the edge of the table and waited while Casey poured the hot brew.

"The eggs are ready." Casey filled her mother's plate with eggs, bacon, and a slice of white bread, lightly buttered just the way she liked it.

"Took you long enough, girl. You look kind of funny to me this morning."

Casey froze in her tracks. "Sorry, Momma. That thick bacon takes a bit longer. Ronnie likes it. I thought he'd be here to eat with you."

Casey knew any mention of Ronnie would hush her mother. Anything for Ronnie. Casey couldn't understand the unnatural relationship they shared.

"I don't think you have enough to do at that hoity-toity school. And you make sure you get home on time. I'm going out tonight with *Mistah* Worthington," she drawled. "Ronnie will want supper early."

Dread caused her hands to shake, and the plate almost slipped from her hand.

Evie speared a bite of egg and continued to talk as Casey sat across from her, waiting for the usual assault to end so she could go to school to get away from her mother, the house, and Ronnie.

Casey took the long way to school; anything to drag out the minutes. Since it was going to be her last day, what did it matter if she was late? The only reason she was going at all was because her mother might take it into her head to call and check on her. She'd done it many times before.

She turned the corner and saw Doc Hunter picking up his morning paper. She ran over to him. "Doc, do you think you could see me now instead of later? I can be a little late for school if it's all right with you." The old man looked at her over the top of his glasses and nodded.

Thirty minutes later, a dazed look on her face, Casey walked down the path to the sidewalk. She knuckled her eyes as she tried to see past the tears that were blurring her vision.

Her plan was to leave as soon as she finished her last class. She'd walk to the ferry and afterward hitch a ride.

She turned when she heard her name called. She frowned at the sight of Flora, who helped her mother out occasionally. "Casey, hold on. You have to go back home. Your momma's been taken to the hospital." The tiny woman gasped for air as she took a deep breath and rambled on. "I just stopped by to tell your momma I'd help her today. I found her on the kitchen floor, white as a ghost, clutching at her chest. You'll need to be taking some fresh nightgowns to the hospital and a few other things."

"What . . . what's wrong with her? Did they say? Is she going to die?"

"I don't know, child. Can't you make those feet of yours go any faster? Might be the best thing for your momma. Maybe those doctors can *dry* her out."

"I don't know what to do, Flora. Tell me what to do."

"I'm tryin' to, kiddo. First you have to call the hospital. Maybe you should go there. Pack a little bag for your momma. I already called the mill and told Ronnie. Hurry now, Casey. I'll call you later to find out how she is. You might want to take a few posies from the garden."

And then she was gone, almost running down the street. Where did the little woman get all her energy?

Ten minutes later, Casey let herself into the house through the kitchen door. She saw everything at a glance—the breakfast dishes, the overflowing ashtray, the littered counter, the chairs pushed away from the table. One of her mother's slippers glared up at her from under the table. She looked around for the other one but couldn't see it.

Would her mother die? Probably not. Her grandmother had once told her only the good die young. Looking at the card she'd picked up, she decided to call them right away.

The phone was in her hand a moment later. After making her call, she dialed information for the number of the hospital and copied it down carefully. It was ten minutes before she was able to speak to anyone who knew what was going on with regard to her mother. Finally, the charge nurse on the surgical floor told her Evie was undergoing some tests and more than likely would be discharged by the end of the day.

Casey digested the information, thanked

the nurse, and hung up the phone. A few more hours wouldn't make a difference to her getaway plans. She could spend the time cleaning up the kitchen, run the sweeper, and do a load of laundry.

The kitchen door slammed shut. The sound was so loud she heard it on the second floor.

Ronnie.

Of course he would come home. Anything to get out of working. She crossed her fingers that he wouldn't go through her book bag and find her money. Tiptoeing quietly, she left her mother's room, crossed the hall, and walked down to her own room, where she closed the door and slid the chain into place. She was shaking from head to toe. *Don't let him come up here. Please, God, don't let him come up here.*

Her movements were jerky, uncoordinated, as she staggered across the room to open the window. Her hands were shaking so badly she dropped the screen to the ground. She had one leg over the windowsill when she heard Ronnie's boots on the steps. She literally froze in position.

"Open this damn door, Casey. I need to talk to you. I want to know what's wrong with Momma." He could see her through the narrow opening. How much of a chance did she have? Better to drop to the ground and make a run for it.

She hit the ground hard. The breath knocked out of her, she had to wait till her breathing returned to normal. Gasping for breath, she picked herself up and ran around the house. It was her first mistake. Her second mistake was thinking she could hide in the tool shed. She looked around, frantic, for some kind of weapon. She saw the garden spikes leaning against an old wooden table. She thought of it as a spear as she hefted it in her hands, her eyes on the sharp point at the end of it.

She smelled him the moment he burst through the door, his face as hateful as Momma's was sometimes. She knew what he was capable of doing, knew every move because he was brainless and predictable.

He saw her crouching behind the barrel that held peat moss. He lunged, but she held her ground. He lunged again. This time she let him see the spear in her hand. He laughed, a maniacal sound that she'd heard so many times before. This was going to be the last time.

Her shame would stay with her forever. Always.

Like a fingerprint, it was a part of her.

She had to be cunning.

She brought up her arm, the spear clutched tightly in her hand. He lunged and grabbed her arm just as she drove the spike downward into the fleshy part of his thigh. His scream was high-pitched, almost a feminine squeal. She yanked the spike loose and prepared to strike again. He cursed her as he clutched at his leg. She brought the spike down a second time but he rolled away, and the bloody spike hit the edge of the battered table.

He lunged for her, a clay pot in his hand. He whipped it across the side of her face, and she fell to the floor. As she scrambled away, she could feel the warm blood trickling down her neck. *Where are the spikes; where are the spikes?* She crawled toward the door just as Ronnie's work boot shot forward. She took the blow to her stomach and doubled over. He lunged again, but she scrambled backward out of the way.

She was outside now, clutching her stomach as she tried to straighten up so she could run to the house. He was coming after her; she could hear him dragging his injured leg across the rough boards of the garden shed. She could hear him cursing, words she'd never heard before.

She had to get out of there. Stumbling, falling, she made her way to the steps of the back porch, where she collapsed. She reached for the railing to pull herself upright. He was less than twenty yards from her when she saw the broom leaning against the steps. Using every ounce of her strength, she whacked it hard over the banister. The jagged edge of the handle was her reward. She held it out in front of her; it was her lance, and she was preparing to joust. It wavered in her hand.

"Come one step closer and I'll ram this down your throat, Ronnie. I mean it. One more step, and I'll kill you. I'll kill you dead." Either her weapon or her tone of voice slowed him down, giving her just enough time to get into the house and lock the door behind her.

Frantically, she looked around for the portable phone. When she didn't see it, she started to cry. It could be anywhere. Her mother was forever taking it with her, then leaving it. They had to wait for the phone to ring so they could find it. This was one of those times. No, no, that wasn't right, she had used it when she came home. *Oh, God, where did I leave it? Where?*

The only room in the house that had a lock on it was her room.

Her belly was on fire as she made her way to the second floor and the safety of her room, the broom handle still clutched in her hand.

She fell on the bed and for the first time was aware of a trail of blood leading from the door to the bed. She looked down at the bed and saw the pooling blood.

Her blood. She closed her eyes to blackness.

Three hours later, Eve Edwards walked into the quiet house. She felt foolish and even a little embarrassed. Taken to the hospital for heartburn. Still, it had felt like a heart attack. *Better to be safe than sorry. It's all Casey's fault, frying those eggs in all that grease. That girl can't do anything right. Well, it's time she learned.*

Chapter Three

Sweetwater Island
August 1997

Casey took a final glance around the room that had been her home for the past ten years. A sad smile touched the corners of her mouth as she scanned the institutional gray walls, softened somewhat by the dime store prints she'd hung on her arrival in a rare moment of lucidity. The pictures looked desolate and faded. Like her. A shadow of her former self.

Sun trickled in through the small second-story window, its thick glass covered with what she had laughingly termed chicken wire. Severe in its bareness, it remained unadorned. No attempt made to suppress its austerity. No attempt was allowed. The view forever the same. The bars that held her captive awaited their next victim.

Casey heard the rattle of keys and knew it was time. She looked around one last time. Many times she had wondered what it would be like to walk out of the asylum. Her heart gave a sudden leap as Sandra, her nurse, placed a hand on her shoulder. Her wish was about to be granted.

"It's time, baby. C'mon. You have your things ready?"

"Yes. I'm ready." And had been forever, it seemed.

Sandra opened the door and directed her to the hallway. Chipped gray paint covered the walls. In some places you could even see where the plaster had been patched over. Another glob of plaster of paris couldn't disguise the years of neglect. Her heart pounded as she took a final step into the hallway. Fear enveloped her, suffocated her like a plastic cloth. Casey drew in a deep breath in hopes of calming her sudden burst of fear. What would it be like? Could she function outside the hospital? Would the world accept her? Knowing what awaited her on the path to freedom, she paused. Unprepared for the rush of emotion that flooded her, she lingered before taking that final step down the solitary hall of madness. She knew. She'd been there.

Her first clear memory after her arrival was of being jabbed with a needle. Voices, some muffled, some painfully loud, asked if she could remember. Her mouth had felt like cotton balls were lining it. She'd been in a fog, and her eyes felt like hot bricks rested on them. Her legs were heavy, sluggish when she tried to move them. Raw. She remembered being too sore to move. And empty. Then came the nothingness, the hours of trying to focus on the blank state of her mind, all to no avail.

After weeks, or it could have been months, she couldn't recall, Dr. Macklin had left her alone for a while. But that was before the drugs began. And the nightmares. She'd lived in a state of fog for so long, those last weeks seemed unreal. No drugs. She could actually think. And she was starting to remember. Slowly she was returning from her journey into the black pit of hell.

The echoes of the lost ones continued their cries down the lonely halls. Casey heard their desperation. The sadness. This had been her home, its occupants her family. She had to leave. She could never return.

Sandra gently pushed her forward, bringing her back to reality. "Keep going, and you'll be out of here in no time," the nurse whispered.

Tears glistened in Casey's dull green eyes. "I know. I just feel sad leaving."

Wheels on dinner carts whined, and the clatter of metal lids bounced off the flimsy walls lining the long corridor. Mrs. Mullens, or Mrs. M. as some called her, chose that moment to enter the hall.

"You must go, Casey. Meet me in the main hall in ten minutes. Your ride should be here by then. And your clothes, don't forget them," Sandra said as she glanced at her watch and excused herself to tend to the elderly woman.

"Now look, Mrs. Mullens, what are you doing with that?" The nurse's hoarse voice could be heard across the room as she took the bedpan from the petite woman.

"I want to give Casey a gift. She's my girl, you know that? She knows that. Everyone knows that. Don't they? You know that?" Mrs. M. whimpered to Sandra.

Casey watched as Sandra took Mrs. M. to the dayroom and led her to the sagging green sofa by the door.

"Yes, Mrs. Mullens, I do. You sit here, I'll be right back." Sandra's muffled footsteps could be heard from across the hall.

After her arrival three weeks earlier, Mrs. M. had assigned herself as Casey's official mother since she had no family of her own to speak of. Or if she did, Casey pondered, they'd never visited in the short time she'd been coherent enough to notice. She would miss the elderly lady and the unusual gifts she lavished upon her in recent weeks. She walked into the room and sat next to the poor soul. Giving her a last hug, she turned so the old woman wouldn't see her tears.

"Good-bye, Mrs. M. I'll write to you." She wondered if someone would even bother to read the letters to her. Sandra was the only decent nurse in the hospital. She could barely keep up with the patients as it was. Suddenly, Casey had reservations about leaving. What would become of Mrs. M.?

The woman's ragged voice jolted her back to the present.

"Will you? I want those chocolate-covered cherries, the kind with the white stuff." Dull gray eyes held hers, seeking a promise.

"I'll get you the creamiest-filled cherries I can find." She blinked back another round of tears. Casey vowed to herself that she wouldn't abandon this woman who had treated her like a daughter in such a short time. She'd been especially close to Mrs. M. since the doctors had eased up on her medication. She didn't recall being close to anyone before that. Ever. Somehow, she'd arrange for a visit. Sandra told her the hospital frowned on former patients returning to visit, not that she'd ever witnessed any such happenings. Maybe Sandra would help her. With Mrs. M. returning to oblivion, she walked to the doorway, peering into the hall.

Casey spied Sandra with Jimmy John Johnson, or Three Jay as he liked to be called. She caught the nurse's eye and pleaded with her. Hurry.

The rattle of dinner trays continued and could still be heard over the soft moans and wails of the patients. She watched as Sandra tucked a cloth napkin around Three Jay's turkey neck. Recent experience told her this could take hours.

Taking the paper out of her breast pocket, she read her mother's address for the millionth time. Swan House. What kind of place was it? Would she fit in? What would they think of her? She stuffed the paper back into her pocket.

She knew from Sandra it was a short walk into town, the island only a few miles long. She would find her way. Alone. Casey glanced at her drab smock. It would have to do.

Anxious to leave, she gave Mrs. M. a final hug and sped down the hall, not bothering to wait for the change of clothes Sandra promised. She passed several of her friends on the way. Some waved, some grunted and threatened. Some weren't coherent enough to even think.

She felt their emptiness, their isolation, their fear. As she turned the last corner, she stopped and gazed around her. The gunmetal gray walls stood like defeated soldiers, their last bout with chivalry lost. Echoes of the wounded wailed in the ongoing war to survive. She would no longer have to fight that never-ending battle. For her, it was over. She was really going home. A life of her own. They had taken ten years from her. Ten lost years she could never reclaim.

As she stood on the steps of the dilapidated building, she cast a last glance at the second floor and spied her former room.

The chicken wire would imprison another. She'd served her time. A thrill tingled down her spine, and her belly knotted in anticipation. For the first time in her adult life, she was free.

The address on the scrap of paper wasn't at all familiar to her. She had no recollection of ever having lived there. Nothing.

Her mind remained as blank as a freshly erased blackboard.

She was at the edge of Sweetwater Island according to the faded sign nailed on the rotted fence post. Downtown was another mile. Apparently paved roads hadn't reached this end of the island. Red clay swirled around in small whirlwinds at her feet, leaving a thin layer of dust on her hospital-issued sneakers. The August sun beat down on her pale skin, reminding her where she'd spent most of her life. Outdoors hadn't been off-limits, yet Casey couldn't recall spending more than an hour at a time on the hospital's unkempt lawns.

Situated at the southern tip of the island, Sanctuary was as reclusive as its occupants. Brick walls prevented a view beyond the grounds. Casey hadn't dared an attempt to journey beyond them. She surveyed the island as she walked along the dusty road. She searched for a sign of recognition, anything familiar to pivot her stagnant memory into the past and merge it with the future.

Her life at the hospital had been boring, if you excluded the bouts with the doctors, the fights with the needles. Needles that sent her into never-never land. In a constant fog, she often felt she'd been close to remembering something. At times brief, fleeting thoughts skittered along the edge of her memory, only to be snubbed out by the sharp sting of a needle.

She'd had no proof. Nothing. Only the gray images that teetered on the brink of her subconscious.

Now, was another matter. Each dust-covered step led her to freedom. She was getting a late start, but a fresh start. She was free. Free to be. Whatever that was.

With the spring of freedom to her step, she didn't mind the late-August heat, nor did she care that her throat was parched. However, she wouldn't turn down an icy bottle of Coke.

Sandra had given her a brief history of the

island, telling her its inhabitants were a close bunch, and many could trace their ancestry back to Thomas Carnegie, who in the late eighteenth century purchased Sweetwater Island, known as one of the Golden Isles in its day. Carnegie, Sandra said, had built many a mansion on the island, and though it no longer was quite the social gathering place for the nineties, some of the traditions were still very much in place. Casey wondered what those traditions were. South Georgia continued to cling to an ignorance that was better left forgotten. Or by her standards. Though she'd been locked away, Casey had read the newspapers in her moments of lucidity and knew trouble in the form of racism and hatred still lurked beneath the murky waters of Southern gentility. She wondered how the fine folk of Sweetwater would receive *her*.

Casey spotted two boys coming toward her on bicycles. Risking injury, she stepped into their path. They stopped and eyed her expectantly.

The bigger of the two, who looked to be around twelve, snickered as he glanced over his shoulder to a smaller version of himself. Brothers, she thought. Both wore clothes too large, their shorts barely covering their backsides. T-shirts displaying rock stars hung to their scraped knees, and several silver hoop earrings dangled from their ears.

"Hi, uh . . . sorry, do you guys know this address?" A slight tremor caused her hand to shake as she held the scrap of paper out to the older boy. Casey had no recollection of ever being around children.

The boy took the offered paper from her hand.

"Yeah, I know where it's at. Go three blocks, then turn left. It's about a mile, then another left. Once you're at the gate, just tell them who you are, and they'll let you in."

"Tell who?" she asked.

"The guard, loony-tunes. You live there?" the older boy asked, then looked to his brother, rolling his eyes upward in an exaggerated movement.

"Uh, yes. Thanks." She turned in the direction the boy pointed out to her. Loony, he called her. Was it obvious? She looked at the drab brown shift she wore, the white canvas sneakers. *Not the current style,* she mused. Its having been the mode of dress for so long, she'd never questioned it. Until then.

On the pocket of the shift, in faded black letters, it read: *Sweetwater Sanctuary for the Mentally Disabled.*

No wonder they looked at her funny. The benefactors of the hospital hadn't been kind in their assessment of the facility's functions, and all who were unfortunate enough to wallow away behind its walls were given the same clothes to wear, telling the patients that trouble stirred when differences arose.

Casey could never understand the logic of such a statement, but she hadn't cared. She'd only existed. Her life a means to an end. Yet, she'd never quite figured out just exactly what the end was. Until two months ago, when she'd been told of her upcoming release.

She walked to the end of the street, took the left turn, and hoped the boy had given her the right directions. She paused. Spying the reflection in the window of a lone car, she stared at the blurry image. Her black hair, once long and shiny, jutted out in all directions. Her face appeared washed-out and sunken. Hairstyles and appearances hadn't been a primary concern over the last ten years.

The creak of a rusted sign indicated that

Sweetwater Island had a population of two thousand. Casey viewed the small scenic island surrounding her. She needed to prepare for the encounter she had come to dread. The visit that she hoped would cast a light on her past. A past she could only remember as faded and gray. The visit with the one woman who had answers. Yet, if the past was an indication of the future, Casey wasn't sure how she would extract answers from the unwilling woman. Or, she mused, if she figured a way to get answers from her mother, she felt sure they wouldn't come forth freely since she had never wanted to talk about Casey's past. Casey had been too crazy to care. But that was then.

She strolled down the sun-baked street, guessing the shops were closed for the day. No shoppers littered the sidewalks. Children apparently were under lock and key, and all those who might have braved the August sun found it too hot, or she thought, in a town that size, they were all waiting, lurking behind their lacy curtains, fanning themselves in anticipation of a look-see. An occasional peek through their ancestral sheers would soon provide them with the view they'd expected. Casey mentally berated herself. These people weren't expecting her. They were probably at home taking care of their families. What had she expected after all? A parade? The release of Sweetwater's most famous inmate. The crazy girl.

Shops lined the narrow street. Some housed in older homes, others sported a modern look, their newness out of place in the midst of the town's old-fashioned appearance. Clay pots of geraniums barred the glass-paned doors of Bentley's Real Estate Office, their protection a joke to a would-be trespasser.

Smells of mesquite drifting from a smokestack caused her mouth to water. Tempted, she hurried along the sidewalk, the scent of BBQ her guide. Crossing at the intersection of Main and Sweet Way, she followed the scent to Big Al's. On the sign in big letters it read:

Best BBQ in the South. Come inside, treat your mouth.

If the smell was any indication, Casey told herself she was in for the treat of a lifetime.

A glance at her shift told her she'd have to change before she could enter the restaurant. In pursuit of a clothing store, Casey scanned the street and spotted a sign proclaiming *Haygood's Clothing Store* to her north. She should have waited for Sandra to give her clothes. At the time leaving was her only concern. At present, however, she wished for a simple dress. Hunger continued to gnaw at her insides.

She turned back toward Main Street and wandered north, locating the store. Casey stopped in front of Haygood's and eyed the window display. A bright, flowered dress draped a lifelike mannequin whose breasts jutted out at her, beckoning her to come inside so she, too, could wear such a dress. Casey doubted she'd fill one out quite as provocatively as the mannequin, whose man-made nipples appeared abnormally large. But she imagined that was the enticement. Men would purchase such clothing for their lovers in hopes that they would fill the upper portion of the dress out as well as the chunk of plaster that displayed it. She eyed the dress one last time before entering the store. She wondered if she'd ever worn a provocative dress for a man. A boy in her case, since she'd been only eighteen at the time of her incarceration.

About to step away from the window display, she stopped. A shadow caught her eye as she peered into the shaded glass. Two women stood behind her, their heads together, whispering.

One of the women, tall and thin, pointed a clawlike finger at her. Rooted to the ground, Casey stood still, hoping they would leave. She continued to stare at the contents of the window display until her eyes watered. Casey strained to hear their hushed murmurs.

"I know that's her, Cora. I heard Evie talking. For a mother it didn't sound like she was too happy about the return of her long-lost daughter. Said she needed more time to prepare. She's only had ten years!"

She felt the gaze of the thin woman burning a hole in her back.

"Well, I say, once a nut, always a nut. I always knew that family would come to no good. And look at that Evie, all high-and-mighty now that she trapped poor old John into marrying her. History will prove me right, you just wait."

The second woman, rounded with one too many dollops of ice cream, bored an even deeper hole into Casey's back.

Casey turned to look at the two gossips. The thin woman raised her pointed chin a

notch higher and grabbed her companion
by the arm.

"Come along, Cora, I don't have time for
talking to trash."

"But, Vera, I thought you said we were
going . . ." The heaviest woman didn't get to
finish whatever it was she was about to say.
The scarecrow woman pulled her away from
the window and sped down the street, stopping once to stare and point her stubby finger at Casey.

What had she done? She had never laid
eyes on the women, yet they eyed her
openly, discussing her as if she were a freak
in a sideshow, not caring that she watched
them and heard what they'd said.

Deciding it was best to ignore the gossipy
women, she entered the store and found its
cool air refreshing. Rack after rack of clothing caught her eye. After ten years in the
same style of dress, it was a welcome sight.

Silver and gold dominated the decor.
Heavy silver curtains discreetly sectioned off
the dressing area. Queen Anne chairs covered in gold awaited gentlemen, young and
old, to grace their plush cushions, rears covered in Fruit-of-the-Looms and some in fash-
ionable cotton boxers. Mirrors trimmed in

gold adorned the entire back wall of the store, beckoning all who could to come and view the array of elegantly displayed clothing.

Casey scanned the store, a display of printed dresses capturing her attention. Some were patterned in sunflowers, others in tiny purple irises. She marveled at the brilliant colors, the casual elegance of the simple designs. Briefly, she wondered if she could fill out the front bodice as well as the mannequin. A glance downward told her the answer was no.

She removed the iris print dress from the rack and walked over to the full-length mirror. As she held it in front of her, admiring the tiny purple flowers, a salesclerk appeared out of nowhere and snatched the dress from her.

"Put that back!"

Stunned at the clerk's rudeness, Casey turned to her. "I was going to . . ." Intimidation prevented her from finishing the sentence. Did the woman treat all of her customers so badly? She reached for the dress, hoping the woman would let go of it.

As the salesclerk released her hold on the dress, an angry puff of air escaped her brightly painted mouth.

"It really is you!" Taking small, deliberate steps, the woman inched herself into a corner. Painted fingernails covered lipstick-reddened lips.

Not wanting to cause a scene, Casey took the dress from the woman and placed it on the counter.

"I want this dress. Do you want to take my money?" Her hands trembled as she reached for the folded bills.

The hateful woman stared at her a moment longer, then hesitantly walked to the cash register.

"I suppose I'll have to if I don't want to report you to Sheriff Parker." Hostility coated the clerk's harsh words.

Feeling she had no alternative, Casey asked in a hushed tone, "Do you know me? Have I done anything to you in the past?" She could tell by the blush staining the clerk's cheeks that she was taken off guard by her questions.

The clerk cleared her throat. "Don't you dare play innocent with me. I know you, and I knew Ronnie, or have you conveniently forgotten him, too?" Chipped red nails fumbled with costume jewelry encircling her jowly neck.

Ronnie. Her pulsed raced. With unsteady hands she placed her money on the counter and waited for the clerk to take it.

"What's wrong, Casey? Do you have a conscience after all? Poor Ronnie. God rest his soul. I'll bet he's doin' flip-flops in his grave right about now."

Casey scooped up the wad of bills and ran to the door, the dress forgotten. She had to escape. Her pulse pounding, she felt as if her chest would explode. Once outside she drank in sweet gulps of fresh air, her heart rate slowing to a normal beat as she mentally talked herself down from the panic attack.

She took one last cleansing breath before she headed in the direction given to her by the boys. The dress and her hunger forgotten, she suddenly found the halls of Sanctuary calling her. In her eagerness to leave the confines of the hospital, she hadn't considered what she would be up against on her own, without Sandra as a buffer. She wished she'd waited for her ride.

Casey headed south. In her peripheral vision she noticed a glossy black vehicle snaking its way along the deserted street. She figured more lookey-loos were coming out of their hiding places to watch the freak show. She walked faster, desperate to break into a run, then slowed her pace as the sleek machine crawled alongside, nuzzling close to the curb. Hesitant to leave the security of town such as it was, she stopped in her tracks.

A sudden wave of dizziness caused her to stumble. The image of the car swam before her. Fearful that she would faint, she reached for a parking meter to steady herself. It was as if her bones had chosen that moment to liquefy. A bright flash of red flickered before her vision, then nothing. A sudden heaviness made it hard to breathe.

"No! I said no! Get away! Leave me alone!"

Casey rubbed her eyes, as if that would remove the unwelcome vision. *What is happening to me?*

"Do you need help?" a voice from the vehicle inquired.

She must be experiencing aftereffects from the panic attack.

"Can you hear me? Dammit, lady, speak up." Impatience laced the husky drawl.

Moistening her mouth, Casey cleared her dry throat.

Strangely enough, she felt anger that a

total stranger would speak to her in such a manner. She lashed out without thinking. "What do you want? Can't you people just leave me alone!"

The stranger got out of his car and walked over to her, his gaze questioning. "Look, lady, do you live around here? You look awful. Are you all right? Are you ill?"

Casey stepped back, panic pouring through her. Not wanting to be the star of another freak attraction, she turned, and muttered, "I'm fine. I think the sun just got to me."

Was she in for another round of insults? Did she know this man? She felt his gaze lingering on her as he continued to stare at her. A shiver ran the length of her, and a flame of heat settled in the pit of her stomach. All at once she was desperate for recollection.

"My name is Blake Hunter, I'm the doctor here in Sweetwater." The voice that had sounded coarse only seconds before now softened and was full of concern.

A doctor? He didn't look like a doctor. At least not the ones she'd been in contact with at Sanctuary. Certain he was lying, Casey let her gaze rake him from head to toe. No way. He looked too good to be a doctor. She knew what they looked like. He didn't fit the picture.

Casey was intense as she viewed the man before her and realized the only way she was going to rid herself of this bothersome stranger was to answer him. If all male specimens in Sweetwater were this large, they'd better send whatever they were feeding them to the hospital, since the male species there had a tendency to be thin and scraggly. Shoulders, broad as an oak tree, filled out the worn denim shirt, and trunklike legs defied the elasticity of the khakis. Casey felt another pull deep in the pit of her stomach as her eyes rested on the brown leather belt that cinched the man's tapered waist.

"Have we met before?" She smoothed imaginary wrinkles from her shift as she waited for his reply.

"I don't believe I've had the pleasure. Can I offer you a lift?" He walked over to the passenger-side door and opened it, indicating she should get inside.

Not knowing what to do, she went with her gut instinct. *Don't get in the car with strangers.* Someone must have told her that. Was it a memory? Or another factual thing she just knew.

"No thanks, I'm walking home. I was supposed to get a ride, and well . . ." She was rambling. Not having had a conversation with a normal male in so long, maybe never, she wasn't quite sure how to brush him off.

"In this heat, you've got to be kidding! This humidity is too high for you to be walking about. In other words, it's not a great day for a Southern stroll. I wish you'd take me up on the ride." He looked at her and smiled, revealing even, white teeth. The grin reached dark brown eyes that crinkled at the corners, telling her smiling was a way of life for him.

Should she? He seemed harmless enough. It was only a short distance. After the hateful reception at the clothing store, his kindness was welcome. Pushing short strands of hair behind her ears, she stepped toward the car.

"Good decision." He hunched to fit his large frame in the confines of the car. Starting the engine, he shifted into gear, leaving a trail of dust in his wake.

She couldn't believe she was doing this! Barely away from the hospital an hour and already she was doing crazy things. Maybe she *was* crazy.

"Do you have an address? I've spent

most of my life here in Sweetwater. I should be able to get you home." Humor laced the deep voice. Curious, Casey turned to the man and handed him the slip of paper with her address.

"How far do I have to go?" She watched as he scanned the address.

Emotions danced along the sculpted face of her benefactor. Shock. Surprise, then astonishment. Did she know him? Were they connected somehow? Casey stared at the stranger, amazed at the whirl of emotion dancing in her belly. And below.

"My God! I should have guessed! Your dress." He glanced at her shift pocket.

Casey looked at him as if he had lost his mind. Maybe she shouldn't have accepted a ride after all. Weirdos came in all shapes and sizes, according to Sandra.

He turned to her, questions simmering in his maple-colored eyes. His mouth, the upper lip as full as the lower, almost a pout, moved, yet no sound came out. He raced along Sweetwater's untraveled roads, silent.

What now? She didn't know how much more public scrutiny she could take. And in such a short time, too. She wanted to question him, but something held her back.

Glancing out the window, she tried to admire the scenery. Having had the same view for so long at the hospital, an eagerness to discover anything new overwhelmed her. Realizing her freedom held no boundaries, she turned to Blake. Her question still lingered, unanswered. Anxious to get home, she asked again. "Is it far?"

Apparently he hadn't heard her. Annoyance turned to alarm as she watched him maneuver the car off the shoulder. Oak trees stood along the length of the road, giving a would-be rapist plenty of protection against an outside view if he chose to drag her into the wooded area. Casey cringed at the imagined scenario and forced the horrific image from her mind. She stuffed her trembling hands into her pockets.

"I can't believe it! What did you say your name was?" His eyes were wide with amazement.

"I didn't." Did it really matter? As Blake studied her, she sensed he was truly curious. The look on his handsome face was too shocked to be that of a rapist or serial killer. Sandra had been big on educating her charges with tales of what went on in the outside world.

"It's Casey Edwards." The air was thick, almost electric.

A flick of his wrist silenced the engine. A stillness penetrated the confines of the car.

"No wonder! I got busy at the office when I realized the time. Do I ever feel like an idiot." With an elbow on the steering wheel, he palmed his forehead, shaking his head from side to side, loose black curls resting on the collar of his shirt. Casey was captivated by this stranger as she'd never been by another. At least she didn't think she'd ever been captivated by a stranger, or anyone else for that matter.

"Why?" She couldn't figure this strange man out. She wasn't sure she wanted to.

"You really don't know?"

"What am I supposed to know?" *Do I have a psychic hot line number posted on my forehead and am not aware of it? I don't think so.*

"I should have told you. It was rude of me not to." He looked at her, shock still etching his sharp features.

"Then do it, now! Please, all this . . ." She threw her hands out in frustration. *What sort of game is he playing?* "What exactly do you know about me?"

"You're a mystery in the medical community for starters. And locally, too." His gaze never wavered.

"How do you know this?"

He hesitated before answering. He eyed her up and down, then cleared his throat.

"I read a few articles about your case in medical school. Amnesia of your caliber is almost nonexistent." He let the statement hang in the air.

"Just who are you?" Had she misunderstood the implication of his statement? Was he really a doctor? Had this been planned?

"I told you my name. And I'm not saying anything, other than what the entire medical community has said for years. Your case is unique."

"Take me home." She didn't want to hear any more. For years she had been subjected to every form of hypnosis, trances; anything they could do, they did, until she was no longer willing to play guinea pig for the doctors. It had been months since an attempt was made to poke and pry into the recesses of her empty memory bank. Except the drugs; they'd never stopped until recently.

"That's where we're headed. A few more minutes." The engine purred at his command. He pulled back onto the road, not bothering to look for traffic. Not that there was any. The residents of Sweetwater remained hidden behind lace curtains and locked doors. Casey observed an older couple on an afternoon stroll braving the sultry heat, no doubt for a look at the latest sideshow.

And what did he mean?

"We?" she questioned.

"I guess you really don't know." His voice held a trace of excitement.

"Enlighten me." Sarcasm spewed from her mouth, surprising her.

"Look, I'm sorry. Eve should have told you. She'll be back in town tomorrow." Blake tramped on the accelerator, and the car lurched with a sudden rush of speed.

"Stop!" Angry with herself more than anything, she wanted Blake to answer her. Now. He seemed quite expert at avoiding her questions.

"Casey," he paused, and looked at her for a moment before turning his gaze back to the road. "You really *don't* remember, do you?"

Chapter Four

"No, I don't." Confusion shook her. She looked at Blake. A flash. A brief splash of vibrant red, then nothing.

Trees passed in a dark green blur as they sped along Sweetwater's dusty roads. "I'm Adam's best friend. He's your stepbrother."

Unaware she'd been holding her breath, Casey relaxed, a sigh escaping her tight lips.

Blake's brown-eyed gaze traveled the length of her, stopping to rest on her face.

Wondering if he perused all women in such a manner, Casey asked, "Well?"

"I'm lost." He smiled at her again, and like a magnet to metal, in spite of her confusion, she found herself drawn to her newfound . . . friend?

"How do I measure up?" This boldness was new to her. She discovered she liked

speaking her mind, never having been allowed to do it at the hospital. A sense of
freedom washed over her like a tidal wave,
drenching her with questions.

Blake turned to her, his gaze probing. The
warmth of his slight smile echoed in his voice.

"You're not what your mother said you
were. Or your stepfather. Of course, he only
knows what Evie tells him."

"I don't understand." Casey stared out
the window, the scenery passing in a col-
ored blur, with an occasional house emerg-
ing out of the shelter of tall oaks draped with
Spanish moss.

"He was never allowed to visit you after
the first time. Apparently it was a disaster.
He never tried again. Besides, your mother
was always so upset after the visits, John
just tried to stay out of her way."

Curious now, the questions pummeled
her as fast as the passing trees.

"When did he try?"

"I don't remember. I was away. I didn't
come home that often, at first. Adam will be
able to tell you more. Do you remember
Adam at all?"

Puzzlement replaced his smile of moments ago. She shook her head.

"At first? I don't understand." She let the question hang.

"After you were . . . hospitalized. Your mother, Evie, married John. Adam and I were away at Emory University in Atlanta. Adam's practice is there now." He turned to her, his embarrassment obvious. Casey felt sure he didn't want to explain her family's history, and for a moment she was sorry for this man who had been asked to deliver her home. To the unknown.

Casey pondered Blake's remark, and asked, "If he did visit me, I don't remember."

"I think at the time, Evie wanted you to get well. She stayed with you those first few months, day and night. You were out of it, according to her. After a while, the doctors told her it might be best if she stayed away."

Blake turned the wheel with the ease of one used to being in control. He drove up a slight incline, making a sharp right turn. Another mile and they stopped. Blake spoke to the guard at the gatehouse. The boys had been truthful, after all. The small brick guardhouse caused her insides to clam up. A fine line of sweat beaded her upper lip at the sight of the heavyset man. His navy pants and blue shirt reminded her of the guards at the hospital. The only adornment this man had that hospital security hadn't displayed was the revolver strapped to his rounded hip.

A laugh from the man inside the gate-house and a loud whoop from Blake said the two were on friendly terms. *And why wouldn't they be?* Casey wondered. *All guards weren't the same. Were they?*

Blake sped through the iron gates as they opened. For a minute Casey felt as if she were Jonah about to enter the whale. Now where had that thought come from?

Would she have the courage to confront Eve? It was hard to think of the strange woman as her mother. Last month during her visit she acted as if Casey were simply visiting a luxury hotel, soon to return home. No talk of why she was there, what she would do when she came home and took her place in the family. Casey secretly had hoped her mother would pull her into her arms and comfort her, telling her how wonderful it would be to have her home again. Of course, she told herself, she wasn't a little child anymore. Maybe she had never been a little child. If she had been a child, why couldn't she remember. Did she expect too much?

The cloud of mystery surrounding her return was becoming dark and ominous. Despair descended on her, resting on her shoulders like a thick fog.

"What do you think?"

Blake's question brought her back to the present. Surprised at the unexpected view before her, Casey drew in her breath as she admired the scenery.

Oak trees parted gracefully, their wide arches shadowing the dirt-covered road. Sun filtered through the leaves, briefly shooting flashes of light through their lace-like pattern. Blake slowed the car. Nestled in a bowl of green below them stood Swan House. Dozens of magnolias surrounded the red brick mansion. A circular drive outlined a bouquet of vibrant colors. Never had she seen such a display of flowers. Their colors were so bright, she felt gray and dull in their presence.

Casey continued to gaze in muted silence at the structure below. Surely she would have remembered if she had ever lived there. The house looked as if Scarlett had lent a new and improved blueprint of Tara to an architect, and, together, they designed the antebellum mansion of her dreams. Another thought she couldn't explain. How was it she knew about Scarlett and Tara but couldn't remember other things?

Casey closed her eyes. She could visualize carriages, ladies in satin dresses, their hooped skirts billowing out before them, bonnets resting on their heads with colorful ribbons fluttering in the warm summer breeze. She imagined she heard the high-pitched squeals of young girls' delight as they trotted down the dust-covered path on their way to destinations unknown.

"What do you think of your new home?" Blake asked.

"I never imagined it so huge! It's almost the size of the hospital."

Thick white columns held up the balcony that wrapped around the entire front of the mansion. Standing at attention, eight perfectly lined columns ran the length of the dwelling.

A glimpse to the right told her the columns ran around the entire structure. Red brick chimneys peered out from the cover of oak trees. As if in mock salute to her arrival, the tree branches waved gently in the late-afternoon breeze.

"It's been in the family for hundreds of

years. Generations of Worthingtons have left their trademark. John added on another eight or ten rooms, a ballroom, and a sunroom. Then he added the indoor pool a few years back. Swan House has all the amenities." His last comment was almost mocking.

After the severity of the hospital, with its lack of warmth and general bleakness, she wondered if she could ever get used to such a lavish lifestyle.

Roughly, Blake shifted the car into gear. As they traveled downhill to Swan House his quiet voice filled the confines of the car.

"Appearances can be deceiving, as I'm sure you know." Casey felt his mood change. Friendly before, he seemed dark and threatening. His comment sent shivers down her spine. Feeling a sense of unease, she ignored his remark.

"I can't wait to explore the grounds. There must be a hundred acres!" Her forced enthusiasm must have jarred Blake out of his mood. When he glanced at her, his smile was back in place.

"Actually I think it's one hundred and fifty, but who's counting? You'll have plenty of time once you get settled in."

They reached the bottom of the hill and

stopped at the edge of the circular drive. Wooden doors burst open and a small, spritelike woman ran down the brick steps, her arms held out, as if trying to embrace the world.

Blake got out first and walked around to Casey's side of the car. The door was barely open before Casey felt the little woman tugging at her hands, crushing her in a surprisingly powerful hug. Did she know her?

The small woman stood back as Casey got out of the car. Feeling as though she were under inspection, she stood ramrod straight and stared at Blake, who by then was standing behind the unknown lady, barely containing his laughter.

"Well, I'll be damned! It really is you! Oh pardon me, I don't usually cuss like that, well not often anyway." Just a smidgen over four feet, the little white-haired woman reached for her flowered apron and touched a corner to her shimmering blue eyes.

"Yes, you do." Blake's affection for the woman was etched in the crinkle lines of his smile.

"Stop interrupting, darn you. And who asked you anyway?" The woman looked up at Blake and smiled.

"See? That mouth of yours will be the death of you yet. Casey, meet the mouth of the South, Flora Farley, our . . . I don't know what she is! She looked after you on occasion and helped your mother when you were a child." He affectionately placed his arm around Flora's shoulders.

"Mouth of the South? Is that what you're callin' me now? Why you just wait, Mr. Blake. When you want one of my famous pecan pies, I'll give you one all right—filled with shells!"

Casey watched as Blake continued to tease the little woman. By the looks of it she was enjoying every minute. Her smile revealed apple cheeks and a perfect set of dentures. Flora affectionately pushed Blake aside and grabbed Casey in a motherly hug.

"Come along, Casey, we've got work to do." Flora directed her to the double doors, pulling her along behind her. Blake shook his head.

Casey found her tongue. "Work?" Not that she would mind, but she thought a day or two of rest, getting used to Swan House and reacquainting herself with her mother, would be first on the agenda. Did her mother expect her to work for her keep? If so, she'd show her she hadn't a lazy bone in her body.

Flora led her up the oak stairs covered in well-worn carpet. She didn't bother to stop at the three landings leading to the top floor. Flora continued to pull her along. Obviously, she hadn't heard her, or she chose to ignore her comment.

They walked to the end of a long hall on the fourth floor. Casey barely had time to stop before she slammed into the elfin woman.

"I've put you here." Flora nodded toward the double doors. "I know it's far away, but you'll thank me for it later. I thought you would want to be as far from the noisy kitchen as possible, after the hospital."

Flora opened the door to the bedroom. Casey gasped at the view. All that separated her from the lush gardens below was a sheet of glass. She'd never seen such a panorama. Admiring the beauty, Casey walked over to the window and gazed out at the lavish gardens. A visual display of flowers she couldn't begin to name were scattered about the lawn, a kaleidoscope of nature's splendor.

"Well, Missy, I can see by the looks of you, I'm not going to have trouble getting you to listen. You haven't uttered a single word. They are something, aren't they?" She gestured toward the window. "Mr. Worthington tends to them when he can, but Hank's our head gardener. You better watch out for him, too. Just because he was a gardener in England to some duke or something, he thinks he's king of the manor here. He does a fine job, though."

Enchanted with the glorious gardens below, Casey scarcely heard Flora's prattle in the background. As she turned to face the woman, a sense of unease invaded her. Casey looked back at the window. In the center of the gardens she eyed a stone path leading to a large fountain. A glint of sunlight caught a cascade of water in the smaller fountain perched in the middle of the garden. Curiously, she felt drawn to the light. Not understanding, she stepped closer to the window, the rays of light beckoning, as if daring her to merge with their brightness. Drawn into the vortex of sunlight, she went with it, no longer hearing Flora's constant chatter.

She huddled in the dark on the closet floor. Jackets touched her painfully thin shoulders as sobs racked her. She squeezed her eyes shut, trying to block out the pain. He prom-

ised he wouldn't hurt her again. Momma saw them this time. She just looked at her in that way she always did, especially when she had that glass. She said it was water but she knew better, she was nine years old, not a kid anymore. Remembering the last time was enough. Rubbing her sore thighs, she hiccuped and wiped another tear from her face. He promised he would do worse next time. He said that the last time, too, she remembered. Still, she wasn't about to take a chance. What he did was bad enough. What could be worse? He was gone. The back door slammed, and she heard Momma holler. That meant she could come out of her hiding place. Opening the door a narrow crack, she peered through the slit of light. From out of nowhere a hand reached for her, covering her mouth, trapping her scream.

"No!" Casey ran from the window to the door, yanking at it, only to find it stuck. Her desire to escape was so strong, nothing mattered. Not the woman who stood staring at her as if she'd just seen a ghost, and she wasn't sure she hadn't. It didn't matter, she had to leave. Flora's bantering became a shout as she continued to pound on the jammed door. Flesh met with wood, her fists scraped and raw, she slowed her beat to a soft knock. Overpowered by defeat, she slumped to the floor, rivulets of tears streaming down her pallid face. Weak and confused, she focused her red-rimmed eyes on the scene around her.

Flora stood in the middle of the room, apparently speechless, for once. She looked at Casey as if she had gone mad. Maybe she had, or was going to. Was this the beginning of a breakdown?

The sun that had taken her hostage minutes before was now slinking behind a dark cloud, out of sight, however temporary. She remembered being drawn to the warmth of the rays. Then she felt as if she were being sucked through a straw. Then nothing. Like an epidemic, a black fear rooted itself, coursing through her veins, resting heavily in her heart. She began to shake as fear racked her body. Wrapping her arms around herself, she tried to control the tremors, but it was useless. Like an unwelcome visitor, terror took hold of her and implanted itself, daring her to defy it.

"Casey! What's the matter, girl, you look like you've seen a ghost." Flora was back in action, her chatter welcome. Casey wouldn't have to think. Reaching behind to massage the stiff muscles of her neck, all she wanted to do was lie down. Inching her way up, using the door for support, she stood and wiped her tear-stained face. Embarrassed at her display of craziness, Casey cleared her throat before speaking.

"I'm sorry, Flora. I don't know what happened. One minute I was admiring the gardens, the next, I'm beating on the door. You must think I need to go back where I came from. I feel like a fool." She brushed away another tear and ran a hand through her short ebony curls.

"Well, it's no wonder, dear. You ain't had a proper home in ten years. And then all of a sudden here you are"—she thrust her small arms out—"in this mausoleum. It's enough to make me cry sometimes. Though I can't understand why the door wouldn't open. Must be stuck, the humidity does that sometimes. In all its splendor, Swan House is still just an old house. I'll tell Mr. Worthington; he'll see to it."

Casey thought Swan House could never be just an "old house" and told Flora so.

"That's true, but like all homes, it comes equipped with its share of problems. I think I hear Blake. Do you want to freshen up before you come downstairs?" Flora slapped her forehead before she continued. "Of course you do! Mrs. Worthington purchased some things for you. I hope the sizes are right. She does have a way with clothes, that much I'll give her. Let me see." Flora walked to the end of the room and opened mirrored doors, revealing rack after rack of clothes.

Shelves piled high with sweaters, shoes, nightclothes, hats, and some things she wasn't close enough to see. Casey walked over and stood by the door, waiting, as Flora surveyed the contents.

"I guess she did you justice, after all. I wasn't sure she would go all out."

Casey stood inside the closet and came back out, speechless. She pointed to the racks of clothes, then her slim finger tapped her chest. Eyes as wide as saucers, she viewed the contents again.

"These are mine?" she whispered.

"It appears that way, Missy. Tell you what, I'll run a bath while you enjoy looking through the clothes. Pick something real nice out, you'll want to look your best at dinner tonight. Mr. Worthington can't wait to meet his daughter."

"Sure, uh . . . okay."

Casey entered the closet. Her room at the hospital would have fit in there. Twice. She smiled. Talk about going from one extreme to the other. She walked the length of the closet, running her hand along the tops of the dresses, blouses, jackets, and all the finery that was hers. Never having had such a wardrobe, or if she had, she had no memory of it, she felt like a kid at Christmas. She pulled a peach-colored silk blouse from the hanger and held it in front of her. Matching silk pants, along with satin slippers, completed the outfit. A note pinned to the blouse told her matching underthings were in a drawer at the end of the closet. Was this what it was like to be rich? She knew she had never lived this way before. Finding the drawer, she opened it. Expecting the undergarments to be on top of the pile, she searched through the soft, ruffled finery. For a moment, she felt like she was prying, then remembered, these were *her* things. In all the silk and lace she felt a sheet of something. Cardboard? She was sure it wasn't supposed to be there; after all, someone had gone to a lot of trouble to arrange the feminine, delicate underclothes in just the perfect order. Probably left over from a packet of panty hose. Pulling it out from under the soft pile, Casey saw that it was a photo, with handwriting on the back. Not wanting to be nosy, but wanting to return it to the rightful owner, she read the childishly scrawled message on the back:

To The Best Mom Ever,
Set this on your bedside and
think of me in your dreams!

Happy faces were scribbled around the message. *Who wrote this?* she wondered, as she turned it over in her hand. It was a picture of a young boy, his age unclear. She turned the picture over again. In the bottom right corner, a signature was barely visible. Casey didn't see how she'd missed it before. Walking over to the window, she held the photo up to the light, trying to read the name.

Turning the picture around for another perspective, she stopped. Leaning closer to the window, she could barely make out the letters. R-N-I-E.

She looked at the photo again, hoping to jar her memory. The face that stared back at her wasn't familiar to her at all. Even though the picture looked innocent, somehow she knew it was evil. Whoever this person was, she sensed there was evil in his soul.

A flash of red distracted her from the picture. Shaking her head, she went back inside the closet. As she laid the picture on the chest, a hot spear of pain rammed into the back of her head. She cradled her head in her hands, wincing. She dropped onto the floor, writhing in agony.

"Casey?"

As quick as the pain came, it was gone. Had someone called to her?

Dear God, what was happening to her? She searched the room. She was alone. There were no voices. First she was swallowed up by light, then the pain that surged through her head, powerful, almost electric. Maybe she shouldn't have come home so soon. If that was how her memory was going to come back, she wasn't sure she wanted it.

That smile. There was something familiar about the picture. She looked at it again. The smile was a smirk, almost hateful. Why was this familiar to her now? She looked at the letters again. R-N-I-E.

Ronnie.

The clerk at Haygood's had mentioned the name Ronnie. Was it supposed to mean something to her?

She threw the photo on the floor as if she had been burned. The name spewed from her lips like spit. Had someone placed this evil picture, knowing she would find it?

And just who *was* Ronnie?

Chapter Five

Casey put the picture in the pocket of her dress, intending to give it to Flora later. Flora might know who the boy in the picture was. She decided there was nothing she could do about it right away anyway, so she gathered her underclothes from the drawer and went back to the bedroom.

Flora was in the bathroom, preparing her bath and talking at the same time. Not wanting to yell, she stood in the doorway, watching as the little woman put out big, fluffy towels and fragrant soaps on a padded stool next to the tub.

The opulence amazed her. A spa-sized tub that looked as if it would hold a dozen people filled one-half of the room. On the opposite wall, a vanity area covered the other half. Shades of pale pink, cream, and gold covered the remaining walls. Stacks of towels, thick terry robes, and bars of soap in the same matching shade as the wallpaper were stacked in a glass cabinet next to the pedestal sink. The commode was hidden behind a cream-colored wall, along with a glass-enclosed shower. Feathery plants occupied empty corners. Casey couldn't wait to sink her stiff muscles in the warm, scented water.

Casey took a bar of soap from the basket placed at the foot of the spalike tub and inhaled the scent of gardenia. Her favorite. *How did I know that?* Dr. Macklin said smell could be one of the triggers in gaining her memory back.

"Flora, who picked out these soaps?" She continued to inhale the floral scent.

"Mrs. Worthington, I believe. You don't like it?" Flora placed a terry robe on the stool by the dressing table.

"As a matter of fact, it's my favorite. I just wondered who knew it."

"Eve loves to shop. She must have remembered it was your favorite. A mother knows those things."

Casey placed the soap on the edge of the tub when she remembered the photograph.

Reaching into her pocket, she pulled the picture out and looked at it one last time before handing it over to Flora.

"I found this. Do you know who it belongs to?"

Flora took the picture from her and looked at it. With her clear blue eyes downcast, she muttered something unintelligible and hurried back to the bedroom, stuffing the picture in her apron pocket.

Even having known Flora for less than two hours, Casey knew her behavior wasn't normal. For two solid hours the little woman had done nothing but chat, offer friendly advice, and an opinion or two. Now her behavior was the complete opposite. And she hadn't answered Casey's question.

She went to the bedroom and found Flora in the closet, searching the drawers.

Not wanting to startle her, Casey said in a soft whisper, "Flora?"

The spritelike woman spun around, knocking a shoe box off the shelf.

Casey could see Flora's pulse pounding in her neck. She was afraid! Had the picture frightened her?

"Oh my . . . I'm sorry, dear, I . . . you surprised me." Running her hands over her starched apron, Flora edged out of the closet and hurried back to the bathroom to turn off the water.

Casey followed, her question still unanswered.

"Who is that person in the picture, Flora? I seem to remember, yet I can't actually place him, only that there is an air of . . . evil about him." She shrugged. "I don't know, it's just a feeling I have."

"Well you know what they say about feelings, get one, go with it. Ask your momma, she'll tell you."

"Why do I feel like you're avoiding my question? Is the identity of the boy in the photograph a big secret? I've barely been home three hours, and I feel like a zombie. I know nothing, I don't even remember this"— she whirled around the bathroom, her hands gesturing out to her sides—"monster of a house. I'm being sucked up by light. I'm telling you, it's straight out of a Stephen King novel!" Who *was* Stephen King? "Then to top it all off, my head feels like a split melon, and now, you won't even tell me who's in the picture. It's too much." Casey walked to the bed and plunked down, not caring what Flora thought of her at the moment. She was sick of being treated like an idiot. Just because she had no memory of her life beyond ten years ago didn't mean she was crazy. They had thought that at first. All those fine doctors in that fine hospital. That much she did remember. But never once in all her years at the hospital did they ever tell her exactly why she was there, only that a tragedy had occurred causing her to lose her memory.

"I'm not avoiding your question. I was instructed by Mrs. Worthington not to answer any questions regarding your past. She said she would tell you what you needed to know. I understand what a confusing time this is for you, dear. As much as I hate to, I do have orders to follow, and if I'm wantin' to keep my job, I have to do as the missus instructs."

Casey was ashamed of her outburst. The last thing she wanted to do was cause trouble for the one person who'd actually treated her like a normal human in the past few hours. She eased off the edge of the bed and placed an arm around Flora.

"I'm sorry. I don't know what came over me. I don't usually vent my frustration that way. Or I don't think I do. The past ten years are a blur sometimes. I should know better. I feel like I'm on a mental merry-go-round, and it's spinning faster and faster."

Flora patted her on the back as if she were a child. Taking her by the hand, Flora led her into the steamy, gardenia-scented bathroom.

"I think a hot soak will do you more good than anything. I'll have a snack ready for you when you're finished, and we'll forget this conversation ever took place. Now enjoy your bath."

Flora swished out of the room, their conversation over. And still Casey had no idea why seeing the boy in the picture had upset her so. His identity remained a mystery.

Casey removed the rough brown shift and looked for the hamper. Hidden underneath the vanity, she found a small wicker basket. Wadding the garment in a ball, she stuffed the ugly thing in the trash, glad she would never have to wear the disgusting rag again.

Easing herself into the deep, warm, scented tub, Casey sighed and realized it was the first real bath she'd had in ten years. She smiled, thinking of the cool, short showers she was accustomed to. She could get used to this.

She found several disposable razors,

along with an aloe-based shaving cream. Shaving her legs was prohibited at the hospital, for fear that the patients would try to commit suicide—like she would kill herself with a Bic. This was an unexpected treat. Lathered with the thick cream, Casey delighted in the silken feel of her skin as the razor glided over her long legs. Uncommon as it was for her to be shaving her legs, she felt she had done it in the past and would continue to enjoy this small pleasure in the future.

With her neck fitted in the bath pillow, Casey closed her eyes. For the first time in a long time, she was totally relaxed without the benefit of drugs or the supposed hypnosis sessions with Dr. Macklin. Not giving much thought to what she would do once she arrived home, Casey realized she couldn't stay in limbo forever. What *exactly had* she done in the past? Finding out had to be her first priority. She had to, so she could move forward. Whatever had happened, was it so terrible that she could never live it down? She couldn't live with Eve indefinitely. She needed a life of her own. And besides, what did she really know about her mother? The few times she had visited the hospital were a blur. A peck on the cheek, followed by a whiff of some exotic perfume, then she was gone. Though her mother never failed at each visit to ask her the same question Dr. Macklin, Mr. Bentley, the director at the hospital, and Sandra all asked her on a daily basis: "Remember anything today?" For ten long years. Day after day, week after week, month after month, year after year.

Wrinkled and baby pink, Casey stepped out of the deep tub and pulled her foot back before she stepped on the thick carpet. Placing a hand towel on the floor to prevent a wet mess, Casey remembered that she didn't have to do that. Not sure that she would ever get used to the luxuries in her new home, she stood on the small towel and rubbed herself dry.

Tempted by the array of bottles displayed on the vanity, Casey spotted a bottle of her favorite gardenia-scented lotion and proceeded to slather the pleasant-smelling cream all over her body.

At first she felt a slight sting, then a prick, as if she were jabbed with a needle. Another sharp prick. Then another. Casey was careful when she'd shaved. She hadn't felt any of the prickly sensations as the razor skimmed over her legs. She poured a generous amount of lotion into her palm and began rubbing the cool cream over the backs of her arms.

"Ouch! Damn, what the . . ." Casey stood in front of the mirror, dropping her towel to the floor. She stared at her reflection in the steamy glass.

Thin rivulets of blood snaked down her legs. Turning to the side she saw streaks of red surfacing on the backs of her arms, like tiny spider veins that had somehow surfaced to the top of her skin.

With the washcloth she had just used, Casey dabbed at the blood on her legs and arms. Tiny cuts dotted her arms and legs. She'd been *careful* with the razor. And that still didn't explain the cuts on her arms.

Casey wiped the foggy mirror and reached for the switch to turn on the lights. On closer examination she saw that her arms were covered with tiny, diamondlike cuts. She ran her hand along the back of her arm. Several minuscule objects jutted out from under her tender skin.

She pulled the drawers open, slamming them one after the other until she found what she was searching for. Tweezers. She leaned into the well-lit mirror and, with a steady hand, plucked the glistening objects from her arm. Tiny pools of blood channeled the length of her arms.

Nude and covered with blood, Casey sat on the counter and continued plucking the tiny slivers from her body. Slim, red ribbons inched their way down her legs, splattering the carpets. Minutes ago her concern had been keeping the floors dry. Now, as she dripped blood on the cream-colored rug, that was the least of her concerns.

Finding a bottle of peroxide under the cabinet, she removed the glass from her skin and rinsed her wounds. Telling herself an infection was the last thing she needed, she searched the drawers until she found an antibiotic cream. Careful not to rub the stinging cuts too hard, she gently dotted the ointment over her skin.

Her eye caught the bottle of lotion she had left opened. As she was about to place the lid on the jar, she noticed several clumps of something at the surface of the bottle.

With surgeonlike skill Casey took the tweezers and pulled one of the larger clotted lumps from the top of the cream. Rinsing the cream from the small object, she plucked another from the jar, then repeated her action. Not caring what kind of mess she made, Casey took the bottle of scented cream and dumped the contents in a soap holder. Just as she thought. Tiny sparkles of glass.

Knowing it was nearly impossible for the glass to shatter and wind up in the closed jar, a new jar at that, she knew the glass had been placed in the jar. Like the picture. Someone wanted to scare her. And harm her. She could have been seriously injured. Was that the goal of her unknown enemy?

With her cuts treated, Casey wrapped her tingling body in the thick robe. Back in her room, a feeling of unease inched its way up her back, settling in her neck. Muscles that were relaxed from the warmth of her bath were now tense.

"You finished in there, girl?" Flora's singsong voice filled the room as she nudged the door open with her foot. She carried a large tray loaded with the makings of what appeared to be a feast. Casey hurried to help.

On the wall opposite the window above the gardens, Flora placed the tray on top of a small cherry table.

Hungrier than she cared to admit and not wanting to spoil her appetite for dinner with Mr. Worthington, Casey eyed the food, her fear temporarily forgotten.

"I think this should hold you over until dinner. Mr. Worthington likes to follow the routine used by his ancestors." Flora poured rich chocolate from a pink, rose-patterned pot.

Casey watched Flora fill her plate. Munching on a crisp slice of cucumber, Casey asked, "What routine?"

"Dinner. Usually we serve at nine. Mabel provides a late snack to hold you over. If this isn't enough, just ask. She usually has a variety of goodies."

Casey couldn't imagine what dinner would be like if this was just a snack. A platter filled with fresh, raw vegetables took up half the tray. Another with croissants and a pot of butter with strawberry jam. A second plate held meats, cheeses, and warm bread. A small silver platter held three slices of pie.

"Did you make the pecan?" Remembering Blake's earlier teasing, she wondered if Flora hadn't had the pie ready and waiting.

"Yes, but don't tell Blake. It wasn't easy, either. Mabel rarely lets me in the kitchen;

her domain, she says." Flora sat in the chair opposite and helped herself to a croissant. Casey took one of the tempting rolls and did the same. Butter dripped from her mouth and rolled onto her chin.

"Mmmm, I don't think I've ever had anything this delicious. I'll be the size of an elephant if I continue to eat like this." Casey took another bite of the soft bread, savoring the rich buttery taste.

"I doubt it. Your mother is a small woman, and so was your father. I think you need a little meat on your bones, girl. Eat another, it'll be a while before dinner."

Flora stood up. Casey didn't want her to leave. The fear she felt earlier was back. Not wanting to explain, Casey motioned for Flora to stay.

"What exactly is your job? I thought you did the cooking."

"Only on Mabel's day off. Usually something light. I organize the staff. We have the gardener, the one who thinks he's in England, and of course Theresa and Millie come once a month. They do the heavy cleaning. Or so they say, but I often have to clean up behind the two of them. It isn't like it used to be. Most of their time is spent trying to seduce Adam or Blake. I don't see why John keeps them on." Flora shook her mop of white hair.

Casey laughed out loud. She liked the feeling. She wanted to get used to it. Flora was good medicine for her.

"Well, I guess if Adam and Blake want to uh . . . mess around with the girls, they'll take matters into their own hands." Somehow, she didn't think Blake was the type to fool around with the help, but you could never tell.

"Blake has more class, but he does not like to tease. Adam, I don't know about that young man. He has everything in a dress panting after him, young and old alike. If I were thirty years younger, I'd go for him myself." Flora wiped butter from her mouth and continued.

"Now, Mr. Blake does have his moments; he's the only doctor in town since his father passed on. And, of course, Adam, but you know what kind of doctor he is. Not much call for him around here. He stays in Atlanta, doesn't visit as often as he used to."

Not wanting to end the conversation, Casey buttered another croissant, and asked, "When do I meet Adam?"

"He'll be here soon. You know the two of them have been friends since they were young boys. Blake's father was the only doctor on Sweetwater for years. He died a while back. I think Rose, the first Mrs. Worthington, was a bit overprotective of young Adam. He was in and out of Doc Hunter's office on a weekly basis." Flora took another bite and gulped at the hot cocoa.

"Adam became friendly with Blake, and, as they say, 'The rest is history.' "

Casey was intrigued with her new family. Like a dry well, her empty mind was desperate for news, anything to fill the hollow corner where memories should have been. Would she gain her memory back? Or would life actually begin for her at twenty-eight?

"You'll meet him tonight," Flora said.

"Who?" She had been on another planet, not paying attention to the soothing banter.

"Adam. He can't wait to see you. Hearing so much about your case . . . uh, I mean you, I think he is anxious to meet you."

"And I'm anxious to meet him, too. Though I'm a bit nervous about Mother. For some reason I feel like our relationship in the past has been . . . strained. I don't know anyone anymore. I feel so lost. I just hope

we can be friends. I'm sure if Adam's anything like Blake, he must be nice." What had
given her the idea that she had a *strained* relationship with her mother?

"You should rest, Casey. With Blake and
Adam coming, there's no telling how late an
evening you'll have. I must get those trollops
organized before Mr. Worthington comes
down. I'll be downstairs if you need me." As
Flora left the room, a trail of her words could
be heard down the length of the long hall.

Casey nibbled at a slice of the pecan pie
and decided she liked knowing Flora would
come to her rescue.

A nap sounded like a great idea even
though it was her first day at home. There
would be other days to take walks and explore her new surroundings. She yawned
elaborately. With all the discoveries she had
made, she was mentally exhausted. The
bed beckoned. The moment she curled into
a ball she felt as if weights were resting on
her eyelids. A second after she closed her
eyes, she slept.

Casey felt the dream, the nightmare from
her past coming as she drifted off. Unable to
fight the images, she let go, her subconscious in total demand.

It was dark. The feeling of being closed in was almost suffocating. She shifted around in the small space and tried to stretch out. Leaning back against the wall, with her legs out before her, she was still too big. She thought by now they should know she wouldn't fit in the closet anymore. She also knew if she remained quiet and didn't put up a fight, she wouldn't have to stay in the closet very long.

It was hot and the air was steamy-like. Kind of like when she got to take a shower and used the hot water. That was okay. But she didn't like this kind of heat. Her throat felt tight and all closed up. She tried not to think about the air, or if it was being all sucked up. This always scared her. She feared she wouldn't have enough air. They said she would die. She believed them. Sometimes. Sometimes she wished she would die; then maybe they would be sorry for what they did to her.

Taking another deep breath, she felt something heavy weighing down on her thin chest. She closed her eyes. Afraid now, she was too weak to push it away. Her air was almost gone; she couldn't breathe! Gasping, she tried to push the heavy thing from her. It wouldn't move. It was there like before, sucking up her air. She pushed at the heavy object, kicked the closet door. Maybe they would come. She needed air. She would die!

Panting now, her breath came in ragged gasps. She kicked and screamed; the massive form resting on top of her was too much. She squeezed her eyes tighter, wishing to be someplace else. It never worked. Her raspy voice howled like a trapped animal. That's what she was. Trapped.

She shoved at the form. Opening her eyes, one at a time, she stared at the thing. It was wet. Not wet like water wet, but thick, like oil. And it smelled. Eyes like those of a dead fish stared back at her.

Seeing the silent stare above her, she remembered. A sheer, black fright took hold of her, possessing her. She gave in to the pure, raw fear.

And screamed.
And screamed.
And screamed.

Chapter Six

Casey sprang up in the bed, drenched in sweat. Her breath came in short, uneven spurts. Recalling the horror of her nightmare caused her entire body to tremble. Her pulse pounded from the imagined fear. Or was it imagined? Not knowing frightened her.

The claustrophobia she had experienced was certainly real. As if she were still locked in the dark corners of her dream, Casey walked over to the window and assured herself the fear was an illusion.

The mellow sunlight cast a golden halo over the grounds. She needed the wide-open space to soothe her shattered nerves. The beauty of the grounds at Swan House, the lush green lawn weaving through a multitude of color calmed her almost immediately. Everything was so open and *normal*-looking.

Rubbing her sore knuckles, she winced. The backs of her arms were tender from the pin-sized glass cuts. Casey reflected on the day's events. Had it only been a few hours since her release from the hospital? Things were happening too fast. Unsure of anything at the moment, she walked over to the table and picked at the remains of her minimeal left by Flora.

Should she burden Flora with the afternoon's events? Thinking of her, she smiled. Flora was a genuine, kind-hearted soul. Casey was surprised when she learned Flora had taken care of her as a child. At least she wasn't a total stranger there. Not that her mother was a stranger to her, but Adam and Mr. Worthington were. What did she really know about these people?

Blake seemed nice enough. Though they had only just met, she felt some sort of camaraderie existed between them. She thought he might have felt it, too.

Anxious to meet her stepfather, she wondered what he was like. She knew Evie had married him after she was hospitalized, and they'd been an item before that. Blake told her he'd visited her once. Would he approve of her? She hoped so. And if he didn't? That didn't bear thinking about since she was dependent on him and her mother. Soon she would find a job and a place of her own.

Questions. She needed answers. *Patience,* Casey told herself. *I'll learn soon enough.*

Tomorrow her mother would fill in the gaps for her. Then she would decide what she would do.

Casey heard the knock on the door and almost jumped out of her skin.

Evie smoothed the pale yellow Chanel suit before lifting a manicured hand to knock on the door of the guest room. She would give her daughter the privacy she deserved.

Angered that her trip to Atlanta had been cut short, she knew it was going to be difficult to put on her motherly cloak, and even more difficult to wear it convincingly. It had been so long.

She remembered the phone call.

"Evie, she's out," the voice on the other end of the phone had whispered.

"What! I thought it was next week. You said . . ."

"I know what I said, goddamn it! I can't

keep fixing things for you, Evie." The speaker sighed, frustration apparent.

"Yes, I know. And I can't continue to cater to your expensive tastes." She slammed the phone down in the cradle.

She hadn't counted on Casey's early release. Oh, it had been mentioned by Dr. Macklin. With her influence she was sure nothing would come of it. She was wrong. And she didn't like being wrong. Evie knew what she wanted and got it. Whether by her own hand or one she had learned to master like a puppeteer, she always got her way. It wasn't about to change. *She* wanted to be there to greet her daughter. *She* wanted to be the first one she came to when her memory returned. *If* her memory returned.

She heard the footsteps hesitate on the other side of the door. Casey was still the little mouse she'd been as a child. At least that hadn't changed. Mice needed guidance through their tunnels.

Casey paused before opening the door. A deep sense of foreboding twisted her insides. Fear left over from her dream? *I have nothing to fear,* she told herself. *It's probably Blake, ready to introduce me to Adam.* She smiled, glad that she had him as a friend.

Swinging the door as wide as it would open, Casey stopped cold in her tracks.

"Welcome home, Casey. Are you settled in?" Evie stepped inside the room, her exotic perfume wafting behind her. She pulled Casey in a light hug and kissed the air on either side of her face.

Casey didn't know what to say. Her mother was a stranger to her, after all. The perfectly coifed woman proceeded to walk around her room, surveying it as if it were the first time she had actually seen it.

She watched in silence as Evie continued to inspect her surroundings like an army general. She stopped at the closet.

Turning to Casey, she asked, "How do you like the clothes? I picked them out myself. Nothing but the best, I told them. I wasn't sure of the size, but from the looks of you"—Evie scanned her from head to toe—"it appears I was accurate. When you're up to it, I'll take you to Lord & Taylor in Atlanta. We'll make a weekend of it. From there we'll go to Stefan's; he's the best stylist in Atlanta." Evie lifted a limp strand of Casey's hair as she said this.

Unable to mutter a single word, Casey watched her mother. She didn't look as though her silence bothered her. In fact, she looked like the cat who killed the canary.

"I'm sorry, I wasn't expecting you. Blake said you were in Atlanta."

Evie turned so abruptly, Casey felt the air whip around her.

"Blake says all sorts of things, Casey. In time you will learn not to listen to him. He's trouble. Watch out for him. I've been lucky. You may not be. Trust me, please."

Blake. Trouble?

"Why shouldn't I trust Blake, and of course I trust you, Mother," she said quickly.

"Because he's jealous of Adam and his wealth. Since day one he's been nothing but trouble. Questioning John and Adam about everything. Still, after all these years. He doesn't come here that often anymore, not since Adam set up his practice in Atlanta, thank God." Evie smiled at Casey, revealing perfectly capped teeth. Mother Nature had been kind to her. Or a surgeon's knife. Her mother could pass for forty. A petite woman, her slender figure was a perfect match for the elegant linen suit she wore. Pearls graced her delicate neckline and tiny pearl studs decorated her earlobes. Not an ounce of gray glistened in the golden cap of her flawlessly cut pageboy. Nothing about her said "Mother."

"I just met him. He seemed nice enough." Not wanting to start off on the wrong foot with her mother, Casey smiled and walked over to the closet.

"Can you help me pick out something? Flora said we dress for dinner. I haven't . . . well, you know how long it's been." Casey nodded toward the rows of clothing, hoping Evie would rise to the bait. She wanted her mother to be her mother. To tell her how happy she was to have her daughter back. Tell her how much she had missed her. Tell her how much she loved her and that no matter what, she would be there for her.

"I'd love to." Evie shoved satin-padded hangers along the length of the rack. A silk, teal blouse with matching pants, a dark green sheath dress, and a pale blue skirt with a matching angora sweater were her choices. She tossed the expensive garments on the bed haphazardly, apparently unconcerned about their care.

"You can pick from these. You'll need to learn what to wear, Casey. We have a position to uphold in society, dear. We must dress the part. You're twenty-eight years old. I'm not about to start babying you at this late date, but I will see to it that you have the proper guidance in what we Southerners deem as socially correct. Now, my dear, I must run. I haven't seen John since my arrival. He's been ill, you know. I have a feeling poor John won't be around much longer. I'll see you at dinner." A brush to her cheeks and she was gone.

A plush cream carpet under her feet could have been a bear trap. Casey couldn't move. Surprise didn't describe what she was feeling. Strange. Her mother *was* different than she remembered from her visits to the hospital.

Casey threw the clothes in a pile and stood staring at the contents in the closet. It was a wardrobe befitting a queen. Yet, for all the care her mother had shown in picking out the expensive designs, she hadn't shown a shred of regard for their care.

In the bathroom Casey searched under the cabinet for the ugly, brown shift she had discarded only hours before. Suddenly, its scratchy material was silken, its drabness exquisite. This was her. Not the silken garments hanging from padded hangers. This was the Casey her mother visited in the hospital. This was the person she was, at least for now. For the moment, she couldn't bring herself to touch the new clothes. It was betrayal. Though of what, she didn't know.

Evie paced the dark confines of John's room. Flora said he was showering. He was actually going to come downstairs for dinner. Maybe she had underestimated him. At seventy-three, he's been as spry as a forty-year-old. Until the last few months. He no longer tended his precious gardens. He stayed in his room most of the time, taking his meals in bed.

Worthington Enterprises continued to flourish without his dictatorial hand. Evie wondered what the reaction of the board would be the day she took her seat at the head of the table. At forty-nine, she was looking forward to a new career. Not that she wished poor John an early demise, she just needed to be in control. While John was a most generous husband, he still pinched the purse strings if he felt she was living too lavishly, as he put it. Tossing his wealth about wasn't uncommon for Evie. Coming from a poor family in Sweetwater, as a child she often dreamed of being rich. . . .

She remembered the long days spent taking care of her four brothers and three younger sisters. As the eldest, the responsibility of raising them had rested on her shoulders. Her parents worked at whatever odd jobs they could find. Many times they were dependent on the charity of others. Evie would never forget the first day of her junior year.

The pale blue dress had graced the window of Barnaby's for weeks. Evie passed it on her occasional trips to town. She wanted that dress more than she wanted food. If only she had a job. She would save every penny for that dress. But, unless she was available for baby-sitting, there wasn't much opportunity for her to work. She had her hands full as it was with the brood at home.

It was rare when she had a day to herself. This particular day, a Saturday, her mother had insisted she get out of the house, telling her it was her chance to hang around with her friends. She jumped at the chance. Though she didn't tell her mother about her lack of friends. Not many wanted to hang with the Tilton bunch. Poor white trash they called them. Evie fumed when she heard those remarks, but deep down, she knew it was true. Someday, she would show them all.

Crossing the dust-covered street, Evie wandered over to Barnaby's. The dress was gone! Her heart dropped to her feet. She'd had such hopes for that dress. Maybe Robert Bentley would notice her. Evie had had her eye on him since the previous summer. His father owned the only real estate office in town, so right away Evie knew he was off-limits, but that didn't deter her. She was sure if she had the right clothes, he would notice her.

She trudged back home, her heart heavy with resignation. She wanted so much more. Babies and worries. Her mother, at thirty-eight, looked twenty years older. Worn-out before her time. Not her. No way would Evie let that happen. No matter what she had to do, she would never live like her mother.

Evie was surprised to see her father home on Saturday. He was usually out begging for work from one of Sweetwater's better families. A part of her admired him for his tenacity to provide for his family, no matter the cost. Another part of her wanted to shout at him and ask where his pride was. Did he have no shame? Still, he was her father, and she loved him, as much as she was capable of loving anyone. Evie had admitted to herself long ago that she could never love anyone but Evie. Look what happened to her parents, who professed to be in love. Eight children. The sacrifice was too great.

Her father smiled and walked toward her with a glint in his steel gray eyes. Maybe he had a real job. Evie hoped so, then maybe she would be accepted. He held a brown paper bag out in front of him.

"This is for you." Her father handed her the sack.

Evie peered at the contents in the bag.

"I can't believe it! How did you know?"

"I've seen you stop in front of Barnaby's."

Evie took the pale blue dress from the bag. She searched for the price tag, but couldn't find it. She eyed her father, her gaze questioning.

"It was donated to the church. I got it from Edith; she's seen you admiring it, too."

Evie was instantly filled with rage. She tossed the swirl of blue on the ground. Charity? Did she want the dress that bad?

Without another word, she went inside,

angry at her lot in life. She had coveted that dress, but now that it was hers, she didn't think she could wear it. But if she did, maybe Robert would notice her.

Yes.

Pride lodged in her throat, and she swallowed deeply. Just this once.

Monday morning arrived. Evie was nervous, yet excited. She was sure this year would be different.

Evie slid into the small desk, her new dress sliding up her slender thigh. She'd taken her bra off in the rest room earlier. Not caring what she revealed, she scooted around in her seat, waiting for Robert. She couldn't wait to see the look on his handsome face when he saw her breasts bursting out of the tight dress. She knew he had this class with her. She'd looked on the bulletin board first thing.

Barbara Richards, the most popular girl in school, was the first to notice her. As the classroom filled, Evie became more uncomfortable. Hushed whispers, an occasional giggle. She felt the eyes of the entire class on her. Robert Bentley stared at her, too. He looked at her breasts, then smirked right along with the rest of the class.

Barbara stood up from her desk in the front of the room and swaggered over to Casey's desk. She centered her ice-blue gaze on her.

"Did you get the grease stain off the shoulder?" Barbara asked, then looked at the rest of the class. Laughter exploded.

Evie ran from the classroom.

Never! She would never go back to school. One day, she would show them all.

Chapter Seven

"Eve, darling, you're back," John said as he embraced her.

Evie cringed at the sound of her husband's voice. Adjusting the scowl on her furrowed brow, she fell into his outstretched arms.

"I didn't expect you until tomorrow. I know you're anxious to see Casey."

John patted her on the back, went to the mirror, and adjusted his tie. "I'm quite nervous myself."

Evie watched as he primped, a smirk hardening the lines around her mouth. Did he expect Casey to care what he looked like? Poor thing could barely manage to dress herself.

"You look wonderful, John. I hear you're coming down for dinner. Oh, darling, I'm so glad you're feeling better. I think if you continue to improve, we will take that trip we're always talking about." Evie stood behind John, wrapping her slim arms around his waist, alarmed at his frailty. John had been a big man when she married him. And fit. Well over six feet, and, at sixty-three, he'd had the physique men twenty years younger would've envied.

"Don't be too hasty, dear. These old bones aren't up to that, at least not yet. We shall see. Now tell me about your trip." John shuffled over to his recliner and eased down into the soft, worn leather.

A man's room, done in dark greens, browns, and soft beige. The one room Evie wasn't allowed to change. Old leather and the lingering smell of cigars marked the room as John's. Evie had refused to share this room when they married, saying it didn't fit her feminine needs. John gave her a free hand and she redecorated the suite across the hall. It worked out perfectly. Excluding the few times John requested a conjugal visit, their arrangement was ideal.

"Just the usual," Evie said. "I shopped, had lunch at Fuddruckers with Patricia. I do hate that name. I left early to prepare for

Casey's return. I'd hoped to arrive before she did, but it appears Rob . . . Mr. Bentley, saw to her release without notifying us." She hoped her disgust wasn't obvious.

John held out a branchlike arm and gestured to the phone on the bedside table.

"Oh, he did call. I guess Flora forgot to tell you. Blake found her walking downtown."

"Walking? Did something happen at the hospital?"

"Evidently Casey got tired of waiting. I called and asked Blake if he'd mind fetching her. I think he was running behind. You know him. Nevertheless, she's home, and I can't wait to see my beautiful daughter."

Beautiful? He hadn't seen her. And she wasn't his daughter. He acted like he *wanted* Casey there. Evie had thought the intrusion into their life would upset John. Obviously, she was wrong. She schooled her face into a practiced smile.

"That's so typical of Blake. You would think after all poor Casey has been through, he could do something right for a change. I just don't understand that man. I hope you said something to him." Anger settled in the lines she tried so hard to hide. She was glad now that she was standing behind John.

She walked to the door and faced her wan husband, her outrage under control.

"Eve, we've been through this before. Not now. I thought you would be overjoyed. My God, your daughter has been institutional-ized since we've been married. That's all I've heard for years, you wanting your daughter back. Now your dream is a reality, and you continue to complain about Blake." Huffing from his long speech, John gasped for each breath.

He slumped back in the chair, his breath-ing still labored. Eve watched in horror as John clutched his chest. As he struggled to convey his urgency to her, his arms flailing and legs stretched out before him, Evie stood transfixed.

Panic glazed his eyes. "Ugh, 'elp. Eeeh!"

John's incoherent call for help finally jos-tled her into action.

Running to his side, Evie shouted at the top of her lungs, praying Flora would be in the hall.

"Flora! Call 911, it's John!" Her shout was met with hurried footsteps.

She placed a shaky hand on John's brow. Sweat beaded his forehead. As he tried to sit, Evie pushed him back into the recliner.

"Shhh, it's going to be all right. Help is coming."

Evie saw the pounding pulse in the veins of his neck. Faster and faster. *My God! Is he having a heart attack?* She ran to the door.

"Help! Someone . . . *now!*" She peered down the hall and saw Blake's mad dash up the stairs.

Breathless, he entered the room without a glance at Evie.

He gripped John's pale hand and looked at the designer watch on his wrist. Damn. He should have seen it coming. Hell, he was a doctor. He counted the pulsating heartbeats.

"Don't just stand there, Eve, call an ambulance. Now!" Blake shouted.

"Damn you, Blake, I have. Rather, Flora did. What kind of monster do you think I am?"

"Have Flora get Adam. He's at the stables." He turned back to John, whose skin was an unhealthy gray color.

"Hang on John. You're going to be fine." He brushed a hand through his damp hair. Holding his fingers against the throbbing vein in his best friend's father's neck, he was reassured for the moment—the pulse was steady.

He heard Adam bound up the stairs. Thankful for his arrival, Blake stood back as his friend entered the room. The smell of leather and hay clung to him, reminding Blake of what Adam had been doing before his call to duty. The horses.

Casual to a fault, Adam sauntered over to the chair where John lay, his pale skin lathered with perspiration.

"Hey, bud, what have you got yourself into now?" He touched a dirty hand to his father's forehead. His nonchalant perusal gave Blake a moment of reprieve.

"Flora called the ambulance; it should be here any minute. Oh dear, this is so awful." Evie went down on her knees and placed a hand on John's chest.

Adam searched for Blake's eyes over the blond crown of hair.

Too shaken to respond, Blake raised a winged brow, and mouthed, "Not now."

Blake shifted John into a reclining position and removed his shoes. Reaching behind him for the footstool, he gently propped his feet up. Comfort was uppermost in his mind. He hadn't ruled out a heart attack yet. John's pulse continued to throb at a steady pace. Until the proper tests were run, he wasn't going to dismiss anything. Feeling Adam's fear, he looked into the face of his best friend and motioned for him to leave the room.

"Come on, Evie, I need you to get up." Blake took her by the hand and gently pushed her in the direction of Flora, who remained in the doorway. For once she was too shocked to utter a single word.

Clearing the room was no easy task. They all loved John and wanted to be at his side. Blake didn't want them to see what might be coming next. John Worthington was like a second father to him, and even more so since his own father's death three years before.

The high-pitched wail of sirens in the distance allowed Blake to convince Evie and Adam to leave.

"Do what I say. I'll take care of him." He knew if it were his own father, he would've wanted to stay in the room, but as a doctor, he also knew what affect watching a loved one die could have. He knew. Firsthand. If at all possible, he would spare this family that pain.

*　　*　　*

Casey heard the sirens and ran out into the hall, where her mother and a strange man stood leaning against the wall. Flora was standing at the top of the steps. All were statue-still.

"Is something wrong?"

Adam looked at Flora, then Evie.

"My father may be suffering a heart attack. We don't know anything, yet. Blake is with him now."

Casey could see that worry rested in the deep crevices around his blue eyes. She longed to reach out and smooth away the worry lines. She didn't think he would welcome her touch. Not now. How awful that her first meeting with Adam had to be under such tragic circumstances.

"I didn't know, I'm so sorry." Distraught at the scene playing out in front of her, and not knowing what to say or do, Casey could only stare at the trio, praying that what Adam told her wasn't true.

"There isn't anything we can do. Evie, I hear the medics. Let them in." Adam's command left no room for questions.

Casey observed her mother's compliance and realized there was more to her relationship with Adam than that of stepmother and stepson. Something much deeper. Was it fear she saw in her mother's eyes?

Evie ran down the steps, her heels creating a soft thud on the plush steps.

The medics vaulted up the staircase, intent on their rescue. Casey watched in silence as they entered what she assumed was her stepfather's suite of rooms. Her mother jumped as the door was slammed behind them.

Who closed the door? Was John Worthington dead? Was Blake trying to spare the family further distress?

Unsure of what her role was, Casey returned to her room. Feeling childish at her earlier behavior, she looked down at the outfit she wore and quickly changed into the teal pantsuit. What was she thinking of? She couldn't go around looking like an escapee from the loony bin.

Casey left her room and closed the door behind her. She would show respect for the man who provided her with the clothes and the home that was more impressive than anything she could've imagined.

Flora motioned for her to join her at the top of the steps. They watched in silence as the paramedics carried a gurney down the staircase. Adam and Blake followed behind.

"It looks to me like Mr. John may have suffered a stroke. We won't know until tests are done. Poor man, God bless him. He doesn't deserve this." Flora's blue eyes were drowning in unshed tears.

Casey reached for the woman who in such a short period of time had reached out to her and offered comfort. She wanted to return the same comfort if she could. She wrapped her arms around Flora, taking pleasure in how good it felt to share a human touch.

Flora sniffed and dabbed her eyes with the hem of her apron.

"I'm sorry, I just don't want anything to happen to John."

"I know. I don't either. I'm sure Adam and Blake will see that he has the best care possible."

"You're right, you know. I just hate to think of Swan House without him. It's bound to happen, but still." Flora reached for the railing and started down the stairs. "Let's go in the kitchen. Maybe I can talk you into another piece of pie."

"That sounds nice. Do you know where my mother went? Why don't I ask her if she wants to join us."

Flora reached for her arm and stopped her before she could walk away.

"She's in John's room. I'd leave her be for now. And one other thing, Casey. Your mother *never* enters the kitchen."

"Why is that?"

"Says she cooked enough as a child. She had the full responsibility for her seven siblings growing up. I don't think Ms. Evie had much of a childhood." Flora shook her head either in denial or lack of understanding.

Together, they entered a gleaming black-and-white kitchen. A stainless-steel refrigerator surrounded by stark, white cabinets was blinding to the eye after the heavy darkness of the other rooms.

An island in the center of the kitchen was scattered with mini flowerpots, and what looked like herb seedlings. Bright copper pots hanging from the ceiling gave the kitchen a homey, lived-in look. But it was the red-and-white-checkered curtains and seat cushions that drew Casey's eyes. The room looked so cheerful, and it smelled heavenly from fresh-baked bread. She knew she was going to spend a lot of time in that room.

Casey sat at the scarred oak table, thinking it out of place, and yet it fit perfectly. Kind of like her.

Flora opened the cabinets and pulled out bright red plates, cups, and saucers. A pot of coffee appeared from out of nowhere, and soon Casey was munching on sweet pecans.

"Mabel must love the kitchen. It's so cheery."

Flora nodded as she sipped her coffee. "I think so. You'll often find Adam and Blake here. Not for the cheeriness, mind you, but the food. The two of them eat like horses and never gain an ounce."

"Growing boys, I guess." Questions lodged in her throat.

"Flora, did I know either of them?"

"Not that I know of. You may have encountered Mr. Blake a time or two at the doc's, but other than that, I don't think so."

"I wish I remembered. In time I'm sure I will. I want to talk to Mother. I need to understand why I was . . . gone for so long."

Flora dropped her fork, the pinging sound giving off an echo.

Casey started to take another bite, then stopped in midair. "What did I say?"

"I was about to ask you. Did you say what I thought you said?"

Casey was tired. Tired of talking. Tired of games. As much as she liked Flora, she just wished she would be straight with her.

"I said what you heard, Flora. I'll repeat it. I don't know why I was put away in that place. I didn't then, and I don't now. But, I'm going to find out. Is that clear enough?" Casey took her cup and saucer over to the sink and observed the twilight through the window. Dusk was settling over the grounds, bathing the rolling hillside in soft pinks, purples, and blues. How long had it been since she'd seen such a landscape? Too long and maybe never.

Disheartened since her arrival, she wondered if coming home had been such a good idea after all. Then again, she hadn't been given any other options. Maybe she should ask her mother to lend her the money to rent an apartment of her own. When the time was right. If ever there was such a time.

Flora swallowed the last of her coffee when Casey turned to face her.

"I think Mrs. Worthington has the answers you're looking for."

"I'm sorry. I shouldn't have snapped at you, but it seems since my arrival, everything that could go wrong has gone wrong. First the picture, then the glass, and now poor John. Maybe I should have stayed at the hospital." Disgusted with her display of self-pity, she chastised herself. Things could be worse, she supposed.

High heels clicked against the ceramic tile floor, startling both Casey and Flora.

"Mrs. Worthington?" Flora seemed stunned by her mother's arrival.

Her mother stood in the doorway. Her eyes were glassy with unshed tears. She'd aged in a matter of minutes.

Casey wanted to rush into her mother's arms and ask all the questions she'd wanted to for so long, but the last thing she wanted to do was cause her more worry. Now wasn't the time. Perhaps later, when John recovered.

"I'm sorry, I don't know what to say." Casey walked over to her mother and wrapped her arms around her as she had done with Flora earlier.

Her mother stiffened in her embrace, then relaxed. Her petite frame suddenly shook with sobs.

"There is nothing you can say, Casey." Her mother pulled a lace handkerchief from her pocket and dabbed at her eyes. "It's not your fault." She sobbed. "John is just getting old."

Casey released her mother and gently placed an arm about her shoulders. "I'm sure he'll be just fine. Blake seems very competent."

"You don't know him. He frightens me!" A demented glint flashed in her mother's gaze. Brief, but there.

Her mother looked around the kitchen. She peered from left to right. Casey had been around enough crazy people to know her mother's behavior was what the doctors would term paranoid. She looked as if she were waiting for Blake to walk through the door with an axe in his hand.

"Why, Mother? What did he do?" Casey looked searchingly to Flora. A sense of doom settled in the pit of her stomach.

Suddenly, Evie laughed, the sound wicked to Casey's ears.

"He's a murderer, that's what he is!" Her mother's abrupt change in behavior alarmed her.

"Blake? But who, how?" Casey questioned.

Evie laughed. "I think I should ask you

that." Her frenzied glare scanned Casey, then rested on Flora, who watched in silent shock.

Casey felt a fear so deep, its enormity took her breath away.

"Ask me what, Mother?"

Flora chose that moment to speak. "It's all right, dear. Here let me help you." Flora steered her sobbing employer out of the kitchen and gave Casey a "don't-ask-I'll-tell-you-later" look as she left the kitchen.

Casey couldn't remember anything. Absolutely nothing. *How can I live like this? Why won't they tell me whatever it is they're trying to keep secret?*

Casey trembled, then began to shake with uncontrollable rage as she slammed her tender fists against the oak table. Damn the doctors.

Damn them all!

Chapter Eight

Casey felt as if she had been punched in the gut, the force of it taking her breath away. She couldn't breathe. In. Out. In. Out. She was reeling from her mother's strange behavior and her accusation against Blake.

Murder? What kind of cruel joke was she trying to play?

Flora returned to the kitchen, her face a mass of lines and shadows.

"Will she be all right?" She wrapped her arms around herself, hoping to still the tremors.

Flora leaned against the oak table and shook her head. "As right as she'll ever be."

Puzzled, Casey sat across from Flora and reached for her hand.

"Why did she accuse Blake of murder? It's bizarre."

"I wish I knew, Missy. There's no tellin' what goes on in that head of hers. Your momma hasn't been well. She has spells. Started having them not long after you were put . . . after you were hospitalized.

"At first, it was just little things," she went on. "You know, like, she'd forget where she put something. Sometimes she and Mr. Worthington would be havin' a talk; I'd hear this, mind you, I wasn't eavesdroppin', just listenin'. He'd be tellin' her about his day and she'd act as if she never heard a word he said. She'd start talking about somethin' different, as if they'd been talkin' about it all along.

"She was on some kind of medication, I'm not sure what it was, but Mr. Worthington thought that explained her forgetfulness and her odd behavior. Me, I thought the pills were *for* the odd behavior, but I never said anythin'. Then Mr. Worthington took her to a specialist in Atlanta, and for a while, she was her normal self. I don't know what the doctors did; I never asked."

Casey tried to absorb everything Flora said. Her mother had never acted abnormal on her visits to Sanctuary, or if she had, Casey wasn't aware of it. Of course back then, anything other than what she herself was experiencing was normal.

"I still don't understand why she would accuse Blake of murder even if she's not in her right mind. Who is he supposed to have killed?"

Casey heard Flora's intake of breath as she struggled to get up from the table. She walked over to the sink and stared out the window.

"Years ago Sweetwater was the scene of a horrible murder. Blake had nothing to do with it. I'm sure Mrs. Worthington is confused. In her state of mind we never know what she's thinking."

Flora seemed different now, Casey thought, not the bursting-with-energy chatterbox she normally was. Flora acted like the steam had blown out of her engine. Maybe she was just tired.

The shrill ring of the telephone startled her.

Flora grabbed the portable phone at the edge of the counter, her back turned. Casey strained to hear what she was saying. Flora finally turned to Casey.

"It looks like Mr. John is going to be fine. Dr. Foo seems to think he suffered a slight stroke, though they won't be sure until the tests are complete. He's asked that you forgive him and hopes to welcome you home as soon as the beasts let him. That was a quote from Blake." Relief rested on Flora's face, removing years.

"Thank God. Should we tell Mother?" Casey asked.

"I heard her pick up the extension. Blake will tell her."

Casey felt drained. Meeting her family and learning her mother wasn't the woman she appeared to be, and now this, her stepfather's illness, all were too much. She needed to think, clear her head. Something nagged at her subconscious, leaving her feeling on edge. As if something bad were about to happen.

"Flora, you never said," she paused, not wanting Flora to accuse her of meddling where she shouldn't, but the question continued to nag at her. She had to ask. "Who was it that died?"

The little woman scampered around the huge kitchen, opening cupboards, peering inside. She opened a canister and grabbed a bowl from the countertop. She dumped flour from the canister. Taking milk and eggs from the refrigerator, Flora cracked the eggs and dumped the milk into the large bowl. Casey watched as she pulled a wire whisk from the drawer. She felt sorry for the beating the eggs were taking.

Casey placed a hand around hers. "Flora. Stop."

Flora did as she was told and looked into Casey's eyes. "Missy, I might be speakin' out of turn, but I'd best say this now and get it over with. No matter what you hear about that day, don't believe it. And trust me, when word gets out you're home, you'll hear all sorts of things. It's in the past, and it's best forgotten. People were hurt. Just leave it be, Casey."

Casey ran her hands through her hair and flashed an aggravated look at Flora, who stood frozen in place.

"Why?"

"Like I said, you'll have to trust me. It's a day the residents of Sweetwater want to forget."

A sharp pain sliced through Casey's head, leaving her stunned.

Then blackness.

The lights were so bright. She wanted them off. Her clothes were wet and clung to her skin.

They kept pulling her along.

She smelled. Gross, she thought. She'd started her period and it was all over her.

"Over here." Someone shouted.

Flashbulbs were going off everywhere. Red dots danced before her eyes.

She wanted them to leave her alone.

They wouldn't stop pulling her. Someone lifted her up, then pushed her down.

She was cold. Her hands and feet felt like ice. Her hands shook.

Someone tugged at her arms.

The lights continued to flash, blinding her.

Metal.

Heavy and cold.

She tried to wave her hands about and couldn't.

She screamed.

Casey glanced around. Pushing herself into a sitting position, she saw the worried look on Flora's face. "What happened?" Her head felt like it had exploded.

"There now, it's all right. You're gonna be just fine." She helped her into a chair. "Way back when, they called it swooning," Flora said, and mopped Casey's forehead with a cool cloth.

"I fainted?"

"Seems so. You've had too much excitement."

Casey agreed.

"Let's go upstairs. You need to rest." Flora took her by the arm and helped her stand. A wave of dizziness washed over her.

Casey allowed Flora to lead her through the dark halls. She hated the dark. Even as a child, she'd hated the dark. And the closet.

The closet?

She stopped in the middle of the formal dining room. The cobwebs that clouded her mind only seconds ago were gone.

"Blake said you took care of me as a child. Do you recall me being afraid of the dark?"

She watched as Flora struggled with her answer.

"I remember you were. When you stayed with me, it was always at my house, and if you recollect . . . never mind that, you were never there at dark. Your mother or father always came to get you then."

Fear gushed through her. She was truly terrified, and she looked around the room as if seeking refuge from her thoughts. Seeing the room for the first time, she took in the dark, heavy furniture. A formal dining table that could seat at least twenty graced the middle of the long room. Gold wallpaper covered the walls, and at the end of the vast space, a fireplace dominated the entire wall. She doubted a fire could warm the gloominess that surrounded her.

She was still having trouble with Flora's statement. She wandered aimlessly around the long room, her thoughts jumbled.

Determined more than ever to solve the puzzle of her life, she walked over to Flora, who sat at the long dining table. She sat down next to her.

"My father?" Casey waited for another explanation to her blank life.

"I guess you don't remember him, either. He was a kind man. Too bad he died so young."

"Only the good die young," her grandmother once said. Where had *that* come from? She listened as Flora went on.

"He was such a hard worker, always helping those less fortunate than he even though he didn't have much himself. In the end it cost him his life."

"How?"

"On the outskirts of Brunswick, down at the railroad tracks late one night, I think he was on his way home from the mill, there was a horrible car accident. Your father, Buzz, stopped to see if he could help. There were three or four cars involved."

"My father's name was Buzz?"

"Yes." Flora smiled at her, seeming not to mind the interruption. "Or at least that's what everyone called him. He always wore a crew cut, but his real name was Reed.

"Buzz loved children. One of the boys in the accident was barely alive. By the time the ambulance got there, they were so busy, they were askin' for volunteers to take the injured to the hospital and the dead to the morgue. Your father took the little boy and drove him over to Peach County. They were the best back then. I think we call them trauma centers today.

"They say Buzz raced as fast as he could to get the youngster in the hands of the doctors. I'm sure he must have been afraid the child would die, or he wouldn't have taken such a risk. When he entered Peach County they had been informed of the pileup, and sent their ambulances to help. If I remember, there were fourteen people involved.

"Reaching the intersection a block away from the hospital, he never bothered to stop. I don't know if he didn't hear the sirens, or if he was just too anxious to get to the hospital. They hit head-on. Your father didn't survive. He was killed instantly, a blessin' some say."

Casey felt tears flow for a man she had no memory of, but who gave his life trying to save a child.

"And the boy, did he die, too?" Casey rubbed her eyes.

"Oh, no. He lived."

"That was a very heroic thing to do." There was decency in her family. Thank God.

"Most of Sweetwater thought so, except for your mother," Flora said.

"It must have been hard for her. Losing her husband with two small children to raise."

Casey jumped out of the chair as if she'd been poked with a cattle prod.

"Did you hear that?" The shock of what she said hit her full force.

"I heard," Flora said.

Casey covered her mouth with her hand. "I remembered something!" She wasn't sure if it meant anything, but it was a start. The sooner she had her memory back, the sooner she could start her new life.

She hugged Flora, who was still seated at the table, a smile plastered on her face.

"Do I have a brother or a sister? Are they here? Do they know I'm home?"

Again Flora took on that faraway look. "It was a boy. He was older than you. He died many years ago. It's a sad topic, and not one you'll want to be talkin' about to the members of Swan House."

"What *can* I talk about, Flora? Why all the secrets? What is everyone hiding? I finally remember something, something I think is important, and you're telling me I can't talk about it. You sound just like Dr. Macklin at Sanctuary. Whenever I felt I was on the brink of remembering, he would knock me out with a pill or a shot."

"This isn't the hospital, Casey. But trust me, when the time is right you'll get your memories back. I'm not so sure it's a bad thing, you losin' your thoughts and all. It's like the good Lord has given you a chance to start life with a clean slate. You'll have a choice in the memories you'll be makin' for yourself, Missy."

"I hope you're right." Casey knew it wasn't the time to pursue the past. She would wait. She'd waited for ten years; another few days wouldn't matter. She resigned herself to it and changed the subject.

"Flora, you didn't say. The boy, the one in the accident," she paused considering her question, "does he still live around here?" Casey hoped he hadn't survived only to live life maimed or lame.

"Indeed he does. And what a fine young man he turned out to be."

Casey released her breath, relieved that her father's efforts hadn't been in vain.

"Maybe I will get to meet him when I get my life together."

"Oh, don't worry about meeting him, sweetie. You already have." Flora wore a grin as wide as Texas.

"I have?" She didn't recall meeting any strangers. Maybe she was losing her short-term memory, too.

"You sure did, honey." Flora paused. "It was Mr. Adam."

Casey's eyes popped wide open. Her jaw went slack at the same time.

"I'm shocked. This family truly amazes me. It seems at every corner there is a new revelation. It's almost frightening. Then that explains how my mother met John. At least I think it does." She watched Flora nod, her assessment of the story correct.

"Mr. Worthington was still married at the

time. However, because Buzz was employed at the paper mill and of course it was owned by none other than John, he felt responsible for your mother and you kids."

They must have been a great comfort to one another, Casey thought.

Flora stood up and walked to the end of the room. With her back to Casey, she resumed her tale.

"Mr. John gave your momma a large check. Supposedly it was enough so she would never have to work again. Your mother began to make weekly visits to Swan House after that. She and Mr. Worthington became fast friends real quick.

"By this time, I think a year had passed since your father was killed. Evie wasn't aware of the sadness that had descended on Swan House. Mrs. Worthington had just been diagnosed with cancer, and the prognosis was grim. It was a sad time around here, let me tell you." Flora lifted a silver frame from the mantel and stared at the image.

Casey waited for Flora to continue.

"Mrs. Worthington's only concern was for Adam. She wanted to make sure he was taken care of. She made me promise I would stay on and take care of him. Sure wasn't a hard promise to make. It was a joy workin' here. I couldn't have children of my own, so I was delighted."

Casey watched as a brief wave of sadness came to rest on Flora's gentle features.

"I was here night and day. Fortunately for the family, Mrs. Worthington passed on quickly. There was no lingering, no sickroom. I knocked on the door one morning, and her usual welcoming call never came. Alarmed, I went inside. She was in bed, her gold hair spread across the pillow like sunshine. She looked like an angel. I went over to her and touched her cheek." Flora stopped and paused, as if the memory were too much.

"She was so cold. She must have died early the night before. Mr. Worthington was beside himself with grief. After the funeral it was months before he went back to work. Adam forgot he had a father, so as promised, I took care of him and did my best. That's about the time Evie's visits became a daily event. I have to say this much for her, she brought the sparkle back into Mr. Worthington's eyes."

"How long was it before they got married, Flora?" Maybe the chronological sequence of the events would help her remember.

"Oh, it was years. Your mother was having personal problems. John took care of her finances. He still felt it was his fault that your father died, and like the fine man he is, he took responsibility."

"What about me and my brother? Where were we while all this was going on?"

"Oh, you were always with your mother. Your brother never came."

"Swan House is so enormous, I think I would remember if I ever lived or visited here." Casey looked around the huge dining room. She knew she had never been in that house before. She could feel it.

"It's odd that you say that. I don't recall Evie bringing you inside. She made you wait in the car. She would never come to the drive in the front of the house; instead she would park at the gate and walk."

"I knew I hadn't been in here. Then my mother and John must have dated for a long time." It wasn't a question, but Flora answered it anyway.

"I don't think I would call what Evie and John did dating." Flora's cheeks flamed red.

"Evidently it was more than dating. He married her," Casey said.

"While Mr. Worthington was charmed by

her . . . he wasn't foolish. He knew it wouldn't look right if they married so soon, especially after the murder." Flora paled at her apparent slip of the tongue.

"What murder, Flora? You keep bringing this up and don't explain yourself. Please, tell me. I won't tell anyone you told me. Flora I need to know," Casey begged.

Flora appeared deep in thought, as if weighing her answer. "You're right. Evie should have told you, but she's so confused these days."

Flora's gaze never wavered as she spoke. "It was your brother, Casey. He was murdered."

Chapter Nine

"Who in the name of God would murder my brother? More to the point, why would someone *want* to murder him?"

Casey paced the dining room, her movements jerky and flat-footed. She stared at the dark furniture, which looked even more somber than it had moments before. Her mood was starting to turn as dark as the furniture.

"This is all so confusing. Isn't Adam my stepbrother?" Casey ran a hand through her hair in frustration.

"He is. The real brother . . . it's a long and tragic tale. This is another story that should be comin' from your momma." Flora held up a hand to silence her as Casey opened her mouth to pose another question.

Did Flora know anything about her

brother's death? A brother she had no memory of. A brother whose life was taken in a moment of anger, vengeance, or what? What made people kill?

"I don't think my mother is in a position to tell me anything, Flora. Whatever I learn, I'm going to have to learn it on my own. No one seems to think I need to know what kind of life I had. I just don't understand all the secrecy."

Who were these people who were supposed to be her family? Her life, blank slate that it was, was becoming more and more riddled with puzzles and unanswered questions.

Casey was tired; she wanted nothing more than to sleep and forget about her life, at least for today. Tomorrow she would make a plan. Tomorrow she would decide what she should do with . . . the rest of her life.

Sun flickered through the thin crack in the heavy drapes. With sleep still skimming the surface of her subconscious, Casey rolled over and observed her room.

The silken comforter was soft and felt

lush against her skin. She nestled deeper into its warmth. Slinking lower, she pulled the blanket over her face to block out the rays of light and tried to return to the blissful state of sleep.

There she wouldn't have to think, or plan, or make any life-altering decisions.

But her mind was buzzing and wouldn't stop. With a heavy heart, Casey threw the covers back and went to the window. The thick drapes parted easily. Golden sunlight streamed into the room, bathing the furnishings in a soft glow.

She stood back and viewed the garden below her. A rainbow of colors greeted her early morning vision. She smiled. Maybe she could work in the garden with Hank. She'd ask. At least her hands would be busy.

The questions and doubts that had plagued her before bed returned. She tried to block them by filling her mind with the splendor of the gardens below, but couldn't.

Her heart started to race. Back at Sanctuary, Sandra had always told her if she wanted to find out something, she had to search for the answer. Maybe she needed to go back to that other life for the answers. But before she did that, maybe, just maybe, she could find out something here at Swan House. If the answers she sought failed to surface, only then would she go back to the doctors and the hospital that she had vowed never to visit again. If she failed in her attempt, she would permit the doctors to experiment on her, anything to help her uncover events prior to her hospitalization. Determined to learn the reason for her loss of memory, she hurried to the shower, her decision hastening her along. She'd start immediately. If she was lucky, maybe she'd find some answers.

She stood under the warm spray from the shower and let her mind wander.

Adam had been late returning from the hospital the previous night. When Flora poked her head in the door to say good night, she'd told her Mr. Worthington would be home in a few days. She'd said Evie was staying the night at Worthington Enterprises, where John had a small apartment. She hadn't mentioned Blake. Flora had seemed contented with her news and had left her alone with her thoughts. Then the day's events caught up with her and she fell asleep moments after her head hit the pillow.

                    *   *   *

Casey turned the water off and stood naked in the warm, steamy room. It felt eerie, like yesterday, when she'd encountered the ground glass in the jar of cream. Flora hadn't been a bit surprised when she'd told her what happened. She'd looked at the scratches and cuts, clucked her tongue a few times, and nothing more was said. Any thought of how the glass shards had gotten into the jar seemed of no importance. It was as if she had imagined the entire incident.

Casey stared at the mirror. The mist from the shower prevented her from viewing the dark circles she knew existed under her eyes. Wiping the fog with one hand, she glanced at her reflection. Wet hair clung to her neck. She looked like a scrawny drowned rat.

She ran the towel along her arms and legs, wincing at the sharp tingle where her skin still smarted from cuts and scrapes from the day before.

Who had placed the glass in the lotion? And why?

A last quick swipe with the nubby towel and she was ready to get dressed. In the closet she reached for a pair of panties and a lacy bra. She no longer appreciated the designer clothes that Evie had gone to so much trouble to purchase. She dressed with one thought in mind: starting her search. Now. It was time to rediscover the life she'd had prior to the ten years she spent at Sanctuary.

A stab of fear settled in the pit of her stomach. Was her earlier life one she even wanted to remember? Without Evie to explain her childhood, she'd have to rely on Flora. Maybe Adam. While her heart told her she could trust these people, she knew in her gut she shouldn't trust anyone just yet, even Mother and Adam, until she knew what they had to do with her past. If she needed their help, she would ask for it. She hoped it wouldn't come to that. She crossed her fingers that she would have the mental as well as the physical stamina to handle whatever it was she found in her search.

One last glance in the mirror told her it was as good as it was going to get. At least for the moment. Her appearance wasn't a major concern. When she had her life back, then she'd think about clothes and all the girly things she'd missed.

She peered out in the long hallway; all was quiet. With Mr. Worthington in the hospital, it seemed that the light of Swan House had temporarily dimmed. And she hadn't even met the man. Flora told her he ran a tight ship, but with a loving hand. As she walked down the stairs, she heard the soft murmur of voices echoing off the kitchen. An older woman was openly crying as Casey approached the doorway leading into the kitchen. Apparently Mr. Worthington was well liked by his staff. Casey felt sad for the man she didn't even know. She made a silent promise to herself to find the way to the hospital so she could visit him.

She entered the kitchen, clearly the heart of the house. Flora was directing a young woman about her age, showing her how to fold cloth napkins. Smells of chocolate and baking bread gave the room a cozy feel.

She observed the daily routine at Swan House. Here she wouldn't have to clam up when a patient was administered a mega-dose of Valium. Here in this cozy, comfortable kitchen she wouldn't have to cover her ears to block out the terror and the screams of the insane. She wouldn't have to hold her breath, waiting to see if the dreaded footsteps would stop outside her door. No, here she could walk about freely. Here, she could think and plan and not worry about someone watching her every movement. She could go outside if she wanted. With that thought in mind, Casey made her presence known with a robust good morning.

Flora jumped and placed her hand on her chest. "Oh dear, you gave me a start."

"I'm sorry. I didn't mean to frighten you. It all looks so . . . normal." She felt herself blush as the rest of the staff stopped to stare at her. She instantly regretted her words. This is what they would expect of her. From this moment forward, she'd show them. She wasn't crazy. She was as normal as they were. The only difference was, they had a memory of their past and she didn't. The girl folding the napkins looked embarrassed. Casey thought she looked to be around her age. She would need a friend; maybe this was a start. She walked over to the young woman and held out her hand.

"I'm Casey Edwards." The girl fumbled with the pile of napkins and held a work-reddened hand out to Casey.

"Julie Moore. Nice to meet you." The girl apparently was over her moment of discomfort. Warm brown eyes brightened, and her smile revealed a dimple etched in the groove of her cheek. *Cherry red cheeks,* Casey thought. *I like this girl already.*

Casey knew she would have to take the initiative if she were to make friends at Swan House. Her past had preceded her, and there was nothing she could do about that, but she could see to it that her past didn't follow her around like a dark shadow.

She reached for Julie's offered hand. "Thank you." Wanting and needing to know more about her new acquaintance, Casey formed her next question.

"What is your job at Swan House?" Casey watched as Julie added another napkin to the pile. She looked to Flora as if asking her permission. Flora took Julie's hand and led her to the table.

"Time for a break. Casey, would you mind entertaining Julie while Ruth and I go over the linen list?"

Ruth, a short, heavyset woman with a too-tight bun, followed Flora out of the kitchen. Mabel, the cook, continued to fill bowl after bowl with ingredients, oblivious to the actions of those around her.

Casey poured hot chocolate into rose-patterned cups and carried them to the table.

"I guess Flora thought I needed a break. Actually, I'm not tired at all. I hope she doesn't think I'm a laze-about. This is my first week here, and I don't want to mess up because I really need this job. My husband, he'd be so angry if I . . . well, let's just say I need the work." Julie fiddled with the place mats on the table.

Casey smiled. "Me too. I've never had a job. . . ."

Julie laughed, and Casey joined her.

"I guess we both need to learn when to open our mouths and when not to. It's just . . . I felt when I saw you we could be f—," Julie sputtered.

"Friends?" Casey finished for her new friend.

"Yes. We even think alike." Julie said.

"I thought so, too." Suddenly, Casey felt happy for the first time in years. Before they could have a friendship, she needed to clear the air. If Julie had questions about her past, she wanted her to feel free to ask them.

"I know most of the staff is aware of . . . where I've lived for the past ten years. If you have any questions, please don't be afraid to ask. If I can answer them, I will. I've lived under a dark cloud too long. I want to walk in the sunshine again." Casey stared across at Julie, her gaze intense.

"I'm glad you brought this out in the open. I overheard Mrs. Worthington talking the day before you came home. I was curious." Julie glanced down at her hands resting on her lap. She looked uncomfortable.

"About what?" Casey inquired.

"I don't like to gossip. I just thought someone should know. Until I met you, I wasn't sure who I should tell." Julie stared at the table.

"What is it?" She hated how anxious she sounded. She hoped her new friend wouldn't pick up on the anxiousness. In the end, though, it couldn't be any worse than what she'd already heard and been through the past twenty-four hours.

"Your mother was whispering on the upstairs phone. There's a phone in the main hall; you may have noticed it in an alcove. If you didn't know it was there, you'd miss it. I wasn't intending to eavesdrop; I want you to believe me."

Julie's former cheery disposition was gone, replaced with . . . fear? Casey was apprehensive. Did Julie have another tale to add to the burgeoning stack? No matter what this young woman said at this point, she would believe her.

"Tell me Julie, what exactly did you hear?"

"I heard Mrs. Worth . . . your mother talking about your brother. She said you weren't going back to Sanctuary, no matter what."

"Which brother? And of course she knows I'm not going back to Sanctuary."

Julie looked confused for a moment. "The one who died. It's just that . . . never mind."

"I've just learned about his existence myself. Prior to coming here, I didn't even know I had a brother. No one wants to talk about him. At least to me they don't. Why are you telling me all this?" Casey asked.

"You asked. I want you to be careful. Watch who you talk to, what you say," Julie cautioned.

"Then how do I know I can trust you? How do I know you're not just telling me this? I don't know who or what to believe. I've been warned, yet I remember nothing." Casey threw her hands in the air. "Do you have any idea how frustrating all this is?"

Julie's face reddened before she spoke. "Frustration, I understand. Warnings, I understand, but the loss of memory, I can only imagine. Casey, I want to be your friend."

At that precise moment Casey wanted to grab Julie in a bear hug, but was afraid she'd think she was truly nuts if she acted so spontaneously.

"Thank God! You can't imagine how wonderful this makes me feel. Just to have someone to talk to, to be there for me, is going to help me more than anything in the world. I can feel it."

"You better wait before you give me too much credit. Spend a few days in this house, then come back and praise me." Julie's words came out fast, like a stream of bullets. After they were out, she looked at Casey, waiting.

"What do you mean?"

Julie allowed her gaze to sweep around the kitchen, apparently making sure Mabel was ear deep in flour. She leaned across the table and cupped a hand to the side of her mouth. "There's an evilness in this house. I felt it the minute I got here, and I've only been here a week. Soon you'll see for yourself what I'm talking about."

Julie took their cups to the sink and resumed her task of folding the napkins. Flora and Ruth returned to the kitchen at that moment. All thoughts of further questioning were put on hold.

Flora looked at Julie, then Casey.

"Is everything okay?" Flora asked, her gaze settling on Casey.

Summoning a smile, Casey looked at Julie, then Flora. "It couldn't be better. I think Julie and I hit it off pretty well."

"Good. Young ladies need friends. Real friends, not just women whose idea of friendship is gossiping and competition. I've had those kind of friendships, and trust me, you can do without them."

Casey sensed an underlying message in Flora's words and hoped she wasn't trying to warn her about Julie. She said as much. "No need to worry. Julie and I have much in common."

Casey watched Julie as she continued to fold the napkins into pyramids. A smile touched the edge of her mouth when she lifted her head. "I think you're right, Casey, we do have a lot in common." Casey sensed that Julie wanted to add more, but felt the timing was wrong.

Flora gave a satisfied nod in Casey's direction, pleased with their response.

"What do you plan to do with your day, Casey? I'm sure any plans you might have made with your mother will have to be put on hold since Mr. John is in the hospital."

Casey was wondering that herself. She remembered the promise she'd made to visit her stepfather. With Evie hovering by his bedside and especially in her mental condition, if you could call it that, she didn't think she could manage the pretense required for a visit. At least not that day.

She wanted to learn about her past.

"Does Sweetwater have a library?" she inquired.

"Well, for Pete's sakes, Missy, we're not that uncivilized. Right by the courthouse it is. If you're looking for something to read, Mr. Worthington has a fine library, filled with volume after volume of books."

"Thanks, but I wanted to do some research, you know, about Sweetwater and all. Maybe something will prod my memory."

"Well, then, tell Lilah you don't want to be bothered. That woman lives to gossip."

"Is Lilah the librarian?" Casey asked.

"Yes, sad to say. I think she's read every book in that library a thousand times, or at least the ones on Sweetwater. She's probably hoping she'll find some missed piece of hundred-year-old gossip that she could use against someone. Actually, she's quite sweet once you get past her wagging tongue."

Casey couldn't believe her luck. A gossipy librarian could save her hours of research.

"If you want a ride, Hank's going to town. I'll see if he's left yet."

Flora hurried out of the kitchen in search of Hank. Julie folded the last of the napkins and whispered to Casey on her way to the linen closet. "Be careful and watch Lilah. She's nice, but she's also a social climber. She'll do anything she can to raise money for the library. I think it's to protect her job. Your mother has donated large sums of money to the library. I saw the write-ups in the paper. There's even a plaque hanging in the entrance to the library. Just thought you should know."

There was no time to ask any more questions. Hank appeared at the door, his keys in his hand. Casey waved as she followed the gardener out to his truck.

* * *

Hank was a tall, wiry man of few words. His skin had darkened and leathered from the many hours spent in the sun. He looked older than his fifty-nine years. A touch of a British accent mixed with a Southern dialect usually made people stop and listen when he spoke.

Casey's silence didn't seem to bother him. He accepted her compliments on the gardens at Swan House but hadn't muttered another word. Humid air blew in through the truck's open windows, leaving Casey feeling hot and sticky. She hoped the library had air-conditioning. She asked Hank. He shrugged. She took that to mean he didn't know.

Hank slowed the truck to a crawl as they entered the village of Sweetwater. He glanced at her, his eyes dark and cold, like black circles of ice. Casey shivered, in spite of the heat.

"I know what you're after, young lady, and if I were you, I'd stop before you stir up any more dust. Things have settled down. Mrs. Worthington isn't going to like it when she hears about your visit to the library."

Casey was stunned. If he'd shoved her out of the truck and run her over, it wouldn't have surprised her half as much. She felt at

a loss for words. Thinking of Hank as nothing more than a country gardener was obviously a mistake. With his warning, she now
had to consider him another clue in the mystery of her former life.

She would have answers soon, she
hoped, courtesy of Sweetwater's library.

Hank parallel-parked in front of the library.
Casey opened the door and turned to him.
"Thanks for the lift. When you report back to
my mother, tell her I'll be very discriminating
in choosing what to read."

She slammed the door, not bothering to
wait for Hank's reply. Why the warnings?
The picture, the glass, the clerk in Haygood's. And now Hank. Julie was right. A
definite evil lurked beneath the Southern
gentility of Sweetwater.

Sweetwater's library boasted more books
than Casey could ever recall seeing in one
room. Floor-to-ceiling shelves lined the walls
and covered the windows. Fluorescent lighting provided a dim, murky light. Lemon oil
mixed with mold and what Casey thought of
as an *old* smell scented the room. Mildew
and dampness.

She spied a small desk piled high with books and walked toward it. Peering over the stack, she stepped back when she realized she wasn't alone.

"You must be Lilah." Casey took a minute to compose herself. She wondered how long the woman would have let her roam the library before introducing herself.

Small, pudgy hands cleared the heap of books off to the side. Casey saw why Lilah remained seated.

She had to weigh at least three hundred pounds. Folds of fat hung from the sides of the chair. She had a triple chin and Elvira black hair that had been permed, or rather fried, to a frizzy mass. Piercing blue eyes held Casey's gaze and never wavered.

"I know it's a shock. It always is when you're not expecting it," Lilah squeaked. Casey had to cover her mouth to hide her grin.

"That, too. And don't tell me I remind you of that little fat woman in *Poltergeist.* I've heard that so many times I could gag. You know if I were her, I sure as hell would work at that voice, you know, losing it and all. Her being an actress. But me, I'm the librarian, and I like being different." The rotund Lilah huffed and drew in a breath as if it would be her last.

Casey held out her hand. "I'm Casey Edwards."

"My God! The last time I saw you, you were covered—well never mind that. What in the world brings you here?" Lilah's already high-pitched squeal sounded several octaves higher.

Casey briefly wondered if she'd ever live her reputation down. Whatever it was.

"I'd like to learn a bit about Sweetwater. I thought if I were to read up a bit, something might jar my memory."

"Then it really is true?"

"What?" Casey asked.

"You really don't remember, do you? I'd say it's a blessing, though some wouldn't. Why I tell you I remember that day like it was yesterday. The lights flashing, Sheriff Parker, practically a boy then, and your poor momma, why it was awful, I tell you, just awful."

Casey couldn't believe her good fortune. Lilah had opened the door, and she hadn't even knocked.

"I don't remember anything about the past."

"Let me tell you this, little lady, some things are best forgotten. Now that memory of yours, it's doing the right thing, shutting down on you and all. A young girl like you shouldn't have those kind of memories. Of course, a young girl like you shouldn't have had to do what you did. I always thought there was more goin' on than what was said at the inquest. So did everyone else in this town."

Casey felt as if the air was being sucked out of her lungs. *An inquest?*

"Then there must be a file, records, newspaper clippings, something. You said this sheriff, what's his name, is he still sheriff?" Casey's heart slammed against her rib cage.

Lilah rolled her large frame away from the desk and crossed flabby arms over an ample bosom. "Yes, he is, as a matter of fact. Why do you want to know?"

Casey knew a challenge when she heard one. Lilah the librarian wasn't going to display loose lips today. At least not yet.

"I would think it obvious. I'd like to know what happened that day." Casey heard the desperation in her voice. She tried to take a deep breath to steady herself. It didn't work. She felt on the brink, desperate.

"I'm thinkin' it's not my place to tell you about that day. Ask Evie, she'll be the one to tell you. She is your mother, young lady."

"I don't think it's a good idea right now. Mr. Worthington suffered a mild stroke last night. Mother is with him at the hospital."

"Oh, that poor woman. I tell you, she's had more to bear than most. She's always been such a generous soul. When the chance came for the library to purchase our microfiche machine, your momma donated the money. Poor, poor John." Lilah heaved another deep sigh.

Taking a chance that Lilah's tongue might loosen if pulled, Casey asked, "You see why I can't ask my mother. But I'm sure she wouldn't mind if you told me what *you* remember."

Lilah seemed to be in deep thought. "I guess I could do that. Why don't you pull up a chair." Lilah pointed to the chair behind her.

Casey sat down and waited. Excited, yet fearful, she needed to hear this woman's account of a time that her mother, Flora, and apparently anyone connected to Swan House refused to talk about.

"It was a real fall day as I recall. I'd had

dozens of trick-or-treaters that started out early in the evening. The little ones. I remember running outta candy. I'd just turned on the television to watch my favorite talk show."

Casey waited patiently while she ran on and on about her favorite soap star who was appearing that day on her daily talk show.

"The sirens scared me half to death. You don't hear them much in Sweetwater. I remember wondering what in the world could have happened to cause such a ruckus. Being alone and all I needed to know what happened, so I called Vera. She's Sheriff Parker's dispatcher. It was the only instance I could ever recall where Vera was speechless. That woman's mouth usually wags a mile a minute."

Casey smiled. Took one to know one.

"She could barely talk. Said the sheriff had gone out to the Edwards place. Well, right away I knew something awful happened. I always told your momma that boy wasn't right in the head. Buzz knew it, too. Course by that time, your father'd met his maker and Evie was left alone with two little ones to raise. The boy not being hers and all just seemed to make it worse."

"Wait! What do you mean, the boy not being hers?"

"I thought you knew." Lilah shook her head, her fried locks slapping against plump cheeks. "Buzz was just a youngster when he married Carol Conners, his high school sweetheart. Talk was they had to get married. Some said Buzz wasn't the father, but who knows? They did that back then. Men accepted their responsibility. Not like today. Babies having babies, then going on national television and talking about how they did it. It sickens me, truly it does. Buzz did the right thing, no matter what they say.

"Ronald wasn't right from the git-go. Your father took him to see some doctor in Atlanta. Never told anybody what was wrong, but it sure didn't take a genius to figure out little Ronald wasn't right. Seems like it wasn't too long afterward that your father and Carol divorced. Never knew why, Buzz never talked about it, and Carol moved to Tennessee.

"A few years later Buzz met your momma. Boy, what a looker she was. The men couldn't get enough of her. Buzz thought he was the luckiest man alive. I remember seeing him once walking down Sweetwater Way all smiles, like he knew the answer to the greatest secret in the world."

All ears, Casey eased to the edge of her seat.

"I can't remember how long they dated, but it wasn't long after they married that Carol died. Ronald being the way he was, none of her family wanted to take him in. Of course since Buzz claimed to be the father, they expected the child would live with him.

"He must have been around seven or eight when he came to live with Buzz. Evie was pregnant with you, I remember that. I admired her, takin' another man's child to raise, especially in her condition."

Lilah pulled a drawer open and removed a half-empty bag of Snickers and offered one to Casey. She took the offered chocolate and waited for Lilah to continue.

"Right after you were born things started to change. Evie was havin' a hard time with Ronald, and Buzz, if I remember correctly, had just got laid off from the mill. Your Grandma Edwards took you whenever she could. She still worked, cleaned houses for Sweetwater's finest folk. Let me tell you, she did one hell of a job. That's what paid for that condo.

"Things just went from bad to worse in that family. But I'm gettin' ahead of myself. Back to the day all hell broke loose, that is what you want to know, isn't it?"

Chapter Ten

"That seems to be the day no one wants to talk about. You might as well start there." Casey took another chocolate bar from the bag, anything to keep her trembling hands busy.

Lilah shoved her bulk from the chair and waddled to the back of the library. She motioned for Casey to follow.

"I have some papers I kept. There were several articles in the *Sentinel*. Don't know why I kept them. I guess I knew this day would come."

An ancient wooden file cabinet contained the papers Casey hoped held the secrets to her past.

The librarian thumbed through several papers before she found what she was looking for.

Casey stood next to her, wanting to peek over her shoulder but afraid to do so.

"Let's sit down." Lilah hobbled back to her desk.

"The inquest. Surely the paper covered that?" Casey prompted.

"Let's not be in such a hurry. You'll learn soon enough. Remember I'm telling you what *I* remember of that time, not what the papers reported." Lilah removed several newspaper clippings, all yellowed with age. She flicked through them, careful of their condition.

"Here it is." She skimmed the article. Casey knew that if what Julie and Flora said was true, Lilah had memorized the contents of the articles.

She passed the washed-out paper to Casey.

October 31, 1987
On a day usually reserved for cele-
brating the awakening of the dead, resi-
dents of Sweetwater mourn the death
of Ronald William Edwards. The twenty-
six-year-old male was found slain in the
family's home. Evie Marie Edwards, the
victim's stepmother, was too distraught

to comment on the death of her step-son. When asked about a suspect, Sheriff Roland Parker refused to com-ment. At the time of this writing there have been no arrests.

The rest of the story told of the shock and horror the residents of Sweetwater felt about the murder.

Casey laid the article on the desk. "How horrible for Mother. This"—Casey pointed to the newspaper—"doesn't tell me anything, other than that a crime was committed. Don't get me wrong, I think it's tragic, and worse that it happened on Halloween, but really, Lilah, this doesn't give me the first clue to my past."

Lilah smiled, showing beautiful white teeth. "Maybe not now, but who knows about later?" She looked through the folder and gave Casey several more articles from the *Sentinel*. All said the same thing. A mur-der was committed. Nothing about wit-nesses or suspects. Casey viewed the dates. All were written during the week after her stepbrother's death.

"This is it? What about the inquest? Did they ever find the killer? You can't commit murder, have the entire town in an uproar, then come to a dead stop." Casey flopped the papers onto Lilah's desk. It was like a big joke. On her.

"If you recall, I said I'd let you look at what *I* had. I said I'd tell you what *I* remember. That's not to say someone else doesn't have more information. You'll learn something sooner or later to nudge that missing memory of yours."

"I'm sorry I wasted your time. That day seems to be so important, yet I keep getting the same answers. It's almost like everyone is going out of their way to hide something."

"You can probably get the transcript of the inquest at the courthouse. I'll call over there and see if Marianne can get the files pulled. She's the clerk. If anyone can get their hands on information, she's the one to do it."

Lilah thumbed through a large Rolodex. Satisfied, she dialed the number and turned, leaving Casey staring at her broad back. She couldn't hear what Lilah said, and wasn't sure if she wanted to.

What kind of place is Sweetwater? What evil lurks in the minds of those who live here? And what is so wicked about my past that I can't remember? My stepbrother was savagely murdered. I should have some recollection of that, shouldn't I? My God, I've been in a mental hospital for ten years and have no idea why. I never questioned it. Until now. I must truly be insane. Why would anyone in their right mind continue as I did for all those years and not question it? At least I should have asked my mother. Or Sandra. Sandra would have told me.

But Casey had her answer: Sanctuary was a mental hospital. Obviously, she hadn't been in her right mind or they would have never put her there. And who were "they"?

"Says she'll look, but you'll have to hurry. She was about to go to lunch."

"I'm sorry. What?" Lost in her thoughts, Casey hadn't heard Lilah.

"Go on over. She'll look for you, but hurry. When you leave, turn right, walk two blocks. You can't miss it."

"Uh, sure. And Lilah, thank you. Thank you for taking the time to share your memories. We'll talk soon."

"Anytime, Casey."

*   *   *

After the dark library, the August sunlight was blinding. Casey shielded her eyes against the glare and spotted the court-house just up the street.

The color of red dirt, the brick building appeared to be at least three stories high. Thick white columns surrounded the building. At the very top of the courthouse four clocks could be viewed from any angle, their chimes creating an echo. She smiled. Couldn't call in late for work if you worked at the courthouse. Casey was sure the court-house boasted a porch, or at least that's what it looked like from a distance. Lush green lawns sprawled at least a hundred feet on either side of the official-looking building. Sprinklers soaked the deep green grass. Casey wondered if Hank would approve.

She climbed the stone steps and entered the building. Very well maintained, the halls were quiet that hot afternoon. She could hear the click of typewriter keys and the swishing sound of a copy machine.

Her heels clacked against the black-and-white marble floors as she followed the click-clack of the typewriter to an office at the end of the hall. Perched in the traditional feet-flat-on-the-floor-elbows-in position from typing class, sat a woman about her age. Casey cleared her throat.

"Yes?" the woman said. Casey was glad her mother had purchased the fine clothes she now wore—a dove gray skirt with a matching blouse. She knew, and she didn't know how she knew, that this woman judged people by their appearance. Maybe it was the woman's piercing gray eyes.

The woman gave an impatient glance at the slim band of silver on her wrist. "I'm about to go to lunch. Is there something I can do for you?"

"I'm not sure." Casey decided to take her time. After all it was only one o'clock, and they weren't about to close the courthouse this early. Casey eyeballed the woman. A gold clip held white-blond hair in a tight French braid. Pale skin, untouched by cosmetics, as colorless as her hair. Thin lips formed a phony smile. Casey thought she needed color. She expected her foot to start tapping at any moment.

"Lilah sent me over here," Casey said. If this pale, lackluster creature was the Marianne who could find anything, Casey thought she'd be better off looking for the transcript herself. She didn't relish the thought of spending a second more than necessary with the frozen mannequin.

"Yes, she mentioned you were coming. However, Marianne had to leave. You'll have to come back tomorrow."

With an irritated edge to her voice, Casey asked, "I wanted to see a transcript. Is there anyone other than Marianne who could help me?" Casey looked for a name tag or some type of identification.

"It's not your concern, Miss Edwards. Now if you'll run along, I have a luncheon appointment. If you had paid closer attention, you would have observed the sign on the door. Lunch hour is from one to two. Now if you'll excuse me." Casey felt like a child being dismissed and was suddenly fed up. Fed up with everyone in this hateful town.

Leaning over the wooden counter, Casey grabbed the woman by her sleeve. "Look, I don't know who you are, and I don't really care. I simply came here for some information. For some damn reason you and every other small-minded person in this town have treated me like yesterday's garbage. I want to look at a transcript. Now, either you get it for me, or I'll go to your superior. And if that doesn't work, then I'll go to their superior. Do you understand, Miss . . . whatever-the-hell-your-name-is?" Casey released her grip on the woman's arm. Outraged by her own behavior, yet feeling as though it was justi-fied, Casey didn't waver as her green glare met ice.

The woman shook Casey's hand off her arm, then reached under her desk for her purse. A moment later she was walking to-ward the door.

"You haven't changed a bit," she said over her shoulder. "Still crazy as a loon."

She didn't get to finish whatever else she was going to say because Blake Hunter walked through the door at that precise mo-ment.

"Ah-ha. I saw you go inside the library earlier. Lilah said I'd find you here. I'm free for a while. Thought I'd see if you were inter-ested in lunch." Casey felt her heart drop to her feet and race back upward when Blake smiled at her. His eyes. They were gorgeous. Milky Way brown.

Casey watched as Miss Ice melted. Red splotches blossomed on her pale cheeks.

"I'd love to. However, I'm trying to get

Miss whoever she is to retrieve a transcript. Seems no one except the sainted Marianne can find it." Casey's eyes looked daggers at the Ice Queen, who remained rooted in the doorway.

Blake took charge. "Brenda, is there some reason why Miss Edwards can't get what she wants?"

Casey sensed the woman's discomfort. She almost felt sorry for her.

"Marianne was told to take care of her. I've been instructed to follow those orders," Brenda explained.

Blake smiled at Casey. "Seems like Brenda has the courthouse confused with the military. Who gave you those 'orders'?" There was no humor in Blake's line of questioning.

"You'll have to ask Marianne." Brenda paused, then added, "Lunch at Big Al's again? I can't tolerate that BBQ. We'll have to go elsewhere tomorrow, Blake." She trotted out the door, her chin so high in the air Casey was sure she'd suck in dust from the air-conditioning vents.

Blake looked embarrassed. "It's not what you think," he said as he led her into the hall.

"You don't have to explain," Casey said.

"I know, but I want to. Let's get out of here," Blake said.

They walked downtown on Sweetwater Way, very much a pair. Blake casually took her hand. Casey liked the feel of his hand in hers. The butterflies in the pit of her stomach were good butterflies, not her usual knot of anxiety.

"I just happened to have the last booth available at Big Al's the other day. The place is packed at lunchtime," Blake explained.

She remembered the smell coming from the smokestack yesterday.

"I invited Brenda to join me. I knew she only had an hour for lunch and thought it the gentlemanly thing to do. That's it. Nothing more." Blake held her hand tighter as they crossed Main Street. She liked the way he took charge.

Casey was glad she'd run into Blake. Glad he'd invited her to lunch. Glad Brenda wasn't more, though she obviously wanted to be. She wondered if Brenda really had a "luncheon appointment" as she called it. Or had she been hoping to run into Blake again?

"I can attest to your 'gentlemanliness' if there is such a word. I really appreciate the ride yesterday." Suddenly, her chest felt heavy, and her hands were trembling.

"Hey, you okay?" Blake asked, as they entered Big Al's.

Another panic attack. Taking a deep breath, Casey shook her head. She removed her hands from Blake's grasp. She had to get out of there. She needed fresh air. Pushing the door open, Casey inhaled. Her heart started to race for no apparent reason. She had to concentrate on something, anything, until the pounding stopped, until the fear disappeared. Focusing on the weeds growing out of the cracks in the sidewalk, Casey counted the many shades of green and brown. She counted the cracks. When she was up to thirty-five, her heart rate returned to its normal beat. She could breathe again.

Blake came outside and stood next to her. "Let's go inside and get a cool drink."

Casey nodded as Blake led her back inside the restaurant. After the hot sun, the coolness of Big Al's revived her. They seated themselves in a booth at the rear of the diner. Fake red leather seats covered in duct tape and tables topped with red-and-white-checkered tablecloths crowded the small room. It reminded Casey of a picnic setting.

The smell of BBQ wafted throughout. Until this minute, she hadn't realized just how hungry she was. A waitress dressed in tight jeans and red T-shirt that read "I do Big Al's" in black letters plunked down two glasses of water.

"Watcha gonna have?" she asked, pen poised over her light green pad.

"Give us a minute, Della."

"Sure thing, Doc." Della sauntered over to the next table, where her customers weren't as patient. Casey could hear them grumbling.

"What happened, Casey?" His eyes searched hers for an answer.

"I had a panic attack. I thought they were under control since I haven't had one in years, then I had one the day I left the hospital. I don't understand why I'm getting them now."

"Everything is new to you. I'm sure you're feeling somewhat anxious over your situation. I can prescribe some Xanax if you think it will help."

"Thanks, but that's the last thing I want. I had so many drugs at Sanctuary, it'll take years to get them out of my system. Dr. Macklin taught me some relaxation techniques that work just as well as medication. I'm okay." Casey picked up the menu, hoping to change the subject.

"Try the pork, I'll guarantee it will melt in your mouth."

"Sounds delicious. I'm starved."

Della came over at just the right moment, took their order, and seconds later delivered two tall glasses filled with sweetened iced tea.

Casey drained her glass and wiped her mouth with the checkered napkin. "I needed that."

"Apparently so. Casey, tell me something." Blake paused as if contemplating his question. "What transcript are you looking for?"

Casey thought it should've been obvious. "The day Ronald Edwards died. I want to know what happened. No one wants to tell me. I figured I would find out from the transcript of the inquest."

Again, Blake appeared to think before his next question. "Who told you there was an inquest?"

"Lilah."

"Son of a bitch! I can't believe she'd tell you that. There wasn't an inquest, Casey. At least not a formal one." Blake raked a hand through his hair.

"But . . . why? Why would she tell me that? Surely, she has nothing to hide."

"No, you're right. She doesn't. Have you talked to Evie since your return?"

Here we go again, Casey thought. *Someone else telling me nothing.*

"Yes, but if you mean has she told me about my past, no. With Mr. Worthington in the hospital, the timing and all didn't seem right. She has too much to deal with as it is. If there wasn't a formal inquest, then there isn't a transcript?"

"Exactly. However, there is a record. There has to be. I can't believe Evie would make you wait. You have a right to know what happened. It just might be the key to regaining your memory." Blake glanced around the diner. Leaning over the table, he whispered to her, "Can you stop by my office, say around four this afternoon?"

Della approached the table, a heavy tray balanced above her shoulders, saving Casey from a reply. She stared at plates piled high with BBQ pork, a mountain of fries, and huge scoops of coleslaw.

"This looks delicious. I don't know if I can

eat all of this." Casey speared her fork into the spicy pork, surprised at her appetite. After a panic attack the last thing she wanted to do was eat. But that was back in Sanctuary, this was Sweetwater. Everything was different in Sweetwater, even her panic attacks.

Between mouthfuls of the succulent pork, Casey asked, "Why do you want to see me in your office? Why not here or Swan House?"

Blake spoke softly, again glancing around as if he were afraid someone might overhear their conversation.

"I have something I think you should see. It has to do with your past. If my father's suspicions were correct, it could help."

"Did I know your father, Blake? When everyone talks about this person or that person, I feel so . . . empty, like they know all my secrets. What did he know that would concern me now?"

"It's your medical records. When you were a child Flora used to bring you in for yearly physicals, shots, that sort of thing. I was going through Dad's old records when I ran across them. I think it's something you should look at." Blake's tone held no traces of his earlier lightheartedness. This was Dr. Blake Hunter, not Blake the man she hoped would be her friend.

Casey dipped her last fry in ketchup. She'd eaten everything and felt sick. Even sicker when she thought of what might lie in wait for her at Blake's office. This was what she wanted: answers to her life, anything to spark a memory, a memory to a past she didn't recall and a memory of what she'd hoped for in her future.

"I'll be there. But first, I need to apologize to Brenda. I was ready to pull her arm off when you came in."

"I'm sure you were justified. She can be a bitch, trust me. Rumor has it at one time she hated you. High school stuff." Blake reached for his wallet, tossed a few bills on the table, and escorted her to the door.

"No wonder. I really have to apologize now. Who knows what I might have said or done back then? This is what I'm talking about. My life is an open book, and I'm the only one who hasn't read it."

They stood in front of the restaurant continuing their conversation. Casey wished he would take her hand again and ask her if she wanted to go for a walk.

Blake glanced at his watch. "Don't be too hasty. She was a bitch then, too. I don't think it was anything serious, like I said, high school stuff. Brenda has a fear she'll never marry and won't be able to join the Married Ladies Club."

"The what?"

"This is the South. Traditions are important. Society life is all some of these ladies have. When their husbands take the ferry over to Brunswick to the real world, many of them are left alone. This club is important. You're someone if you belong. At least that's what most of them think. If you have the best china, the best maid, the best cook, the ladies look up to you. People in Sweetwater know it's Brenda's dream to be accepted in this club. But first, you have to be—"

"Married." Casey finished for him. Brenda must have her eye on Blake.

"You're a quick study, Casey. I've got a few things to take care of before four. I want to check on John and see what we can do to help you get that memory back." Blake cupped her chin in his hand. A new and unexpected warmth surged through her.

Searching for her voice, Casey mumbled

a meek okay before Blake walked away, leaving her to stare after him.

Blake put the phone back in its cradle. The news from the hospital was encouraging. John was progressing nicely. So far, the only serious damage he seemed to have suffered was an impairment to his voice. If he continued to improve at this pace, he'd return to Swan House within the week.

He glanced around his father's former office, now his own, for Casey's file. Blake had no desire to move to any of the new modern buildings in Brunswick. Like his father before him, the idea of walking up a flight of stairs to find himself in comfortable living quarters when he had a lull in his day suited him just fine.

Hardwood floors still gleamed from weekly polishing. His father's desk, his desk now, held several files, an appointment book, and his grandfather's antique clock. The walls were painted a soothing cream color and covered with pictures of delivered babies, some still living, others not. The opposite wall held his medicine chest. An ancient mortar and pestle made of wood sat atop the chest, along with dozens of old jars bearing strange symbols burned into them. Bright red geraniums blossomed outside in a window box. He'd never bothered to cover the window; he liked the view. Both young and old found Blake's office relaxing. His examination room was the same. No sterile chrome for him or his father. He preferred the laid-back atmosphere, and so did his patients.

He found the file beneath his desk blotter and read it one last time. He had to make sure he'd interpreted his father's suspicions correctly.

Casey had suffered enough already. Blake didn't know what to expect when she learned of its contents. He'd be there for her, he knew, no matter what. He felt very protective of Casey.

Maybe it was her eyes. He couldn't forget how she'd looked at him outside Big Al's. Jade green, with gold flecks. She'd captured a small piece of his heart when she stared back at him, innocent in one sense and worldly beyond her wildest dreams in another. He'd wanted to comfort her, tell her everything would be all right. But he couldn't, because he didn't know if it ever *would* be all right.

He glanced at his watch. Four-fifteen. Casey was running late. She must've really smacked on the apology to Brenda. Too bad, because when Casey's memory returned, she'd recall what a bitch Brenda was.

Casey was about to enter the building in search of Brenda to apologize and had second thoughts. Instead, the window display at Haygood's captured her attention a second time and she decided to throw caution to the wind and go shopping. The iris print dress now belonged to her, along with matching earrings, and sandals. She knew her mother wouldn't mind; actually she'd probably approve since she herself, according to Flora, was addicted to shopping. While she'd hated to ask the clerk to bill her mother, until she had a job she had no alternative. She'd pay her back. The hateful clerk from yesterday must've had the day off. The elderly saleswoman in the store hadn't been overly friendly, but she hadn't been rude. This is what she needed, something as mindless as shopping. Anything to take her mind off her dreaded encounter with Blake. What could his deceased father possibly have in his files that would have any bearing on the present?

The courthouse clock chimed quarter past the hour as Casey stood on the corner of Sweet Way and Main. She was late for her appointment with Blake. She jiggled her packages, trying not to make one arm more heavy than the other.

Her foot had barely hit the pavement before a sleek black sports car roared past her. She felt herself being hurled back onto the sidewalk. She cringed as her shoulders slammed into the sidewalk. Gravel and dirt flew from all directions, blocking any chance of identifying the car, its occupants, or the license plate. The packages that only moments before had been such a great joy to her were now armed torpedoes digging into her, their pointed edges like knives.

She managed to push herself into a sitting position. Across the street the elderly clerk from Haygood's stood under the canopy, watching. A young girl pedaled by, her long braids billowing behind her as she stared at Casey. A quick glance across the street told her Brenda had finished with her luncheon appointment. For a moment Casey thought she'd suffered a head injury.

Surely the citizens of Sweetwater weren't going to stand by and watch?

Her silk blouse in shreds, Casey brushed the gravel from her back and knees. Her clothes were ruined. She scooted around the sidewalk, picking up her purchases. Piling the boxes in front of her, she took a minute to examine her injuries. Other than a few scrapes, she was fine. Seeing she only had one shoe, she searched for its mate but couldn't find it.

Casey scooped her packages up with bruised arms and crossed Main Street. Rage didn't come close to what she was feeling. Murderous rage? Maybe.

She couldn't believe no one had offered to help her. No one asked if she'd been injured. She could've lain on the sidewalk and bled to death for all the concern Sweetwater's proud citizens had shown her.

The sports car . . . Frantically, Casey peered up and down Main Street. There was no evidence of the automobile. It had disappeared without a trace. Abruptly she stopped to peruse Main Street. The elderly clerk had returned to her post. The young bicycler could've been imagined. A scene straight out of the *Twilight Zone.*

Something was definitely wrong.

Casey limped along, searching for Blake's office that he'd pointed out to her on their way to Big Al's. Had it been only two hours since Blake had left her? Only two hours since her heart had raced as he'd gazed into her eyes? She remembered thinking it was as if he'd reached down into her soul, searching. She'd felt drawn to him and knew he felt the same.

Spying the older home with its green shutters and welcoming porch, Casey saw the sign proclaiming Dr. Blake Hunter was indeed in his office.

She barely made it up the short flight of steps without losing her packages. Tossing them onto a wicker rocker, she lifted the brass door knocker.

Blake himself answered the door.

"My God! What happened to you?" he asked as he pulled her inside.

Her legs felt like Jell-O as he escorted her to the back of his house. She didn't get a chance to see the apartment on the second floor where Blake lived because the next thing she knew, he hoisted her up in his arms and ran down a flight of stairs and into his office.

Gently, he placed her on the examination table. Her eyes chose that moment to fill with tears. She couldn't help it.

Blake embraced her in a compassionate hug and smoothed sweaty tendrils of hair behind her ears.

"Shhh. It's all right. Try and relax." He rubbed the lower part of her back in soothing, circular motions. Casey felt herself relax at his touch and leaned into him.

Hesitant to leave Blake's embrace, Casey knew he must think her an idiot. He patted her as if she were a child. She pulled away, brushing her tear-stained face with the palm of her hand.

"I'm sorry. I rarely cry." She laughed. "At least I never did at Sanctuary. The past twenty-four hours is a different story." She sniffed, and Blake offered her a tissue.

Leaning against the examination table, Blake crossed his arms in front of him and waited.

"Want to explain this?" He nodded at her disheveled appearance.

"I'm sure it was an accident. I went to Haygood's. I decided not to apologize to Brenda. Or at least not yet. Instead I went shopping." Casey blotted her eyes.

"That's a very normal thing for a woman to do. But I don't think the prices at Haygood's are so terrible they'd make you cry." Blake grinned.

She laughed. "I wouldn't have anything to compare them with. It all happened so fast, I'm not sure if I imagined it or not."

"If these injuries are supposedly imagined, you've done an excellent job. Maybe I can hire you to 'unimagine' some of my patient's ailments. Now, do you want to tell me how you came to have all these scrapes and bruises? I know Laura can be an old hag when she wants to be, but I don't think she did this to you." Casey heard the humor in his comment. Suddenly, her ordeal didn't seem so terrifying.

"You're right, she didn't. And I'm not sure who did." Casey explained to Blake how she'd stepped off the sidewalk onto the pavement right into the path of an oncoming car.

"Did the car actually hit you?" Blake asked.

"I'm not sure. The next thing I knew I was lying on the sidewalk. I remember looking around to see if anyone would come to help me, but no one did." Casey shook her head in disbelief. "What kind of people live here, Blake?"

"You mean no one bothered to see if you were all right?"

"No. Oh, they might've watched me crawling around on all fours and figured it out then, but right after I hit the pavement, I saw Laura. She simply watched. And Brenda, she must've just finished with her luncheon engagement. She saw me, too. And the girl. There was a young girl on a bike—she looked at me and kept on going."

"Right now I'd like to look at your wounds." Blake was the professional again, all talk of her accident put on hold for the moment.

"Why should I mind, you're a doctor, aren't you?"

"Yes. I just wasn't sure how you felt about doctors at the moment."

"You're not like the doctors at Sanctuary."

Blake removed Betadine, a package of sterile gauze, tape, and scissors from a drawer.

"How do you know?"

Casey thought for a minute.

"Women's intuition, I guess. I don't seem to recall you saying you practiced psy-

chiatry, so that pretty well tells me something."

Blake gently pulled her blouse away from
her scraped flesh.

"Ouch!"

"Sorry, just a little more." Blake tugged at
the material.

Blake ran his fingers through his dark hair.
For a moment Casey thought of the handsome doctor from *ER.* George Clooney.
That's who he reminded her of. She told him
so.

"Well, unlike the hospital hunk you watch
on television, this doc doesn't have any
magical potions to get this blood-crusted
blouse off without hurting you. Would you
mind going into the patient's dressing room
and taking it off? It probably won't hurt as
badly if you do it yourself, you know, kind of
like yanking a Band-Aid off."

"Sure. Lead the way." Casey slid off the
table, and Blake pointed to a room at the
end of the hall, no bigger than a closet. A
bench held a stack of disposable gowns
and a box of Kleenex. She peeled the peach
creation away from her skin in seconds.
Wrapping the paper gown around the lacy
scrap her mother called a bra and suddenly

anxious to leave the small confined room, Casey hurried back to Blake's examination room, bloody shirt in hand.

Blake patted the table, indicating she should climb up.

"If you'll just lie on your stomach, I'm going to clean your wounds. You're still bleeding, so I'm going to clean around the wounds, not inside them. The blood removes the dirt as it flows, so chances for infection are slim. Tell me if it stings, and I'll stop."

Casey tensed as Blake doused her back with disinfectant. What she thought were surface cuts apparently went much deeper.

"Almost finished," Blake said.

She relaxed. Closing her eyes, Casey let Blake bandage her wounds. A slight sting here and there, but certainly nothing she couldn't stand.

Blake's hands were no longer on her back. She felt his slight touch as he examined her cuts from yesterday.

"Casey, what happened here?" he asked, pointing to her arms, then taking a tweezer as she had done yesterday. She felt a slight pinch as he removed a shard of glass. She wasn't sure if she should tell Blake about the previous day or not. She'd put it behind her.

Pushing up on her elbows, she looked at Blake, who stood at the head of the table, hands folded across his chest. She knew her feeling of trust wasn't misplaced. She could tell this man her secrets.

"I found a bottle of lotion; it was gardenia, my favorite scent. I rubbed it on the back of my arms and legs. It . . . the jar had glass inside." Casey hoped he believed her.

"Who did it belong to?" Blake's gaze darkened at her words.

Casey laughed. "I'm not sure. Flora suggested I take a hot bath. I'd had a . . . I don't know, I guess you doctors would call it a 'spell.' It shook me up. Flora ran a hot bath for me. I'd noticed a basket of gardenia soaps. Because it's my favorite scent, I asked Flora about it. She said Mother bought the soap."

Blake inspected the previous day's damage. Retrieving a box of round Band-Aids, he stuck several on her arms.

"Looks like you'll live."

"I'm glad for the prognosis. However, I have another dilemma." She slid off the table.

Blake, deep in thought, looked right through her.

"And that is?" He'd heard her after all.

"My blouse. Here." She handed Blake the bloody material.

Casey felt the floor swim beneath her. Grabbing the edge for support, she was too late as she fell to the floor.

Dim lights whirled before her eyes. She thought of Dorothy. Was this how she felt when she received that knock on the head? The room was spinning out of control. She'd just entered the Land of Oz. . . .

Hands ripped the wet gown from her body. She was nude and trembling. A woman led her down a dark hall. A metal door to their right opened. Water spewed from the wall. A shower? The woman pushed her forward under the scalding spray. Another woman adjusted the temperature and shoved her beneath the stream of water. A rancid stench filled her nostrils. She held her breath, hoping the smell would go away. A stiff brush was placed in her hand along with a bar of soap. She began to scour her arms and legs. When she reached the V of her body, she took the brush and ran the soap up and down the stiff bristles.

"Casey, it's all right. I'm here."

Blake removed the ammonium carbonate capsule as Casey came to.

She was in Blake's office. He'd been examining her, then her world had gone black.
Lifting herself into a sitting position, she saw
the worried look on Blake's face.

"What happened? What's that smell?"
Her throat felt like sawdust.

"You fainted. And it's an ammonium capsule. Smelling salts."

"Seems to be a habit these days."

"What do you mean by that?" Blake
asked, his brow deepening with concern.

"Yesterday. At Swan House. It happened
then."

"Here, let me help you," Blake said as he
pulled her into his arms. "We need to talk."

He gently lifted her off the floor. Casey
was amazed at his strength. He carried her
up the stairs as if she were light as a feather.

She relaxed when he placed her on a
beige sofa. Big, soft cushions hugged her.
She viewed the room, done in browns and
greens. Casey thought the room a reflection
of Blake. Masculine, yet gentle. Clay pots of
all sizes filled with blooming African violets
rested along the windowsill. A forest green
recliner sat opposite the sofa. Next to that a
brass table lamp held the latest medical
journals. The late-afternoon sun streamed in

through the sheer curtains at the windows, bathing the room in a cozy afternoon glow.

"Don't move. I'll be right back."

She smiled at his order. Moving was the last thing she wanted to do just then. Wrapped in a cloak of comfort, Casey relaxed as she heard Blake in the kitchen opening cabinets and running water. Closing her eyes, she thought she could get used to this. It seemed odd. She felt light and peaceful, her familiar knot of anxiety gone.

Blake returned, carrying a tray with two steaming mugs and a plate filled with cheese and crackers.

"Drink this." Blake handed her a mug of herbal tea.

"Mmmm, it's good. I like this." She took a cracker from the plate and waited for Blake to get comfortable. He sat next to her on the edge of the plush sofa.

Taking his cup from the tray, Blake swallowed, then turned to her. "Now. Tell me about yesterday, the fainting."

"It was just like today. One minute I'm standing there, and the next I'm waking up. There's not much to it."

"Sometimes when people faint, they can

actually 'dream,' or have flashbacks. Does anything like that happen?"

Casey considered the possibility. "No, I don't think I dream. I do seem to be afraid after I wake up. At least yesterday. Today, just tired."

Blake paused and took a drink before his next question. "Casey, would you consider undergoing regression therapy? This can sometimes give you a full memory return, or it can nudge you in the right direction."

She'd undergone every kind of therapy possible, but didn't recall this particular name.

"At this point, I'm willing to try anything. I may have already tried this, I'm not sure. At Sanctuary I was a guinea pig."

Blake paced the room. "I remember in medical school, Adam telling me about this 'regression therapy.' We suggested it to Evie. She told Adam she'd tell your doctor. Maybe they tried."

"Can't you check my medical records?"

"Of course, with your permission. You do know what this means, Casey?"

"What are you talking about?"

"Your records. If I do this, I'll be acting solely as your physician."

"And? I'm sorry, I don't get it." Casey felt ignorant, out of her league.

"Anything more will have to wait. It's kind of an unwritten rule I have."

He felt it, too. She wanted to shout with happiness. She felt the chances were good with Blake's medical knowledge her memory would return. Maybe then she would have a chance at a normal life.

"I understand. Now, I have to go back to Swan House. They're probably wondering where I've been." Casey leaned forward, placing her mug on the table. When she stood up, she felt another wave of dizziness wash over her and quickly sat down.

"You're in no condition to leave. I'll call Flora, tell her not to expect you for a while. When you feel like it, I'll drive you home. Doctor's orders."

Casey gave a halfhearted salute. "Yes, sir."

Blake carried the tray with him into the kitchen. She could hear him talking on the telephone.

"Flora says to tell you you're in good hands. She'll not worry. Said to tell you Evie is spending the night at the hospital, so no need to hurry back."

"What a sweetie she is. I wish I could remember her. I imagine she took very good care of me. Which reminds me, Blake, the reason you asked me to your office in the first place." She let the statement hang.

Blake sat in the recliner across from her. Running a hand through his dark curls, he looked like a man torn. "Yes. I'm just not so sure now is a good time."

"It was before," Casey replied.

"I know. However, as your medical doctor, I'm not sure it's wise at this point to pursue it."

"Look, Blake. I'm twenty-eight years old, a grown woman. I'm not some teenager who's going to freak out on you. You've got to understand, just because I lived at Sanctuary my entire adult life doesn't mean I need constant protection from the world. Don't you realize, I've witnessed more than most could ever imagine. While Sanctuary might be a privately funded home, trust me, its residents were anything but normal."

Blake considered what she'd said. "You're right. While this goes against my better judgment, as your friend, I can't find a reason not to show you my father's file. At least not a physical reason."

"There you have it. Now, let's see what you think is so important." Casey felt her strength returning, the shakiness gone. She walked over to the windowsill, her back to Blake as she stared down at the beautiful African violets.

"All right. I'll just be a minute."

Casey turned to face Blake. Something in his voice caused her to pause. Was it that horrible? What could possibly be any worse than spending your entire adult life in a mental hospital. Casey smirked to herself. *I know what could be worse, you crazy loon. Not knowing why you were in that crazy house in the first place.*

Blake returned to the living room carrying a thick manila folder. The edges were frayed with age. He placed the file on the coffee table that only moments before held the delicious tea and crackers. Casey looked at the file. The word *forbidding* came to mind.

She sat on the sofa and opened the file. She scanned its contents. Some she understood, some she didn't. Apparently she'd had the usual childhood illnesses. Nothing out of the ordinary. The date of her last visit stood out. *October 1, 1978.* She read the spidery scrawl of the former Dr. Hunter. Then read it again. Her hands shook as she held the thick folder. She looked at Blake. Her lips moved, but the words never came.

She dropped the papers to the floor.

"Who?" she mouthed.

Chapter Eleven

"Apparently my father had his suspicions back then." Blake took Casey in his arms, forgetting the doctor-patient vow he'd made.

Casey shook her head and pushed him away. She inhaled, drawing on the techniques Dr. Macklin had taught her. Relax. Exhale. Again. When she felt calm enough to continue, she said, "I would have been nine. What about Mother, did she know?" Casey couldn't imagine her mother not knowing. Anger started to build in her.

Swelling in the vaginal area. Patient, age nine, had no explanation when questioned about tenderness. Will talk to mother.

"You'll have to ask her. Or Flora. She usually brought you in for your checkups."

"None of this makes sense, Blake. Why wouldn't my mother take me to the doctor? If I'm right, it means she was more interested in my stepbrother Ronnie than me."

"You know about that?" Blake asked her. His voice was full of surprise.

"Yes. Lilah told me."

"Figures. I guess since he was your mother's first child technically speaking, she may have felt closer to him. It would be natural for her to want to give him that something extra since he'd lost his own mother."

Casey thought about what Blake said. He was right. Her mother had taken a child who, according to Lilah, was slow, possibly mentally challenged, and loved him like her own. Losing his own mother must have been devastating for the boy.

"You're right. I guess I'm just shocked." Casey indicated the pile of papers now scattered on the floor.

"I know. I wish I knew if Dad talked to Evie. I'm sure he must have. It wasn't like him not to follow through with something this serious."

"You mean the molestation?"

He looked uncomfortable and nodded.

"Yes, Casey. If my father's suspicions

were correct, he thought something along those lines may have occurred."

"The question is, who?" Why would anyone want to harm a child? She'd spent ten years of her life locked away from society. Had she lost those years because of a deranged pervert?

"When can I see this doctor who specializes in regression therapy?" Agitated, she paced the room as Blake had minutes before.

"I'll check your records at Sanctuary. If they haven't tried this particular therapy, I'll have Adam arrange for an appointment."

"I'd like to get started as soon as possible." She wanted to put an end to her life as it had been. She needed to close that particular door, so she could open a new door to the future. A future she hoped would include Blake.

"I think I should take you back to Swan House. I'll call Becky later and get a copy of your records." Blake stooped and gathered the contents of the file. "I'm going to keep this for now. It might be best if you didn't mention any of this to anyone until we're sure."

"But, I thought . . ."

Blake placed the papers back on the desk. He pulled Casey to him. "Shhh." He smoothed the nape of her neck and continued to hold her. *I could stay this way forever,* she thought as she buried her face against his shoulder. She inhaled the clean, spicy scent of his aftershave and simply enjoyed the feel of his arms around her. Casey drew in a deep breath, as Blake lightly kissed the top of her head.

He gently pushed her away from him, his deep brown eyes traveling over her face, searching. For what? Her heart started to pound, not the sudden frantic pulsing beat caused by her panic attacks. The quickened beats she was experiencing, were from . . . anticipation? She could feel her face redden as Blake continued to stare at her.

"You better take me home." Casey stepped out of his embrace and, for a moment, felt an overwhelming emptiness. She wrapped her arms around her middle to insulate the leftover warmth from Blake's arms.

Blake shoved his hands in his pockets and grinned. "I'm sorry. I was out of line."

"I just need a little time, Blake. While I've been locked away all these years, I'm not immune to attraction. Don't apologize. I'm flattered that you want to be with me."

"Trust me, Casey, holding you wasn't the

only thing on my mind. That's for another time and another place. I'm not a schoolboy. Those packages you tossed on the porch"—he nodded behind him—"is there something in there you can wear, or do you need to borrow something?"

Casey realized she was still wearing the paper gown. "I have a dress in one of those boxes if you wouldn't mind getting it for me."

Blake grinned and did a perfect Groucho Marx with his eyebrows. "No telling what the genteel ladies of Sweetwater will think if they see you standing on my porch with a paper gown." Blake grabbed the packages from the porch and tossed them on the sofa.

The humor of the situation hit Blake at the same time it hit her. They doubled over with laughter, both falling onto the plump cushions. Tears glistened in Blake's eyes as he watched her rip into the packages.

"I wonder what Brenda would—"

"Think of this?" She glanced at her paper dress. "This wouldn't win any brownie points from the Married Ladies Club." She went into another fit of laughter. Blake howled, as they visualized the prim and proper Ice Queen dressed as a tablecloth.

Delighted with the humorous turn of

events, Casey took the package containing the iris print dress from its tissue wrapping and shook it out.

"You can change in here if you want. I've got to get something from the office. I'll be right back."

Blake had provided a few moments' reprieve from her thoughts. He'd also given her something else to think about. Their future relationship.

Robert Bentley pulled a starched linen handkerchief from his breast pocket and mopped beads of sweat from his forehead. He'd been close, but not close enough.

Damn her!

This hadn't been in his plans.

He'd prepared for this day for ten years. Now that it was finally here, he wasn't about to let some loony bitch fuck it up.

In twenty years his routine hadn't changed one iota. Nor had his plans changed. He'd been adamant about his rigid routine. A half hour on the treadmill, an hour of weight lifting, and a healthy diet assured him he didn't look his fifty years.

He'd continued to operate his failing real

estate business as he had when it had flourished for his father. Poor old son of a bitch. If he knew what had become of the business he'd worked so hard to establish, he'd sink to sea level proportions in that swamp he'd been buried in.

And Norma, his wife. God, what a pathetic woman. The Fultons had been one of the wealthiest families in Sweetwater and could trace their ancestry back to Plymouth Rock. Robert had taken a sudden interest in Norma right after high school. When they married, her father hadn't quite accepted him into their family. He'd stare down that long patrician nose of his as if Robert were little more than a pile of horse shit.

Robert had secretly desired more than running his father's real estate office. He wanted the power that went along with old wealth. Just knowing how close he was at the very moment to achieving a goal that had taken years to materialize gave him a charge that even *her* powers of seduction couldn't quell. He wanted all the citizens of Sweetwater to look up to him. He wanted the women to fall at his feet, and that hadn't been a problem. He'd had so many of Sweetwater's female population, he sometimes had a hard time remembering just exactly whom he'd bedded. Norma sure as hell hadn't cared for sex. When they were first married, Robert had tried to be patient with her, telling himself she'd been a naive young virgin. Thirty years later, the dried-up bitch still hadn't had an orgasm. Or at least not to his knowledge. He'd often wondered if she knew what she'd missed. Poor Norma.

Then there was the other bitch. She'd sashayed her ass right in front of him in high school. Then she'd been nothing more than poor white trash. His eye had been on dollar signs at the time, not a piece of ass. He knew she'd be a hot one though. Tits that seemed to defy gravity, and her legs were the sexiest he'd ever seen. Social constraints had been the only thing that kept him from plowing that bitch's field.

When Reed Edwards married her, Robert secretly thought him the luckiest man in Sweetwater. He didn't have to pretend to understand a wife who was afraid of sex. That much he knew, because it wasn't long after they married that Evie became pregnant. He remembered the day she came to his office. It wasn't long after she'd delivered her nutcase daughter.

He was alone, going over some paper-work. The door to his office opened, and he looked up, thinking it was Norma there to nag him as was her daily habit. When he saw Evie, he knew his teenage fantasies were about to come true.

Dressed in a short denim skirt and tight pink T-shirt, her long blond hair tickling a firm ass, all he could do was stare. He'd been even more surprised when she walked over to the French doors and locked them. Primal instinct had taken over at that point. Drawing the shades, he turned and motioned for the vixen of his dreams to follow.

He remembered her voice had been husky and seductive. "Aren't you going to ask me if I need anything? I thought that's what all you real estate men do. Provide a service." She let her statement hang in the air. The air crackled with electricity. He felt himself harden at the innuendo. He didn't give Norma a second thought.

"Well, Mrs. Edwards, I do provide a service to the community. I sell their homes, rent their offices when space is available. Are you here to tell me you've got something to sell?"

Evie, evidently confident in her sexual

prowess, walked around his desk and traced a pink-tipped nail across his belt buckle.

He inhaled and almost forgot to exhale.

She looked at his erection. Smiling, she proceeded to remove his belt. He stood motionless, letting her hands roam his body. She skimmed her hand along the head of his penis poking out of the top of his undershorts. When she licked her fingertips and traced its glistening tip, he almost exploded.

"You know what I'm selling, Robert?" she asked.

Oh, hell yes, he knew what she was selling, and he was damn sure buying.

"Tell me." he said through clenched teeth as she found his balls. She cupped them, almost too hard, but he realized at that moment, he wouldn't have cared how hard she squeezed.

"This." She slid on top of his desk and revealed her merchandise.

His heart rate quadrupled when he saw she wore nothing under her short denim skirt. She parted her legs, and Robert gasped at what he saw.

"You like?" she teased.

Like didn't cover it.

She lifted her top, displaying firm round breasts with small nipples.

He'd had plenty of sex in his lifetime, but he couldn't wait any longer. His penis throbbed as if it were ready to blow up. He wasn't sure that wouldn't happen when he came. He held back, wanting to enjoy every minute of this sexual fantasy come to life.

He lifted her skirt up around her waist, not caring about anything except delving his tongue into her hot center. He licked her until she writhed in ecstasy. His tongue felt like a hot spear. He darted in between her soft folds. She bucked up and down, thrusting herself at him. Her body shook as she climaxed. She almost choked him to death with her legs wrapped around his neck.

"My God, Robert! Look what you missed in high school," she said when one last shudder racked her body.

Robert was about to slip his engorged penis into her, when she slid off the desk.

She adjusted her clothes and laughed. She walked out of his office, leaving him with a hard-on so big, he had to resort to his boyhood practices. . . .

Now, lost in his sexual daydreams, Robert

barely had enough time to cover his erection when Becky, his secretary, came in reminding him of his current dilemma.

"Haven't I told you to knock?" he snapped.

"Sorry. But I thought this was important."

It'd better be or she'd have to go. Break a rule, say bye-bye. Rule number one: Never come into his office without knocking. He'd instilled that rule years ago, since he still had occasional sex on his desk.

"What is it, Becky? I have work to do."

"Dr. Hunter just called. He's asked to see Ms. Edwards's medical records. He left his fax number for you. He faxed over a medical release form signed by Ms. Edwards."

Now, when things were just beginning to fall in place, that psycho stepdaughter of John Worthington's had to come home. He'd been unable to stall any longer. She was out.

He'd spent his years as director of Sanctuary doing everything in his power to prevent her release, and now, that doctor he'd hired fifteen years ago was about to ruin everything.

He'd chosen only the most incompetent staff to work at Sanctuary. When a position opened up for a psychiatrist, Robert made damn sure to hire a doctor who had a blemish on his record. Like that bastard Dr. Macklin. Although he'd surprised him this time.

Robert had insisted that the Worthington family wanted Casey to continue with the therapy and her medication as usual. He'd explained the tragic circumstances that led to Casey's commitment. He'd also told the doctor to report any progress to him. Robert had explained that her charts were to be locked away each night and only he and Dr. Macklin were to have the key. Unbeknown to Dr. Macklin, Robert had kept a duplicate copy of her chart. Never mind that a few things had been added here and there.

This had been fine until Robert learned that Dr. Macklin had outsmarted him.

Early in his career Dr. Macklin had been fired from Mercy Mental Hospital in Savannah. He'd allowed a patient diagnosed as a paranoid schizophrenic a weekend furlough. Apparently the patient, a young black woman in her early twenties, went berserk. A search found her in the home of her ex-boyfriend. She'd hung herself.

Dr. Macklin had been termed a "no hire." He'd been only too glad to do as Robert instructed, although Robert knew he could never reveal too much. A bonus here and there, an occasional cruise, kept Dr. Macklin in the palm of his hand. Until two months ago.

Robert had been busy trying to save face with Norma, who'd recently learned of his many indiscretions. He hadn't noticed the sudden withdrawal of Ms. Edwards's medications as noted on her chart. Nor had he noticed her walking about the corridors of Sanctuary. He had no idea that she actually helped the staff with the domestic chores required at the small hospital, and had been doing so off and on for weeks.

To preserve his and Sanctuary's reputation, he'd told the Worthington family on more than one occasion of all the experiments they'd tried and how the outcome had always been a failure. If Casey were ever to regain her memory, it would be by some other means than medical science.

Then the good Dr. Macklin had requested a meeting with him, which in itself was unusual.

It seemed the family of the young girl who'd committed suicide hadn't believed their daughter would do such a thing. She'd been sick long before her family admitted her to Mercy. They knew their daughter, and she would never take her own life. They went on to say that Dr. Macklin, whose judgment they'd trusted immensely, told them Amy might even be able to function in normal society. She was improving daily, according to the doctor.

When Dr. Macklin was fired from Mercy, the family begged and pleaded with the local police to investigate Amy's former boyfriend, Jason Dewitt.

The Savannah police ignored their multiple requests. It actually became a department joke, Robert heard.

Finally, after coming into some money, the family hired Dick Johnson, a private investigator who'd spent sixty years living in Savannah. His mother, once a Vegas showgirl, had traveled to the South in search of her wandering lover. Never finding him, she'd met and married Richard Johnson, one of the first black attorneys to practice in Savannah or at least the first one accepted into the white circle of law. The occasional reference to "zebra," "Oreo baby," and "half-breed" went hand in hand when Dick's name was mentioned.

When the dead girl's family came to his

detective agency in search of answers, Dick was too well trained not to listen. The case appealed to him. The family hadn't seemed the kind who were looking to place blame to clear their daughter's sinful deed. They believed more had happened between Amy and her former boyfriend than the police reports revealed. Being a poor black family hadn't been in their favor, either.

Dick managed to pull in a few favors. According to the autopsy report, Amy had been hanged, but there were no rope marks on Amy's neck, and a rope was never found. Further investigation showed Jason Dewitt, Amy's white lover, had just learned Amy was pregnant. Dick was convinced Jason had killed Amy in a fit of rage, choking her to death, then trying to make it appear as though she'd committed suicide.

When Jason's grandfather, the Honorable William James Dewitt learned of the murder, he'd pulled and tightened every string in Savannah to cover up his grandson's crime. Jason Dewitt's punishment was being sent to Harvard.

After Johnson's investigation, fifteen years after the incident, Dr. Macklin had been cleared of all suspicion surrounding Amy's death and had started practicing what he'd been trained for. Psychiatry.

Robert pondered his current circumstances. If Blake Hunter wanted Ms. Edwards's medical records, something was up. He wondered whose cheeks he'd have to spread to find out. He'd kissed many asses in his lifetime on this small island. Those days were about to end.

Becky, with her greasy brown hair and sloped shoulders, remained in the doorway. Sometimes Robert felt sorry for the woman. Today wasn't one of those days.

"Then get them, Becky. My God, do you think this hospital pays you to lurk in my office? Do what the man asked, get the records and fax them to him. Blake's a doctor; he should know Sanctuary normally doesn't fax medical information."

"He faxed the release form," Becky whispered.

"Then do it, dammit!" His stupid secretary reminded him of Norma.

He had nothing to worry about. The records were as they should be. He'd checked them himself when he'd learned of Dr. Macklin's story. At least the man hadn't

tried to sabotage the hospital. Not that Robert really cared. It *was* a nuthouse after all, albeit an expensive one. An old rundown mansion that some poor relative of one of Sweetwater's better families had left the state. The funding required for remodeling the old mansion listed on the National Historic Registry had been enormous. They'd turned the aging dump into a mental hospital. When the citizens of Sweetwater needed a director, they asked Robert. At first he'd said no. Then he learned it would be a salaried position, and he would only be required to spend a few hours a week on the forgotten grounds. He'd accepted the position and had held it ever since.

Sanctuary had been just that to him many times over the years. When Norma complained or whined too much, he suddenly had work to do. God, how he wished she'd been able to have children. She might have been happy. When her father died four years after their marriage, he'd not only left Norma his house, but left her all of his holdings, which were enormous. A stipulation in the will—the firm of Goldberg, Willoughby, and Ruskin had complete control. Robert remained indebted to Norma. Her father's es-

tate left Norma wanting for nothing and him for everything. That was about to change.

Casey placed the last of her recent purchases in the closet where she'd discovered the evil picture.

She hoped Blake discovered something in her medical records. She couldn't recall the tests that had been administered. For years she'd been on medication that left her in a fog. Some days when her thoughtless conscience reminded her, she'd flush the pills down the toilet. Then her days weren't quite so foggy. She could think. At other times it almost seemed like she could remember. She'd told Dr. Macklin, and each time he'd pricked her with a needle. Any hope of recovery was snuffed out by the obliterating sting.

Then a few months earlier something happened. Dr. Macklin instructed Sandra to ease off her medication. Casey remembered waiting for the sounds of the orderly's footsteps each evening. Would he stop with his needles and give her the expected return ticket to never-never land? She'd been almost joyous when the orderly passed her door.

A few weeks later she'd learned of her upcoming release. Though she was sad at the thought of leaving her funny family, the clearheaded part of her told her there was something in her life she had to come to terms with. Just what that was, she didn't know at the time. Now, it was a different story. With Blake's help and her own determination, she was about to find out.

Flora practically swooned when she learned of Casey's accident. She'd asked if it really was an accident. Casey assured her that it had been, but the more she thought about it, the more suspicious she became. One would think after nearly plowing down a pedestrian, the person behind the wheel would return to the scene to make sure he or she hadn't injured anyone. Laura, Brenda, and the young girl hadn't offered their help. They'd stared at her like roadkill. The vehicle had disappeared in a cloud of dust. She'd had no hope of identifying its driver.

Flora had sent her up to bed, promising to bring her a tray.

"Casey?"

Startled, Casey opened the door.

Flora carried a tray filled with food. Casey helped her remove the plates from her bulky load.

"If you keep this up, I'll be as big as a house," she said.

"You need some meat on those bones, child. You always was a skinny little thing," Flora said as she placed the tray next to the bed.

"Flora." She didn't know how to phrase the question she wanted to ask, so she just blurted it out. "When I was a child, you took me to the doctor. Did Dr. Hunter, Blake's father, ever tell you he suspected anything . . . untoward may have happened to me?"

Flora's rosy cheeks were suddenly the color of Mabel's flour. "What in the world makes you think that?" she asked, her voice high-pitched.

"Today before the accident, Blake asked me to visit his office. We had lunch together. He said he had something he thought I should see. Apparently, he'd cleaned out his father's patient files and found mine." Casey waited, expecting Flora to finish the story, hoping she'd have an explanation for the awful suspicions the elder Dr. Hunter had.

The housekeeper remained silent, wringing her hands like a damp dishcloth.

She persisted. "Blake told me you used to take me for checkups, that sort of thing. I told him I couldn't understand why my mother didn't do this."

Flora sat down on the bed, something Casey knew she wouldn't normally do.

"After your grandmother Gracie died, Buzz would send you to me. His hands were full with Ronnie and your momma. They always seemed to be in some kind of mess. Nothin' to concern yourself with, but it was always somethin'."

Casey noticed Flora's Southern accent became more pronounced when she was upset.

"Ronnie'd get in some sort of scrabble over at the school, then Miss Evie would go an' try to make things right. She'd end up in as much trouble as the boy."

"It seems strange to me my mother would go to such trouble, especially when she couldn't be bothered with me. I mean a simple visit to the doctor's office couldn't have been half as stressful as her apparent confrontations where Ronnie was concerned." Casey heard the childish whine in her voice, but couldn't help herself. She'd been without her mother for so long.

"You were no trouble, Casey. For me or your momma. I enjoyed every minute you spent in my care. You were such a good girl. Always doin' as you were told. Never a minute a sassin' like your brother. Though I think your momma secretly delighted in fightin' with the teachers. Seemed she would egg 'em on whenever she could. Then a course with Buzz dead and all, Miss Evie had way more than she could handle. That's when she took to drinkin'."

"I wish I remembered, Flora, but I don't. I think the information in that file might be the key to unlocking my memory." Casey paused for effect. "Could you possibly help turn the key?"

She could see Flora in a mental battle with her conscience. She took a deep breath. Her conscience won. "You'd been acting strange. Remember I said what a good girl you were? Little by little I noticed you becomin' a bit rebellious. I'd ask you to do somethin', and you'd tell me no. You quit talkin' my leg off. And when bath time came around, why you was downright ornery. You'd hide in the bathroom until I promised not to come in. I never believed in locks, just trust. You knew this, too.

"One afternoon your momma called, all upset, and asked me if I could come and get you. Of course I told her I would. When I got there, it was obvious you'd been cryin', and your momma looked like she was about ready to pull her hair out. Ronnie was nowhere to be found.

"I took you back to my place. I remember you never uttered a word. Earlier that day I'd made your favorite peanut butter cookies. I'd been plannin' on takin' them over to you that evenin'.

"A bit of a spark returned to those bright green eyes of yours when you spied those cookies. Then it was snuffed out like a candle. I remember thinkin' that was odd."

Casey interrupted, "Why did you think that? Maybe I just wasn't hungry, maybe I didn't like them anymore." Casey knew that couldn't be true because to this day peanut butter cookies remained her favorite.

Flora took her hand and patted it. "I look back now and think that day was one of the worst in my life. You were like my own daughter.

"You asked me if it was okay if you took a

bath. I told you of course it was. I thought your askin' me to bathe odd. Usually I had to drag you into the tub.

"I fixed you a plate of cookies and told you your clean panties and a fresh romper was in the top drawer like always. I kept several changes of clothes for you at my house. You bathed, then came to the kitchen and had your snack, all the while, you hadn't mouthed a word. I was thinkin' a callin' Doc Hunter, then I thought better of it.

"I went to the bathroom to clean up, and that's when I knew I'd better call Doc Hunter." Flora squeezed her hand and took a tissue from the box next to the bed. She blotted her eyes and went on with her story.

"You'd left your clothes in a pile behind the door. As I was puttin' them in the hamper, I noticed your little underwear was dirty. They were your new pink day-of-the-week panties I'd bought you. While Miss Evie wasn't the greatest housekeeper in the world, she'd always seen to it that you kids bathed and that your clothes were washed proper. I thought this just another strange thing in an already strange day. I was about to drop your panties in the hamper when I noticed the blood."

"Blood! My God, surely I was too young to menstruate?"

"That's what I thought, too. You were nine, if memory serves me right. Though it did explain your odd behavior. I thought it best to take you to the doctor, just to make sure there wasn't nothing else wrong." Flora blushed as she said this. Casey's palm dampened. Flora took her used tissue and patted her hand with it.

Suddenly Casey saw flowers. Pink tulips. And a blue background.

"What is it?" Flora asked.

Casey stood and walked to the window. The gardens stretched so far back Casey couldn't see their end. She turned quickly and looked at Flora.

"Does Hank have tulips planted? Pink ones?" The words rushed out of her mouth.

Flora's already white face whitened more. She put a trembling hand to her mouth. "Hank don't have no tulips that I know of, Casey. Why are you askin'?"

"I've seen them before." The room became silent.

Flora drew in a deep breath. "That's what you was wearing that day."

"What day?" Casey spun around. Suddenly she knew; she just needed to hear it from Flora.

"The day I took you to see Doc Hunter."

"I remember. The dress, it had a sky-blue background. Pink tulips. The material was covered in pink tulips." Casey's eyes pooled with unshed tears. She'd actually had a clear memory.

Flora took her in her arms and rocked her. Maybe like the child that came to her that day so long ago, looking for comfort?

Casey blew her nose and smiled. "This is good. I don't remember much else, but I recall that dress. I think it might have been my favorite. Was it?"

"It sure was. Your grandma Gracie made it for you. She made a lot of your things when she had the time."

"This is so wonderful, I can't wait to tell Blake." She hugged herself, wishing it were Blake's muscled arms around her.

"You can. Tomorrow. You've had a long day. I think you need to eat and get some sleep."

"Oh, no you don't." Casey said, as the little woman readied herself to leave the room.

"Don't what?" Flora inquired, her face a mask of feigned innocence.

"You're not about to leave me hanging this time. Sit." She gently pushed Flora back to the bed. "You can share this with me." Casey indicated the platters of food. "There must be enough here for ten people." She filled the plates with cold roast beef, juicy ripe tomatoes, and Caesar salad. Slices of garlic bread were still warm. Casey handed Flora a plate.

"Where was I?" Flora asked.

Between bites of ripe red tomato and tangy Caesar, Casey filled Flora in.

"Oh, yes. My memory, old age an' all. Gettin' back to what I was tellin' you. I thought you was much too young to be bleeding. It was about time for your checkup. I called the doc, and he told me to bring you right over.

"You fought me at first. I'll never forget you kickin' and screamin'. You told me you hated me and never wanted to stay with me again."

"Oh, Flora, I *was* an awful child. I'm sorry."

"No, sweet thing, you wasn't a bad child. You were scared and hurt. That was just your way of gettin' it out. You never said a word when we walked downtown. Seems like that particular day all of Sweetwater was out and about. They looked at me like I'd hurt you."

"And you should have. You should've spanked my bottom, Flora. I was awful to you."

"That wouldn't have helped matters.

"Doc Hunter saw you wasn't your normal self. He thought it might be a good idea if he talked to you alone. I'd already told him on the phone what I suspected. He took you in his office. My Lord, you were there forever. Doc Hunter finally came out and asked where your momma was. I told him about her callin' me and havin' me come after you.

"He'd given you a puzzle to work and sent you upstairs to wait in the front room."

Casey had felt a sense of déjà vu in Blake's living room before. Now she knew why.

Chapter Twelve

"I could tell by the look on the doctor's face the news wasn't good. We were in his office, the one Blake uses now. He told me to sit down and not to say a thing until he was finished."

Flora looked at Casey, her gaze direct.

"He said, 'Flora, we've got a problem. Something's going on at the Edwards place. I think you and I both know what it is.' I wasn't real quick, but after a minute I followed what he was gettin' at. He told me the blood I'd discovered wasn't menstrual blood. Said you put up such a fight he almost didn't get to examine you. He said he suspected you'd been . . . hurt. Though that wasn't the word he used," Flora explained.

"There seemed to be some tearing inside you. I asked the doc if it could've happened from that bad fall you'd taken on your bike the week before, but he said no. I'd hoped that's all it was, but I knew there was more.

"I asked him if he thought you'd had . . . intercourse." Flora blushed at the word and fidgeted with the blanket at the foot of the bed.

"He told me that's what he was afraid of. My heart fell to my knees. My little girl, so innocent, so fun-lovin'. All that gone by the hand of some evil bastard." Flora cried, and Casey grieved for her lost innocence even though she had no memory of it.

Flora's muffled cries filled the room. Casey didn't know what to say. Rage took over coherent thinking. Doc Hunter had been right. Who would do something so vile and evil to a child?

No longer able to control her anger, Casey took her plate and hurled it against the wall. Then she took Flora's and did the same. Not caring, she then took the tray and sailed it like a disc through the air. With a thud it hit the wall, exposing the drywall.

"Why?" she screamed. "Why did Momma let it happen?" Gut-wrenching sobs sent her to the floor. She cried until her eyes felt like sandpaper. Her breath burned deep in the back of her throat. At that moment she knew what murderous rage felt like.

Flora took that moment to slide up the bed, next to her. With Flora holding her, Casey wept for the childhood she'd lost, cried for the physical pain she must have felt, and, more than anything, a slow, simmering rage began to boil. Rage at her loss of innocence and the person who'd stolen it from her.

She felt weak. With her chin resting on Flora's shoulder, she looked out the window through eyes now reduced to tear-swollen slits. The sun set low on the horizon, the last twinkle of light dancing across the gardens. Beauty maintained by wickedness, the thought came to her.

Surrounded by broken glass and the remains of her unfinished meal, Casey untangled herself from Flora and began scooping up the evidence of her fit of rage.

"Here, let me do that." Flora swatted her hand at Casey.

"No, Flora. I'll take care of it. I'm sorry. I don't know what's happening to me. For years it seemed I was no more than a ghost walking around in shadows. Now those dark, wispy images I've lived with for so long are becoming real to me. I'm afraid when I do remember. What will I do?" Casey held out her arms in search of answers.

"You'll do what the good Lord planned for you. You'll forget those terrible things and put them behind you. You'll start a new life. You're a young woman with a bright future ahead of her. Don't let the blackness from your past color your future." Flora dumped the last of the glass into the wastebasket.

"You're right. It's just hard to fathom something like this could've happened to me, and I can't remember it." Casey plopped down on the bed, hugging the pillow to her chest.

"Stop thinking about it now or you'll drive yourself insane." Flora's pearly white face turned a deep shade of crimson.

"See? Everything you or anyone else says all comes back to the one thing I'm supposed to forget. Where I've spent the past ten years. I can't do that, Flora, no more than you can forget your past. The hospital *is* my past. I just need to remember why I was sent there in the first place." She leaned back onto the plump pillows. She felt the weight of the world on her shoulders, and there didn't seem to be a damned thing she could do about it.

"And you will. Right now you need to rest. Do you want me to run a hot tub?" Flora asked.

"No, I'll have a quick shower. I'd probably fall asleep in the tub and drown I'm so tired. Don't worry Flora, I'm fine really." Casey sat up on the bed and a touch of a smile lifted her mouth. "Go on, I know you're exhausted."

"We'll talk more tomorrow."

"I'll look forward to it. By the way, Flora. Dr. Hunter's notes indicated he might've known who was responsible for molesting me. Did he happen to mention a name to you or my mother?"

Blake tossed the flimsy fax paper on the table next to him. He'd gone over the records so many times he'd memorized them.

Ten years and nothing. Not even a spark of recognition. There'd been a few articles on Casey's medical history in some issues of the *Journal of the American Medical Association*. Adam had shown more of an interest than Blake had at the time because of his area of specialization. Blake hadn't given much thought to it other than he'd remembered Casey coming into his father's office as a child. Now, however, he wished he could remember what they'd said.

Day after day, month after month, and year after year—nothing. It seemed this Dr. Macklin had done all the required tests, given all the medications required for a patient suffering from trauma-induced amnesia, and still no results.

All of that changed about two months ago. Dr. Macklin's attitude appeared to have changed. Casey's records were much more detailed. Dr. Macklin noted on several occasions he'd been amazed at Casey's sudden recovery. Casey was able to converse normally; she kept herself scrupulously clean, according to his notes, and even helped the staff with domestic chores. The doctor had been optimistic but cautious. He'd eased her off the medication. When Casey's mental health appeared to equal his own, Dr. Macklin had recommended her release. Then nothing. Her medical records stopped there.

Blake looked at his watch. Ten o'clock, too late to call. He'd tried to call Dr. Macklin twice that evening and hadn't been able to reach him. He'd hesitated about leaving a message on his machine. He wanted to talk to the doctor. Something didn't feel right.

He thought about going to Bentley and demanding the records, but he couldn't stand the sight of the pompous ass. He'd call Adam and have him arrange a visit with Dr. Dewild, or was it Dewitt? He couldn't remember. Casey would be in good hands. According to Adam, this young doctor was the best in the South.

He put aside Casey's mental health and thought of her as the woman who in just a few short hours had managed to latch on to his heart. Twice that day, an overwhelming sense of protectiveness consumed him. He'd wanted to block out the world and keep her with him where he knew she'd be safe. When she'd cried in his arms, his libido kicked in, reminding him that good doctors didn't get aroused when they offered their patients comfort.

Who in the hell were you trying to kid, Blake old boy?

When Casey's memory returned, he would consider their possible future.

A little voice whispered in his ear, *You*

know there's a chance. You saw the look in
her eyes. What other evidence do you need?

Evie snapped the gold compact shut and
tossed it back into her Chanel bag. The hospital lighting was horrid. Plastering a smile
on her face, she entered John's room.

In the middle of the private room the standard metal-framed bed held her once-robust
husband. Pale blue miniblinds prevented the
morning sun from removing the gloominess
Evie always associated with hospitals. Disinfectant couldn't cover the smell of death,
disease, and urine. A vase of yellow roses
from the garden at Swan House rested on
the bedside table next to John. She'd had
Hank clip them for her the day before.

A pencil-thin nurse took John's blood
pressure, and Dr. Foo, his neurologist, removed the metal chart attached at the foot
of his bed.

"One-thirty over ninety, Doctor." The
nurse released the cuff, and Evie heard the
gush of compressed air being released.

"Very good. I see our patient is following
orders quite well." Dr. Foo said. Evie waited
in the doorway. If it were she, no matter how

great Dr. Foo's reputation was, no way would she allow a foreign doctor to touch her. She didn't trust them. Look at Vietnam and that Korean thing. *My God,* she thought, *they could be planning to slowly kill every American they touched.*

"Eehhie," John screeched as he tried to sit up in the bed.

Dear God, if this was all that was left of him, maybe Dr. Foo's plot to kill the Americans should begin with John.

She smiled and walked to the side of the bed. "Dear John." Evie smoothed a strand of white hair from her husband's forehead and cringed. His skin felt like parchment, and his hair was limp from lack of washing. *This* wasn't her John. *Her John* had been meticulous in his personal hygiene habits. Who was this shrunken clump of gray matter?

"What is his prognosis?" Evie asked as she turned to the doctor.

Dr. Foo, a small man in his mid-fifties, with thick black hair and glasses that perpetually slid down his nose, placed John's chart at the foot of the bed.

"It is good, Mrs. Worthington. The only damage is to your husband's speech. With therapy, I'm sure in time you'll come to understand him." He smiled at John. "We'd like to send you home in a few days."

Evie watched some of the old sparkle enter John's eyes. And it made her sick. She'd assumed he would remain an invalid. He'd give her power of attorney, name her president of Worthington Enterprises, and at the end of her busy, decision-filled days, they'd share her victories and battles over a glass of Chardonnay. Of course John would merely listen. Any thought of him advising her washed away with the stroke of a . . . stroke. Evie laughed inwardly at her wicked sense of humor. Then, when she'd finished her wifely performance, she'd be free.

Free to mother Casey.

"Mrs. Worthington?" Dr. Foo said.

"Yes, I'm sorry I got lost for a minute. You were saying." She gave Dr. Foo her best smile.

"I think in time John will fully recover."

Evie felt as if she'd been struck by a bolt of lightning.

"What?" Her hand fumbled with the pearls at her neck. She stepped away from John's bedside.

"Provided John gets his therapy, he should be as good as new."

"Yes. Yes . . . of course. I trust that he will." Evie felt like a deer trapped in blinding headlights. Rooted to the floor, her mind gyrated like a child's spinning top.

This certainly changed the direction her thoughts had taken. Last night she'd even slept in that god-awful plastic olive green chair, hoping the doctors and nurses would see what a devoted wife did when she truly loved her husband. She'd revised her plans, right down to the last detail, and that last detail hadn't included John's full recovery.

All that and for what? John would be home in a matter of days. She'd actually sacrificed a night's sleep and probably ruined a Versace original. Not to mention the fact that a perverted orderly kept entering the waiting room to spy on her. Evie was sure he'd been peering up her dress.

Dr. Foo mumbled a few words to the nurse, and together they left the room, giving her the privacy she needed with her husband.

She went back to John's bedside. Was it possible that John could age so in a mere twenty-four hours? He looked his full seventy-three years and more. Dr. Foo must be wrong. The thought gave her hope.

"Ome," John said, his word garbled, and Evie leaned closer to him in an effort to understand him. "Ooome." He pointed to the door.

"I'm sorry John, but you'll have to try harder. You sound like a caveman grunting." Evie turned her head in disgust.

John kicked the foot of the metal bed. Evie jumped. He certainly wasn't slow in learning the role of caveman.

"John, listen to me. Don't try to talk. If you understand, nod."

His white head bobbed up and down.

At least his faculties were functional.

"Worthington Enterprises needs family at the helm. Mort Sweeney isn't family. The production at the paper mill has decreased, and I just learned Mort and his family left for Europe. I know we've talked about this before, John, however this time you're unable to have a say in the matter." Again, Evie smiled at her play on words.

She watched John's expressive blue eyes. Vibrant and alert. Evie watched the heart monitor. The little green beeps were moving fast. The sudden alarm sent Evie to the door.

The skinny nurse pushed her aside as she bolted through the double doors.

"Please, outside." She shoved Evie farther into the hall.

Dr. Foo galloped at breakneck speed to John's room.

My God! What in the world were they fussing about? She stepped outside the room, where the nurse took John's blood pressure, and Dr. Foo read a slip of paper as it rolled out of the heart monitor.

"What's happening?" Evie demanded from her position outside the open door. She rushed into the room, demanding to know exactly what was going on.

Dr. Foo muttered something to the nurse and scribbled notes on John's chart.

"Mrs. Worthington, could you step outside, please?" Dr. Foo asked.

"Certainly." Evie felt her own pulse start to race.

Dr. Foo took her elbow and guided her to the waiting room. He poured himself a cup of coffee the candy stripers had just made.

"Please, sit down." Dr. Foo pointed to the ugly green chair she'd slept on during the night.

Evie stood. She wasn't about to take orders from this . . . this foreigner.

"Thank you, Doctor, I prefer to stand.

Now what exactly did you want?" She left no room for small talk. She wanted to get this little speech over with and continue her conversation with John.

"Your husband's blood pressure just soared to dangerous levels. I'm not sure why, but until I find out, I can't allow him any visitors."

"Are you saying I had something to do with his blood pressure?" Evie scoffed. She used her best clipped Southern lady-of-the-manor voice.

"No, Mrs. Worthington, not at all. These things happen. It's usually best for the patient not to have any distractions for a few days. I'm sure you'll want us to do what we think is best for your husband, and right at this moment, I think he needs to concentrate on getting well and nothing more." Dr. Foo's tone of voice was purely professional, but Evie sensed an underlying meaning. The good doctor looked to her for a response.

"I want to do what's best for John. I don't know how he'll feel about my leaving. He wants me here, you must understand that. Why I actually spent the night in these horrid chairs just to be close to him."

"I'm glad you understand." Dr. Foo stood,

looked at his watch, and thanked Evie for her time. He left her standing in the waiting room, the scent of scorched coffee filling her nostrils.

Dismissed. The little foreign weasel had *dismissed* her.

"You can't . . ." she sputtered. God, she sounded like John.

She didn't need John's signature to take control, at least not just yet. A meeting with the shift supervisors was scheduled for two o'clock. She'd be there. With bells on.

Casey applied a touch of blusher to her pale face, then tossed the pot of cream on top of the vanity.

Casey dressed in khaki slacks, topped with a red shell, and matching Keds. Her mother's size selection was amazing. Everything was a perfect fit. One last glance told her she'd do. That day she had other problems to concern herself with.

She would find answers. Then again, that's what she'd said the day before.

Blake had called earlier from his office and said he was on his way to Swan House. They were going to go over her medical records, go back to the courthouse, see if the reliable Marianne could produce some sort of written document on her case. She wanted the empty spaces filled in.

Blake's willingness to provide a ride couldn't have come at a better time. Flora didn't drive, Julie was busy working, and she'd be damned if she'd suffer another ride from Hank. Her mother remained at John's bedside.

She waited on the brick steps. Roses scented the morning air, their colorful blooms adding a bright splash of color to the overcast sky. Grass, freshly plowed dirt, and the incoming scent of rain filled the humid air. Casey hoped the weather wasn't an indication of how her day was going to turn out.

Expecting the sleek black automobile she'd ridden in before, Casey was surprised when she saw the bright yellow Volkswagen wind its way down the hill. With a screech and a grind, the vehicle came to a halt.

Blake hopped out of the little bug, wearing faded denim that clung too tight in places that shouldn't have been filled out so much. Casey felt a spark of desire flicker as she scanned the rest of him. A white dress shirt couldn't hide the muscles that rippled with his every move. A light dusting of black hair poked out from the top of his shirt. She wondered what it would be like to touch him there, to feel the heat from his body.

"Well?"

Casey looked into his maple brown eyes, her thoughts suddenly jumbled. She quickly stood, brushing her backside as she did.

"Sorry, I was on another planet." She took Blake's offered hand.

"Then I'd say it's time to land. You ready?" he asked.

"Yes. I told Flora I'd wait out here. Mother is still with John, so there wasn't any reason for me to stay inside. And besides, I wanted to enjoy the flowers." Casey nodded in the direction of the garden.

"I can see that," Blake said as he helped her with the door, which stuck, before climbing into the driver's seat.

"This is from my college days. I drive it now and then, keeps the battery charged. Hope you don't mind. There's no air-conditioning."

"I love it," Casey exclaimed, settling herself in the cracked seat.

Blake shifted into gear and sped off.

Once they exited the gates of Swan House, his lighthearted mood turned serious.

"I called Adam. He's scheduled an appointment with Dr. Dewitt."

Casey felt her heart accelerate for a second and feared another panic attack. She took several deep breaths before answering.

"Then I take it you've read my medical records." She watched Blake maneuver the compact car with ease just as he handled the luxury vehicle days ago.

"I did. Sanctuary faxed them to me late yesterday."

"And?" Casey prompted.

He removed a hand from the wheel and placed it on her thigh. Casey was sure his hand would melt into her skin. His touch seared through the khaki material, and, again, she felt a tingling in the center of her belly.

"I didn't see any evidence of you ever undergoing regression therapy. Adam says Dr. Dewitt is sure RT will help you. If you don't experience a full recovery, you will at least have some recollection. I think it's worth a try."

Was it? Would her memory recall the horrors that caused it to shut down in the first

er. She didn't want them trampled with bad
ews and dire warnings.

She opened the door before turning to
lake. "Yes. Now, if we could get started."
he wanted to add, "The sooner I'll be in
ur arms" but couldn't. Not yet.

"I don't get it," Casey said as she tossed
e faxed copy of her records on the table in
nt of her. "For years, nothing, then boom.
. Macklin's entire attitude changes, and I
agically improve. Almost overnight. Then
discharged. If these records are correct,
medications were changed often. I won-
r why." She picked up the faxed paper
ain and read. "Haldol, Stelazine, Trilafon. I
w nothing about these drugs. The
mes alone sound potent."

"They're antipsychotic drugs," Blake
lied.

But why? I thought I'd suffered, it says
e"—Casey scanned the records—
auma-induced amnesia.' "

That's right, it does say that. Casey, what
ctly did you mean by 'if these records
correct'?"

don't know. A slip of the tongue, I guess.
?" She looked at Blake and didn't like
t she was seeing in his expression.

place? And if so, could she cope with the
revelation?

"When do I see Dr. Dewitt?"

"Day after tomorrow. There's a catch. His
office is in Savannah. That's a bit of a drive
from here. It might be best if you made it an
overnight trip."

"That's fine, Blake . . . but, I don't drive. At
least, I don't think I do." There she'd said it.
Twenty-eight and she had no idea how to
operate a vehicle.

Her statement seemed to amuse him. He
laughed, the sound rich and warm.

"I assumed as much and took the liberty
of rescheduling my appointments tomorrow.
I thought we could leave early in the afternoon, arrive in time for a nice dinner, do a bit
of sight-seeing. Your appointment is scheduled for ten the next morning."

He'd taken care of everything. Was she
being wise to allow him to take control of her
life? Was she being too trusting?

"I guess all I have to do is show up."

Blake glanced at her. She turned away.
She didn't want him to see her like this, exposed, with no control over her life. For so
long she'd allowed others to have power
over her life. Did she want this to continue?

"I hate to see you go through this, but Adam and I both think it's best. If you're serious about wanting your memory back, this is the way to go."

Casey frowned. She'd never really asked for Blake's or Adam's help. What did they have to gain? Or did they have something to lose?

She had to take the chance. It was the only way to see who won and who lost.

Chapter Thirteen

"If this is the only way I'm go able to get on with my life, I need stand who I am and what I am. I must think I'm crazy, but these days I've learned so much, an means nothing. Nothing substant I'm also aware that what I learn past could be devastating to my willing to take that chance."

Blake parked in front of his clicked the ignition key off befo her. "You're right, you know." hand to trace her jawline. Time his gaze held hers.

She trembled and wished look at her that way. She wan and simple. Her feelings for th she'd only met days ago were

place? And if so, could she cope with the revelation?

"When do I see Dr. Dewitt?"

"Day after tomorrow. There's a catch. His office is in Savannah. That's a bit of a drive from here. It might be best if you made it an overnight trip."

"That's fine, Blake . . . but, I don't drive. At least, I don't think I do." There she'd said it. Twenty-eight and she had no idea how to operate a vehicle.

Her statement seemed to amuse him. He laughed, the sound rich and warm.

"I assumed as much and took the liberty of rescheduling my appointments tomorrow. I thought we could leave early in the afternoon, arrive in time for a nice dinner, do a bit of sight-seeing. Your appointment is scheduled for ten the next morning."

He'd taken care of everything. Was she being wise to allow him to take control of her life? Was she being too trusting?

"I guess all I have to do is show up."

Blake glanced at her. She turned away. She didn't want him to see her like this, exposed, with no control over her life. For so long she'd allowed others to have power over her life. Did she want this to continue?

"I hate to see you go through this, but Adam and I both think it's best. If you're serious about wanting your memory back, this is the way to go."

Casey frowned. She'd never really asked for Blake's or Adam's help. What did they have to gain? Or did they have something to lose?

She had to take the chance. It was the only way to see who won and who lost.

Chapter Thirteen

"If this is the only way I'm going to be able to get on with my life, I need to understand who I am and what I am. I know you must think I'm crazy, but these past few days I've learned so much, and yet it all means nothing. Nothing substantial anyway. I'm also aware that what I learn about my past could be devastating to my future. I'm willing to take that chance."

Blake parked in front of his office and clicked the ignition key off before turning to her. "You're right, you know." He lifted a hand to trace her jawline. Time stopped as his gaze held hers.

She trembled and wished he wouldn't look at her that way. She wanted him. Pure and simple. Her feelings for this man whom she'd only met days ago were new and tender. She didn't want them trampled with bad news and dire warnings.

She opened the door before turning to Blake. "Yes. Now, if we could get started." She wanted to add, "The sooner I'll be in your arms" but couldn't. Not yet.

"I don't get it," Casey said as she tossed the faxed copy of her records on the table in front of her. "For years, nothing, then boom. Dr. Macklin's entire attitude changes, and I magically improve. Almost overnight. Then I'm discharged. If these records are correct, my medications were changed often. I wonder why." She picked up the faxed paper again and read. "Haldol, Stelazine, Trilafon. I know nothing about these drugs. The names alone sound potent."

"They're antipsychotic drugs," Blake replied.

"But why? I thought I'd suffered, it says here"—Casey scanned the records—" 'trauma-induced amnesia.' "

"That's right, it does say that. Casey, what exactly did you mean by 'if these records are correct'?"

"I don't know. A slip of the tongue, I guess. Why?" She looked at Blake and didn't like what she was seeing in his expression.

"Just a thought." Blake stood with his hands in his pockets, looking a million miles away.

"Then expand on it. I don't like the way you look."

Blake gave a short laugh. "Hey, I can't help what the good Lord dished out."

Casey tossed a green-striped throw pillow at him. "That's not what I meant."

"Then you approve?" he asked, a glint of humor in his eyes.

"Oh, for crying out loud. You're just like Flora. How is it we can be in the middle of a serious conversation one minute and the next, we're teasing back and forth?"

"You tell me," Blake said.

"See. There you did it again. Seriously, Blake." Casey kicked her tennis shoes off and tucked her feet beneath her. "I've got all the time in the world. At least I think I do. The drugs, Blake. Why would Dr. Macklin give me antipsychotic drugs? That wasn't the normal course of treatment for my condition."

Blake appeared deep in thought. "I've spent most of the night wondering why myself. The drugs mentioned are usually prescribed for severely disturbed patients.

Suicidal, delusional, and sometimes halluci-
national."

"I was all those things?" *Please, Dear
God no! Not suicidal. Life is too valuable.*

"I don't know. It doesn't say so in your
records. I tried to call Dr. Macklin last night. I
tried again this morning. It seems he's no
longer the staff psychiatrist at Sanctuary."

"What?" Casey exclaimed.

"I know. I was surprised myself. I called
Bentley's office. He's nowhere to be found
this morning. The staff at Sanctuary haven't
seen him, either."

"When did all this come about?"

"Apparently the day you were released."

Casey stood up and walked toward the
window. She felt as if she'd done this before. She recalled the feeling of déjà vu from
yesterday and Flora telling her she'd been
there before. She stuck her finger in the dirt;
the pots of African violets were dry to the
touch. Casey went to the kitchen and filled a
glass with tap water. Blake followed her and
watched.

Back in the front room the silence between them was thick, both lost in their own
private thoughts. Casey poured water in the
plants, then set the glass on the windowsill.

"How did you know where the glasses were?" Blake asked.

Casey turned around so fast the glass she'd placed on the sill fell and shattered on the hardwood floor.

"I forgot." She said as she bent to pick up the pieces. "I recalled being here once before. The day Flora brought me here. The day your father examined me."

She watched Blake clean up, mopping the water with a lace doily from the end table. He tossed the wet fabric onto the coffee table and took her by the hand.

"We have to talk. Really talk, Casey. Not this back-and-forth bullshit. It's leading us nowhere. You want answers, I want you to have them. Let's put our feelings aside and pretend to be detectives for a few minutes. Do you think you can do that?"

"Sure."

"Okay. Let me tell you what we have so far. And Casey, I'm going to tell you something you should've been told a long time ago. It's not my place, but right now I don't think it's important who tells you, just that you know. What I'm about to say isn't pleasant. So, tell me now if you'd rather I stop this conversation before it goes any further."

"I can take it, Blake. Go on."

She just hoped he wasn't about to start another story with no relevance to her present situation. She said as much to Blake, as he adjusted the cushion behind him.

"I wish it were mere inconsequential things I had to tell you. I don't want to do this, but someone has to. Your mother is with John, and it's my understanding from Adam that she's going to take over Worthington Enterprises while John is ill. It doesn't look like anyone involved in this atrocity is willing or able to enlighten you at the moment. As your doctor and your friend, I'm willing to suffer the consequences of my actions."

"God, Blake, don't sound so gloomy. After what I've witnessed and been through the past few days, trust me, this should be a breeze."

"Maybe. When you asked Brenda for that transcript, did you know there wasn't a formal investigation, never mind an inquest? It was ruled an accident." He paused and ran a hand through his thick hair, something he did when he was stressed.

"So I'm told." She was frustrated, tired already, and the day had barely begun.

"I ask for your patience."

"Go on," she said.

Blake seemed to be doing battle with himself. He stood up, jammed his hands back in his pockets. *Another habit,* Casey thought as she watched him pace the living room.

"It's essential for you to get your memory back, Casey. You and only you can fill in the gaps, but for now, I'll tell you what little I know. I was in Atlanta at the time, at Emory. Adam called me and told me what had happened. I remember thinking what a terrible thing to have happened on Halloween of all days. And my father was so distraught, I seriously thought he might suffer a heart attack."

"How awful for you and your family."

"Yes, it was. But not as bad as for your family. After your father died Evie did the best she could under the circumstances. You were well provided for, don't get me wrong. But I think Evie wanted more than money. I think she truly wanted to be married again. She'd been seeing John, and Adam didn't like it. He'd been close to his mother and couldn't imagine how his father could possibly be interested in another woman.

"Your grandmother Gracie took care of you when your mother couldn't. Then, Gracie died, and Flora did a lot for your mom, cleaning and taking care of you.

"Ronnie was in high school, so you must have been in third or fourth grade. Certainly big enough for Ronnie to look after without your mother having to worry. He took care of you sometimes. Flora spent as much time with you as she could, but she worked for the Worthingtons and couldn't take off as much time as she liked.

"Fast-forward about eight or nine years. Evie and John had announced their plans to marry. Adam was angry. He and John fought. They cooled it for a while. I heard your mother went off the deep end for a spell. Then they got back together. It was a long time after Evie and John were married before Adam even bothered to visit his father at Swan House.

"I'm getting ahead of myself. Flora said you'd changed. Said it was like day and night. I guess you were the center of Flora's life for a long time, especially after Gracie died. She'd noticed things."

"Flora and I talked about the molestation last night," Casey said. "I actually remembered the dress I wore to your father's office that day."

"Did you recall anything else?" His eyes were alert as they searched hers.

"No, that was it. But it's the first honest-to-goodness, drug-free memory I've had. Or at least I think it is. The other instances didn't seem quite as vivid."

"Then it's a start. Flora and my father were very concerned about you. I don't know if Dad ever told Evie his suspicions, but I plan to find out. Flora said you were never right after that. Quiet, withdrawn, always jumping at the slightest noise." Blake combed a hand through his hair. "I'm not sure if I should go on." He looked to her for the answer.

"You can't do this to me! I've sat here waiting patiently, and now this!" She slung her hands apart. "Let me ask you something, Dr. Hunter. Do you know what it's like not to know what your favorite ice cream was? Did I like cartoons, what color was my bike? Did I even have a bike? Did I have a diary? Friends? What were my secrets? Did I play Monopoly with my brother? Did Mother tell me sweet bedtime stories? Did I like school?" She stomped across the wood floor, a finger pointed accusingly at Blake.

"You!" she cried. "You know what else I can't remember?" She wiped her nose on the hem of her red shirt. Tears streamed down her face, and she felt her lower lip tremble.

Blake sat back down on the sofa. "Tell me, Casey," he said, his voice full of concern.

She swallowed back another round of tears and sat next to him.

In barely a whisper she uttered, "I don't even know if I've ever made love."

"I don't know if anyone told you this, but you were engaged once. His name was Kyle. Right after you were sent to Sanctuary, he left town. Last I heard he'd been married three times. His mother died a couple of years ago. So, whether the two of you . . . *were close* in that way, I couldn't tell you."

Blake took her in his arms and rocked her. She sobbed and felt her tears dampen his shirt. She inhaled, loving his scent. His shirt smelled like sunshine and Clorox. She'd wondered about making love since the first time Blake held her. And the funny thing was, she couldn't ask anyone. What would she say? " 'Oh, excuse me, you look about my age. Do you know if I slept with a fiancé I can't remember?' " She gave a wry laugh. "It doesn't get any better than this, does it, Blake?"

"Shhh, it's okay, baby. I promise, it'll be okay." His words soothed her, his broad chest felt like protective armor against her breasts as he held her tight against him. She could get used to this. She sighed and pulled away from the only comfort she'd known in years, maybe in her life.

"Please, Blake. I've got to know," she pleaded.

Resigned, he shifted his position and continued. "Like I said, Flora knew there were things going on in your life. Things that shouldn't have been. The molesting. The obvious changes. She couldn't do anything except watch you. You'd be okay for a while, then nothing. Flora said you sometimes went days without speaking a word. This went on for years."

Casey thought her behavior must've been typical of a molestation victim. Who would want to be friendly and outgoing when inside they were shattered?

"Your mother told you and Ronnie a date

had been set for her and John's wedding. Poor Eve, she was so excited; this I do remember. Adam still hated the idea, but enough time had passed. His grief wasn't as fresh and raw as he got older.

"That's when it happened. Right after Evie announced her engagement. Halloween of all days. Maybe it was an omen of things to come, who knows. Ronnie's death changed a few things. Of course John and Eve postponed the wedding. Your mother wanted to go ahead with their plans, but John wouldn't hear of it. Adam was delighted."

Casey couldn't help interrupting, she had to know. "Why didn't Adam like my mother?"

"As I said, he'd lost his own mother. The last thing he wanted was someone trying to take her place."

"But you just said he was older, he'd gotten used to the idea of his father's remarriage."

"You'll have to ask him yourself. He may have thought Evie had ulterior motives for marrying his father."

"What 'motives' could my mother have possibly had?"

"Casey, please. Let's not go there. Talk with Adam, I'm sure he can explain what he

felt at that time. Do you want me to go on?"
he asked.

"Of course."

"Sweetwater hadn't seen anything like it.
Sheriff Parker wasn't much older than me at
the time. New to the office, I'm sure what he
saw that day changed him forever. Grady
Wilcox, the former sheriff, didn't even bother
to run against him. Said he was too old,
Sweetwater needed some young blood. I
look back and think Roland made his first
mistake when he didn't ask for Grady's help.
Grady might've been an old coot to Roland,
but he knew his profession. He'd practiced
law way back when. He gave it up, though,
and no one even asked why." Blake sighed
and pinched the bridge of his nose.

"Flora said you'd been acting more
strange than ever. She even thought you
might've been high on drugs. Marijuana,
LSD, she didn't know, she said. I don't know
any other way to tell you this Casey, I've
prolonged it as much as I can. I'm going to
blurt it out and suffer your wrath."

He smiled, a sad smile. He took her hand
in his and she felt his warmth, his firm, yet
gentle grip. She looked at his hands. He had
nice hands. Nice nails. Short and even.

His voice filled with anguish as he continued. "The day Sweetwater so desperately wants to forget, Casey, is the day you allegedly killed your stepbrother." His eyes darkened with pain as he stared into her own.

Allegedly killed your brother. Allegedly killed your brother. Allegedly killed your brother!

In her heart she knew it had to have been something like that. She felt as if an invisible hand were about to close around her neck, making it difficult to breathe. Panic unlike anything she'd ever known lodged in her throat, making words impossible. Wrapping her arms around herself, she began to rock back and forth as chilling images built in her mind.

She stopped. Her thoughts paralyzed her. No! He was wrong. They were wrong. They had to be!

"Casey." Blake's voice sounded like it was coming through a tunnel.

She stared at the wall. And rocked. Faster and faster so it would go away.

The clothes they gave her were stiff and rough against her tender skin. She was cold. All over. A haze clouded her vision, making everything appear as if it were floating. She glanced at her wrists. Leather, like a belt. Too tight. Her arms were strapped to her sides. Why? Suddenly, she heard voices.

"Doc Hunter says she'll sleep for a while. I hope whatever he gave her will knock her for a loop. My God, I've never seen anything like it." A woman's voice.

"Yeah, well jus' wait till you see the boy, then say that. A person should never have to see what we saw out there today. And that poor mother. She's lost both of her young 'uns. As much as I hate to say it, this one here ought to burn in hell."

She was cold, she couldn't burn. Didn't they know that? And just who were they? She tried to get a closer look, but all she could see were their backs.

"Dammit, Casey! Listen to me!" Blake shouted.

She jerked forward and turned to Blake. Her voice felt raw and scratchy. "Hmm?"

Numb, that's what she felt. She couldn't look at Blake. How could he do this to her after all she'd been through in the short time she'd been home? He was like all the others. Mean and cruel. She wished she'd stayed at Sanctuary.

"Listen to me," he continued. "You're suffering from shock. I'm going to give you something."

"No! I don't want anything. You're just like the rest of them." She reached for her shoes and jammed her feet into them, not bothering with the laces, and ran to the door.

Blake grabbed her arm and pulled her to a stop. "This is the last thing you expected to hear, I know. Maybe I was wrong to blurt it out the way I did. I'm sorry, but it had to be said. Please, Casey, trust me."

She stopped. He was right. Why would he make up such a thing? The more she thought about it, the more sense it made. Why else would she have remained at Sanctuary for ten years?

"I'm sorry. I can't . . ." She flung her arms out loosely in front of her.

"I know. It's a lot to swallow. But I'll help you. We can deal with this, Casey. I promise. Once we talk to Dr. Dewitt, he'll help you. Then you can put this behind you and go on with your life."

He said "we." Did that mean he'd stand behind her, *even if she was a murderer?*

She nodded and sat back down. All the strange looks she'd received since her return. The rude clerk, Brenda. It all made sense now.

She was a killer. A cold-blooded, thoughtless killer.

What good would it do for her to remember? She'd apparently been insane, killed poor Ronnie, and, by the grace of God, her memory of that day had been wiped clean. She should just leave it at that. She *wanted* to. But something nagged at her conscience. Like a sore thumb, it was there. A fleeting thought. She'd think of it later. Right now she just wanted to absorb what Blake told her.

He hadn't uttered a word. She stared at him, expecting to see fear and disgust. What she saw totally surprised her.

"Why are you looking at me that way, Casey? I've always known about this. It doesn't change anything." He reached for her.

"This is a living nightmare! One minute I think I'm this, . . . I don't know what, and the next minute I learn I'm a murderer." She let him hold her. She felt safe and secure. All she wanted was to be safe. She didn't want him to see her fall apart again. She would get through it. Somehow.

"I can only imagine how you must feel. We'll investigate. I'm going to find Dr. Macklin. I'll talk to Bentley; we'll get those reports from Marianne if they even exist. And Dr. Dewitt. We aren't going to sit around doing nothing, Casey." He dotted light kisses along her jawline. She drew in a deep breath. Oh, God, how she wanted to believe him. How she wanted to forget what he'd just revealed.

"Does it really matter now? It's not going to change what I did," she said, despair in her every word.

"This isn't the end of the story." Blake stood and began his all-too-familiar pacing.

"Why, Blake? Why does it matter now? After ten years. I've served 'my time' so to speak. What good will dredging up the past do me? You tell me."

"I think something more happened the day Ronnie died. I think the entire town of Sweetwater believes that, too. Adam and I have discussed this for years, and we both believe something was covered up. We just don't know what."

Can it be possible? she wondered. *A spark of hope. Maybe there is more to the story.*

She was confused. "When I . . . when I killed Ronnie." She hesitated, the words sounding foreign to her. "When I did this . . . Why didn't I have a trial?"

Blake turned to her. "That's part of the mystery. While I have my suspicions, I was never privy to the so-called police report. The report Marianne and Brenda can't seem to take the time to look for. That's why I think it would be good to talk to Roland. See what he says after all these years."

"What are your suspicions?" Casey asked, anxious to hear his answer.

"Remember, these are just my suspicions. When you allegedly killed Ronnie, my thought has always been you did it in self-defense."

"Forget it, Blake. I'm sure if that were the case, I would've had a trial, and who knows what. Don't forget, I haven't a clue as to what happened. It would certainly explain the medications I was on. Maybe I am crazy." She shrugged and gave a hollow laugh. "Maybe it's not such a good idea to question the sheriff. He apparently did his job. For whatever reason, I lost it that day, right along with my memory. Maybe we should just leave it at that." A part of her believed those words. Another part of her wanted to investigate, with a vengeance.

"Then how will you know?" he asked.

Maybe she should at least give it some thought. If Blake and Adam both felt something more had happened, she owed it to them to validate their suspicions. And she was sure, when all was said and done, she'd still be the crazy lady without a memory. The crazy lady who had killed her brother.

"I suppose it can't hurt to ask a few questions. But Blake, I don't want to stir up trouble. The citizens of Sweetwater haven't been too welcoming as it is. And with John ill and Mother stuck at his bedside, the last thing I want to do is upset either of them."

"I agree. That's not my intent. Do you think you're up to a talk with the sheriff? I think that's the most logical place to start. Depending on what he says, if you want to continue, I'll hold off canceling the appointment with Dr. Dewitt. Your call."

"I might as well. But remember I don't want to do this at the expense of someone getting hurt. And I want to see Dr. Dewitt no matter what." She'd made her mind up in those few seconds. Even though she'd killed, she was going to find out why, because if she didn't, how could she possibly live with herself?

He'd seen her yesterday loaded down with packages. Though she'd been across the street, he could see that the years had been good to her. He hadn't expected her to look so normal. Not after everything that happened that day. He remembered that day all too clearly. And he wanted to forget it.

The buzzing of the intercom interrupted his thoughts. He was glad, since he didn't like the direction his thoughts were taking him.

He pushed the button. "Yes, Vera?"

"Dr. Hunter is here. He'd like to see you."

He sighed. "Send him in."

He'd always liked Blake Hunter, but something about the man made him feel inadequate.

The door opened. Grateful didn't describe what he felt for his battered desk chair at that moment. If it weren't for its dilapidated support, he'd be flat on the floor.

The woman in his thoughts stood next to the doctor. The distance he'd viewed her from yesterday had deceived him. Not only did she look normal, she looked like she'd stepped right out of a fashion magazine. Though her hair had been longer, and he didn't remember her being so pale, ten years in Sanctuary hadn't taken their toll on her beauty.

Suddenly he wished his brown hair wasn't so thin and that he'd refused that last hot dog. He sucked his gut in as he stood and held his hand out to Blake.

"What can I do for you?" he asked, his eyes flickering back and forth between his two visitors.

"Mind if we sit?" Blake asked.

Shit, why now of all times did I forget my manners? And why hasn't the cleaning crew been in lately?

"Sure, go ahead." He motioned to two chairs across from him. They weren't in any better condition than his own, but at least they were clean. He quickly glanced at his desktop. The usual clutter. Files, a mug claiming he was the boss, and splatters of spilled coffee covered the surface. A gold ashtray in the shape of a star filled with overflowing butts and stubbed-out cigars. A ceramic Elvis wearing chipped blue suede shoes sat on the edge of the desk. Nothing had changed in the eleven years he'd been in office. The office looked exactly as it had the day Grady Wilcox walked out, leaving him in charge of the well-being of Sweetwater's finest.

Blake and Casey seated themselves, and he did the same.

"Now, what can I do for you?" the sheriff asked Blake while he looked at Casey.

Blake shifted in his chair and looked at his companion. "I guess you know Casey."

Roland knew her well. Too well. But now wasn't the time. He coughed. "Uh, we've met."

"Casey is aware of the crime she was accused of, Roland. We've come here to get some answers. I hope you don't mind."

Roland drew in a deep breath and tucked his shirt in. "What kind of answers are you looking for?"

Casey chose that moment to speak. "The day Ronnie died." She looked down. When she lifted her head, her deep green eyes were filled with tears. Blinking them back, she braved his stare. "I need to know what happened. And the report. I'm sure there had to be something filed with your office."

Roland felt like he'd been kicked in the gut.

He would never have expected it. And so soon. Hell, she'd only been home a few days.

"There is a report. Somewhere. God knows where. Before we had computers, you know. It's been so long, I'll see if I can get Vera to look for it." He punched a button on the intercom.

A crackly voice replied, "Yes?"

"Vera, see if you can find the Edwards report. It should be packed away with the files we stored in the attic a few years ago." He released the button.

"Good God, Roland, that'll take days to find!" the voice squawked.

"And you're overloaded with work?" He smiled at Blake and Casey as he waited for Vera's reply.

Nothing.

"She'll find it. It just might take her a few days."

"I'll check back. Roland, I have a few questions to ask. Do you have time?" Blake inquired.

He'd put the noose around his neck for sure. After telling Vera she had nothing better to do in so many words, he hadn't thought of his own escape route. He'd put the road-blocks up himself.

He made a pretense of looking through a pile of papers. God! A crossword puzzle from three weeks ago. *Important stuff here, Parker.* He glanced at his cheap plastic watch. "I've got a few to spare."

"Tell me what you remember about that day, Roland," Blake prompted.

He leaned back in his chair and prayed the usual fart noise wouldn't make itself known. It did. He felt his face turn red. God-damn it! He'd have a new desk chair before day's end. He looked at Casey. A hint of a smile, nothing more. Blake remained as rigid as possible.

"There isn't much to tell. Casey, uh . . . Ms. Edwards here went . . . God, Blake, I can't say this in front of her!" He looked from Blake to Casey. How much humiliation could a man stand in one day?

She spoke. "Sheriff Parker, I don't re-member what happened that day. Don't worry that you'll embarrass me. I just need the facts, nothing more."

And she'll get nothing more, he thought.

"I was on my way home when Vera dis-patched the call. I'd been in office barely a year. I remember thinking finally some ex-citement on this island. I'd been bored that day. Not much crime in Sweetwater. The usual drunks, teenagers speeding. An occasional domestic call, that was about it.

"When I arrived at your place I recalled my earlier thoughts and wished to God I could've withdrawn them." He shook his head. Not even in his nightmares could he have called up an image so hideous, so unthinkable.

"It must have been around eight or so. It was Halloween, and I tell you both, there isn't an October that goes by that I don't think of that day as I'm sure most of Sweetwater does. Your momma, now Mrs. Worthington, was waiting on the porch.

"I've never seen a woman shake so bad. I thought she'd pass out on me, but she didn't. She led me inside the house. The downstairs was dark as I recall. We went upstairs." He looked at Casey to see how she was holding up. She stared straight ahead, almost as if she were looking through him.

He continued. "I saw you, Ms. Edwards, huddled in the corner of the hallway. Your mother didn't say anything. She just kept shaking.

"At the end of the hall, a door was partially opened. There must have been a night-light or something, I don't remember. Just that there was a light of some sort. I do remember the smell."

"Copper!" Casey shouted. "I remember!"

Blake motioned for him to stop. "What else do you remember, Casey?" Blake asked her.

Deep in thought, Roland waited for her to answer.

She shook her head as if trying to clear her mind. She looked at him. "Sheriff Parker, tell me if I'm wrong. My God, I can't believe this!" She felt dazed, as if she'd been knocked over the head with something. "Maybe I'm losing it again or my memory has crossed into another dimension, who knows. But I swear I remember seeing Robert Bentley that day."

"What?" Blake shouted.

"Hold on, Blake," Roland said as he got up and closed the door.

Back at his desk, he watched the pair in front of him. Silent as night, both lost in their own thoughts, both unaware that he scrutinized their every move.

"There must be some other explanation, Casey. Why would Bentley have been there? I don't think he even knew your family then."

"Don't be too hasty, Doc. Ms. Edwards's memory isn't as bad as you might think. At least not on that account. She's right. Bentley was there that day."

Chapter Fourteen

Blake turned back to stare at the sheriff's office, a frown building between his eyebrows. He opened the door for Casey before he walked around to the driver's side and climbed in. "I've always suspected there was something more to that day," he said as he maneuvered the Volkswagen along Sweetwater's dusty back roads.

"Why would he have been there?" If she could only remember. She was the only one with answers. Except for her mother. With things as they were now, she wasn't about to question her.

"If Dewitt is as good as Adam says he is, maybe by this time tomorrow we'll have our answer."

"I hope so. Did you try Bentley's office again?" she asked.

"Yes, I got his answering machine. I tried Sanctuary, too. Becky said he hasn't been in today." He shifted into passing gear, and the little car climbed uphill effortlessly.

She hadn't been to this part of the island because developers had yet to cut through this area of lush tropical greenery. She dreaded seeing high-rise buildings and ricky-ticky fast-food joints with equally tacky neon signs. Nothing was forever, it seemed. She turned to Blake.

"Where are we headed?"

"Adam's place."

"But I thought he lived in Atlanta." She drew in a deep breath and sighed. "Why?"

Blake tossed a glance in her direction. "He called me. Apparently his Jag died on him. Took it to Poorman's. I'm giving him a ride to the hospital. I forgot to mention it. Sorry. And he does live in Atlanta, this is his home away from home."

"Poorman's?"

Blake gave a hearty laugh. "It's the only auto repair shop on the island. Don't ask about the name. Old Jaybird they call him, has been in business for years. That's it ahead." He pointed to a weather-beaten wooden structure that looked like it hadn't seen a fresh coat of paint since the turn of the century.

Blake pulled into the parking lot. Dozens of automobiles surrounded the place. An elderly man peered up from beneath the hood of a pickup truck as Blake turned off the engine.

"You lookin' for Mr. Adam, Doc?" The man had to be in his seventies, Casey thought as she looked out the window. He wore coveralls that might have been blue at one time. Now, they were covered in oil, grease, and multiple colors of what she thought must be paint.

Blake hopped out of the car and walked over to the elderly man. She couldn't hear what they were saying, but the sudden addition of a third voice caused her to pay closer attention.

Adam, her stepbrother.

Decked out in summer whites, he was the picture of a Southern gentleman. Casey thought all he needed was a straw hat to complete the picture, and he'd look like Gene Kelly in *Singing in the Rain.* Now where in the world had *that* come from? Had she been a movie buff? Just one more unanswered question.

Blake and Adam both shook hands with Jaybird before they headed for the car.

She opened the door and lifted the seat to crawl into the back.

"That won't be necessary, Casey." Adam's voice stopped her cold. "The backseat is fine. I just need to get to the hospital." Adam's tone was disapproving; the contempt could've been heard by a deaf man.

Casey leaned out of the car, stood aside, and watched as her unfriendly stepbrother scrunched his six-foot-something self in the cramped backseat.

She looked over the VW's top at Blake. He lifted an eyebrow, shrugged before he slid into the driver's seat.

Having no other choice, she got in the car and yanked the door shut. Suddenly, she felt on edge, the way she'd felt when she found the picture in the closet. The picture of Ronnie.

"I appreciate the ride. Darned luxury cars are anything but," Adam said to Blake.

"That's why I kept this girl." Blake lovingly patted the bug's cracked dash and looked at her. "She never fails to do just what I want her to do." He winked at Casey.

She couldn't help but pick up on Blake's

jovial attitude. She was glad for it; she didn't like the direction her thoughts were headed. "Then why did you tell me earlier you had to drive her now and then to keep her charged up?"

Adam smirked. "I thought as much."

Blake's middle finger shot in the air.

"And here I thought you two were the best of friends, or at least that's what you both have Flora thinking." Casey found herself enjoying the light sparring between the two, but didn't understand Adam's reserved attitude toward her.

"Flora's made one too many beds," Blake said as he swerved into the hospital parking lot.

A three-story stucco building, the hospital's dazzling whiteness, trimmed in a calming blue, stood out against the dark green leaves of the many trees scattered on the property. Dozens of angel oaks created an archway over the stone walkway leading to the front entrance.

Nothing modern here, Casey thought.

She got out of the car and pulled the seat forward for Adam.

Blake stepped out and looked from her to Adam. "Do you want to see John, Casey?"

Though she hadn't planned on it, she thought now was as good a time as any. "Of course. And Mother, is she here, too?" She'd barely seen her mother since her return.

"She's at Worthington headquarters in Brunswick,"Adam said, his words clipped.

She looked to Blake. "I thought you said she was here with John?"

He gave Adam a scorching glare. "I thought she was."

The three of them walked single file down the stone path leading to the hospital's front entrance.

Inside, the lobby was dim and dark. A wooden desk dominated the center of the room. Rose-colored carpet muffled their footsteps as they stood in front of the desk. A young woman sat behind the desk, her face hidden behind the pages of a romance novel. Casey smiled to herself. *Fun job,* she thought. *They must not be dying today.*

The young girl placed the book on her lap. "May I help you?" she asked as she swept her gaze from Casey to Blake, finally resting on Adam.

"Oh, sorry Doctors, I was uh . . . busy." She scooted farther beneath the desk. Pale blue eyes looked from Blake to Adam.

"We're here as family"—Adam looked at the nameplate on the desk—"Karen. Could you tell me what room they have my father in? They've moved him to a special care unit."

The girl scanned her ledger. "One-fifty-four."

"Thanks," Adam said. He turned to the right, and together they walked down the hall in silence. The atmosphere was hushed, as if death lurked around every corner. Life-saving and life-taking machines rested outside doors of patients whose lives could be snuffed out or rejuvenated with the snap of a button. A sharp left, an immediate right, led them to John's room. Adam turned to them before entering.

"Give me a minute?" He placed his hand on the door, not waiting for their response. The constant blip of a monitor and the in-and-out whir of a ventilator were snuffed out as the door closed behind him.

"I'm dying of thirst. You want anything? There are machines right around the corner," Blake said.

"A pop would be nice."

She watched Blake as he sauntered down the hall. Nurses stopped him, a patient waved, and Blake threw his head back in a gust of laughter. She smiled. She really liked the man. Apparently the staff at the hospital liked him, too. *It would be hard not to,* she thought.

Raised voices caused her to turn away from Blake's retreating back. Not wanting to appear nosy, she sat in the plastic chair outside the door and picked up a copy of *Redbook*. The pages were a blur as she thumbed through them. She couldn't help but overhear the angry voice inside John's room.

"Dammit, Dad! I told you years ago to cut her out of your will. You don't even know the woman, for Pete's sake. And you want to leave this to her?" Adam bellowed.

Casey heard the sound of something dropping on the floor followed by a muffled voice.

"I don't care what Evie says. You know what I think of her," Adam's angry voice continued.

She didn't want to hear more. She got up and paced the hall, looking for Blake. Ready to search the halls, she breathed a deep sigh of relief as she saw him turn the corner, bottles of Coke in hand. She almost rushed to meet him.

"Hey!" he said as he handed her the soft drink. "You look like you've seen a ghost. You okay?" Blake questioned.

She didn't want to tell him what she had overheard. "Yes, I'm not feeling well. I don't think I should stay." She needed time to think. Alone. After her recollection in Sheriff Parker's office, she needed to sort things out. By herself. Coming here had been a mistake.

Blake didn't question her sudden change of heart. "Let me tell Adam."

Casey nodded and walked away from the door. While part of her couldn't wait to meet her stepfather, the other part of her was glad for the postponement.

Who had Adam wanted out of John's will? My mother? Why?

"He'll get a ride. I think I'd best get you back home. You don't look so hot."

"Gee, and I thought you liked the way I looked," she said lightly.

"I do. I just don't like those worry lines creasing that beautiful forehead of yours." He gave her arm a quick squeeze.

"Thanks for your concern. I think I'm just overtired," she said, as they neared the hospital's exit.

"You need to relax." Blake unlocked the car and opened the jerky door for her. "I'm still hoping to talk to Dr. Macklin and find out where Bentley's hiding."

Casey eased into the seat, leaning her head against the neck rest. "What makes you think he's hiding?"

"I don't know, but I plan to find out. You still want to go to Savannah tomorrow?"

"Of course. I want this nightmare to end. I hope Dr. Dewitt can help me." She didn't want to tell Blake the thoughts she'd been having lately. She, too, was starting to think something evil had happened on that fateful Halloween day ten years ago. She'd experienced a brief flashback in Sheriff Parker's office. Right now, she wasn't sure what to make of it. But tomorrow was another day. She would find out everything she needed to know sooner or later.

Chapter Fifteen

"Couldn't you have picked a better meeting place? You know I hate this fucking ferry!" He grabbed on to the railing, firmly planting his feet in place, not daring to move. He hoped his fresh fruit salad didn't make a return visit.

At least the ID fans were in working order, Robert thought as he viewed the Georgia coastline. After a trip through the scrubbers, clean white smoke billowed out from the paper mill's smokestacks, leaving behind a smell he'd never gotten used to. He held his breath for a moment, then exhaled.

"And you have a better idea? From what I've seen the last few days, I think you need to rethink any ideas that pop out of that feeble mind of yours," she chastised him.

Right now, Robert hated this woman,

hated the hold she had on him. Soon, he told himself. Soon, he'd have this bitch over a barrel, maybe literally—he'd always wanted to rough her up a bit.

He gave what passed for a rueful laugh. "You're right. I'm sorry. I don't know what's gotten into me." He smiled at his companion as he edged her closer to the ferry's railing.

Standing in front of her, blocking the passengers' view, he snaked his hand down her cream silk blouse. He found her nipple and pinched. Not hard, just enough to elicit a twinge of pain.

He watched her intake of breath, saw the veins in her neck pulse, and felt the flutter of her quickened heartbeat against his own.

"You're sick, you know that?" Her words were laced with disgust.

He laughed and thrust his hard penis against her. Tossing a glance behind him to make sure he didn't attract anyone's attention, he reached for his zipper and jabbed up against her stomach.

He saw the glazed look in her eyes and knew no matter how prim and proper this bitch acted, she liked this public, indecent foreplay as much as he did.

Inching his hand up her skirt, he slipped

her lacy panties to the side. With his fingers he proceeded to massage her, sliding his fingers to her center, finding her wetness. *Yes,* he thought, *she won't refuse this. Ever.*

He continued to stimulate her. She took him in her hand and slowly trailed her fingers down his swollen length. His nostrils flared as she began to pump him fast and hard.

He shoved her hand away. "Not yet."

His fingers were extensions of his penis as he shoved three, four, then all five inside her. He saw her wince, and experience told him it wasn't from pain, but pleasure.

Warm wetness closed over his hand like a glove. He felt her throbbing as he removed all but one finger from her moist insides. Her juices drenched his hand as he rubbed her sensitive center. Her body shook as her orgasm racked her body.

He removed his hand, and whispered in her ear, "Now it's my turn."

Again, she took him in her hand. He came on the front of her pink blouse and watched with wicked delight the look of horror on her face.

"Here," he said, handing her his handkerchief.

She dabbed at his semen and looked

around, apparently trying to make sure no one witnessed their actions.

"Now, Robert, we must talk. Hank told me he listened in on Lilah's conversation at the library the other day. He said Casey was asking questions. I'm sure you're aware of this since your little drive-by failed to produce results. And that excuse for a spy you've got in the clerk's office, well, let's just say you need to do something about her." She gave an evil smile. "Fuck her if you have to, Robert. That dick of yours has always been your most redeeming quality. You might get better results if you used it more often."

God! If she only knew. He'd banged Marianne in the courthouse hundreds of times. If anyone knew he'd once done it to her in her office with the American flag spread out beneath them, he would've been arrested for defacing the flag. Kind of like his secret hero, Larry Flynt.

He gave a curt laugh. "This," he said, patting his crotch, "is yours and only yours. We've talked about this before. I promised you, there are no others." He seriously thought he might choke on his own words. As long as she continued to believe him, he'd keep feeding her his lies.

She flashed him a look that told him she didn't believe him. As long as the words didn't actually come out of her mouth, he'd assume she was as gullible as he thought.

"What's next, Robert? We have to hurry. This ferry ride is almost over. I don't know when we'll be alone again."

"Adam recommended she see Dr. Dewitt. I'm going to call him today. You can say what you want about Adam, but right now he's doing us a big favor."

The ferry was about to dock. "I think the good Dr. Dewitt will follow my instructions to the letter if he wants to continue practicing medicine in the state of Georgia."

"What are you talking about?"

He laced an arm around her as they prepared to go ashore. "He specializes in regression therapy. Several years ago, I think the practice started sometime in the mid-fifties, doctors used what they call LSD-25. Evidently this hastened patients on their so-called journey into their past lives." He secretly thought all this nothing more than bullshit, but if Adam endorsed it, there might be something to it. For once his drug connections were about to prove useful.

"How's this suppose to help us?" Eve

asked, as they walked down the wooden plank.

"Dr. Dewitt believes RT can actually jolt patients who've suffered different forms of amnesia into regaining their memories. And if they don't experience a full recovery, he feels his patients are able to at least benefit in the sense that they've supposedly got a better chance for remembering; I guess it opens the subconscious. At least that's what I got out of it."

"I still don't get it," Eve said, as they walked to their cars.

"Do I have to draw a picture for you? A dose of LSD, a large dose, just might send Ms. Edwards back where she should be, maybe never to return." He gave her a look he knew would prevent further questioning.

Eve's eyes sparkled as she centered her gaze on his own. "Make sure this time, Robert. We don't have room for another mistake."

If anyone were to observe them, they would have thought they were discussing the weather or the latest movie.

Not in a million years would a bystander believe they were plotting to drive someone insane.

*   *   *

Anticipating the day's journey, Casey checked her bag one last time, making sure she'd packed everything she needed.

Yep, she said to herself as she went through the stacks of clothing. Two pairs of slacks, a sweater, and just in case, a black silk pantsuit, a navy T-shirt and slinky night-gown, and three pairs of lace undies. She stifled a grin. Was she packing for a day at the shrink's office or for a seduction?

Flora was busy in the kitchen with Mabel, and Julie had a much-deserved day off. Casey had just learned the poor girl worked fourteen-hour days to make ends meet. Casey knew there was more to her new friend than met the eye. She guessed if Julie wanted to tell her about her life, she would. Until then, Casey would remain quiet and be her friend.

Her mother hadn't returned to Swan House. Flora said she told her she wouldn't leave the hospital until John's condition im-proved. She said she intended to spend the night at Worthington headquarters, where John had a small apartment. *It makes sense,* Casey thought.

A glance at the clock told her Blake would be there any minute. While a part of her dreaded her appointment with Dr. Dewitt, another part couldn't wait to get started. The sooner she had answers, the sooner she could get on with her life.

Just the thought of Blake made her heart start to race. He'd been gentle with her yesterday on the ride home. Not asking questions, just allowing her to relax and, for a short while, enjoy their shared silence. And today, he'd rearranged his calendar for her.

Hope, it seemed, was all she had at the moment. Nothing concrete, or at least not until she became a patient of the great Dr. Dewitt.

Dewitt, the name rang a bell. She wondered if he'd ever been to Sanctuary. Maybe that's where she'd heard his name. Maybe he was one of Dr. Macklin's colleagues.

Another mystery, Dr. Macklin. He'd been the staff psychiatrist since Casey could remember. On the day of her release, he'd simply disappeared. Blake tried calling his home several times and hadn't gotten an answer. He'd mentioned a possible stop at Mercy Hospital, where Dr. Macklin worked before coming to Sanctuary. Casey wondered what he'd think of her if he saw her now. After the three short days she had been at Swan House, she wasn't the same woman who'd left Sanctuary afraid of her own shadow. It seemed so long ago, almost a lifetime.

A different lifetime, she reminded herself.

She heard voices below and hurried downstairs, not wanting to keep Blake waiting.

At the bottom step, she stopped before he noticed her just so she could drink him in unobserved. His dark hair was still wet from his shower, and Casey imagined she could smell his musky aftershave across the room. He wore tan slacks with a red polo shirt. She thought he looked good enough to eat. She must have made a noise because he saw her standing at the foot of the stairs. He walked over to her, his hand outstretched, ready to retrieve her overnight bag.

"You look great, Casey," Blake said as he led her to the front door.

"Thanks." She was glad now that she'd taken those extra minutes to blow-dry her hair and apply makeup.

"Here," Flora said as she hurried out from the kitchen. "Mabel says this'll keep you from stoppin' at those 'horrid fast-food joints' as she calls 'em. I think she's got enough here to feed an army." Flora handed Blake a white wicker basket. Red-and-white-checkered napkins were packed in a side compartment, and a plaid Thermos bottle rested in a special place all its own.

"Tell her thank you for us, Flora; she certainly didn't have to go to all this trouble," Casey said as she waited for Blake to adjust his load.

"'Twas no trouble. That woman cooks enough to feed the entire island. You two get on now. Call me, Casey, if you need me."

"I will. Not to worry," Casey assured her as she gave her a light hug. She knew Flora was anxious about her, especially after she discovered how much Blake had told her.

She'd questioned Flora about the police report after Blake brought her home. She had no idea where it could've gotten to. She promised to ask Evie as soon as John's health improved.

They suffered through another round of hugs, and Casey smiled.

Blake's car, what she now knew as a BMW, sat with the trunk open in the driveway. Apparently the VW couldn't withstand the trip. He packed their baggage along with

Mabel's goodies basket in the trunk and walked around the front to open her door.

"You all set?" Blake asked, as they buckled in.

"Yes, just a bit nervous, though."

"I would be, too, Casey. If this doctor is as good as Adam says, we could have this all wrapped up in a matter of hours."

"I know. I'm just afraid, Blake. Afraid of me, the person I was. Somehow I don't feel like an evil person. I don't feel like those women I read about in the news. Do you think I'm right, or is this just more wishful thinking?"

"I think you're right. I knew you a bit when you were little, you sure as heck didn't seem like . . ." He ran a hand through his hair.

"A murderer? It's all right, you can say it. I'm sure at seven or eight most killers don't look like the murderers they'll later become. I don't feel like one. How long to Savannah?" she asked, hoping to change the subject. They'd be there soon enough, then they could explore the dark emptiness of her mind. Until then, she wanted to enjoy the beautiful day, have fun, and be . . . a woman? Maybe what she needed to do was . . . flirt the afternoon away with Blake. Just the two of them, without interruption.

"Not far. Relax, Casey, while you have the chance." He reached for her hand and squeezed. He was right. This might be the last peaceful day of her life.

Dr. Jason Dewitt, graduate of Harvard School of Medicine, admired the framed certificates on his freshly painted walls. Solid oak frames, nothing but the best. An antique desk, a Chinese silk rug and a Tiffany lamp completed the picture of the well-bred young and upcoming professional. Two Queen Anne chairs and a love seat for those patients who felt an upright position prevented them from the total feel of a psychiatrist's office were arranged in a comfortable setting, all in hopes of relaxing whoever might be experiencing distress. It sounded pathetic, even to his own professional ears. *Experiencing distress.* A term learned in medical school. The Easterners liked that term better than nuts or crazy.

Behind the desk a door led to a large bathroom. A shower, sink, and a full bar assured Dr. Dewitt that even while working, he would have all the comforts of home.

Almost, he thought as he reached to

straighten a perfectly aligned frame. Almost.
Grandfather had made sure of it. The Judge
as he referred to him. The Honorable William
Dewitt. Respected by Savannah's legal pur-
veyors for over fifty years.

He walked to the window and examined
the view. His office, located on East Bay
Street, faced the Old Cotton Exchange
building. The riverfront had been turned into
a tourist trap. What once constituted Savannah's downtown now attracted tourists from
all over the world. Shops sold the famous
pecan pralines and homemade taffy. Local
artists displayed their latest creations in
stores designed to entice, provoke, and,
Jason thought, basically rip off the con-
sumer. Ever since the release of *Midnight in
the Garden of Good and Evil* Savannah had
become the South's version of Disneyland,
where one could, for a price, glimpse inside
the private lives of Savannah's finer and not-
so-fine folk.

He pulled the shade down halfway.

Seated at his desk, he reviewed his appointment book. *Nothing today.*

While the Judge thought setting up his
practice in Savannah a smart business move,
Jason knew none of the great citizens of the

city would want to bare their souls. He'd relented and, against his better judgment, allowed his grandfather to make his decisions as usual. His parents had died in a small plane crash when he was three, and the Judge was the only parent he'd ever known. He'd spent his entire life deferring to him. No more. With the Judge six feet under, he controlled his own destiny. A move to Atlanta should do the trick. Oh, he had a great reputation, patients from all over the country came to see him. He'd helped many people recover from phobias and irrational fears and come to grips with their lives. Past and present. He'd published many papers on that very subject. Yet he wasn't satisfied. It took more than work to satisfy him. He'd shared that desire with no one, other than the Judge.

A soft tap on his partially open door brought him out of his reverie.

He pretended to be absorbed in a medical journal as he gave a quick, "Yes" to the interruption.

Jo Ella, his receptionist, stood in the hall just outside his office, waiting for him to invite her inside.

"What is it, Jo Ella?" Jason removed his wire-rimmed glasses and rubbed his temples. The glasses were nothing but a prop. At thirty-three he looked twenty-three. Medium brown hair cut close to his scalp, average blue eyes and not much of a beard gave Jason his look of youth. He hated the fact that nothing about his appearance said "doctor." He was average in every way. Average height, average build, average everything.

"You've got a call on your private line from a Robert Bentley. He says it's urgent."

"Doctor?" Jo Ella prodded.

"Uh, yes, take a message." He looked down at the journal he pretended to read.

"I did. He said it's a matter of life and death." Jo Ella smiled, revealing perfectly white teeth.

"Isn't it always?" Jason joined in the receptionist's unspoken humor.

"What do you want me to tell him, Doctor?"

"Put him through." Jason watched as Jo Ella returned to her desk. When the employment agency sent her over the previous year, Jason had already told Tara Hodges she had the job. Tara was perky, blond, and robust, all the traits he despised in a woman. Until Jo Ella walked in his office, Tara had been perfect because she didn't appeal to him in the slightest. Jo Ella was his idea of perfection. He'd forgotten all about his promise to Tara and hired the young woman on the spot. When the employment agency called days later to complain, he'd told them to mind their own business and reminded them just whom they were dealing with.

He looked at the phone on his desk as Jo Ella transferred the call to him. He wondered how this Bentley fellow had found his private number.

He punched the button and picked up the receiver. He'd worry about it later. "Dr. Dewitt," he said in his most professional voice.

"Well, I'll be damned," the voice said.

"Who is this?" Dewitt asked, irritated at the interruption.

"Robert Bentley." The voice repeated in the same cool tone.

"And that's supposed to mean something?" Jason snarled into the phone. He hated game playing. He removed the phone from his ear, ready to slam it back in its cradle, when the voice rose to a shout.

"Does the name Amy Woods mean anything to you?"

Jason felt like he'd been sucker punched

in the stomach. He swallowed deeply and drew in a breath before asking, "Who are you, and what do you want?"

"Amy. Ring a bell, Dr. Dewitt?" Bentley prompted.

Jason saw his entire life flash before him. His plans to relocate to Atlanta down the drain like dirty dishwater. A split-second thought raced through his mind—*Thank God the Judge isn't alive.*

"How much?" he asked. He sounded like the gutter trash that stalked the tourists after dark. Perspiration dotted his upper lip, his Pierre Cardin shirt was suddenly damp with sweat.

Bentley gave a hearty roar. "I'm not asking for money, Dewitt, at least not yet."

Jason took a handkerchief from his breast pocket and blotted his face. "Then what are you asking for?" He hated the way his voice trembled. He sounded like a wimp. Hell, just then he *was* a wimp.

"Your services."

"Do you need to see a psychiatrist?" He almost felt relieved, but not quite. Bentley had mentioned Amy.

"Some say I do." Another peel of laughter.

"Either you tell me what this is all about or

I'm going to hang up." *Right, you chicken shit, right.*

"Robert Bentley. I'm director of Sanctuary in Sweetwater. One of our former patients scheduled an appointment with you."

"And?"

"I need to know when. I'll hold on. The last name is Edwards."

Jason pushed the hold button and saw that his hands were shaking. He couldn't let Jo Ella see him like this. He buzzed her, something he only did when they were extremely busy.

"Yes, Doctor?" Jo Ella asked.

"Uh, yes. I have a new patient. The name is Edwards. When is the appointment scheduled?"

He heard the shuffle of papers while she searched.

"Tomorrow morning at ten."

"Thanks."

He opened his desk drawer and grabbed a bottle of Valium. He swallowed two before he picked up the phone.

He cleared his throat. "Tomorrow. Ten o'clock."

"Wonderful. Now listen and listen good because I'm only going to say this once. Ms.

Edwards has suffered trauma-induced amnesia for ten years. She's never undergone
regression therapy of any kind. That's what
she's coming to you for. While she stayed at
Sanctuary we were fortunate enough to
have Dr. Philip Macklin on our staff." The
voice paused. "While that name may or may
not mean anything to you, it meant a hell of
a lot to the Woods family. He released your
friend Amy for a special weekend furlough
so she could tell her lover she was pregnant.
Seems she never returned. I can't seem to
forget this, nor could the board of directors
at Mercy."

"I see."

"You do? And just how clearly do you
see, Dr. Dewitt?"

"Crystal." He sighed. "What do you want
me to do?" He'd find out just who this bastard was, and he'd be sorry he ever picked
up the phone and called him.

"I think it should be obvious. For reasons
that don't concern you, I want you to assure
me Ms. Edwards doesn't come close to remembering her past. It seems I read somewhere you can treat patients with LSD-25.
That would send Ms. Edwards on a trip."

"My, God! That hasn't been practiced in

years. It's extremely dangerous to the patient."

"We think alike, Dr. Dewitt. I don't think I need to say more, do you?"

Jason felt his gut clench and unclench. *Damn this man, I'll kill him if I get the chance.*

"Where am I supposed to get LSD? It's not like I can write a frigging prescription for it. What guarantee do I have that you'll keep quiet?" He hated himself for asking the question.

"Now, now, Doc. Don't get all huffy on me. I've thought of that, too. Tonight when you go home to Grandpappy's mansion, you'll get a delivery. Answer the door yourself. The rest should be simple. As far as the guarantee, you can just forget it." The click on the other end left no room for arguing.

Son of a bitch!

Jason hadn't thought of Amy in years and didn't want to think about her at all. He'd put that part of his life behind him the day the Judge sent him to Harvard, where he'd worked his ass off to make the Judge proud. And to forget.

He remembered when his grandfather called him and told him Dr. Macklin had been relieved of his duties and why. The

Judge never told him anything more until he died. He'd made Jason promise never to let anything tarnish the Dewitt name, no matter what he had to do. The subtle hint hadn't gone unnoticed.

Jason went to the bar and poured himself a shot of scotch. As much as he didn't want to admit it, the old man still controlled his life. Right from the grave.

He would do what needed to be done. The Dewitt name remained safe. Because Jason was very good at keeping secrets.

Relief didn't describe what she felt when Blake handed her the key to her private suite and told her his was right down the hall. On the drive over it occurred to her that Blake might want to share a room. She wasn't ready for that yet.

The Gastonian Inn, located in Savannah's Historic District, didn't look like a hotel at all. To her it looked like someone's old mansion that had gone to seed and been refurbished. Blake laughed, and said she was on the money.

Casey looked around her room with its king-size canopied bed, fireplace, and huge

marble tub. It far surpassed the luxuries at
Swan House. Blake was taking her out to
dinner, and from there they were going on a
moonlight riverboat cruise. She felt like a
young girl getting ready for the prom, minus
the corsage, minus the dress and stiff hairdo.

Dressed in black silk lounging pants complete with matching blouse, Casey slipped
sling-back sandals on and applied a dab of
coral lipstick. Her mother had been generous choosing her wardrobe, her taste im-
peccable. She spritzed gardenia-scented
perfume behind her ears and her neck.
Catching her reflection in the full-length mirror, she nodded her approval. It continued to
amaze her that she was the same woman
who'd left a mental institution just days ago.
Then, she hadn't a glow to her cheeks, her
ebony curls were limp and flat. And her eyes
were as dull as her life. Now, those same
eyes sparkled, their deep jade color reflect-
ing her mood. She even looked like she'd
put on a few pounds.

A light knock sent her scurrying for her
purse. She opened the door and gasped.
Blake was decked out in a black dinner
jacket and tapered dress slacks. In place of
the standard white dress shirt, he had cho-

sen black. He reeked of sexiness. His dark eyes were filled with humor as Casey stood in the doorway gawking.

He dared a look downward. "I'm zipped." He laughed.

Her face flickered with embarrassment.

"I'm sorry. You look very handsome tonight, you caught me off guard," she said, and closed the door behind her.

"Good. I like keeping you on your toes. Now, my lady, our carriage awaits."

Hand in hand they walked down the long hall. Sconces cast a golden glow over them, and vases of yellow and white roses scented the air with their heady fragrance.

Casey couldn't believe her eyes when they stepped onto the portico. Blake had been serious when he said "our carriage awaits." A carriage with two powerful chestnut horses, and a driver wearing authentic-looking livery. They climbed aboard.

Casey inhaled. Horse, straw, and leather permeated the inside of the carriage.

She looked to Blake. "This is so overwhelming. I can't believe you'd go to this much trouble."

The clip-clop of the horses' hooves against the cobblestone road, the warm evening breeze wafting in through the small open windows, and Blake seated very close to her gave Casey such a feeling of happiness, that she wondered if she would ever know such complete, utter contentment again.

The next day she would know, but that was a long way off. She wasn't going to let anything spoil that night. It belonged to her and Blake. It might be the only night of its kind they'd ever share.

"I didn't go to any trouble. I made a call, told them my Visa number, and *voilà*!" He gestured to the carriage.

"What's a 'Visa'?"

"Oh, it's a credit card. You know like a Master Charge. Only now it's called Master-Card. It's actually better than cash."

"Guess I've been locked away long enough for the world to change." She sighed and peeked out the window as they rode through Savannah's Historic District.

"That's Forsyth Park," Blake said as he saw her lean closer to the window. Draws a lot of tourists."

"It's gorgeous," Casey said, as they passed the famed park.

"Yes, it is. Old Savannah offers plenty of entertainment. You can tour some of the historic mansions. They even have a few ghost tours." Blake grinned.

"It sounds fun. Another time, I'd like to come back and do all those things. Right now"—she turned to him—"I just want to enjoy this." She leaned into the surprisingly plush seat and smiled. The continuous clip-clop of the horses lulled her. The carriage came to a sudden halt, jolting Casey out of her relaxed state. A view outside told her they were on East Broad Street.

Blake tipped the driver and helped her down. Her heels were no match for Savannah's cobblestoned streets.

He placed an arm around her as they maneuvered their way through the crowd of people gathered in front of the Pirates' House.

"We don't have to wait?" Casey questioned as they entered the restaurant.

"I made a reservation yesterday. I thought you would enjoy this. A lot of history here. Those gardens we saw outside were the first experimental agricultural gardens in America. This used to be an inn for seafarers in the eighteenth century."

Casey could believe that as she viewed the rough ceiling beams. A sign to her right told her a nail hadn't been used in the beams, that they were joined with wooden pegs. She smiled, realizing Blake was full of surprises.

"Something funny?" he asked, as the hostess led them through a maze of halls.

"You. I would never have guessed this would appeal to you."

"It does. I've always loved history. What do you think?"

"It's wonderful. I had no idea such a place existed."

Seated in their own private dining room, Casey relaxed for the second time that evening and allowed Blake command.

He ordered for them both. Casey had never seen so much food, excluding the picnic basket Mabel packed. They'd nibbled on the ride, and now she was thankful that's all they'd done.

Plates of crab, king crab, blue crab, and Alaskan crab filled the table. Jumbo shrimp with the sweet smell of Old Bay served atop piles of cracked ice and smaller shrimp ladled over beds of rice, all this accompanied by a fresh green salad; the greens were from the restaurant's own private garden, the waiter told them, and if that wasn't enough, tiny loaves of bread in clay pots tempted them. Small pots of homemade butter completed their feast. A second bottle of wine was discreetly placed in its container.

"Do you think we'll eat all of this?" Casey asked as she reached for a crab leg.

"Something tells me if I bet against it, it would be a sure thing," Blake said as he peeled a shrimp.

The meal wasn't one that allowed them lingering looks and small talk. They had to work for the precious bites of crab and shrimp. Twice Casey felt the prick of a crab's claw and Blake the expert showed her how to pull the shell away, using the claw as a handle.

Two hours later they were aboard the *Georgia Queen* along with a few hundred others who'd decided to spend the evening drifting along the Savannah River's coast.

Casey looked out over the water and again felt an indescribable feeling of peace overwhelm her. Blake stood next to her, apparently lost in his own thoughts. A slight breeze tossed her short curls about and cooled her heated skin.

It wasn't hot, she reminded herself as she sneaked a side glance at Blake. It was *him.* For the past two hours her mind hadn't registered anything other than her growing desire for the man who'd spent the evening making sure her every need was met. *Except this,* Casey thought. This deep, tugging sensation in the pit of her stomach. Her body felt heavy and overly warm despite the cool caress of the coastal breeze.

She risked a peek at Blake. Her heart fluttered.

She knew then. He felt it, too, she was certain. Words weren't needed as their eyes met. All that she'd contemplated in the last few minutes were mirrored in his eyes. He stepped forward and pulled her into his arms.

Casey leaned into the hard expanse of his chest and wound her arms around his back. She was safe with Blake. He wouldn't let anything happen to her. He laced his arms around her and under the moonlight they swayed to a distant melody as it wafted up the stairs, accompanied by a low, soulful voice singing the blues. Casey couldn't make out the performer's words; she didn't need to. The bittersweet lilt of the entertainer was a symphony, as she and Blake continued their slow dance across the deck of the ship.

Out of sight, ensconced in the comfort of the starlit night, Blake tilted her chin up.

As if in slow motion Casey watched his lips as they sought her own. When she felt their smooth warmth lightly touch her mouth, she pressed her lips against his. His mouth tasted warm and sweet from the wine they'd consumed. Ecstasy came to mind as Blake's kiss aroused her to heights a mere kiss shouldn't dare. She heard her own intake of breath as his tongue teased the fullness of her lips. Seized by a boldness unfamiliar to her, she kissed him back with a hunger she hadn't known she possessed.

His intake of breath sent shudders of desire rippling through her. Their kiss suddenly urgent, both lost control, their passion their guide. Tongues met, warmth covered warmth, hunger met hunger.

Their desire reached a crescendo, before spiraling downward, making Casey aware of each and every fiber in her body. Blake's embrace slackened as his kisses became soft and light. She drew in a deep breath as he nipped at her neck, leaving behind fiery pools of heat where his lips touched.

Reluctant to let go, Casey felt empty, yet more alive than she could recall when Blake stepped out of their embrace and leaned against the ship's railing. His black hair stood out against the blue-blackness of night. Lights from the riverfront reflected in his smoky gaze as he watched her. Casey wished she could paint the moment. She had never seen a more perfect man. He'd removed his jacket earlier, loosening the top button of his dress shirt, revealing a V of dark hair that Casey knew would be soft to the touch. Daring, she raised a hand and, with the pads of her fingertips, touched the soft darkness. *Soft as down,* she thought, as her fingertips trailed the broad expanse of Blake's chest.

He took her hand in his and placed wet kisses on her palm. She knew she had to stop because she couldn't guarantee what would happen right there on the fourth deck if she didn't. Pulling her hand back, she stepped away from Blake. He jammed his hands in his pockets and shook his head.

"Casey, I can't seem to do anything right when I'm around you. I made you a promise, and look at me. I'm still acting like a schoolboy."

"Stop," she said as she placed a finger over his mouth. "I like schoolboys. Look, Blake," she said as she rested her arms on his shoulders, "stop apologizing every time you touch me. I liked that kiss as much as you did. I didn't stop you." She peered around him. "It looks like the *Georgia Queen* is ready for bed. I think that means we should think about departing, too."

Blake captured her hands in his. "You're right. And Casey, I want you to know I haven't enjoyed myself this much with a woman . . . hell, there I go again. What I meant to say . . ."

"Shhh, I know. I feel it, too." His arms felt like protective armor as they left the riverboat, content with their thoughts.

Chapter Sixteen

The dream came again but she couldn't control it. Drifting on the edge of sleep, she took that final plunge into nothingness, where the subconscious ruled and dreams dominated.

She was back in the closet. She could feel the jackets and sweaters drape the back of her shoulders. She scrunched into the corner, pulling her legs up close to her, and rested her head on her bony knees. She knew they'd come for her soon. She promised herself she wasn't going to scream and cry. Not this time. It never mattered. They'd let her die in here. She hated them. She wished her momma acted like Flora. She wished she would bake her favorite peanut butter cookies and play games with her. And him! How she hated him. He always looked at her that way when Momma wasn't around. Sweat dribbled between her shoulders. It'd been a long time since Momma left. Maybe they were really going to let her die this time. Maybe this time, she'd really leave her. He said that to her all the time, hoping to scare her. Well, she was good and scared all right. Her lower lip trembled, and her eyes flooded with tears she'd promised not to shed.

It was there again. The fish eyes. They bulged, like someone had reached in and poked them so they'd stick out.

Hard to breathe again. And that smell, she'd smelled it before. Metallic. A thick, wet substance clung to her white cotton gown. She pulled the material away from her skin. Bruised and raw. Had she had another bicycle accident? She looked around the closet. He opened the door. She wanted to shout to Momma, but was stopped when a hand came over her mouth.

She couldn't breathe!

He really wanted to kill her!

She looked up at him from her hiding place and made a quick promise to herself: If she lived, if he let her live, she'd tell Flora how Robert Bentley came in her room.

Casey woke, disoriented. Another bad

dream. She rolled over and fell asleep again but not before she said a prayer asking God to let her forget the awful dream she'd just had.

Caught in a tangle of sheets, Casey bolted upright, her heart pounding in her chest. For a moment she couldn't recall where she was, and it frightened her. Then she remembered. The Gastonian Inn. Savannah.

Soon she would have her answers when she kept her appointment with the great Dr. Dewitt.

She squinted to look at the clock on the bedside table. Six-thirty. She'd shower and wait for Blake. Something tugged at her subconscious as she untangled herself from the sheets. Giving herself a mental shake, she headed for the bathroom.

The pulsing stream of warm water soothed her aching shoulders and cleared the cobwebs of sleep. Still, the nagging feeling that she was missing something remained.

She washed her hair, shampoo lather spiraling down the drain as she leaned into the stream of the shower.

Then it hit her like an elephant slam.

The dream!

Wrapping herself in a thick robe provided by the inn, Casey twisted a towel around her hair as she sat down on the edge of the bathtub to think about her dream.

She knew what she experienced in dream form wasn't just a dream. It was too real, too frightening. Another memory was surfacing in the guise of a dream. She had to pay attention.

She was that little girl in the closet. She was the one who had been hurt by someone. Her mother, maybe? No, it couldn't have been her. But she'd been there. And that bastard Bentley! Why would she dream about him anyway? Just where did he fit in all this? Had he hurt her? Was he the one who sent her over the edge? And Ronnie, her stepbrother, where did he belong in this puzzle? Or was he just a jagged edge waiting to cut?

Determined to find answers, she quickly dressed and went downstairs in search of coffee.

She found Blake seated at a corner table reading the paper, his hair still damp from the shower. She imagined she could smell the woodsy scent that she now associated with him from across the room. He wore dark green slacks with a cream-colored sport shirt. It fit, she thought. He looked like a doctor, was her second thought. A doctor on his day off. Casual, but prepared, just in case.

He must have felt her gaze because he looked up, then motioned for her to join him.

"I thought I'd let you sleep. We had a late night." Blake filled a delicate cup with coffee and handed it to her.

"Mmmm, I needed this." She took a sip of the hot brew and felt almost human. "I'm an early riser." She paused and looked at him, not sure if she should burden him this early in the day. "I had the dream again last night."

"The dream?" he asked as he topped off their cups.

"I've had it off and on for years. Sometimes I think it's just that, a dream. Other times I think it's my memory returning for a quick visit in hopes of nudging my conscious self into remembering.

"I'm always in a closet. I couldn't be more than nine or ten. And I'm so afraid of not being able to breathe. I think someone must be trying to suffocate me." She gave a dry laugh as she watched Blake. He didn't laugh. He looked angry.

"Good Lord, Casey! Do you realize what you're saying?" Blake leaned forward and took her free hand in his.

"I know it sounds crazy, but I can't think of any other explanation for the feelings I have. In the dream I'm struggling to breathe. Something is on top of me." This sounded insane even to her. Her mother would never have let such a thing happen to her. Nor would Flora.

Blake appeared deep in thought. "Today, we'll have answers." He took a deep pull of coffee and glanced at his watch.

"You don't believe me, do you?" His sudden change of attitude alarmed her.

"It's not a question of believing you, Casey. I can't imagine this could happen to a child and a parent not be aware of it, that's all."

"I thought of that, too. I don't think Evie knew anything was going on. What I'm having a hard time with is understanding how Robert Bentley knew when I was locked in the closet." She jerked backward when she saw the impact her words had on Blake.

"Slow down a minute," he shouted, then lowered his voice as he looked around to make sure the other patrons hadn't over-heard him. "Bentley saw you?" Blake asked, a look of disbelief on his face.

"I'm sure of it. In the dream I remember thinking I hated him, and I couldn't under-stand why he appeared at such odd times."

She wanted Blake to believe her more than anything.

"Nothing fits, Casey. I have no explana-tion for that. Other than your mother, I don't know of anyone who would know if Bentley was there or not, and if he was, I would want to know why."

"If, Blake? *If.* Surely you don't think I'm making this up? Granted it all comes from a dream. But I know in my heart"—she jabbed her thumb against her chest—"he was there. And today, I'll prove it!"

She pushed her chair back, almost top-pling it over, and ran out of the room, not caring that the other diners stared after her.

Blake signed the credit card receipt and realized he'd just had his first disagreement with the woman he loved.

Loved.

There, he'd said it. He didn't know how,

but his feelings for Sweetwater's so-called crazy woman had intensified to a depth he'd never imagined possible. And in such a short time.

He questioned his feelings, wondering if they were mixed up with pity. Somehow he knew Casey Edwards wouldn't want pity from him or anyone else, no matter what her past life had dealt her.

And that reminded him of why he'd traveled to Savannah in the first place.

Dr. Dewitt.

At nine-fifteen Blake tapped on her door. A tear-streaked Casey opened the door and left him standing in the long hall. He stepped inside, not wanting to be the cause of another bout of speculation with the inn's guests.

He looked at the king-size bed in the middle of the room. The sheets were rumpled, and the pillows were tossed on the floor.

She must've had to fight her way out of the nightmare. Or, he mused, she'd been dreaming of the wild time she'd had in his arms. He liked the second scene better.

"What's so funny?" she asked, coming out of the bathroom, blotting her eyes with a washcloth.

She saw the direction his gaze traveled,

and she gave a brief smile. "I'm a fighter in bed."

Her face reddened. She looked from him to the bed. "The dream. I toss and turn when I have it."

"Casey."

She looked at him with those jade green eyes and his heart flip-flopped. She had good cause to be upset and embarrassed, and all he could think of was how he was going to get her into bed.

"I believe you. About Robert Bentley."

"I know it sounds crazy, but I'm absolutely sure he was there. I've done nothing but think about him since I woke up. I recall him being at our house a lot. I guess that's a good sign, huh? This should make Dr. Dewitt's work easier." She went over to the vanity and applied a touch of powder to her red nose and reapplied her mascara.

"You really do believe me?" she asked as she put her cosmetics away.

"Yes. Now let's forget about all this. We'll have the rest of the day to think about it. Right now"—he led her to the rumpled bed—"I want to hold you."

Blake sat on the edge of the bed and pulled Casey onto his lap. She fit; like a fork and spoon their bodies meshed together. He knew they'd fit well in other places, too.

With her small round rump residing on his crotch, it only took seconds for him to get hard. He tried to move so she couldn't feel him, but it was too late.

She adjusted herself right on top of his groin and he had to dig deep for control. His schoolboy days were over, he reminded himself as he gently removed Casey from his lap and laid her back on the bed.

"Blake."

He silenced her with a kiss. He felt her relax into the plump bedding. He wanted nothing more than to ease himself on top of her. He leaned over her, not daring to touch her with his body. He kissed her closed eyes, her nose, and with his tongue he traced the fullness of her lips.

She sighed and opened her mouth. Warm and hot, their kiss deepened, and Blake wished they didn't have to leave.

He pulled away from her and leaned against the bedpost.

Casey managed to look sexy as hell and innocent all at the same time. *Women would pay good money to bottle that look,* he thought. And what made her even more sexy in his eyes was the knowledge that she had no idea how provocative she looked.

She sat up, adjusting her blouse and smiled at him. "I guess we should go, huh?"

"Yeah," he muttered, his voice hoarse with desire. "Give me a minute."

She looked in the direction of his downcast gaze, and her eyes quickly darted back to his face. "Oh, sure. I'll go . . . comb my hair."

"Dr. Dewitt's office is only five minutes away, take your time." What he really wanted to say was, no matter how long you're in there, I'm still going to want you when you come out.

"Sure." He'd acted like a horny teenager. He smiled to himself because something told him she enjoyed his touch as much as he enjoyed hers.

"Ready?" Her hair was brushed and her blouse tucked in properly. One would never know she'd just left his arms.

"Let's do it." This time, Blake felt his face redden with embarrassment.

Casey took his hand and led him out of her room. "We might someday."

"Open mouth, insert foot. I seem to be doing a lot of that lately, at least when I'm with you."

"You don't have to be so careful, Blake. Please, don't think you have to watch every word you say. I'm an adult. I think I'm relatively normal, so please, just be yourself."

"You're right," he said, and signed the credit card slip. He had a few words with the inn's manager to make arrangements to have the luggage brought down later, then they were off.

Blake parked two blocks away from Dr. Dewitt's office, one block north of River Street on East Bay.

Casey felt her heart hammer as they made their way inside. Blake took her hand and squeezed, his silent way of telling her he'd be there, no matter what. Or that's what she wanted to believe. That morning after their near lovemaking, Casey examined her feelings for this man who made her feel almost normal. More important, he made her feel like a woman. Not an experiment, not a crazed lunatic. He made her feel like she was Casey as Casey would've been had she *been* before.

A discreetly placed sign told them Dr. Dewitt's office was on the third floor. As they stepped into the elevator, Casey prayed that this new doctor could help her. Now that she had Blake, she really had a reason to live.

Jason Dewitt looked at the Rolex on his wrist for the tenth time. Nine-fifty. In ten minutes he could possibly be on the road to losing his medical license.

Last night had gone off as expected. At eight o'clock he answered the door and felt a box being shoved in his hands. It all happened in less than a minute, and he never had a chance to identify the person. It didn't really matter, he thought as he crossed to the window again. He'd lain awake all night, hoping that by some sheer stroke of luck the patient wouldn't keep her appointment. It happened a lot. People thought they were ready to confront their pasts and when the time came, they often backed out. He sincerely hoped that's what would happen.

The stash of LSD remained in his pocket, just in case. He hadn't yet figured out how he would explain the need for drugs. Regression therapy, at least the kind he practiced, didn't require medication. He'd worry about that if and when.

He heard the click of the door opening in

the outer office and knew his patient had arrived. Suddenly filled with rage, Jason made himself a promise. He'd find Bentley, and when he did, he'd kill him. It would be simple, really. He had access to all sorts of heart-stopping drugs.

Yes, that's what he would do. With that in mind he seated himself behind his desk and put the bogus glasses on.

"Doctor?" Jo Ella's voice crackled from the box on his desk. "Ms. Edwards is here for her appointment."

He cleared his voice before replying, "Please ask her to come in."

Ms. Edwards didn't look anything like he'd expected. A picture of health, she didn't look troubled in any way, though looks could be deceiving, as he well knew. And the man with her. No one told him she'd be bringing a guest. He'd handle this.

He stood to shake Casey's hand, then that of her companion.

"Please, sit down." He motioned to the two Queen Anne chairs across from him.

"Thanks," the woman said. She looked nervous, as if she wanted to bolt. Jason hoped she would. He'd tell her friend how this sometimes happened and be done with it. Then he'd find that son of a bitch Bentley and shut him up for good.

"I'm sure you want to know all about regression therapy. It's actually nothing new. Medical science has been aware of its merits in treating many forms of mental illness for quite a number of years now." He looked at the couple seated across from him and thought they weren't buying it.

"Dr. Dewitt, I'm Dr. Blake Hunter from Sweetwater. I'm Ms. Edwards's primary care physician."

A doctor? What a joke. Or was it?

Jason felt his armpits start to dampen, something that always happened when he was nervous.

"Then I'm sure you've told Ms. Edwards about the benefit of RT." Jason smiled at the two of them, hoping to impress them with his relaxed attitude. He wanted them to feel the choice was theirs. He'd never had to push patients to do something they weren't comfortable with. Until then. He could tell the woman was uncomfortable with the idea. He wondered why in the hell she'd made the appointment in the first place.

Did she know the trouble her memory loss caused him? *Of course not,* he answered himself. He needed to lie on his own couch.

Calm down, he told himself. *It won't do to arouse Dr. Hunter's suspicions.* He'd just met the man and didn't like him. Briefly he thought it might be because he looked like a doctor. Jason didn't see beads of sweat dotting *his* upper lip—an upper lip that already looked as if a second shave wouldn't hurt.

"I've explained it all to Casey, Dr. Dewitt. Adam Worthington, a colleague and friend, told me about your past successes. I'm impressed. Actually, Adam is the one who called and scheduled this appointment. I hope you can help Casey."

"Adam, ah yes. We attended a few of the same conferences a while back. I trust he's doing well?" The last was said as a perfunctory courtesy. He could not have cared less about his former acquaintance. If memory served correctly, he'd been nothing more than a smart-ass, totally full of himself.

"He's practicing in Atlanta and doing very well. I'll tell him you asked about him."

Casey continued to sit in the chair across from him. She had yet to speak.

"Do that. Now, Ms. Edwards, would you

like to tell me about yourself?" Jason inquired.

She glanced across at her friend, or more likely her lover, Jason thought, and looked back at him. Still nothing. He watched as she twisted her hands, then begin to pick at one of her cuticles. She was nervous. They were always nervous the first time. He sighed.

In a hushed tone she asked, "Could I have a moment with Dr. Hunter, please? Alone."

Did this woman really expect him to leave his office? She remained seated, so he assumed she did. He sighed again but got up and walked out into the reception area.

Alone now, Casey turned to Blake. "I can't do this."

"What do you mean?"

"That man. He gives me the creeps. I'm sorry, I can't." She hung her head forward, embarrassed to look at Blake.

"Shhh, hey, if you don't like the guy, it's fine by me. We can always go back to the inn. Checkout time isn't until three o'clock."

She made a halfhearted attempt to laugh at his humor in a situation that in no way should have been humorous. Leave it to Blake.

"Do you think we could slip out the back door?" She'd do it if he would.

"I'm game." Blake crept to the door behind the doctor's desk. He opened it and went inside.

"A bathroom and what looks to be a fully stocked bar. Want one for the road?" He didn't give her a chance to answer. He slipped through the door and came out with two frosted bottles of Budweiser.

"Blake, put that back," she whispered loudly, and laughed. Then she got it. As usual Blake had her in mind. He knew she didn't want to be there, knew she'd been frightened, and until they were completely alone, he would humor her. She liked this, and he must have known it, because he chose that moment to shove one of the chilled bottles down the front of his pants. His intake of breath sent her off in a fit of giggles.

"Stop! Let's get out of here before he returns."

"Okay, but the beer goes, too." Blake stuffed the second bottle in her purse. He opened the door and peered out into the reception area.

"Now," he whispered as he grabbed her arm. "The elevator."

They bolted to the elevator just in time to avoid the doctor, who was wandering down the opposite end of the hallway.

When the doors opened on the ground floor, they ran out into the street, laughing like children.

"I can't believe we did that."

Blake placed his arm around her shoulder as they walked down Savannah's famed streets. "I can't believe it either, Casey." He stopped in the middle of the sidewalk and turned her so that she faced him. "What was that all about?" He jerked his head in the direction of the building behind them.

She shook her head. "I don't know. I had a bad feeling when I saw him. I can't explain it other than I knew, no matter what, I knew I wasn't supposed to stay there. I couldn't allow him to probe in the protected corners of my mind. He made me feel . . . cold and afraid. Just thinking about him sends shivers down my back despite this heat."

"It's always been your choice, Casey. Adam thinks this guy's the best. I hate to admit it, but I have to agree about the cold part. When I shook his hand, his palm was sweaty. I felt like he was trying to make an impression."

"Then I was right to leave," she said, as they picked up their pace.

"Maybe, maybe not."

"You just said you felt . . ."

"I know what I said," he interrupted. "That doesn't mean the man isn't a good doctor. Adam respects his opinion. That alone has to count for something."

"Why does Adam care? Since my arrival he's done nothing but avoid me. What would it matter to him if I have my memory or not?"

She recalled the angry voices coming from John Worthington's hospital room. What kind of son would yell at his father, who'd just suffered a stroke? She wanted to tell Blake about the argument she'd over-heard, but found that she couldn't. She didn't want to hurt him.

"Adam can be strange. He's not an easy person to get close to, but once you're in, you'll never have a friend like Adam. And I don't think he's deliberately trying to avoid you, Casey. I truly believe he's upset about John's health, among other things."

She could just guess what those other things were. Like how many people would John Worthington be willing to cut out of his will to make his only son happy.

"I suppose." It sounded lame, and she knew it. She felt sorry that she couldn't share Blake's enthusiasm about Adam.

When they reached the car Casey felt like a total failure and disappointment. Blake had rescheduled his appointments in the hope of helping her, and now this. Because of a strange feeling, she had left the one man who possessed the power to help her. Did she really want to remember? Was this her way of protecting her from herself?

They headed to the inn for their luggage. Blake suggested they return to Sweetwater and forego their stop at Mercy Hospital.

Casey wondered if by leaving Dr. Dewitt's office she had tossed away her chance for a relationship with Blake. Were his feelings contingent on her so-called return to normalcy?

Chapter Seventeen

With Jo Ella gone for the day, Jason finally had the chance to wind down and plot his next move. He'd been delighted when he returned earlier to find both patient and doctor gone.

He knew Bentley would call. This time he thought he had the upper hand. He was the puppet master, and if he played his cards right, Bentley wouldn't bother him—or anyone else—again.

The phone startled him, causing his pulse to race. He drew in a deep breath and picked it up on the third ring.

"Dr. Dewitt, can I help you?"

"I hope you already have."

Bentley.

Jason knew the risk he took when he said his next words. "It went well," he said tersely.

"Then it's your recommendation that it's in Ms. Edwards's best interest to return to Sanctuary?"

Jason heard the hope in Bentley's voice. He barely controlled his urge to laugh.

"Most definitely. However, I'm not sure we're on the same page here. We need to meet. Your former patient managed to reveal a deep dark secret. You interested?"

"What do you mean, a secret?" Bentley's voice quivered.

"I don't think I should say any more on the phone. We need to meet. Tonight."

"Tonight? Hell, with the ferry schedule and everything else, you're three hours away."

Jason could just imagine Bentley's race against the clock to plot and scheme. Then remembered he had the upper hand.

"I'll keep the coffee warm." He slammed the phone down and wondered if he'd done the right thing. He didn't see that he had any other choice. He'd never get another moment's peace as long as Bentley knew about Amy.

He remembered the promise he'd made to the Judge. There was no way he would break his promise.

* * *

Robert's hand shook as he punched in the number. She answered on the fifth ring.

"What in the hell took you so long?"

"I told you not to call me here!" the voice all but shrieked.

"Too fucking bad. There's been a change of plans."

"What are you talking about? I thought you said you had a handle on it, and there was no cause for worry." He liked it when she whined. Next, she'd beg, her usual pattern.

"I did. I still do. There's been a change, that's all."

"And I assume it has something to do with me, or else you wouldn't have risked calling me here."

"Look, we don't have time for your smart-ass shit. I've got to be in Savannah by midnight."

"You want me to drive you there, is that it?"

"You really are out of your goddamned mind, you know that? I want to get there before midnight. That's why I called you. You have the authority to use your husband's private plane. I need it. Make whatever arrangements, and I'll be waiting at the airport in one hour." He glanced at his watch. He could be in Savannah by ten at the latest. Dewitt had something up his sleeve, that much he knew. If Casey freaked out in his office, she'd made a record-breaking recovery since then. Hank reported to him the minute she and Blake returned to Swan House and said she hadn't undergone the planned therapy. He'd heard her babbling to the nitwit housekeeper and laughing about how they'd skipped out. But, if by some chance Casey had remembered something, he was going to find out about it before anyone else got the chance. And if it meant silencing Dewitt, he'd do what he had to do.

"Robert!"

"Yes?" His patience was starting to wear thin.

"What should I say?"

"Figure it out. You've managed to convince me for years what a tragic life you've led. Get out your bag of tricks and convince the hubby's pilot how desperate you are to get to Savannah."

*   *   *

Roland Parker adjusted his heavy weight in his new leather chair and tried to find a comfortable position. As he shifted his bulk, he paused, waiting for the expected noise, and when none came, he relaxed. Yes, this is how it should be. A sheriff should have a good chair when he questioned his suspects. He needed to be comfortable when he dealt with the public or various suspects brought in for questioning. Yessireee, a good chair was important.

He frowned. The subject at hand tonight had the power to wreck his career in law enforcement. If that's what you could call sitting here on your ass all day filing reports and making an occasional trip out to the Berry place to toss old Charlie's home brew on the front lawn after he'd pissed Louise off one too many times.

He'd received a phone call earlier today from that bastard, asking him to keep his mouth shut and his eyes open. What in the hell did he think he'd been doing for the past ten years?

Tired at forty, he'd give his right nut if he could turn back the clock ten years. He'd handed that bastard his balls in a basket when he'd agreed to participate in his scheme. At the time, it had made sense in a cockamamie kind of way. If he needed to justify his actions back then, it was that he'd been too inexperienced and frightened to stand up for himself and enforce the law.

Now, all he could do was hang his head between his legs and hope against hope that no harm came to the girl.

Or, a nagging voice of reason whispered in his ear, *You could tell the truth. Pick up the phone and call him. You didn't break the law*.

He actually placed his hand on the receiver and lifted it from its cradle. He gripped it so hard his knuckles turned white. He couldn't do it. He dropped the phone on the desk, not bothering to put it back in the cradle. He didn't care if he got any phone calls. Vera could handle the office; she practically did anyway. He was nothing more than the typical overweight, uneducated, country island sheriff.

If it wasn't for *him*, he could've been so much more. His stomach rumbled hate.

He'd manipulated him from his first day in office and hadn't let up. At first he'd get a wad of cash in the mail. He never questioned where it came from. Sometimes, he'd even get a note telling him he'd won a week-long stay at his favorite fishing lodge. And then he'd go for months with no contact. When they passed one another on the street and Parker caught his eye, he knew it would only be a matter of days before he received another *gift*.

None of it was worth the anguish he went through every night. For the past five years he couldn't even think about going to sleep until he'd consumed at least a six-pack of beer. He knew it would get worse if he didn't put a stop to it.

He couldn't spend another sleepless night wrestling with his guilt. It was time to salvage his soul.

Casey woke to the smell of brewing coffee. She smiled in her half-awake state and rolled over on her side. The down comforter caressed her, and she snuggled deeper into the soft folds, wishing Blake were there to hold her. She imagined how he would feel next to her. Their skin would be slick with sweat from their passionate lovemaking. She knew that his chest and leg hair would lightly tickle her sensitive skin. And he'd have that woodsy smell that she loved. She inhaled and instead of her imagined scent she smelled coffee. She tossed her fantasy aside as she threw the down comforter to the bottom of the bed.

Out of habit she neatly made her bed and went to shower. She looked at herself in the mirror, expecting to see something other than her usual self.

A murderer, she thought. *What exactly does a murderer look like?* As she toweled herself dry, she watched her movements. She didn't know what she hoped to see, but whatever it was, it didn't magically appear.

She *needed* to remember killing poor, disturbed Ronnie. The day before she had her chance, and she blew it like a snuffed-out candle.

Something about the doctor had made her skin crawl. He barely looked old enough to be a doctor, but that wasn't what bothered her. He'd reminded her of an opossum—sneaky. She'd felt him watching her with his pale blue eyes. No, she'd made the right decision. Drugs force-fed to her over the years had prevented her recovery. She would heal herself without more "therapy."

* * *

Casey was surprised to see her mother in the kitchen, especially after her last visit. Was it only a few days ago that Evie freaked out?

"Mother! I'm so glad to see you. How's John?" She poured herself coffee and re-filled her mother's cup.

"He's had somewhat of a setback," Evie whispered.

Casey watched her mother as tears glazed her eyes. *Eyes so like my own,* she thought.

"I'm sorry to hear that. What do the doctors say?" She hoped she didn't sound as empty as her words, but she didn't know what else to say. After all, she'd yet to meet her stepfather.

Evie blotted her eyes with a cloth napkin. "His blood pressure is elevated; they're not sure why. That Dr. Foo, I'm not sure about him." Evie sniffed. "I wish John had an American doctor."

"Mother! What on earth do you mean?" Casey asked.

"He's a Jap or Chinese, I don't know. I just think Americans take care of their own."

Then she should meet Jason Dewitt, Casey thought. "I'm sure he's a good doctor. Blake and Adam seem to like him."

"That's not saying much as far as I'm concerned, dear. Adam is so secretive about everything, and Blake"—her mother actually huffed—"doesn't take life as seriously as he should, so as you can see, I don't put much stock in either one of their opinions."

Casey shrugged. "I guess we all have our reasons for what we do and don't do." She knew it probably wasn't the time, but she'd seen her mother so little since her return. She had to ask her now. Another opportunity might not present itself for a while if John took a turn for the worse.

"Mother, I need to ask you something."

"What is it, dear? I just came home for a change of clothes. I have to hurry back to Worthington Enterprises. We've a meeting scheduled today. You do know I've had to hold the fort down as they say. I can't disappoint John."

Was this her mother's way of saying now isn't a good time? It didn't matter. What she had to say needed to be said.

"I know, Mother. Flora told me. I'm sure John is grateful you're there. I imagine having family at a time like this makes all the difference in the world."

"Yes, it does. But the responsibility is

enormous. John and Adam never thought I could handle it. I'll let you in on a little secret," Evie said in a conspiratorial tone. "I've been waiting for this day for years. I've dreamed of being at the helm of Worthington Enterprises. Do you realize just how many holdings John has?" *She looks dreamy,* Casey thought.

Casey felt uncomfortable discussing her stepfather's financial status and wished her mother hadn't brought it up.

"Actually, Mother, I don't. I'm sure they must be substantial, you know, Swan House and all." Casey looked around, hoping her mother would pick up on her unease.

"Not only does he own all the paper mills in Brunswick, he owns dozens of businesses overseas. The man had his hand in everything imaginable."

Casey wondered if her mother was aware that she had spoken of her husband in the past tense.

"I'm glad you found someone to take care of you. I'm sure John's a decent man, with or without his holdings."

"That's true, dear, but he'll never take the place of your father."

"I have no memory of him, but I'm sure he

must've been a fine man, according to Flora."

Suddenly her mother's face turned an angry red. "What did Flora say?"

"Nothing. Just that he was a good man. Please," she placed a hand on top of her mother's. "Don't get upset. Flora didn't say anything. Really," Casey assured her.

Why would her mother care if Flora talked about her father?

"I'm sorry. It's just that Flora troubles me sometimes."

Flora? Her mother must be in one of her "bad states."

"Flora did tell me about a visit to Doc Hunter's office when I was a child." It was time to find out exactly what her mother knew.

She watched her mother compose herself. "What visit are you talking about, dear? Flora took you most of the time. I had Ron."

"I know about Ronnie, Mother. I know what I did." Casey looked at her mother, hoping for some reassurance, something to indicate she'd been wrongly accused, justified, anything. She waited. Her mother remained silent, her expression totally blank.

"You shouldn't have been told!" Evie's voice raised several octaves.

"I'm not upset, Mother. You shouldn't be either," Casey placated her.

Evie licked her pink lips and swallowed. "I wanted to tell you, Casey. With John ill and me running the business, I haven't had time. I thought when everything quieted down, we'd have a talk. But someone," her mother's voice turned hateful, "someone took that right away from me as usual."

"It's all right. I can handle it. What I can't handle is the not knowing. Blake and Flora both seemed to think Doc Hunter thought I'd been . . ." She hated to say it to her mother, it just didn't seem right. ". . . molested." The last word was barely a whisper.

Her mother's face turned white. "Why! I told them . . ." The wind blew out of her sails as she slumped forward, resting her face on her arms. Her small shoulders shook with sobs. Casey was reminded of a time when *her* shoulders had shaken with uncontrollable sobs. Another visit to the closet, another day-trip to fear.

"Mother," she asked, her voice now strong and insistent, "who locked me in the closet when I was a child?"

Evie's face turned ashen, her mascara trailing down her face like two silvery black snakes. She fumbled with the cloth napkin, twisting it into a tight roll. "What are you talking about, Casey? I don't know anything about a closet."

Maybe this wasn't real even though it seemed to be. And the closet was always in her dreams. That alone gave the closet substance. Maybe she should let it go for the moment. While she had her mother's undivided attention, other questions were more essential.

"Mother, did Dr. Hunter tell you he thought I'd been molested? Do you know who could've done something like that to me?" She found it hard to stay calm in the face of her mother's mindless expression.

Evie blew her nose quietly, then took a sip of coffee that had turned cold. "Yes, Casey, I knew. Dr. Hunter came to me the day Flora took you to his office.

"Your behavior was odd, I'll admit, but I never thought it was because of . . . that. When the doctor told me, though, I knew right away who was responsible."

"You did?"

"Yes." Evie took a compact from her

purse and reapplied her lipstick. Composed now, she continued, "After your father died, I more or less lost interest in life. I met a few men, and we dated. They were all very casual, nothing serious. Until I met Marc."

Casey had never heard of a man named Marc. She reached for the pot of coffee and refilled their cups as she waited for her mother to continue.

"Marc was exciting. After your father, who was always concerned with making a living or taking care of his mother or Ronnie, Marc was like a breath of fresh air. I never knew what he did. I didn't want to know. He lived in Brunswick and would take the ferry over on the weekends." Her mother paused, as if trying to recall a time in her life that really wasn't all that long ago.

"We had such a wonderful time together. We'd go dancing, and sometimes we went to Underground in Atlanta and spent the whole weekend. Marc was very friendly to you and Ron. He didn't have any children of his own, but acted so natural around you and your brother.

"I guess we must have dated three or four months before I realized what he'd been doing. I'll admit at first, he had me fooled.

When I noticed how you were acting around him I asked him if he'd done anything to upset you.

"Of course he said he'd done nothing. When Dr. Hunter came to me with his suspicions, I immediately went to Marc because you had told me that day what he'd done to you. It's not something I want to talk about."

"Why didn't you have him arrested?" Casey questioned.

"I wanted to, but you begged me not to. You said you'd just die if anyone else knew all the ugly things he'd done to you. I called Marc, and of course he tried to tell me you'd teased him. I asked him just what a nine-year-old had to tease him with. He said he hadn't really damaged you; after all, it was just fondling. He said there had been no penetration. Those were his exact words.

"I had your best interest at heart, so I agreed not to press charges if he agreed never to set foot on Sweetwater Island again." Her mother snapped her fingers. "He was gone like that." She smiled sweetly at Casey.

She wondered if her mother was in her right mind just then. Seconds ago, she'd just bawled her eyes out and now she looked like she was ready to greet her Married Ladies Club members.

Marc. The name meant absolutely nothing to her. As far as she knew, no one had ever mentioned that name to her. Flora said she'd actually had intercourse. Could Flora have misunderstood Doc Hunter?

"I guess that answers my question," Casey whispered. She didn't know what else to say.

"Good. I'm glad we had this little talk to clear the air. Now"—her mother looked at the delicate band on her wrist—"I've got to go to that meeting, and then it's back to John's bedside. If you need anything, Casey, just ask Flora."

Evie dropped an air kiss next to her right cheek and fluttered out of the room like a bird in flight.

That's it? All the mystery and trauma of what she'd experienced as a child wiped away with a ten-minute conversation. She didn't feel one bit better. If anything, she felt worse. And, down deep, she suspected her mother had lied to her.

Robert Bentley glanced in the mirror and saw that he looked all of his fifty years. His lack of sleep was obvious from the dark, sagging pouches under his eyes. The meeting with Dr. Dewitt had been a total failure.

The Cessna's pilot delivered him to Savannah in less than an hour. He'd taken a cab from the small airport to the former home of Judge Dewitt. Nothing had changed. Still the same pile of bricks, the same hundred-year-old oaks, the same wrought-iron gate. Old. Respected. While Robert related to the former, the latter remained a lifelong desire. One he'd thought marriage to Norma would provide.

He wiped shaving cream from his face and walked into the room they'd shared for more than a quarter of a century.

It remained as it had been when he'd moved in after their wedding. Norma's father had lived on the property, in the guesthouse until his death four years after their marriage. When the coffin closed, Robert had assumed he'd have the power he'd longed for all his life. He'd been wrong. And so, when the final shovel of dirt was tossed on Jacob Fulton's grave, Robert began to formulate his plan. Oh, he'd not planned every detail, but a seed had been planted, and with the passing of years the fermentation process had taken on a life all its own.

She hadn't been part of his plan until that day twenty years ago. But now, he couldn't imagine his life without her. He'd bitched, moaned, and groaned, but in his own sick way he loved her.

The culmination of those hardworking years was about to come to pass. The only wrinkles in his plan: the girl and Macklin. Or so he'd thought until Dewitt entered the picture. He'd beat and banged on his door the night before until his knuckles bled. He'd even climbed a trellis covered with thorny roses to see inside an upstairs window, where he'd spied a light. Hell, he'd damn near killed himself.

The scratches were still tender. In the morning Norma asked how he managed to look like a cat's victim, and he'd muttered something about subduing one of the crazies at Sanctuary. That shut her up. Lately Norma showed an unusual amount of interest in him and his activities. She'd always had her charities and that stupid Married Ladies Club. Enough things to occupy her. Why the sudden interest in his whereabouts and general well-being, he didn't know.

Whatever, she wouldn't get in the way; he'd see to it.

He knotted his tie and mentally reviewed his schedule for the day. He had to make an appearance at Sanctuary. He also had an appointment in Atlanta to show a suite in an office building he'd listed months ago. A small overnight bag he kept packed and ready just in case was waiting in the back of the closet. His tickets were in his briefcase at the office.

All he had to do was put on the mask he wore exclusively for Norma, walk down-stairs, kiss her wrinkled cheek, nod to the help, and be on his way.

The previous night's fuck-up had to be tended to first. While he hated to ask Adam for help, he didn't have a choice. Doctors knew about one another. Adam had arranged for the girl's appointment a few days ago. He might know where Dewitt had disappeared to. It was worth a try.

Adam plugged his cell phone charger into the cigarette lighter and watched the fluo-rescent green buttons glow, indicating he had power. Actually he hated the damned thing but found it was as necessary to his profession as his prescription pad.

Jaybird had the Jag in working order. Adam took a deep breath and relaxed. The Jaguar had that effect on him. The smell of leather never failed to loosen him up. He almost felt like its scent was a requirement for his profession. Luxury car, soft creamy leather, and, yes, the required cell phone.

He glanced down, making sure the power light was on. With his father in the hospital, he didn't want to be out of touch, not even for a minute.

Adam rode the ferry and headed west on 82 for I-75 North. He'd be in Atlanta soon. He'd meet with his patient, then he'd come back to the island in time to see his father before he went to sleep. Being a doctor did have its advantages. He'd wanted to take his father to Emory, but the old man wouldn't hear of it. The old guy could barely talk, but his mental faculties were in excellent working order.

Adam smiled to himself as he thought of his dad. They'd had their moments over the years, especially after his mother died, but as time passed his relationship with his father had shifted to a higher level of understanding. He knew his father enjoyed his company as much as he enjoyed his.

Right after his father and Eve married, Adam didn't think he'd ever walk into Swan House again. He'd thought of it as his mother's home. Not long after his father's second marriage he'd come home hoping to make amends with his father for his past behavior. When he saw all the changes *she'd* made, he'd gotten so angry it was over a year before he could force himself to return to his childhood home.

It wasn't that he hadn't wanted his father to be happy; hell the old guy had a few good years left; it was *her.* He'd never felt she truly loved his father. He knew in his gut Evie loved his father's possessions far more than she loved him. She'd gone from poor white trash to the president of the Married Ladies Club, the office his mother once held. Normally he would have laughed it off, but Evie had taken her role as John's wife very seriously.

She'd practically made herself over. New hair, a face-lift, designer clothing, jewelry. According to his father, Eve spent most of her time shopping in Atlanta, New York, and on occasion would fly to California for a shopping spree. She always returned with little surprise presents for him, mostly silly gadgets that made him laugh.

If it all made his father happy, more power to him. He couldn't have cared less about the money. Until the day his father's accounting firm had called him. His father and Eve had been married about five years when the call came.

Terrence Lowinsky had managed his father's holdings for as long as Adam could remember. He'd questioned Adam about his father's sudden lavish spending. Two new cars, a condo in Atlanta, a small airplane.

Adam remembered how shocked he'd been. While his father wasn't a tightwad, he wasn't frivolous, either. He assured Terrence he would talk to his father. As he'd prepared for a quick flight home, he'd been stunned when he'd spotted Evie and another man at the airport. The embrace he'd seen hadn't been just a friendly one. He'd lingered behind, almost missing his flight, and watched them. *She'd* been dressed to kill, and *he* looked like the cat that ate the canary.

He'd thought and plotted on the flight to Brunswick and decided he'd let them trip themselves up. He'd advise his father about his wife's lavish spending, and that would be it. Over the next few years he watched everything they did, and they were none the wiser.

The jarring ring from the cell phone jolted Adam out of his thoughts. He picked up the contraption and punched the SEND button.

"Dr. Worthington."

"Uh, yes, Adam. I need to talk to you."

"Who gave you this number?" he barked into the phone.

"Does it really matter?" Bentley asked.

It didn't matter, because as soon as he arrived in Atlanta he'd have it changed.

"What do you want?" While they had contact on rare occasions because of their professions, Adam despised Bentley and wished he'd never laid eyes on him.

"Actually, I'd heard you put Ms. Edwards in contact with a Dr. Dewitt. I wanted to locate him myself and was told by his answering service he'd gone out of town. I thought you might know where I could find him."

"Sorry, Bentley. I don't make it a habit to know the whereabouts of the medical professionals in the state of Georgia."

"You're sure? I really need to get hold of him."

"Goddamn it, of course I'm sure. Why

would I know where Dr. Dewitt is? Hell, I barely know the man. He sure as hell doesn't call me with his itinerary." On the rare occasions when they bumped into one another at Sanctuary, he never failed to cringe in Robert Bentley's presence.

Adam punched the END button and tossed the phone on the seat. Something was up; he could feel it. Why else would Bentley have called him on his cell phone? And just what the hell did Dewitt and his stepsister have to do with Bentley?

Casey felt restless. She'd spent the afternoon with Julie and Flora in the kitchen but only felt in the way. She'd tried her hand at piecrust and wound up with a large hockey puck. From there she'd peeled apples, cutting herself three times. After that Flora and Julie both decided she needed something safe. She'd been assigned to wipe out the refrigerator and the freezer. With a plastic bucket of hot soapy water, Casey scrubbed the stainless steel until it sparkled. Then, armed with lemon wax and a pile of rags, she'd polished the dining room table, the banister, and all the little odd tables. After that, she'd attacked the rugs with the vacuum.

Casey was glad for something to occupy her hands. Her mind continued to buzz, but at least her hands were busy. A quick peek at her cuticles told her if her mind remained in its current state without something to keep her busy, she'd be lucky to have fingers.

Instead of feeling relief, her mother's visit had left her feeling empty. When Flora finished with Julie, she would ask her about Marc. She assumed John Worthington had been the only man her mother dated after her father's death. Or possibly Flora didn't know about the other men in Evie's life. Maybe her mother wanted it that way. She could respect that, but she still couldn't shake off the feeling that something wasn't quite right. Something was missing from her mother's story. Or, she thought, maybe she just hoped something was missing. And that something would ease the guilt she'd shouldered since learning of her crime.

A wave of nausea assaulted her as she grabbed on to the staircase railing. Casey slumped down on the bottom step, willing herself not to black out. A deep breath. In.

Out. Just the way Dr. Macklin had taught her.

A whirl of color blurred her vision. Another deep breath. Images, some in focus, some not, danced before her.

A closet. Only this time she was standing. Searching. She pulled a denim book bag from the top shelf. Her hands fumbled around until she felt the metal Folger's coffee can. She stuffed it into the bag.

A sweater, two T-shirts, and a pair of jeans. She went to her dresser and grabbed a few pairs of panties and a nightshirt, crammed it all into the bag.

She couldn't spend another night in that house. She'd die first.

Then he'd come into the room just as she closed the drawer.

He grabbed her bag and searched through its contents.

"Give it back! You've no right to be here. Leave or you won't like what I do!" she threatened. Standing in the middle of her spartan room, she looked for a weapon. Her eye found the coffee can he'd tossed in the middle of her bed.

Filled with a sudden bout of courage, she yanked the bag from his grasp and lunged for the can when his hand caught the side of her face. The sting didn't bother her; she'd been slapped in the face many times before.

But the other . . . She wouldn't tolerate it anymore. She'd die first.

However, she didn't want to die.

His menacing voice filled the room. "Don't threaten me! You hear? I promise the next time I won't be as nice."

Casey trembled. He left her room as quickly as he'd entered. She glanced around her, praying this would be the last time she looked on the walls that held so many secrets.

Secrets. Her entire life had been one big secret.

Excluding the times with Grandma and Flora, she'd spent her life in fear.

Well, no more, she thought as she tossed the contents of the can into her bag.

One last look around her. This was it. She'd wouldn't be afraid anymore.

Softly she closed the door behind her. As she entered the hallway she didn't see the fist coming toward her.

Chapter Eighteen

Casey shook her head, hoping to clear the images. This was not entirely a dream. She remembered *being* in that closet.

"Flora!" she shouted.

The little woman came running out of the kitchen. "What, what is it, Casey?" she asked, her breath ragged.

"I remember being in the closet. I was going to leave!"

"Slow down. Now"—Flora scooted next to her on the step—"tell me."

"I was going to leave. I remember. I had a can of money I'd saved. I don't know where it came from, but I know I'd been saving for a long time. Something happened. I remember thinking it would be the last time. I'd had enough. I'd been to see Doc Hunter. It's weird. I can remember thinking that something horrible happened, but I can't seem to remember just what it was. The feeling of fear is there, though. It still is. I was afraid I'd die, Flora!" Casey placed her head in her hands and thought of Dr. Dewitt. Maybe she should have stayed.

"You stop thinkin' that right now!" Flora admonished.

"I can't help it, I know someone wanted to . . . hurt me. Or maybe, they wanted to keep me quiet!"

"Well, I know that molestin' wasn't somethin' your momma wanted to come out, but I don't think she'd a hurt anybody. 'Specially you."

"And that's another thing. This morning Mother told me who molested me. I thought I'd feel some sense of closure, but I don't. It all seemed too tidy to me."

Flora cleared her throat before asking, "Who did she say it was, Casey?" The housekeeper's lively blue eyes were watchful.

"Marc somebody. But she said he didn't actually . . . What he did, she said, was touch me where he wasn't supposed to touch me. Apparently they'd dated for a few months. She said that when she confronted him he left, and she never heard from him again. Mother said my behavior changed whenever he came around. She told me after Doc Hunter's examination I told her what happened and who did it. Apparently I begged her not to go to the police."

Casey cast a side glance at Flora. Her face, usually so expressive, remained blank.

"I never heard of the man. That's not to say he didn't exist, though."

"You mean you never watched Ronnie and me while Mother went away? She told me they went to Atlanta for the weekends."

"Could have. But I'd guess by then ya'll woulda been old enough to stay by yourselves."

"Flora." Casey's voice filled with excitement. "What about the house? Why hasn't anyone taken me there? If something horrible happened to me in that house, and that something horrible caused me to lose my memory, wouldn't it seem logical I should go back there?"

Flora stood up and smoothed her ever-present apron over her hips. "I suppose that'd be a sensible thing to do. Don't understand why Blake or Adam hasn't suggested that to you."

Casey didn't either. She wanted to go back to her old house, but she wanted to go alone.

"Flora, where is this house?"

"Now, don't you go gettin' any ideas, girl. That place is so old it's about to fall apart. It was old when you lived there. I suspect the place is full of rats and God knows what else by now. I don't think Miss Evie's been back there since she married Mr. Worthington."

"I'm just curious, Flora, that's all."

"Well, you know what they say about curiosity."

"No, tell me."

"That it killed the cat. The old Edwards place is at the end of the island. On Back Bay Street."

"Is that by Poorman's?" Casey asked.

"Yep. How'd you know about that place?"

"Adam needed a lift to the hospital. Blake and I picked him up there."

"You jus' stay away from there. Now, I'm thinking we need to find something else for you to do." Flora pushed a strand of white hair back into place.

Casey would have done anything Flora asked her to do. But now all she wanted was a chance to get out of the house.

"Would you mind if I begged off? I'm feeling a little tired. I think I'd like to rest a while."

Casey crossed her fingers, hoping Flora didn't see through her lie. She didn't like to deceive her friend, but just then she didn't have a choice.

"Of course, dear. I seem to forget you're not up to par jus' yet. You go on up, and I'll have Julie bring you a cup of tea."

"Thanks, but I'd like to rest. I'll come down for the tea later."

"If you're sure," Flora said.

"I am. Thank you, Flora. I'll feel better after I'm rested." Casey gave her a quick hug and had to remind herself she was tired so she wouldn't run up the stairs. She could feel Flora's eyes on her back.

Once inside her room Casey wondered how she could get out of the house undetected. Peering down the long hall, she stepped out of her room, quietly closing the door behind her. Removing her sneakers, she stuffed one under each arm as she ran down the three flights of stairs. She heard Flora and Julie in the kitchen. That day being one of Mabel's days off might make it her lucky day, since Flora would be busy preparing dinner.

When she reached the bottom landing, she made a mad dash for the front door. Careful not to make any noise, she pulled the heavy wood aside and stepped outside.

The sky was overcast, dark clouds hovering overhead. A sudden shift in the direction of the wind caused her to ponder her decision. The atmosphere suddenly seemed charged with electricity. She knew Sweetwater was in for a heavy storm. Flora had said earlier her bones were aching. She slipped her shoes on. A storm and some heavy rain weren't going to stop her.

Casey jogged to the bottom of the hill and stopped. She'd forgotten about the guard at the gatehouse. The small brick house had windows on both sides. If she were to pass without being seen, she'd have to crawl on her belly. Feeling foolish at how she'd look if she were caught, she shrugged. She needed to get out of there, and she'd managed to come as far as she had without being seen. Why stop?

Inching her way to the ground, she met with gravel and red dirt. She couldn't believe what she was doing. As she came to the side of the brick structure, she could hear the guard talking on the phone.

She lowered herself beneath the window and rolled to her side, where the shrubs were so overgrown anyone could hide there. She used her elbows to pull herself through the undergrowth. Relief didn't describe what she felt when she reached the other side of the shrubbery. It would be impossible for the guard to see her, since the land was down-hill.

She brushed the dirt from her blouse and checked herself for damage. She'd survived and was little the worse for wear with the exception of a few grass stains.

The road to Sweetwater was to her right. She picked up her pace and jogged a good three miles before stopping to catch her breath.

When small drops of rain splattered the pavement, Casey knew she had to hurry, or she'd be caught in the storm. It couldn't be more than another mile to the end of the island, she thought as she ran for cover. She could feel the back of her slacks getting drenched as she splashed along the street. *Sweetwater looks like a ghost town,* Casey thought as she slowed to a walk.

Winded from her efforts, she stopped and placed both hands on her knees, holding her head down while she tried to catch her breath. So many years on dangerous drugs and lack of exercise hadn't left her in good physical condition.

Yes, she told herself. *One step at a time.* She picked up her pace again. Her clothes clung to her, and she hoped she wouldn't catch cold. Getting sick was the last thing she needed just then.

Two, three, then four more blocks. The island stopped. The only things to be seen were tall grass and sand. She looked first to her left, then right and through the rain that was coming down in sheets. She could barely make out the sign that read Back Bay Street.

Hurrying, Casey sprinted to her destination. What would she find? And surely there was more than one house on the street. How would she know which one she'd lived in? The questions pummeled her as fast as the pellets of rain slapped against her chilled skin. She passed two small wooden houses, both with lights on, telling her someone lived in them. Flora said her mother hadn't been to the house since she and John were married. Casey slowed her jog to a steady pace. Shivering from the dampness, she was about to give up when she saw it.

She knew for sure, one hundred percent positively, no matter what, that she'd lived there.

Paint peeled away at the edges of the two-story house, its wooden shutters showing dabs of faded yellow here and there. The house might've been a cheery yellow at one time.

It was. She remembered. Her grandmother used to live in that house. She'd painted it herself.

She walked up to the front porch, its surface sagging with age and lack of care. Careful of her step, Casey inched her way one foot at a time across the porch's wobbly foundation. The roof overhung the porch, and Casey was grateful for its protection, no matter that rain dripped in.

She drew in a deep breath. This was it. She grabbed the rusted handle to the screen door. She pulled the door aside, waiting for the expected creak, and stopped.

She remembered something about the house. And it filled her with a dread so powerful she almost turned and ran.

* * *

Roland stopped in his tracks. He thought he heard a noise, but knew no one in their right mind would be out in this weather, and if they were, they sure as hell wouldn't be where he was. He'd spooked himself.

He shined the beam of his flashlight around the room, looking for the rat he'd spied earlier. Gone.

The staircase loomed before him. Not sure of its sturdiness, he knew he'd have to chance it anyway. He needed to go up there.

He hadn't bothered telling Vera where he was headed. There was no need for her to know, and, besides, she asked too many questions. The only drawback, he thought as he tested the bottom step with his weight, was that if the staircase collapsed with him, he'd lie there until he died. Maybe he should have told Vera.

What possessed him to go there in this kind of weather was beyond him, but that nagging little son of a bitch voice kept hounding him until he'd listened.

One foot, then the other. He stopped on the fourth stair and flashed his light behind him. His footprints were clearly visible on the steps as years of dust, rat droppings, and filth crunched under his boots. He didn't care. One more step, then another. He pointed the light above him. The closed door at the top of the stairway beckoned to him.

All thoughts of turning back left. Roland knew a secret waited for him. He had known it ten years before. Maybe he would finally find out what lurked behind that closed door.

He pushed the door open, and that's when he heard it.

A scream?

Slamming the door against the wall, Roland felt the hairs on the back of his neck rise as he heard the scream a second time.

He looked at the bed, blue-and-white-striped mattress discolored with stains.

My God, he thought as he crossed the room, alert now, waiting for the scream to come again. They'd never even bothered to remove the bloodstained mattress. A large circle of orange-brown rust at the top right side and several smaller spots remained on the bed. Another rust-colored smear covered the entire left side of the bed, as if something or someone had been dragged across the mattress.

A noise. He strained to hear. With the rain beating against the roof and the wind gusting through the windows, Roland wasn't sure that he'd heard anything. His imagination was on overtime.

How many times had the wind sounded like a woman's screeching call? He'd always hated the high-pitched wail. That day of all days he didn't need crap. He'd come to . . . investigate and the last thing he needed was to have the bejesus scared out of him.

He splayed his light across the bed one last time before crossing the room to the closet. With one hand on the knob and the other holding the flashlight, Roland jerked the door open.

The closet was empty.

Well, jerkweed, what the hell were you expecting? Ronald Edwards's corpse to jump out at you?

He scanned the inside of the closet. Running his fingers along the top of the dirty shelf, he paused when he felt the rough material. Yanking the cloth down, he saw what appeared to be a purse or some type of carry-all. He hooked his arm through the strap and walked around the room again.

He remembered that night as if it were yesterday. He'd never returned until now. He had no other choice. He flinched under his own guilt as he tried to remember how many other times he'd wanted to go there but hadn't.

She'd been so frightened then. Hell, he was, too. He'd done as he was told and never once questioned his own actions. But only at first. He told himself over the years he'd been young and afraid, but truly he'd just been gutless.

The scene never did set right with him. Even back then, his inexperienced eye knew something didn't quite click.

He'd come back hoping to find out what hadn't clicked.

He mentally reconstructed the room that night to the best of his ability.

Casey had been in the hallway. She'd been wearing a white cotton gown that outlined her figure. She trembled and just stayed in the corner, hugging her legs and whimpering. He'd taken off his jacket and placed it around her. He didn't want anyone looking at her in the state she was in. He remembered how pretty and blank she looked. Like all the life had gone out of her.

He'd gone into the bedroom and almost gagged at the scene. He'd never seen so much blood in his life. It was straight out of a horror movie. Blood, thickened from exposure, oozed on the wall above the bed. Blood spatters were all over the night table. A pink ballerina lamp glowed crimson. He couldn't tell the color of the bedclothes because they were drenched in blood.

Then he saw it.

The body, wrapped in sheets. Parker saw the eyes of Ronald Edwards glare unseeingly back at him when he pulled the covers aside.

Then he puked. Right there at the goddamned crime scene, he emptied his gut of everything he'd stuffed into it that day. Vomit blew out his nostrils, and chunks of his supper spewed from his insides. He couldn't stop.

And they'd simply stood by and watched him.

After cleaning himself as best he could with his handkerchief, it had been difficult to play the role of big bad sheriff.

Bentley knew it. And took advantage of it.

The noise came again, startling him from his reverie. This time instead of a scream, it sounded like a whimper.

Roland moved to investigate the sound.

He raced down the stairs, all concern for his own safety gone. He stopped when he reached the bottom step.

"Help!"

He ran through the front room and opened the door leading to the porch.

It was *her.*

She was bleeding, and her clothes clung to her like cellophane. Her short curls were plastered against her head. She leaned against the house moaning, unaware she'd been discovered.

"Casey," he whispered, not wanting to startle her.

She rolled her head to the side, and he knew he'd scared her when her eyes widened and she tried to stand.

"It's okay. It's okay, Casey." He held his hand out to her.

She took his offered hand and pulled herself into a standing position, using the back wall of the porch for assistance.

The shutters slammed against the rotted wood. Torrential rains pounded the roof. He cast a quick glance upward, hoping the roof wouldn't blow away. The stone path leading to the front door had long since flooded, and the water was rising rapidly. He wished now he hadn't walked; he wished for his cruiser with its radio and heater.

Getting Casey inside and examining her injuries became his top priority. Gently he lifted her in his arms and opened the screen, then shoved the door aside. He scanned the room. There wasn't anyplace to put her. Before giving it a second thought he bolted up the stairs and entered the room that just seconds ago had caused him to shudder.

Carefully he placed her on the stained mattress. She continued to moan and toss from side to side. He could tell by the glazed look in her eyes, that she had no idea what was happening.

He used his already damp handkerchief and blotted her wet face as he searched for the source of the bleeding.

On her right temple he saw a fresh wound about two inches long. Grabbing his flashlight from his hip pocket, he shined the light for a closer look.

The cut looked deep. He'd have to get

her to the hospital or at least over to Blake's so he could stitch her up.

Then he'd have to answer questions. Right now that was the last thing he needed or wanted.

Casey thrashed about as if she were feverish. Hell, maybe she'd been ill, and he didn't know it. And why in the damn hell had she come back there? More to the point, why in the damn hell had he come back there himself?

He'd get answers as soon as she was coherent. He cleaned her wound as best as he could.

"What . . . where am I?"

Parker smoothed back Casey's wet hair and continued to apply pressure to her cut.

"It's okay. You're here with me. I won't let anything happen to you," he said, hoping that this time he really *wouldn't* let anything happen to her.

Casey sat up using the wall behind the mattress for support. He watched as she focused on the room and saw the questions in her eyes.

"Sheriff?" her voice scratched.

"Yes. You need to lie still, you've been hurt." He looked away from her then, afraid she'd read more into his look than that of a concerned sheriff. And she'd be right.

The glazed look left her, and in its place her emerald stare became more questioning and . . . frightening.

"What happened to me? Why are you here?"

"Looks like you were hit by something. A shutter must've come loose, catching you on the side of the head."

"Yes, the wind. But . . . No! I saw a shadow as I pulled the door aside. Then everything went black." She sat Indian style on the bed. The bleeding had stopped, and she took a tissue from her pants pocket and swiped at her wound.

"We need to get you to the hospital, or at least have Doc Hunter take a look at you. You've got a pretty nasty gash there."

"I'll be fine," she said as she eased herself off the dingy mattress. She walked around the room, went inside the closet, came out and stood next to the curtainless window before speaking. Her words were solemn when they came. "This is it, isn't it?"

He didn't have to ask what she referred to. "Yes, it is."

Casey stepped away from the window to stand at the foot of the bed.

Roland saw she was staring at the stains on the bed and realized the stupidity in bringing her upstairs, in this room of all places.

She looked up at him. "Sheriff, could I have a minute alone?"

He didn't think it was in her best interest to leave her in that room, but he'd already screwed up when he brought her up there. What could a couple minutes by herself hurt?

"Sure."

He quietly left, praying he was doing the right thing. He couldn't, *wouldn't* let any more harm come to her.

Chapter Nineteen

Casey looked around the room and tried to remember what it had been like living there, sleeping there, dreaming there, *killing there.* She couldn't.

She viewed her former room through the eyes of a stranger.

The striped mattress was shoved against the wall. A nightstand covered with years of grime stood next to the bed.

Casey looked down at her feet. Hardwood floors, maybe shiny and slick once, were covered with mouse droppings and layers of dirt. What might have passed for a throw tossed at the foot of the bed was nothing more than a thin strip of cloth. She picked up the tattered material and saw the faded pattern. Ducks and rabbits? A child's blanket. Hers? She didn't know.

She put the blanket back and went to the closet. She hesitated.

A flash of a child? No, it was a young girl. Pulling clothes from hangers. And she was angry. Angry enough to kill.

As she stood in the entryway to the closet, Casey knew the girl she saw in her mind was herself. Not wanting to stop the flood of memories, she stepped inside the dark closet and closed her eyes.

She crammed shirts and a pair of jeans into her book bag. She had to hurry.

Today she'd free herself from this hellhole. After a trip to Atlanta, there'd be no evidence left. All traces of him gone. She paused and thought about her plan. Was it wrong? No! She would not question her actions. No one in their right mind would blame her for what she planned to do.

Casey felt hot tears flow down her face. All the shame, fear, and rage she'd experienced as a young girl returned. Only this time, she knew why. And this time, she understood. She was retrieving the past, just as Dr. Macklin had predicted.

*   *   *

Roland strained to hear. It has quiet. Not wanting to disturb her, yet needing to make sure she was all right, he climbed the rickety stairs.

He saw her silhouette in front of the window. She seemed to be in deep thought. He quietly walked over to her and led her to the door.

"Let's get out of this place."

"All right."

Side by side they walked down the steps to the front room. Parker searched for a spot to sit, but the damn room was still covered in filth and garbage, and there was no place to sit down.

He took his jacket and placed it on the bottom step.

"I need to go. Flora will worry," Casey said as she sat next to him.

For a minute he thought she was still dazed from the blow to her head.

"They think I'm napping," she added.

She *was* coherent!

"Let's wait till this storm lets up, then we can hoof it to my office. I'll drive you back to Swan House."

"Hoof it?" Casey questioned with a slight smile.

He laughed. "Just a country boy's way of saying 'walking.' "

"A country boy? I wouldn't have known."

He grinned. "Thanks. I guess."

"You don't seem too happy being a 'country boy,' Sheriff. Why is that?" Casey asked.

Could he tell her? It wasn't the fact that he was from Ellajay—you didn't get more country than that. It was because he'd compromised all he'd believed in. His momma thought she raised a man with backbone and integrity, when in reality he was nothing more than a big coward. If he'd been half the man his mother thought, he'd never have agreed with that son of a bitch. No, he couldn't tell her those things. If he was lucky she'd never know. But, his luck bucket was about as empty as his life.

"Sheriff?"

"I don't mind being a country boy. It's just . . . local politics getting in the way, that's all."

"Well, I guess that goes along with the job. But sheriff . . ." She paused, and he knew what was coming next. "Why are you here?"

"Like you, I've got some unclear memories of that day. I thought coming back would help."

"And has it?"

"Yes and no." He didn't know what to say to her. How could he explain that he was the one responsible for fumbling the entire investigation? His screwup had sent her to Sanctuary for ten years.

"I know what you mean." She took on that faraway look again. "When I was upstairs, I remembered something, yet I'm positive I'm missing the main part. It's like all these little hints are being tossed my way, courtesy of my subconscious, then my conscious self tries to piece them together, and all I'm coming up with are jagged bits of my life. Nothing that explains why I . . . killed Ronnie."

Roland knew the risk he took before asking his next question, but it had just occurred to him what seemed odd about the room, or the mattress to be more specific.

"Casey, do you remember what side of the bed you slept on?"

She looked at him as if he'd lost his mind.

"I'm not sure. Do you think it will help if I have another look?" She stood and headed upstairs to her former room.

"I'm coming with you."

"Of course."

Parker observed her as she looked at the lump of stuffing on the floor. He could see her trying to concentrate, to remember.

She plopped down on the mattress sending bursts of dust particles into the damp air. She rolled from side to side before getting up.

"I'm sorry, Sheriff, I don't. But I do remember I was planning to leave that day. I'd never been so angry in my life. I wanted to kill . . ." She covered her mouth with a shaking hand.

"Stop, Casey." He went to her to place his arms around her slender shoulders. She trembled in his embrace. He inhaled. She smelled of rain and flowers. He took another deep breath before gently pulling away.

"It's over. You've served your time. Quit apologizing."

Her green eyes lit up the dull gray room. "Is it, Sheriff? Or is this just another pipe dream? I don't think it'll be over until I remember everything."

Parker noticed that the rain had slowed to a steady drizzle as he stared out the grimy window. "Then we have to work on getting it back."

*   *   *

"That should do it. It might throb after the anesthetic wears off. If it does, take these." Blake gave her a small envelope filled with white pills.

Casey put the packet on the end table. "I'm fine, you guys, really. I'm sure I'll live."

"Sheriff, I'll take her home. I appreciate you bringing her in." Blake shook hands with Roland.

"Anytime. Now, Casey," the sheriff said before leaving Blake's office, "if you feel the urge to investigate, please call me. I'll pick you up." He tipped his hat and left.

"Sure thing," she said to the closed door. She felt sorry for the sheriff and didn't know why. He'd looked sad as he drove her to Blake's office.

Blake gave her his terry robe to wear while her clothes were drying. "A question," she called from the laundry room off the kitchen, "What's with Sheriff Parker? Does he have a family or anything? He seems so . . . lost."

"He keeps to himself. Always has. As far as marriage goes, I don't think he's ever taken the plunge. Why?"

She stepped out of the laundry room, warmed from the heat of her dried clothes.

"Just a feeling, that's all. I think he had another reason for visiting my former home. I don't think he wanted to tell me."

"That's his right, Casey. Especially if it's police business."

"See, that's it! I thought he might've been there because of . . . well, because of me and what happened. He even said as much."

Blake handed her the phone after he punched in the number. "Flora. She'll be worried."

"Oh damn! I forgot. Story of my life."

"Julie, it's me, Casey. I took a walk. No, really I'm fine. Tell Flora not to call the sheriff. I'm at Blake's now. He's giving me a lift home." She raised a brow at the next question.

"Dinner?"

He gave her the thumbs-up sign.

"Uh, yes, he'll stay. Okay. And thanks, Julie."

Casey returned the phone to Blake. "Julie said to tell you Flora made your favorite. Pot roast."

"Then let's go. We'll talk on the way."

*   *   *

Robert paced the empty office. He'd arrived half an hour early to familiarize himself with the floor plan. All appeared to be in order. He wished his client would hurry. He had more important things to do.

Like locating Dewitt. Dewitt had tricked him last night. Besides Norma, the one thing Robert liked least was to be fucked over. Why the slimy shit even bothered to set up a meeting confused him. Had that insane Edwards woman opened her trap, or was the good doctor playing with him? Most likely the latter, he thought as he crossed the wide expanse of the empty office suite. He stared out of the thirty-seventh-floor window. Peachtree was wall-to-wall traffic. Cars whipped in and out of lanes, and Robert wondered briefly what it would be like to step in front of one. Or shove someone under the wheels.

He'd tried running Casey Edwards down, but it hadn't worked. Maybe he needed to take a different approach. Where in hell was his prospective renter? Didn't she know he was a busy man?

He looked at the lone clock the last tenant

had left hanging on the wall. Five more minutes, then he'd leave. He didn't need this
shit anymore. The real estate business certainly left something to be desired these
days. He consoled himself with the thought
that he would be closing up shop very soon.

Robert was about to pack it in when he
heard the knock at the door.

A woman in her mid-fifties, wearing a
smart-looking navy suit with matching
shoes, held out her hand in greeting. "Helen
Bishop. You must be Robert?"

"Yes." He opened the door and stood
aside.

"I need office space and I need it fast."
Helen walked across the large room, stopping once to look around. "This looks
big enough, and the price is right. One
Peachtree Center is a good address. Let's
do it."

Robert was curious about this woman. A
possible mystery beneath the coifed coiffeur
of Ms. Bishop?

"Would you like to go over the terms of
the lease? I have it here." He thumbed
through a stack of papers in his briefcase.

"No. If it's standard, I'm sure it will be fine.
I'd like to start moving in first thing tomor-

row." She said all this as she wrote her check. When Robert saw she'd paid an entire year's rent up front, he decided to keep his mouth shut, but he was curious. Why did she want the space so quickly when she'd made this appointment with him weeks ago?

"Yes, it's standard," he said. "Tomorrow will be fine." He gave her the required papers to sign, then returned them to his briefcase.

She held her palm out to him. "Good doing business with you, Robert." She clasped his hand. Her handshake was surprisingly ladylike.

"The same here. Now, I'm sure you'll understand if I leave now. I've scheduled another appointment in this building, and I'm already running late."

"Certainly." The new tenant slid her copies of the lease into her purse and left him alone with his thoughts.

The entire transaction had taken no more than five minutes. Robert liked that. This woman, whoever she was, reminded him of himself.

He'd lied about having another appointment in Peachtree Center. Why, he had no idea. Just that he wanted the busy woman to think she was one of many waiting clients, he supposed. God, why did he need constantly to boost himself? What was lacking in his life? He had things most men would be envious of. Norma's family home, *his home now,* would rival any wealthy man's estate. A Lamborghini, the Jag, a classic Corvette, and three BMWs and Norma's Mercedes. His clothes were tailor-made. He and Norma belonged to The Oaks, one of Brunswick's finest country clubs. Outwardly he had all the material possessions most men spent their entire lives trying to accumulate. And he'd never been satisfied. He knew what was lacking. And by God, he'd have it no matter what. Which brought him back to Dewitt. No way would he let the man intimidate him.

The elevator door hissed open, and Robert quickly stepped out. He hated the damn things; you never knew when you'd get stuck in one. Not that he had, but he'd heard of some people actually dying in them.

Bright sunshine and a warm breeze greeted him as he entered Peachtree Center Avenue. Office workers young and old thronged the sidewalks. Hot dog vendors were scattered downtown, and Robert almost wished he weren't so disciplined. He'd like to eat one, maybe two, covered with relish, gobs of ketchup and mustard. But if he succumbed to such primal cravings, he'd be right up there—or down, he mused—with the lower classes who stuffed themselves with the nasty things all the while wondering why their weight couldn't be controlled.

At Auburn Avenue he stopped and crossed with a crowd of workers scurrying toward Georgia's State Capitol building.

He had one more stop to make, and just enough time to do it before his return flight to Sweetwater. He waved his hand for a taxi and seconds later hopped inside the Yellow Cab. He gave the driver the Buckhead address, observing the man as he mentally calculated his fare plus tip. Buckhead being one of the best addresses in Atlanta, it was doubtful the cabbie delivered passengers in this area too often since most residents had their own personal chauffeurs.

Robert took a twenty from his wallet and looked at the ticking meter before he grabbed another. While he didn't want to appear cheap, he sure as hell didn't want the driver to think him nouveau riche. Hell, he doubted the driver even knew what it meant.

"Thanks," the man said as Robert stuffed the cash into the cabbie's outstretched hand, then made a mad dash for the condo.

She didn't know he'd had a key made on their last trip. While she showered, he'd taken the keys from her purse. A wax impression took seconds. The next day, while in Brunswick, Marv, the manager at Ace Hardware, made several copies for him. You never knew when you might lose one.

He slid the key into the lock. A click and the door opened. Perfect.

"You!"

His heart rate tripled when he saw he wasn't alone. This situation could be handled.

She wore a black skirt with a rose-colored blouse half tucked in. Pale pink nylons encased her slim legs. Her shoes were nowhere to be seen. She looked rumpled, as if she'd dressed hurriedly. Normally, there was never a hair out of place. Now, however, her sleek bob looked like she'd encountered hurricane-force winds.

"Yes, me. So what?"

"I didn't expect you."

He gave her a quick glance as his gaze came to rest on her flushed face. "Apparently not. What in the hell have you been doing, or should I ask *who* have you been doing?" He knew her sexual escapades included others besides himself. Since he practiced the very same habits, he could not have cared less whom she bedded.

"It doesn't concern you. However," she called over her shoulder as she walked toward the bedroom, "your presence concerns me. I know you think I'm nuts, Robert, maybe I am." She gave a deep laugh. "But I know I never gave you a key to the condo. That alone makes me wonder what else you've been doing behind my back."

He didn't know if he could hold off any longer. He had to. Just a few more days, and all this would be his.

"Big fucking deal. Did it ever occur to you that I run a business? I'm in Atlanta all the time. You should've given me a key to this place. Sometimes I stay over. I didn't want to ask you for a copy, so I had one made. End of story. Nothing up my sleeve."

"Lots of things occur to me, Robert. More than you'll ever know." She came out of the bedroom looking fresh as a daisy. "I've got things to do back in Sweetwater. Need a lift?"

He'd have to deal with Dewitt later. He'd wanted at least an hour of undisturbed time to make his calls. He needed to get rid of the stash of LSD he carried in his pocket. Airport security would stop him for sure. He had to leave it somewhere. With her in the way, it would be impossible. He'd never been too sure how far she'd allow him to go with their plan. He knew murder was easy for her, but he wasn't sure how particular she would be when it came to the victim. No way would he conduct business in her presence. Dewitt could wait another day. The drugs would be easy to dispose of.

"Sure. You have a car here?" She usually hired a driver on her trips to Atlanta.

"I rented a Benz. I'll leave it at the airport for the rental company."

"Fine. What time is your flight scheduled, or do you have the Cessna?" The obvious hiding place for the drugs suddenly occurred to him: The rental car.

Once outside, Robert looked around, making sure he wasn't being observed. It wouldn't do for anyone to catch them together. Years of planning would be sucked right down the tube if that happened.

"American flight 442, Robert. Same as you." She shot him one of her know-it-all smirks before leading him to the underground parking garage.

The woman surprised him sometimes.

Before opening the passenger door, Robert walked around to the driver's side. Not allowing her the chance to resist, he took her in his arms and kissed her, long and hard. *This* he had control over. This she had *no* control over. At first she resisted, then he forced her lips to part with his tongue. Teasing her, he nipped her lip, then felt her submission as her mouth opened to him. It worked every time.

A Buckhead address in Atlanta signifies being wealthy, or one of the South's trendsetters, or, quite often, both. Normally Adam would lunch at a Waffle House or Shoney's but that day his patient, a wealthy widow in her fifties, newly recovering from agoraphobia, had insisted they meet at Bone's, a masculine steakhouse right in the heart of the Buckhead district.

Black-and-white images of celebrities who'd dined there in the past lined the dark-paneled walls along with framed photos depicting Atlanta through the years. The place was noted for its lobster bisque and extensive wine list. Adam laughed to himself as he waited for Ms. Bishop to return from the ladies' room.

Helen Bishop couldn't embrace her new-found freedom fast enough. Locked away in her family home for more than ten years, after her only son was killed in a car accident on his way home to visit, she'd been unable even to go downtown. For the past two years Adam had aggressively treated her agoraphobia.

They were celebrating the opening of her new marketing business. She'd taken an office on Peachtree and was moving in the next day.

Adam assumed that this was a farewell luncheon, too. Helen had been going out on her own for almost a year, and that day was the culmination of her long bout with the mental disorder that had confined her for so many years.

She emerged from the ladies' room all smiles. Taking her by the elbow, he escorted her to the front entrance of the restaurant, which faced Piedmont Road. She broke loose from him and walked to the street.

"That's him!"

He saw where she pointed. Something about the figure seemed familiar.

"Who?" Adam walked to the curb and stood next to Helen.

"The man I rented my office from." She took another step, almost into the oncoming traffic. Adam grabbed her arm and pulled her out of harm's way.

"Helen, I'd hate to think we've gone through the past two years of therapy to have it wiped out by your curiosity."

"Oh, Lord, Adam. I'm sorry. I thought I'd say hello is all."

Helen looked behind her one last time as Adam led her back to the sidewalk.

"I wonder who she is?" she asked no one in particular.

Adam turned around just in time to see Robert Bentley and Eve Worthington headed for the underground parking lot.

Together again.

While her husband, his father, lay in the hospital.

Chapter Twenty

Blake leaned back in the kitchen chair and patted his stomach. "If I ate like this every day, Flora, I'd weigh a ton."

"Me, too," Casey said as she put the last plate into the dishwasher.

"Well, I say it ain't gonna hurt neither of you to gain a few pounds. 'Specially you, young lady. Another twenty pounds and you'll look as fit as a fiddle."

"No, Flora, I'd look as fat as a house." Casey folded the dish towel and placed it on the countertop.

"Ladies, it's getting late," Blake said. "I think I'd better head on out. I've a few things to catch up on this evening. Thought I might go over to the hospital and check on John. I tried Adam's place here on the island. He isn't there. I'm hoping to catch him with his father."

He stood and gave Flora a gentle squeeze. Casey felt her heart flutter when he centered his gaze on her. She smiled at him. "Then get out of here, Doc. If you see my mother at the hospital, tell her I asked about her."

"I will. Now, I want my two favorite beauties to relax this evening. Watch TV, do facials, paint your nails, you know, girl things." He winked at Casey.

"Are you saying we *need* facials and painted nails, young man?" Flora asked as she swatted Blake's rear end.

"Yes. I'll call you later, Casey." He squeezed her hand and gave Flora another hug. "Tomorrow, Flora, I'll want that pecan pie again." He gave a last wink, and the three of them walked to the front door.

They could have been a family, Casey thought as she stood next to Flora, watching Blake's taillights wind up the hill. She closed the door and went to the kitchen.

With a pot of tea between them, Casey knew Flora wanted to talk. While Blake's innocent images of girl talk accompanied by facials and glorious pink polishes were his idea of how they'd spend their evening, Casey knew better.

"All right, Flora, out with it."

"Well, girl, you sure are gettin' to know my moods. I had a call this afternoon. From that young lady down at the courthouse."

"Brenda?" Casey questioned.

"No, the other one. Marianne. She wanted to speak to you. I told her you'd taken a walk. And by the way, young lady, if you ever decide to sneak out again, you'd best let me know."

"If I did, then it wouldn't be sneaking." Casey laughed.

"You know what I mean. I thought I'd die when Julie came down and said you were nowhere to be found."

"I'm sorry. I didn't mean to worry or upset you. I just needed some time alone. And I wanted to go to . . . that house." She rubbed the small bandage beneath her hair. She'd managed to arrange her short hair to hide her injury. Flora didn't know about her wound, and Casey had made Blake promise not to tell her. She'd think about that later.

"What did Marianne want?"

"Seems you were looking for some records. I told her I'd give you the message."

"Maybe she found the copy of the report

Blake and I were looking for." Casey wondered what Marianne's last name was and if it was too late to call. When she talked to Blake later, she'd ask him.

"She didn't tell me. Just said it was important. She said she'd call back."

Casey took a sip of tea. "You know, Flora, I can hardly believe the past few days. I try to think back to just a few months ago, when I was incoherent from all those medications Dr. Macklin gave me, and now I don't even seem to be the same person. I've remembered things that I never imagined. The day Ronnie died, I saw Robert Bentley in my room. Do you remember hearing anything about that?"

Casey watched Flora's expressive face for a sign of recognition. "No, not that I recall. Of course I have to keep remindin' you that I'm not as young as I used to be. My memory fails me a lot these days."

Casey wondered if Flora's memory failed her only when it was convenient.

"I've been thinking. Mother said this Marc was responsible for molesting me." She used the word with such ease. "Did I ever even hint to you that he'd hurt me? I just feel so . . . oh, unsatisfied I guess. I wanted to know the person, wanted to put a face to him. I guess I need to have someone to center my anger on."

"Like I said, Missy, I never heard of this Marc person. And the day I took you to Doc Hunter's you never said a word about anything or anybody. My thought is this: If you'd wanted to tell someone, anyone, you'd a told me right then and there. I don't see you goin' to your momma and tellin' her that. Those are just my thoughts, Casey, nothing more."

Flora was right. That's what didn't fit. It all seemed so out of character for the child she'd been at the time. Reserved and maybe frightened.

Suddenly her memory of that day was crystal clear.

"Casey, sweetie you've been hurt by someone, haven't you?" Doc Hunter questioned.

She remained quiet, her hands folded in her lap. She counted the tulips on her dress.

Thirty-six, thirty-seven . . .

"Now I want you to listen to old Doc here. You don't have to say anything, you hear? Just listen."

She nodded.

"I know you're just nine, but, Casey, I know what a bright girl you are. Flora tells me how good you do in school, makin' straight As on your report card. So that's why I know you'll understand what I'm about to tell you.

"Sometimes people . . . Men do awful things. Women, too, but men have been known to do things to girls, both young and old. When you're older you'll probably understand this better, but right now you need to know what happened to you wasn't your fault. Men go to jail for doin' things like this to young girls. But, in order for them to be punished, someone has to tell about all the bad things they do."

Then she looked at him, and whispered, "Nobody did nothin' to me."

"Well, Casey, it sure doesn't look that way to me. You see, we doctors go to school for a long time jus' so we can tell when people are hurt and what to do for them. Why, some of us can even tell what's ailin' a person without them ever openin' their mouth."

Frightened green eyes looked at the doctor. "I ain't stupid. Quit tellin' me those baby stories. I ain't believin' it. You can stuff your lies."

"They're not lies, Casey. I promise you. I'd

never tell you a lie. I want you to make me a
promise. Will you do that for me?"

"Why?"

"Well, because I'm your friend, and
friends make promises to each other."

"I ain't got no friends. Don't want none,
either."

"Okay, then. I understand."

"Then let me go!"

"I will Casey. But I'd like for you to go
home and tell your mother what he's doin' to
you. If you do that, I promise he'll go to jail,
and you'll never have to be afraid again."

"What is it Casey?" Flora's words were
laced with concern.

As if she were coming out of a trance
Casey looked at Flora as though seeing her
for the first time. "I remember the day you
took me to Doc Hunter's office. I was so . . .
I guess I was trying to act tough."

"Of course you were. What else would
you expect? Certainly not the little girl that
you shoulda been. That son of a bitch stole
your innocence like a thief in the night!"

"Doc Hunter wanted me to tell my mother
what happened. He wanted me to say who it
was that touched me."

"And did you?"

"No. I was afraid. He always told me I'd die if I told. Sometimes I threatened him. I'd say 'I'm gonna tell Flora.' And he'd lock me in the closet!" The words flowed fast as memories were hurled her way. She could barely keep up with them.

"Dear Lord!"

"I'd stopped believing in everything. Fairy tales, happy endings and . . . peanut butter cookies." Casey shook her head to clear her scattered thoughts.

"They were your favorite," Flora added.

"I know. I thought I didn't deserve anything. Especially the cookies you always made for me. They were warm and so good. I remember thinking when I had those cookies I always felt a part of something. Isn't that crazy?"

"No, not one bit. Those were the times you must've felt safe and secure. See that memory of yours ain't so defective after all."

Casey gave a wry laugh. "It still doesn't explain Marc. Why would Mother tell me he was responsible when there's always been the chance I'd remember who really molested me?"

"You mean to say you *know* who's responsible for soilin'you all those years ago?"

"Yes."

"Well, good grief Missy, who?" Flora leaned forward in her chair, her eyes as wide as the moon.

"It makes sense now. Or most of it anyway." An ocean of tears, built up over the years, now flowed freely as Casey recounted the tragic event that ruined her young life.

"What I can't understand is why!" She sobbed.

Flora walked to her side of the table and placed her hands on her shoulders. "You've got to tell me, Casey. Who was responsible for this?"

Doubt plagued her. "Oh, Flora, I'm afraid I'll open Pandora's box. What if my memory isn't accurate? What if I name this person and later discover it isn't true?"

The little woman continued with her soothing massage. "That's the chance you'll have to take. Whatever it is, it can't be as bad as what happened to you."

Casey debated for a moment. Flora was right. There'd been too many secrets in her life and in this wicked town far too long.

"The boy in the picture I found in the closet, Flora. How old was he then?"

"The picture of Ronnie?"

"Yes."

"I'd guess around fifteen or sixteen. What's that got to do with anything?" Flora seemed dazed, her voice sluggish.

"Everything Flora. Everything, because that's when it started."

"Girl, you're confusin' me. What started?"

"The molesting. That's about the age he would've been when he started coming to my room at night."

"*Ronnie!*" Flora repeated.

"Yes, Flora, Ronnie," Casey replied.

"Merciful, God. Did you tell Blake?"

"No! I can't. Not yet, I'm so ashamed!" Casey cried.

"I jus' can't believe this! It's too crazy!"

"Well, believe it, Flora. I might not be able to recall what color my shoes were back then, but I remember Ronnie. And he raped me. Repeatedly. But I'm still not going to tell Blake until I remember more about that night."

When Blake left Swan House he swore he wouldn't eat another bite until breakfast, but the slab of apple pie Adam carried on his tray looked too good to pass up. He grabbed the last piece from the pie stand, then refilled his coffee cup.

The patients down for the night, the staff members were busy filling meds and tucking in those who couldn't sleep. Blake always liked that time of night. It was what he remembered about his internship. The nights when he actually had a few moments to reflect on his day.

Tonight his reflections weren't of past good times. When Adam told him they needed to talk, he knew it wouldn't be about the good old days.

Adam took the last bite of his pie before speaking. "I asked to talk with you because I think there's something going on you need to know."

"Going on? As in your life or mine?"

"Neither, but it involves us both, indirectly. I took a trip to Atlanta today."

"You live and work there, Adam," Blake said.

"No kidding. Look I'm serious. I wish you'd be serious, too, just this once."

Blake held his palms up. "Okay, okay. Sorry. What's this all about?"

"A former patient of mine invited me to

lunch. At Bone's. In Buckhead." Adam watched him for a response.

"And?" He prompted.

"Dad has a condo in Buckhead. On Piedmont. Remember way back when I told you Terrence, our accountant, asked me to talk to Dad about his 'lavish spending'?"

"Yes. But that was several years ago."

"I know, but he still has the condo. Eve uses it for her overnight trips."

"Well, Adam, it's hers to use, too."

"Let me finish. Helen, my patient, and I were coming out of the restaurant when she ran to the curb. I thought she was going to run out into the oncoming traffic, but she stopped."

"She tried to kill herself?"

"Hell no. Just listen. She saw the guy she'd rented her office space from. It didn't mean anything to me. I saw the guy's back and thought he looked familiar. When Helen made a comment about the woman with him I looked. Good thing, too. I saw Eve and Robert Bentley walking arm in arm to the underground garage at the condo."

Blake let out the breath he'd been unaware of holding. "Whoa. What do you think this means?"

"I think it means a lot of different things. I think it means that what I knew about years ago is still going on." Adam looked older than his thirty-four years then. Blake knew his friend's concern was for his father.

"I'm sure you're right. The question is, what to do about it." Blake arranged the crumbs on the paper plate with his thumb.

"That's what I wanted to talk to you about. In Dad's condition this is the last thing he needs to hear. This could send him over the edge into an early grave. I bet those two would love that." Adam sounded bitter.

Justifiably so, Blake thought.

"Until you're sure, I wouldn't say anything. To anyone."

"My thoughts, too. I talked with Dr. Foo; he says Dad's condition is improving by the minute, but warned me not to upset him. He told Eve not to visit anymore until his condition stabilized."

"You mean she hasn't been here? She told Casey and Flora she hasn't left his side except to attend a board meeting in Brunswick."

"Not since Foo asked her to leave. Dad said she calls him from the Worthington apartment daily."

"I know there's more. Tell me," Blake coaxed.

"I don't want to do this, but right now I think I know what's best for Dad, and staying here isn't." Adam laced his hands together and rested his chin on top of them.

Blake felt bile rise to his throat. "Do you mean his staying here at Memorial?"

"Yes. I've contacted a colleague of mine. He's director of the Carriage House in Marietta. He's agreed to let Dad come on short notice."

"The Carriage House, Adam? That's a retirement hospital. What in the hell do you mean? John's as able as the rest of us to care for himself, or he will be soon. You just said Dr. Foo's prognosis was anything but grim. How could you do this to your father?" He raised his voice, not caring if anyone heard. There were limits to his friendship. And right now he would not allow Adam to dispose of his father.

"I knew you'd react this way."

"You're right on that, old buddy. John's been a second father to me. What the fuck did you expect?" Blake stood up and shoved his chair beneath the table. The loud bang elicited a few unwanted stares from a group of nurses seated nearby. He didn't give a damn what they thought.

"Calm down, dammit! You're too emotional. Let me finish."

Blake watched Adam and could see this wasn't a decision he'd made without thought. *Yet, why? John is on the mend. I'll give Adam one more minute, then that will be it. If I have to petition the court on behalf of the man who treated me like a second son, I'll do it. I won't allow Adam to do this to his father. I can't.*

Blake looked at his watch. "You've got exactly thirty seconds before I start kicking your ass."

Adam smiled.

The bastard actually thought this was funny?

"Blake, I think Dad's life is in danger if he remains here. I want him where no one can find him."

"What?" Blake's adrenaline rush left him like a deflated balloon.

"You heard me. If you'd stop acting like an asshole long enough to hear me out, you might understand and actually agree with me."

"God, Adam, I don't know what to say."

"Nothing for starters. Don't interrupt me. You know how for years I've known about Eve screwing around on Dad. Hell, I think he's suspected it himself but hasn't said anything. When I saw her with Bentley this morning I knew it was still going on.

"Did Casey mention anything about an argument she overheard?" Adam asked.

"No, should she have?"

"That's what I thought. No, she shouldn't have, and she did the right thing. I owe her one. When you brought me here day before yesterday, Dad and I argued about his will. I've never kept a secret of wanting nothing to do with Worthington Enterprises. I just want to practice medicine. I told Dad this years ago. He understood but still wanted some of his holdings left in my care. I agreed to this. I think I said something to the effect I could hire people to manage his fortune. This stroke made him think. He believes he'll die any second. Someone, and I'm sure we both know who, convinced him to change his will."

"Damn, Adam, I'm sorry. I didn't know." Blake slid back into the chair, all thoughts of protecting John from Adam gone.

"I know. I would've done the same thing. I

know how you feel about Dad. God, I can't bear the thought of seeing the old guy in a home, but until I figure out just exactly what's going on, I don't have any choice."

"Have you told him yet?"

"Yes. He didn't seem too happy, but Blake, he didn't fight me like I thought he would. That concerns me, too."

"Why?" Blake asked.

"First of all, it makes me wonder if he's simply giving up on life and doesn't care where he spends his last days. Or, and this is the part that really frightens me, what if *he* believes his life is in danger, too?"

"We've definitely got a problem."

"I'm going to talk to Sheriff Parker when I leave here. Do you want to come along?"

"Sure, but why Parker, what can he do?" Blake didn't have to tell Adam what he thought of the sheriff's reputation. Or lack of one. He knew Adam knew it, too. They'd discussed it often enough.

"I don't know. I need someone to know what we're doing and why. If, God forbid, something were to happen to Dad, I'd like to think I'm doing everything I can to prevent it. I guess this is just that." Adam smiled weakly, all the professional fire snuffed out.

In its place, a man simply concerned for his father.

"You didn't say. Who'd he name as beneficiary?"

"Want ten guesses?" Adam said, as they both tossed the remains of their snack in the garbage.

"Nope, don't need them. I just wonder how she managed to convince your dad."

Adam shrugged, "The usual way women get to men, Blake. Right between the legs."

Chapter Twenty-one

Roland Parker was about to leave the office for the night when he received a call from Adam Worthington. He couldn't imagine what the psychiatrist wanted with him at this late hour, but he sure as hell didn't have anything better to do.

Ten-thirty. He should have been home with a wife and maybe a couple of kids. At ten-thirty he could've been quite comfortable, all snuggled in bed next to a warm body. But, he reminded himself, ten years ago, when he'd listened to that bastard, he'd given up his right to marry. Who would want to live with him after what he'd done? He had no courage, backbone, guts, whatever you called it. He wouldn't ask anyone to share his life. And even if he did, who'd want to live with a spineless bastard? He really had a hate on for himself.

Roland heard voices in the front office just as he got up from his desk. Blake and Adam didn't waste time. That had to mean it was serious.

He stuffed his wrinkled brown shirt into his trousers and adjusted his belt before entering the reception area.

"Blake, Adam," he said, holding a hand out to them both.

Adam spoke first. "Sorry about the late hour, but I don't think this can wait."

"Evidently. Now, what can I do for you?" Parker seated himself and pointed to the two chairs across from him. Adam and Blake sat down, both looking grim.

"I need to have your word before I tell you what I'm about to tell you. I want your promise that it will never leave this office."

"Of course, Adam, whatever you say." Something must be awfully important to bring both doctors out on such a nasty night. The rain had worsened. Hurricane George's gusting winds were reaching them faster than the forecasters had predicted.

"I'm sure you know Dad is in the hospital; he suffered a stroke a few days ago."

"Yes, I heard. I'm sorry. Give him my best when you see him."

"I will. Actually he's part of the reason why we're here." Adam nodded in Blake's direction.

Parker's curiosity peaked. He waited for one of the doctors to enlighten him.

"I think his life could be in danger," Adam said.

Roland felt the blood rush to his head, roaring between his ears. Sure he hadn't heard correctly, he asked Adam to repeat himself.

"I'm afraid someone might want him dead and might not wait for Mother Nature."

"Yes, yes. Okay." He needed to think. This might be his one chance to salvage his reputation, heal his wounded pride. He didn't want to screw it up.

"Tell me"—he looked them both square in the eye—"do you have any idea who might want him dead?" he asked.

Adam and Blake both spoke at the same time.

"Bentley," said Adam.

"Robert Bentley," Blake mimicked, only choosing to use his full name.

Parker felt as if a giant hand had swooped

down and put a chokehold on him. He found it difficult to breathe. He reached down and loosened his belt, then unbuttoned the top three buttons on his shirt. Propriety be damned! He drew in a shaky breath. He'd been right. This chance was meant to be. The door to the past had opened, and while he hadn't planned on it, he sure as hell wasn't about to slam it in their faces.

"It's funny you should mention him. There's something I should have told you a long time ago." Parker settled himself into a comfortable position. This could be a long night.

Trying to immerse herself in the adventures of an eighteenth-century heroine and unable to, Casey tossed the paperback novel on the nightstand and turned the light off.

She'd waited till midnight for Blake to call. When he didn't, she assumed he'd been delayed at the hospital. He probably thought she'd be asleep by then and hadn't wanted to wake her.

She plumped the pillows and rolled to her side.

I used to sleep on the left side of the bed.

Casey flicked the light on and sat upright in bed. Earlier that afternoon, when she'd tried to recall how she slept as a young girl, she hadn't been able to remember. And now, it being the furthest thing from her mind, she'd remembered. Dr. Macklin was right again.

Why had Parker wanted to know? When she remembered the book bag the sheriff had handed her right before they'd left the house on Back Bay, she shoved the comforter aside and raced to her closet.

Earlier, when she and Blake arrived for dinner, Casey had come upstairs to change and shoved the bag in the back of the closet, temporarily forgetting about it.

She found the bag and pulled it out from the corner.

Casey plopped the satchel on the night table and stared at it. Something had been stuffed inside.

Her hand trembled as she reached inside. Seated in the center of her bed, she dumped the contents into a pile, closing her eyes and praying she wouldn't find another picture of him. She opened her eyes one at a time and felt her heartbeat slow to normal when all she saw were . . . *clothes*?

Hesitantly, Casey touched the pile of garments, mildewed beyond recognition. She picked up what might've been a T-shirt, held it in front of her, and sneezed as dust particles danced in the dim light. Not wanting to get dirt on her sheets, Casey took the pile of tattered clothing and set them on the floor next to her bed.

She went through them piece by piece. When she unrolled a pair of faded Levi's, she felt her eyes fill with tears.

These are my clothes! I wore them as a young girl.

Casey stretched the faded denim out in front of her and smoothed the filthy material flat. That's when she felt it. Suddenly, as if her life depended on it, she crammed her fingers in the right front pocket and removed a faded card.

Intrigued, she leaned back so she could see better when she held the card beneath the lamp.

The bold lettering had faded over the years, making it difficult to read, but the words on the card were still legible.

When it came, the memory was as sharp and clear as if it happened only yesterday.

She was going to do it, no matter what

anyone thought. God would forgive her. Flora always told her God would forgive any sin if you let Christ into your heart and asked him to be your personal Savior. He'd been the only Savior she'd had for the past nine years, she thought as she hurriedly stuffed clothes inside her book bag.

She'd been on her way home from Doc Hunter's office that afternoon when she found the card lying on the sidewalk just outside Haygood's. It had to be an omen from God, she thought as she read the card.

Fulton County Women's Clinic.

One phone call, and her plans were set.

Casey stuffed the card inside her purse. Tomorrow she'd show it to Blake and maybe her mother.

She touched the three stitches at her temple and wondered if she should tell Blake her suspicions. While Sheriff Parker said she'd been hit by a loose shutter, she knew better.

Right before she'd been hit, she felt a presence. As she was about to turn around, she felt the blow.

Everything went black after that. But she knew someone wanted to hurt her. Maybe they were trying to scare her away. Or, and the thought of this sent chills down her spine, maybe someone wanted her dead. It was clear someone hadn't wanted her in that house. Were they afraid of what she'd find in the book bag? The sheriff gave it to her, apparently not caring about the contents, or if he had, nothing he found had seemed important.

Why had Sheriff Parker appeared out of nowhere? He'd shown concern for her, but was his concern real? And why had he asked her if she remembered the position she'd slept in? Almost like he'd been testing her. But for what?

In just a few short days her life had turned into one question after another. Casey knew that her mother could answer many of her burning questions, but until John came home, she couldn't ask her anything more.

Casey turned the lamp off for the second time and crawled beneath the covers. All evening she'd tried not to think about her revelation to Flora, but now in the dark of night, alone with her thoughts, she couldn't stop the memories from coming. One minute she would believe herself a murderer and in the blink of an eye, she'd see herself as a victim, a little girl crying to be loved.

Why? she wondered as she pulled the com-forter closer around her neck.

She remembered that day in the closet ten years ago so vividly, yet anything before then still remained a clouded mystery.

The card. She hadn't wanted to think of its implications, but she couldn't stop her-self. She recalled making the phone call, and then . . . as was the norm for her, she drew a blank.

She recalled being so afraid. And a strong need to hurry. But why? Had her life been in danger?

Or had her fear simply been a case of newfound over-protectiveness for her un-born child?

He watched the upstairs light dim for the second time that night. She must be suffer-ing from her nightmares. This thought pleased him. He hoped he'd caused her some discomfort, if not physical, then at least mental. When he'd seen her running through the rain, he followed her. Her desti-nation seemed fitting for his plans.

Sure the blow would keep her quiet for a while, he'd been surprised when he heard her soft moans. He hadn't dared another attempt, at least not yet. Another opportunity would soon make itself known, and he would wait until then.

He would wait for his orders.

Eve parked her BMW in the hospital's parking lot and cursed the hurricane winds that tousled her perfect blond bob as she walked to the front entrance. Eight o'clock in the morning and already she looked a mess. It wouldn't do for John to see her in such a state. She had decided to ignore Dr. Foo's orders to keep away.

Stopping in the ladies' room, she ran a comb through her hair and reapplied her pink lipstick. A glance in the mirror told her she looked her best, as always.

The maze of halls always confused her. She stopped to make sure she'd made the correct turn. Left, then three doors down. John's room.

Before opening the door, she drew in a deep breath and plastered a smile on her face. John liked to see her happy. And he'd want to know how Worthington Enterprises fared with her at the helm now. She'd fired

Mort and couldn't wait to tell John whom she'd hired in his place.

She gave the heavy door a shove and entered.

The blue shades were open, allowing the dreary gray day to seep inside. A fluorescent light behind and above John's bed couldn't dispel the gloomy atmosphere. She smelled Lysol and urine and wondered how in the world John stood it.

She sat down in the fake leather chair next to his bed and waited.

He must be in the bathroom, she thought, because his bed was empty. Actually, it looked like it hadn't even been slept in. The white sheets were smooth, their corners tucked under, sharp and crisp.

She went to the bathroom and knocked. Nothing.

Pushing the door aside, she peered from side to side.

Empty.

Her next thought caused her heart to pound in excitement.

Quickly she hurried out of the room to the nurses' station. Leaning over the counter, she looked down at the skinny nurse who'd ushered her out of John's room just days ago.

"Yes?" The woman looked up, her irritation at being disturbed evident in the scowl that creased her pale forehead. *Too bad,* Eve thought.

"I'd like to know where my husband is. He's not in his room."

"You don't know?" the nurse inquired.

Good God! Her heart gave another leap, and for a moment she thought she might faint.

Had the hospital tried to phone her? After all, she was his wife. A lawsuit loomed in the near future for this ramshackle excuse of a hospital.

"No one bothered to call me. And you can rest assured the director of this . . . this clinic will hear from my attorney before sunset." Eve forced her eyes to water and took a tissue from the box placed beside a vase of wilted chrysanthemums on the countertop.

"Ma'am, I'm sorry you're so upset. I thought you knew."

"Wouldn't you be upset if your husband passed away?" Evie asked. She started to weep, and became aware of several nurses and a few doctors staring at her. She blotted her eyes and blew into the tissue.

"Oh, no, Mrs. Worthington. Your husband

isn't dead." The woman stood up and walked to her side of the counter.

She led her to another group of horrid green plastic chairs. "Please, sit down."

Eve must have been stunned, for it took several minutes for the nurse's words to register.

"Your husband isn't dead."

Suddenly Eve stood up, all thoughts of crying cast aside. "What did you just say?"

"Mr. Worthington is fine. As a matter of fact, Dr. Foo was about to sign his release papers when Mr. Worthington requested he be relocated."

"Relocated? What do you mean, relocated?"

"He's asked the location not be given out. To anyone." The nurse smirked.

"What do you mean, for God's sake? I'm his wife." Shouting now, Eve didn't care that all who happened by were staring.

"Why don't you ask him yourself. Here he comes." The nurse looked down the hall at a tall form approaching. Eve watched as Adam Worthington strode toward them.

Eve rushed to him. "You bastard, what do you think you're doing?"

"Calm down, Eve. Let's go someplace

where we can talk." Adam's usual placating tone infuriated her. She'd not let him get away with this sort of treatment. She'd tell John as soon as she found out where he had been taken.

Adam pulled her inside John's former room and motioned for her to sit. She did. For once she wanted to hear what this hateful stepson of hers had to say.

"You'd better have a good explanation for this, Adam. I've never been so frightened in my life. That dreadful nurse told me John died. I'm going to call my attorney as soon as I leave here. I've never felt my heart pound so. You know, I'm not that young anymore either, Adam." She took a monogrammed handkerchief from her purse and blew into it.

"Stop it, Eve. Save the show for a new audience." Adam sat on his father's bed and stared at his stepmother. Eve was filled with an overwhelming desire to strike him.

"What are you talking about? One minute I think your father, my husband, for Pete's sake, is dead and the next you're jumping down my throat. I won't have it, Adam. I'm tired of it."

"You know exactly what I'm talking

about, Eve. And *I* won't tolerate it. My father is very ill at the moment, that's what concerns me."

"That nurse said Dr. Foo was ready to sign release papers. He can't be too ill if he was going to be discharged and moved at the same time."

"Well, sorry to burst your Cinderella bubble, but that nurse has no idea what she's talking about."

"And I suppose you do?" Eve snarled. He'd always been such a know-it-all.

"Yes. Dad's blood pressure continues to elevate at potentially dangerous levels. He can't afford to be upset. Knowing that certain people hold the power to do just that, he's asked to be moved to another hospital until his condition can be stabilized."

"You expect me to believe that? John would never do anything like this without telling me first. I know him too well."

Adam was trying to upset her. She wouldn't play his game.

"Maybe you don't know him as well as you think. Maybe you've mistaken him for someone you, ah, know a little better."

"What's that supposed to mean?"

"Figure it out. Here's the deal Eve. Take it

or leave it. Until Dad's condition improves—drastically—I'm the only one who knows where he's at. I'll keep you updated on his progress, give him any messages you have, but that's it. I don't see that it should matter to you anyway. With your trips to Atlanta and a big corporation bowing to your every command, I would think my father would be the last thing on your mind."

"God, Adam, you really are a spoiled little bastard. How can you say such mean things? Why I've been nothing but . . . accepting of you. I've tolerated your rudeness. And you know, years back, when you never even bothered to come home for a visit, it was I who consoled your father, Adam, me who he cried to at night."

Adam got off the bed and strolled to the door. "As I said, Eve, save it for a new audience."

He closed the door behind him, and Eve wished she'd struck him when the urge hit her. She would not allow him to run her life. He might think he had the upper hand now, but she knew better.

She'd had a stepson long before Adam came along. And she knew just exactly how to deal with them.

*   *   *

Jason Dewitt had spent the previous evening enjoying the luxuries provided by the Ritz-Carlton in Buckhead. He felt at home among the eighteenth-century antiques and the quiet elegance the Carlton was noted for.

He'd consumed a bottle of wine in the Lobby Lounge, and when he was called to dine in the hotel's noted dining room, he'd practically stumbled to his table.

In the morning, the bottle of wine that had gone down so smoothly the night before came up mixed with chunks of whatever it was he'd eaten.

He retched until he thought his insides would explode. Maybe he had food poisoning.

In the huge bathroom, he filled the white marble bath with hot water and climbed in. After sponging himself liberally with a sea sponge, courtesy of the Ritz, he dunked beneath the surface and almost felt human when he came up and leaned against the cool tiles. Definitely a bitch of a hangover.

Fleeing Savannah had been in his best interest. After serious thought, he'd decided a confrontation with Bentley wouldn't do. He'd needed more time to think and plan. It didn't hurt to know what he was up against. Yesterday when he saw Bentley coming out of Peachtree Center, he couldn't believe his good fortune.

When he inquired about an office in the building, the building's supervisor gave him Bentley's card, telling him he might rent the space he required.

Today all thoughts of renting office space were forgotten. His plans were taking shape. The staff at the house would know better than to ask him any questions; the Judge had trained them well. He'd contact Jo Ella, explain to her he'd be gone indefinitely. His patients could easily find another doctor to listen to their pathetic complaints.

He would fly to Brunswick and, if luck stayed with him, he'd put an end to the threat from Bentley.

Things were definitely looking up. He recalled his promise to the Judge.

Bentley recalled a time when the mere thought of spending a night alone in the dark dampness that surrounded him at present would've sent him scurrying for better accommodations.

When he'd stumbled on this room years ago, he hadn't given much thought to its use. Now he was glad he'd found it. Dozens of passages, winding in every direction, were located under the basement at Sanctuary. According to the history of Sanctuary, he knew these dark passageways were the former escape route for slaves hundreds of years ago. He smiled thinking of it. What excitement they must have felt, knowing all that prevented them from freedom were the walls of dirt that surrounded him.

A trip to the basement hadn't been unusual for Robert. The hospital stored broken equipment, boxes of old files, and just about anything they didn't dare throw away down there.

Robert had been exploring in the basement when he discovered a door guiding him farther into the damp earth. A crude wooden staircase led him straight down into the darkness. Using his butane lighter to guide him, he'd investigated the hidden tunnels. Afraid he would get lost, he'd hustled back toward the stairs.

That's when he located the room.

He would never have noticed it if it hadn't been for a piece of chain protruding from the wall. He'd stopped and pulled on it. The wall moved. He pushed harder. A door.

The room was as large as the entire basement above. The smell of dampness permeated the huge opening, and years of decaying animals scented the room. He'd covered his mouth with the sleeve of his shirt and viewed the area with a discerning eye. Someday he might have use for such a room.

Someday had arrived . . . a long time ago.

Norma couldn't find him there, the staff apparently had no idea what he'd discovered beneath the basement, and the people of Sweetwater, if they knew Sanctuary housed an escape route for what might have been some of their ancestors, hadn't spoken of it either. He smiled when he thought of all the crazies just two floors above him. *They'd love it down here.*

Over time, he'd furnished the room from the basement's store of discarded furniture. Though the pieces were crude, some broken—a chest of drawers missing a drawer or two—it had served his purpose. He even found a small cot and shoved it next to the wall to the left of the door. The dirt walls that provided safety from detection to those who'd inhabited them before continued to work their magic.

For him they provided what he'd needed more than anything.

A place to hide.

When he left Atlanta yesterday he hadn't planned on spending the night in the room. He'd entered his sacred ground without being noticed. When he received the call on his cell phone he'd decided it might be best to remain for the night.

Dewitt was nowhere to be found. Bentley had called the doctor's secretary again, and she still had no idea where he'd gone—only that he called and told her he'd be out of town indefinitely. And *she'd* been occupied elsewhere. Probably pulling the last of their plans together. Robert hoped she wouldn't fuck up as she had in the past.

They hadn't discussed those plans yesterday. He'd explained to her it was possible they could be overheard, and it was better to be safe than sorry. They would only discuss their plans at prearranged times. So far so good.

Things were falling into place, with the exception of Dewitt. But, Robert thought, he might not be a threat after all. He had only the good doctor's word that the Edwards woman talked. He could be bluffing. At this point in the game he just couldn't take that chance. He remembered the packet he had discreetly placed beneath the front seat of the rented Mercedes.

There was more where that came from.

Chapter Twenty-two

Casey took her usual morning shower before going downstairs. Shaded dreams and vague memories had kept her awake most of the night. Her eyes were heavy and her head throbbed.

Coffee. Flora always kept a fresh pot on the counter. A cup or two, and she'd be fine.

Hoping Blake had already called, she hurried down the stairs to the kitchen. Observing the unusual hustle and bustle, Casey wondered why the extra help had been hired and what was going on.

"Mornin', Missy." Flora looked up from her papers at the wooden table and motioned for Casey to sit down.

"Morning. What's all this?" She nodded at the four women surrounding Mabel.

"We're to do the afternoon tea for the

Married Ladies Club. There's about twenty-five ladies coming this afternoon. Your momma bein' the president and all, it's her turn to host the tea."

"I had no idea. Blake told me about the club, but I didn't know Mother belonged. I guess this must be a pretty big thing in Sweetwater."

"Oh, it is. If you belong to the Married Ladies Club you're somebody, that's for sure. The club's been around for more than a hundred years."

"Then I take it Mother will be here for the party?"

"She never misses a meeting. She'll be here."

"Is she still with John at the hospital?"

"As far as I know. By the way, that Marianne called again. She said to tell you she and Vera tore the attic apart down at the sheriff's office, and they haven't found what you were lookin' for."

"Somehow I knew they wouldn't. It doesn't matter, I guess."

"Is it the report you were lookin' to find, Casey?" Flora looked up from her notepad. Worry lines wrinkled her brow. "You know . . . of that day?"

"The one and only. I'm not relying on anyone's written word of what happened that night. I'm confident I'll remember everything that happened, given time."

The screen door slammed, causing Casey to jump. She turned around just in time to see Hank headed for his gardens.

"That man gives me the creeps," she said to Flora.

"Hank? He is a strange one."

"What's his story, Flora? How long has he worked at Swan House?"

"He came right after your momma and Mr. Worthington married. Your momma hired him cause she said he'd been head gardener to a duke or something. He does a fine job. I ain't never seen no weeds or dead flowers, I can tell you that much. He keeps to himself. He stays in that carriage house at the edge of the property." Flora looked at her. "Why the sudden interest in Hank? You thinkin' of takin' up gardening?"

Casey gave a curt laugh. "I might have at one time, but the day he drove me to the library, all thoughts of gardening blew right out the window."

"Why is that?"

"He sort of warned me. Told me Mother wouldn't be too happy if I stirred up trouble."

Flora laid her pen down, appearing to be in deep thought. "Strange. Can't imagine why he'd say somethin' like that. I wouldn't worry about him. He keeps to himself. Who knows what goes on in that head of his?" Flora smiled and returned to her menu, but her smile seemed forced, not reaching her eyes. Casey wondered if there was more to her position in the household than that of head housekeeper. She didn't know where the thought came from, just that it did.

The members of Swan House, both family and staff, continued to act strangely. All seemed to be hiding something and afraid to talk about it. She knew about Ronnie's murder now. Knew that she'd been committed to a mental institution for his death. Why there had been no trial continued to remain a mystery.

"Hey, you," Julie said as she slid into the chair next to her.

"Oh Julie. I'm glad you can take a break. I've wanted to spend time with you, but I've been out of sorts the past few days." Casey patted her friend's shoulder.

"I understand. I had two days off anyway. I heard your trip to Savannah didn't go very well."

"Word travels fast. Who told you that?" Casey hated being the subject of gossip.

Julie's round face turned a deep shade of red. "No one. I was about to leave when I realized I'd left my umbrella. The staff, we all have a place for our things in the closet off the side of the kitchen. There's a phone in there, too. That's when I heard him."

"Heard who?" Casey asked.

"Hank," Julie whispered. She looked behind her, making sure they weren't being overheard.

"Are you sure?" Casey whispered back.

Julie's head bobbed up and down.

Casey cleared her throat before speaking to Flora, who remained seated at the far end of the table.

"Flora, can I borrow Julie for a while? I need some help . . . upstairs. I really trashed the closet last night. Trying on clothes." She felt ashamed at the way the lies rolled off her tongue.

"I don't see why not. Julie, you're finished setting the tables?" Flora inquired.

"Yes, ma'am."

"Then go on up and see what a mess Casey made."

"Thanks, Flora. I'll be down later if you need me. What time do the society ladies arrive?" Casey asked.

"Four o'clock right on the dot. Now off with you two, I'm still tryin' to figure out a darned menu and only have a few hours to do it. Out!"

As they mounted the stairs Casey remembered Blake. Evidently he hadn't called, or Flora would have told her.

She led Julie to her room, thoughts of Blake put aside, at least for a while. He was never totally out of her mind. She didn't want him to be, either.

"I thought . . . you said?" Julie stammered as she surveyed the immaculate room.

"I know. I lied. Good grief, Julie, I'm a grown woman. I don't need help cleaning my room." Casey laughed and sank down on the bed.

"But, you said you'd made a mess."

"Forget it, Julie. Sit." Casey fluffed a pillow and moved over to make room for Julie.

"Why did you ask me up here?"

Casey could see the sudden fear in Julie's eyes and felt sorry that she'd lured her upstairs under false pretenses, but she didn't have any other choice.

"It's about Hank. I need to know exactly what he said. I simply didn't want our conversation overheard. For some reason, I don't trust him."

"Oh." Julie seemed nervous.

"What did you think I wanted, Julie?" Casey questioned, then it hit her like a ton of bricks.

Julie was afraid of her!

How could she be so stupid? While their new friendship hadn't been more than a quick conversation here and there, Casey thought they'd shared an easy camaraderie. Julie had even warned her about the evil in Swan House.

Julie sat on the edge of the bed, picking threads from her skirt.

"Look at me, Julie," Casey demanded. Sorry for her abruptness, yet wanting to set the record straight, Casey felt cruel and mean when she saw how frightened Julie appeared.

"Yes?"

She centered her gaze on Julie.

"Listen up, I'm only going to say this once. I don't know why you're afraid to be alone with me; I can't help that. But what I can tell you is I thought we could be friends. I hoped you would trust me. Whoever or whatever changed your mind, I'm sorry. I asked you up here so we could speak in private, Julie. I'm not the wild raving lunatic you might think I am."

She sat next to Julie and waited for her to respond.

"I'm not afraid of you, Casey. I've been warned, that's all. He said I'd lose my job if I became too friendly with you."

"Hank?"

Julie's brown head bobbed up and down. Casey handed her a tissue from a box on the night table.

"He said this to you when you caught him on the phone, didn't he?"

"Yes," Julie said. "He told me I'd better not talk to you. If I did, I'd be out of a job so fast it would make my head spin. I suddenly got scared when we were sitting at the table downstairs. He was watching me from the gardens. I could feel it."

"Forget about him. He can't fire you, I

promise. I'm going to speak to Mother about him. What do you mean, you felt him watching you?"

"With the back door open, you can look straight out into the garden. Though I didn't see him, I just felt him looking at me. Like a warning. He must know I'm up here with you. I just can't lose my job, Casey, it's all I have right now."

"Oh, Julie, you won't lose your job, I promise. We'll do something about Hank. I haven't cared for him since day one. He gives me chills."

Julie gave a slight laugh. "I know what you mean. But Casey, please promise me something."

"Name it."

"Please don't go to your mother. I'll handle this my own way."

After the way she'd just treated her only friend, Casey felt she should promise her anything. "As long as you know it's against my better judgment."

"Okay."

"Now that's settled, do you remember what you overheard? Hank must've said something he thought incriminating if he threatened you with your job."

"That's just it. I really didn't hear anything that I considered . . . gossipy or whatever you'd like to call it. He just said something to the effect, 'She didn't have the therapy, she appeared upset, and I'll do it the first chance I get.' "

While those words could've been interpreted as innocent by anyone else, Casey knew their hidden meaning, or at least part of it.

"Julie, remember when I sneaked out the other day? You came up to my room to bring tea?"

"Sure, why do you ask?" Julie's frightened look had been replaced by one of curiosity.

"I need you to think. Do you recall seeing Hank around that day?" Casey crossed her fingers, hoping her thoughts were leading her in the right direction.

"Actually I remember he told Miss Flora he had to go to Brunswick for supplies. The storm and all. I remember because he came to the kitchen, something he rarely does. It was like he wanted someone to know exactly where he would be. That isn't like him, or at least I don't think it is. Mabel mumbled something about it, I recall. So I guess it was a bit unusual for him to announce his where-abouts to the staff."

Casey decided to question Mabel later, when the party preparations were finished. "Did you see him when he returned?"

"No, I'd gone home by then. Maybe Flora saw him. She pretty much knows all that goes on in Swan House."

Which brought up the same question again. Flora's position.

"It appears that way. Tell me Julie, what do you think about Flora's place at Swan House? I can't help but feel there's more to the woman than meets the eye."

"You're absolutely right. Another taboo subject, though. It's rumored that Miss Flora is still in love with Mr. Worthington."

"Still?" Another puzzle, Casey thought.

"Supposedly Flora carried a torch for Mr. Worthington long before he married your mother. I guess even when the first Mrs. Worthington was alive. I know Flora was on very good terms with her, because Mrs. Worthington asked her to take care of Adam right before she died. She told me that herself."

That explains a lot. Is that why Flora hadn't married? Had she secretly hoped when the first Mrs. Worthington passed away there might've been a chance with her boss?

"She told me that a few days ago, too. I'll talk to her; maybe she can shed some light on Hank. And Julie"—Casey leveled her gaze on her friend's round face—"please don't be afraid to talk to me. That's what friends are for."

"Thank you. You've been so kind. Now"—Julie stood and walked to the door—"no matter what Flora said, I know she could use an extra hand right now. I'll get back to work and leave you with your thoughts."

"I'll be down in a few minutes myself. Make sure there's something I can do. Something easy." Casey laughed, recalling her last experience in the kitchen.

"Sure thing." Julie left, quietly closing the door behind her.

The threads of her past were beginning to unravel. Thinking her amnesia impenetrable had been a mistake.

So many hints at something sinister! And she'd begun to piece them together. Then there was Ronnie. Though she recalled him raping her dozens of times, she couldn't call up the fear, the anger, and the hate that should've been directed at him. It was almost as if it had happened to someone else, and she just knew about it. Why?

And now this. Hank, Flora, and Julie, all with secrets of their own. The hushed conversations. Again, why?

She needed to talk to Blake, ask him what he knew about Hank. The more she thought about it, the more she thought Hank had been her attacker on the porch of her old house. What could possibly motivate him to harm her?

Too many questions with too few answers, Casey thought. She'd talk to Mabel and Flora. Maybe if her mother didn't have to hurry back to Worthington Enterprises after her party, she'd give her a few minutes, too.

Her mother continued to puzzle her. It had been years since they'd had a normal relationship, and Casey felt she should make more of an effort to spend time with her, to get to know her again. But then, she mused, maybe she'd never known her at all.

She hurried downstairs to assist Flora and Julie with the preparations for the late-afternoon tea. She wondered briefly about Brenda. Somehow she knew the bitter woman would do just about anything to trade places with her. Would she seduce Blake? Possibly manage to get herself pregnant?

Casey stopped when she reached the bottom step.

Why her thoughts had taken such a drastic turn, she'd no idea. Blake cared about her. He'd told her so.

These silly insecurities were just that. Silly.

But then, things had a way of happening even when you thought you had control over your own destiny.

She knew because it had happened to her when she planned her trip to Atlanta, all those years ago. While she'd made a decision that would affect the outcome of her life, circumstances had taken the decision away from her. While she'd finally achieved the end result as planned, evidently she'd had no control over the manner in which it had happened.

Casey entered the festive atmosphere in the kitchen, hoping to dispel her sudden gloomy thoughts. With fresh bread baking, mouthwatering scents simmering in a pot on the huge industrial-sized stove, and the soft giggles of the kitchen help, she couldn't help but pick up on the lighthearted attitude of those around her.

"Well, well, if it isn't the Merry-Mess-Maker herself. You get all cleaned up, Casey?" Flora questioned.

"Yes. Thanks to Julie." Casey looked at her friend, who was scrubbing new baby potatoes at the sink. Julie smiled, their secret safe.

Casey scanned the huge room in search of Mabel and saw her busy at her workstation at the far end of the kitchen.

Casey walked over to Mabel, who looked up from her kneading. Flour dotted the cook's chin, and white flecks of dough peppered her white hair, reminding Casey of snowflakes.

Mabel told Casey what she wanted to know before she even asked.

"I ain't never liked that man since he came here. I told young Julie he's got a mean spirit about him. He came into the kitchen all high-and-mighty announcing his trip to Brunswick. In all the years I been working here, I ain't never seen or heard him tell anyone other than your momma or the Mister his whereabouts. I thought him up to something, that I'll tell ya."

Mabel's lengthy speech surprised Casey.

"Thank you, Mabel. You've answered my question." Casey patted the woman on the arm and wondered if Julie had told her of their earlier conversation.

So, she was right about Hank.

Casey decided to wait before continuing with her questions since Flora and Julie were both busy.

Julie motioned her to the sink where pots and pans were stacked in piles. "You wanted something easy," Julie said, laughing.

"Yes, I believe I did." Casey immersed her hands in the hot soapy dishwater and found the domestic chore therapeutic. She gazed out the window at the meticulously cared-for grounds and wondered if Hank was watching her. She almost wished he was. That way he could see that his attempt to harm her hadn't worked. Maybe he'd just wanted her quiet while he searched the house on Back Bay. That stumped her. As far as she knew, other than the book bag Sheriff Parker gave her and the blood-spattered mattress, there wasn't anything worth finding.

The shrill ringing of the telephone caused her heart to race.

"Casey, for you," Flora said.

Anticipating Blake's call, she dried her hands on a dish towel and took the portable phone from Flora.

"Blake?" she said, hearing the sigh of relief in her own voice. "Hello? Blake is that you?" Casey waited for the sound of his warm voice to reach her. She pushed the phone closer to her ear, thinking they might have a bad connection. "Is anyone there?"

About to hang the phone up, the unexpected sound she heard caused her to hold the phone away from her ear.

A baby crying. Certain that someone had simply dialed the wrong number, Casey spoke into the phone, "Whoever this is, you've reached the Worthington residence."

The cries were louder now.

Casey looked to Flora, who stood by, watching her.

Suddenly the crying stopped.

At first Casey could barely hear the voice. Then it became louder. A child?

Casey strained to hear the youthful voice.

The words were painfully clear when she heard them.

"Why did you kill me, Mommy?"

Chapter Twenty-three

Finished with his last patient, Blake still couldn't quite believe his conversation with the sheriff the night before. Both he and Adam were angry at Parker for his actions, or rather, Blake thought, lack of action. Even though he told Parker he'd understood where he was coming from, it still didn't explain what *really* happened the day Ronald Edwards died.

And this morning, when he'd been going through the last of his father's files, he'd stumbled upon another revelation that might explain Casey's reason for committing murder.

If his father's dates were accurate, and Blake had no reason to doubt them, Casey made her final visit to his father's office on the last day of Ronnie's life.

The puzzle still lacked the main pieces, but Blake knew the parts he held were the clue to the entire picture. Now it was just a matter of putting them together. When he did, it would only be a matter of placing each piece in its rightful place, as in a real puzzle.

And Bentley had the missing piece, he knew it. He'd been at the house on Back Bay the day of the murder. Why? The son of a bitch still couldn't be found. Blake had tried his number last night, after he'd returned from his talk with the sheriff, but there had been no answer. He'd tried again in the morning, and he'd tried him at Sanctuary. He'd even called Norma. She'd told him he'd gone to Atlanta on business and wasn't sure when he'd return. Blake knew she only repeated the lies that Bentley told her.

He'd put in another call to Macklin, hoping to find him so he could shed some light on the situation. After all, he had been Casey's psychiatrist for ten years. He'd learned from Macklin's housekeeper that the doctor had relocated somewhere in Europe and wouldn't return for his things for several weeks. The housekeeper assured Blake if the doctor called to check in, as he was apt to do on occasion, she'd be sure and give him Blake's message.

Blake held the flimsy white sheet of paper with his father's scrawled handwriting.

Six weeks pregnant.

Blake didn't know who the father was, but he had an idea, and the mere thought of it made him want to kill.

He'd arranged to meet Adam in Brunswick later in the day. Maybe with the two of them together, they'd come up with four. He needed to call Casey. He promised her he'd call last night. After leaving the sheriff's office, he'd been so angry he knew he needed to calm down before talking to her. At the moment he felt anything but calm, but he wanted to talk to the woman he loved, just to reassure himself she was all right.

Flora answered on the third ring.

"Hey, girl, I hope to hell you're busy making that pecan pie I like so much," Blake paused, waiting for the little woman's comeback.

"C'mon Flora, cat got your tongue?"

"Mr. Blake, things ain't lookin' too good here right now."

"What happened, Flora? Is Casey there?

Let me speak to her. Is she all right?" He spoke fast, not giving Flora a chance to answer.

"Calm down, Blake. She's fine, jus' had a bit of a scare is all. Someone on the phone. She's upstairs restin'. You want me to have her call you?" Flora asked.

"No, don't bother. I'm on my way."

"You don't . . ."

He didn't give her the chance to finish. He slammed the phone down and hurried to his car, thoughts of anything else on hold. Something had happened to Casey, and that's all that concerned him.

He arrived at Swan House in less than ten minutes. Dave, the guard, must've seen his car because the electronic gates were opening as he sped uphill. He honked the horn as he passed through.

Blake didn't bother to park; he left his BMW parked haphazardly at an angle in front of the house.

Flora greeted him at the door. "Up here." He followed her upstairs.

She knocked on Casey's door and Blake heard a weak "Come in" from Casey.

When he saw her, he knew he would've killed for her. Her green eyes were red-rimmed, and purple-blue shadows rested beneath them. She was wan and pale. Blake forgot his feelings as the doctor part of him took over. He stood next to the bed, taking her hand in his. Her pulse was normal.

"Oh, Blake, did Flora tell you to come?" Casey reclined against a pile of pillows. She looked lost and confused as she stared up at him. They say there is a moment in a man's life when he knows he's met the right woman, the one who makes his heart stand still, the one who takes him to heights of passion he only imagines, the one who holds his heart in her hand. Right then Blake knew Casey was that woman. Even though he'd never made love to her, even though she might not want him the way he wanted her, it didn't matter. What did matter was that he loved her and would stop at nothing to protect her.

He watched her as she observed him. "Blake, you're scaring me. What's wrong?"

Blake got ahold of himself and answered her. "I think I should be asking you that. Flora told me you had a scare."

"It was nothing, really. I can't believe you'd come all the way out here because of a prank call. It's the middle of the afternoon, you've probably got a roomful of sick people waiting." Blake saw through her. He knew what she was trying to do because he did it so often himself. She was trying to make light of a serious situation. He'd done the same thing for her the other day in Dewitt's office.

"Stop, Casey, you know why I'm here. Flora said you'd had a scare. Want to tell me about it?" Tension-filled eyes stared back at him.

"Not really," she said.

"You don't have a choice in the matter." Blake knew the tone he used sounded gruff, but he couldn't help it. He needed to know what happened so he could do something about it.

She looked at him with fear in her eyes, and Blake wanted to kill the bastard who'd put it there.

"Someone playing a sick prank, nothing more. It just . . . reminded me of something."

"Go on," he prompted.

"That's all there is to it, Blake. Isn't that enough?" she explained, her voice rising.

"No, it's not. Casey, I only want to help you, and I can't if you're not being totally honest with me."

"The voice on the phone." She paused. "It sounded like a young child."

Relief washed over him. She was right. *A child's prank, thank God.*

"Why did this upset you so? Kids do this sort of thing all the time."

She sat up straighter, her tension-filled eyes wide as saucers. "I know that. It's what they said that frightened me. The voice sounded like it came through a tunnel or something. I've thought about it and now I believe someone pretended to sound like a child. It had to be because . . . well it just had to be."

Casey got up and walked over to the window. Several minutes passed while she seemed to be contemplating the rest of her story. "Blake, the person on the phone . . ." She paused again. ". . . they said . . . oh hell, they said, 'Why did you kill me, Mommy?' "

Blake felt the air being sucked out of his lungs by an unseen force and took a deep breath before answering. "Jesus. This has to stop. Come here." She practically ran to him and he took her in his arms. Her head rested on his shoulder. She cried softly, all pretense of bravery gone. He smoothed her short curls and mentally plotted the slow, agonizing death of her tormentor.

Casey lifted her tear-streaked face up to him. "I don't understand this, Blake. None of it. I lie awake at night trying so hard to remember it actually hurts. Some things come easily and others, I don't know if I'll ever remember, but this"—she released herself from his hold and sat down on the bed—"this . . . what if what this caller says is true?"

Blake sat next to her and placed an arm around her. "No, Casey, it isn't true. You're no more a killer than I am." He caught his mistake before she had a chance to comment on it. "You know what I mean. You could never harm a child."

She gave a wry laugh. "Maybe you don't know me as well as you'd like to think."

"This morning I went through the last of Dad's files, clearing everything out. I came across something you should know. Hell, I think maybe you already do. The day of Ronnie's death you visited Dad at his office."

"I know, Blake. I know all about it." Casey sounded defeated.

"Then you know you were six weeks pregnant?" he queried.

"Yes, Blake. And I remember what I did to my unborn child. I really am a monster!" Casey clenched and unclenched her fists. Tears rolled down her cheeks, and again he reached for her.

"No!" she shouted, and walked to the closet. Seconds later she returned, carrying a purse. "This is what I did to my child." She shoved a faded business card in his hand. The words were barely legible, but he managed to read them.

He tossed the card on the bed. "You actually believe you had an abortion at this clinic?"

Hysterical laughter bubbled from her. "Well, damn Blake! It doesn't take a frigging medical degree to figure it out. I remember finding the card in front of Haygood's on my way home from your father's office. I remember thinking it had to be some kind of omen. I came home, made a phone call and well . . . I can't seem to recall much more than that. I'd be an idiot to think otherwise, Blake." She slumped down on the bed.

"You're wrong. I told you I found your medical records, the most recent ones. And Casey, you did not have an abortion."

He realized he had said the wrong words when Casey bolted upright on the bed. "Then where is my baby? Is that another reason I was institutionalized? Did I kill my child, too?" She was hysterical, and Blake knew he had to let her cry it out. She wouldn't hear anything he told her until she calmed down.

Blake eased her back onto the bed. Leaning against the headboard he cradled her in his arms like a child. Her cries finally dwindled to soft whimpers. He waited for her to speak.

"I've ruined your shirt with my mascara." She leaned over and grabbed a tissue from the night table.

She could ruin his entire wardrobe as far as he was concerned. "I don't give a shit about my clothes."

"You should, I guess," she said halfheartedly.

"Casey, I need to finish what I was telling you before . . ."

". . . I started bawling like a baby? Go ahead."

"You never gave birth to a child. You never had an abortion." He drew in a deep breath before continuing. "The night you were in jail you had suffered a miscarriage. My father took care of you."

She was cold. Except down there. A liq-uid warmth. The woman removed her damp warmth and replaced it with something dry and thick.

"Casey, are you all right?" Blake questioned. He didn't like the blank look he saw on her face.

She moved her head from side to side and looked at him as if it were the first time she'd ever laid eyes on him.

When she finally spoke her voice was hushed. "I remember."

"What do you remember, Casey? My father?"

She pushed herself off the bed and went back to stare out the window. "I can't seem to place him. Things were fuzzy that night. I remember two women taking care of me. I had hemorrhaged. Blake, who were the two women at the jail that night?"

"Probably Cora and Vera."

"They were so cruel to me. I remember them changing my . . . I guess they cleaned me up after *the miscarriage.*"

"Doc Hunter says she'll sleep for a while. I hope whatever he gave her will knock her for a loop. My God, I've never seen anything like it."

"Yeah, well jus' wait till you see the boy, then say that. A person should never have to see what we saw out there tonight. And that poor mother. She's lost both of her young 'uns. As much as I hate to say it, this one here ought to burn in hell."

"Earth to Casey? Hello?"

"You're right, Blake. Cora and Vera were at the jail. They were talking about me, saying I should burn in hell. How did they manage to . . . to see the body?"

"Hell, the entire town was there, according to the sheriff. I don't think anyone closed their eyes when they brought Ronnie's . . . You get the picture."

"Only too clearly. Maybe this memory loss thing isn't such a bad idea after all. I remember finding out I was pregnant, Blake. I wanted to die. Just absolutely die. I've racked my brain trying to think who the father could be, and I can't seem to recall a boyfriend, a casual date, anything. Then, I have this other vision, and it scares me to death."

"Tell me, Casey," he coaxed.

"This sounds insane, even to me. Could it be possible that Robert Bentley fathered my child?"

Chapter Twenty-four

Jason Dewitt registered at the Days Inn in Brunswick because he didn't have time to locate better accommodations. He wanted to get the nasty job over with as soon as possible so he could return to Atlanta, where he planned to relocate his practice. He hoped Jo Ella would come with him. He'd arrange for her family to move if that's what it took. Discreetly, of course. His passion had almost ruined him once.

Almost.

Which reminded him of his reason for coming to the smelly town.

Robert Bentley.

He'd inquired about a trip to Sweetwater, telling the hotel clerk he only wanted to spend the evening. She'd given him a copy of the ferry's schedule. He pulled it out of his pocket as he reclined on the worn, faded purple bedspread.

Nine o'clock was the next-to-last trip to Sweetwater. The last return was scheduled for midnight. He still had a few hours to kill. He'd have lunch, visit the local mall, then rest. He wanted to be at his best that night.

Midnight.

Midnight seemed fitting for death. He liked the darkness, the anonymity it provided. It had been dark when Amy came to him. She'd told him Dr. Macklin thought she'd be able to come home in time. Said the doctor told her she could live a normal life.

They'd spent the evening making love—celebrating, he'd told her. He'd roughed her up a bit even though he knew she didn't like it. She never complained. Just kept coming back for more.

As they'd dressed she'd had a look about her. At the time he couldn't place what it was, only that she seemed different. Glowing. Radiant.

When it was time for her to return to Mercy, she hadn't wanted to leave. She'd clung to him in desperation. He'd pushed her away and she fell, hitting her head against the sharp edge of the coffee table. She reached behind her and rubbed her head; blood covered her palm as she waved it around.

God, she was crazy, but so beautiful!

She'd continued to look at her bloody hand. Then Jason knew the woman who'd been diagnosed as a paranoid schizophrenic was just that.

She started screaming hysterically, telling him he hurt her. Said her daddy would kill him. Nobody was allowed to hurt daddy's baby.

Then she'd stopped.

The Amy he knew and lusted after returned. She sat on the bed with her arms wrapped around her and swayed side to side like a little girl rocking her doll.

She smiled at him, and he'd never forget her next words. "I've got a secret."

Humoring her, he'd asked her what it was. When she told him, he lost all ability to think, to reason and rationalize.

He'd placed his hands around that beautiful neck of hers and squeezed until he felt the last gasp of air pass between her lips.

Then he'd cried like a baby and called the Judge. He neglected to tell him how aroused he'd become with his hands around Amy's neck.

The Judge said no way would a Dewitt father a black child. He told Jason he would have done the same thing himself. And then, as usual, the Judge took care of everything.

Since then, everything had been perfect . . . until Bentley came along, threatening to expose his dirty little secret. He wouldn't let that happen. Promises were promises.

Blake made his way downstairs, giving Casey a few minutes of privacy to shower and change for the party.

She slipped into a cool white linen shift and chose a pair of silver sandals from the many boxes in the closet. A slim silver chain embedded with emerald stones went around her neck, and tiny emerald studs glistened in her ears. Not wanting to overdo it for an afternoon tea, Casey observed herself in the mirror before going downstairs. Evie would approve. Understated, yet classy.

Where in the hell did that come from? Probably something she'd heard her mother repeat.

Still somewhat shaken from her bout of hysterics, she silently promised herself to enjoy the afternoon and forget about her unborn child and all it implied. Who knew, maybe she would join the Married Ladies Club one day. She laughed. Somehow she didn't see herself socializing in that manner.

"Well, well, don't you look like a future applicant," Blake said as he guided her through the dining room to the kitchen, where the hub of activity continued.

"Future applicant?" Casey teased. She knew exactly what he referred to, but needed this lighthearted sparring, which had become a habit with both of them.

"Don't tell me you haven't dreamed of belonging for years. I thought you and Brenda . . ." Blake let his words trail off.

"Hush! You'll let my secret out, then the entire island will know!"

"Look at you two, I swear, can't keep your hands off one another!" Flora winked at them as she passed through to the dining room.

Casey stepped out of Blake's embrace and followed her. "Flora, can I help? You've worked so hard, it looks absolutely perfect." Casey observed the dining room. The large table had been removed. In its place were ten small tables, each set for five, each covered with pale pink tablecloths. Pink roses surrounded by fresh greenery, Hank's handiwork, no doubt, served as centerpieces. Delicate china plates with swans encircling the rim, along with cream-colored linen napkins and sterling silver, completed each setting. A name card resided at the top of each plate.

Flora scanned the room, her experienced eye possibly searching for anything out of place. "Thanks and no, Missy, I think it's as good as it gets. Don't you go messin' around and gettin' that pretty white dress dirty. Your momma will have a fit. She should be here any minute. She likes to inspect each place setting before the guests arrive."

"I'm sure she'll see it's perfect. Relax." Casey led Flora back to the kitchen, where Blake and Julie were seated at the oak table sipping coffee.

"Sit," Casey commanded, and poured a cup of the hot brew for herself and one for Flora. "Drink this."

"You sure as sin got bossy all of a sudden, Missy. I need to change, won't do for me to embarrass Mrs. Worthington. You all stay right where you are until it's time, you hear?" Flora took one last sip of her coffee and disappeared down the hall to her room.

"Jeez, you'd think this was the inaugural ball or something," Casey said.

"To Flora it is. It's really all on her shoulders," Blake said, serious now.

"What do you mean?" Casey questioned.

Julie spoke for him. "If the tea is a flop, instead of your mother taking the fall, the help gets blamed."

"I see." She didn't, but couldn't imagine how the success of an afternoon tea party could be of any importance.

Julie spoke again. "If the party flops, we all lose our jobs, Casey."

"You can't be serious?" Casey looked to Blake.

He didn't laugh. "She's right, that's why it's so important, in the Married Ladies Club, to have the best of everything. I told you these women take this seriously."

"I guess they do. How often does Mother host the tea?" Casey asked Blake.

He turned to Julie, who was becoming quite the talker. "With as many members as they have now, each has to host the event at least once every two years."

"That's it?" Casey said, refilling her cup.

"Doesn't seem like a lot, but you don't know these women, Casey. Flora says they're treacherous," Julie said.

"If they're that bad, why does anyone even care to belong to such a club?"

"Just the status, Casey. Nothing more. Like I said, lonely women with nothing better to do with their time or their husbands' hard-earned money."

"I can't believe Mother would even asso-ciate with women like that," Casey said to no one in particular.

Julie and Blake looked at her, then Blake spoke. "We never know as much as we think about people, Casey, even those we're closest to."

Casey wanted to ask him what he meant, but Flora chose that moment to enter the kitchen wearing a light blue dress that matched her eyes and clung to a figure that Casey had no idea existed. No longer were her white curls confined in her usual tight bun. She'd expertly shaped her hair into a stunning French twist. A light dusting of cos-metics, earth-toned eye shadow, mascara, and a touch of lipstick and Flora no longer looked like Flora the housekeeper. She looked like Flora, a sophisticated lady of the manor and at least ten years younger. *Regal,* Casey thought.

"Well quit standin' there with your mouth hangin' open. You'll drool all over that pretty white dress."

Blake whistled. Casey and Julie both grinned from ear to ear. "Flora, you look absolutely stunning. Why if one didn't know better they'd think you were . . ." Casey didn't get to finish what she was going to say because Evie paraded into the kitchen, and all conversation came to a halt.

If Flora looked like a lady of the manor, then her mother looked like queen of the castle in a pale peach Chanel suit.

". . . what, dear?" Evie asked Casey.

It took several minutes for Casey to realize her mother actually waited for her to answer. "We were just saying how Flora could pass for lady of the manor." Casey suddenly felt shy around her mother.

Her mother shot a glance in Flora's direction. "And we all know that will never happen, don't we?"

"You never know," Casey couldn't help saying.

"Yes, dear, I do know. Now Flora"—Evie scanned the housekeeper from head to toe—"you might want to put on an apron. I'm not sure, but I don't think Kmart accepts returns covered with food stains."

"Mother!" Casey exclaimed at the way her mother treated her friend.

"Yes, Casey?" Evie asked sweetly.

"Casey, your hair looks a mess, go on upstairs and run a comb through it. Hurry, now, don't keep your momma waiting," Flora said, before following Evie to the dining room, leaving Casey to stare after the two of them.

"I can't believe this! How can you two sit back and allow Flora to be belittled like that?" Casey plopped down in the chair, her cup still in her hand sending coffee spilling over the rim, a spot landing on the hem of her dress.

Julie hurried to the sink and came back with a damp cloth, trying to blot at the stain. "Quit it, Julie, for Pete's sake. I don't give a good shit if this dress is ruined or not. Blake?" He hadn't uttered a single word. Casey had the distinct impression he would rather be anyplace but here in the kitchen at Swan House.

"She's right, Julie. Who gives a good shit about that dress. Evie'll just buy her another one." He sounded angry. He stood up, shoving his hands in his pockets. *Figures,* Casey thought.

"I'm supposed to meet Adam this evening. Do you think you'll be able to manage here without me for a few hours?"

Casey realized he was referring to her mother. Maybe he thought they wouldn't get along. "I'll be fine. You're angry, and I don't blame you. I apologize for my mother. I don't know why she's acting this way."

"I do. She's having one of her so-called spells. That's what she'd like you to believe, or at least that will be her excuse later. Stress, the party, I've seen it before. Frankly, Casey, I think your mother delights in tormenting Flora."

Casey knew she should defend her mother, but Blake was right. She'd treated Flora like dirt, and no matter what kind of "spell" she had, her behavior was inexcusable.

"I don't know what to say."

"It's not your fault, Casey. Enjoy the party.

I hear the best things about these little get-togethers is the powder room gossip." He pulled her close for a quick hug and planted a kiss on the tip of her nose.

"I wouldn't know. Blake, will you . . . will you call me later?" She hated to ask, but she needed him. More than she thought possible.

"Better yet, I'll come back tonight. We can take a midnight stroll through the gardens."

"I'll look forward to it." She hoped Hank would make himself scarce. He was the last person she wanted to see.

"Later." Blake gave her one last kiss. She could hear him shouting his good-byes to Flora and her mother in the dining room. Her mother didn't bother to respond.

If she smiled one more time her face would crack and shatter into a million pieces. Her return home being the topic of conversation, she had a turn with each and every one of her mother's guests.

The ladies oohhed and aahhed over Flora's luncheon. Said they'd never had anything like her forest mushroom strudel with roasted shallot sauce, that Flora really knew her way around the kitchen. The meal was a success and the employees of Swan House could thank Flora for their continued employment.

Casey excused herself while her mother shook hands with the last group of ladies. Headed for the kitchen to help Julie with the cleanup, Casey stopped in her tracks when one of her mother's guests blocked her path. Not wanting to appear rude, she stood aside, thinking the woman might want to go into the kitchen.

"I heard you came out of hiding. I must say," the tall, thin woman said while inspecting Casey as if she were a bug, "you don't look too bad considering the drugs Robert pumped into you."

She took a step back. She didn't remember her mother introducing her to this woman. "Who are you?"

"Your mother never bothered introducing us. Though I'm not surprised. I'm Mrs. Robert Bentley. She can be such a bitch."

"Don't you dare . . ." Casey blurted.

"Stop pretending, Casey. This entire island knows about you, your mother, and good old Robert. They all agree with me,

too. They think she's a piece of trash. They
only come here because of John. Why don't
you ask your mother about Robert? Ask her
about Worthington Enterprises."

For once her mother came to her rescue.
"Norma, don't you have a bottle to visit? Or
possibly your relatives down at the stables
are in need of their afternoon snack of oats?
You know Casey." Her mother looked at her,
then rested her icy glare on Norma. "Ever
heard how animals sometimes resembles
their owner? Why I do believe you and Trig-
ger could pass for twins."

"Mother!"

"Fuck you, Eve," Norma shouted, before
wobbling to the front door. "And leave
Robert alone, you hear!" She slammed the
heavy wooden door behind her. Casey
stood in the dining room waiting for her
mother to offer an explanation for the
woman's behavior.

"It's been fun, Casey, but I've got an appointment. Tell Flora the next time the cream
sauce has another lump, she's history." She
gave her a quick air kiss, patted her head
like a dog, and left the room.

Casey knew her mouth was hanging
open. That was *it?* A guest had just told her

mother "fuck you," and her mother said nothing? And why did Robert Bentley's wife hate her mother so?

This family of hers confused her more as the minutes wore on. Returning to the kitchen, she lost herself in the cleanup. If she didn't keep busy, she would go mad.

She careened uphill at breakneck speed, not caring that she was drunk, not caring that her Mercedes was all over the road. Norma Bentley knew she'd made an ass out of herself in front of Eve Worthington's daughter and didn't care. The vodka she'd consumed, along with that disgusting spiked punch, had given her the courage she'd been lacking for more than twenty years.

Did they really think she didn't know about them? Robert really was stupid. She should have listened to her father and married someone in the same class as the Fulton family. Even though the Bentleys had money and a small name on the island, Norma realized, after it was already too late, that Robert had married her for her money and nothing more. Though thanks to good ol' Daddy's last will and testament, Robert hadn't been able to touch her inheritance. And he'd been pissed at her ever since.

Sanctuary was on her way home. She'd stop and visit him. She knew he was there. He'd gone to Atlanta, but returned yesterday and spent the night in that god-awful hole in the ground. She knew all about his hiding place. She knew everything about Robert. She even knew the last time he fucked Eve Worthington on their little ferry ride. Quite by accident, she'd actually been a passenger that day. She'd seen the two of them together and followed them. They'd stood on the top deck near the bow, and Robert had fucked Eve quick and hard. Something he never did to her anymore.

Today she could practically feel the whispers, the jeers, the crude comments coming from the members of the Married Ladies Club. She'd never felt such humiliation in her life. And for what? She laughed hysterically and answered herself. "So Robert could get his hands on that bitch's money!"

She looked up into her rearview mirror just in time to see Eve Worthington's black BMW gaining on her. Norma tromped down on the accelerator, leaving Eve Worthington behind in a cloud of dust. She looked in her side mirror, expecting to see Eve trying to catch up, but apparently the bitch wasn't following her. Probably on her way to visit poor John and tell him what a horrid day she'd had.

Norma knew what really happened that night ten years ago. Norma wished Eve had died that night.

It was time to have that little talk with Robert.

Eve had never been so angry in her life. When she saw Norma Bentley's tail lights, for a moment she wanted to crash into her, but common sense took over. Now was not the time to lose her head.

She'd been assured by Adam that John's needs were being taken care of at the nursing home. She'd also been assured that she would be in control of Worthington Enterprises when she'd made a trip to see her attorney that afternoon. He promised her it would be a breeze to have John declared mentally incompetent. At first she'd been upset when Adam told her he'd moved her husband, but after talking to her attorney, she realized that unbeknown to Adam, he'd done her a favor.

She smiled. Norma turned in front of her, apparently headed for Sanctuary in search of Robert. Speaking of whom, he hadn't called her with their final plan. A side stop at Sanctuary was definitely in order. She slowed down, letting Norma move on. The charcoal Mercedes disappeared like a mist. Eve turned the engine off. She needed to think. Let Norma spend some quality time with Robert. It just might be their last afternoon together.

Jason Dewitt brushed imaginary dust from his black Levi's. He couldn't figure out why he felt such rage over a pair of pants. They made him itch. The black sweat shirt he'd purchased at the Gap stank with his sweat.

After lunch at the Krystal, he'd gone to the Brunswick Town Center and purchased the outfit he now wore. It wouldn't do for him to be seen wearing his usual Brooks Brothers suit and Calvin Klein shirt. He'd bet not too many people in this hellhole knew what a decent suit of clothes looked like.

Still, he wanted to fit in. The men his age at the mall all seemed either to have the Levi's logo stamped to their ass, or the Gap slapped across their chest. He'd gone to Champ's and purchased a black hip sack to hold his necessities. The vial of LSD-25 so graciously provided by Bentley rested firmly against his belly.

The Sweetwater ferry delivered him to the island at nine-thirty sharp. Passengers were allowed to disembark before the vehicles, and Jason immersed himself in the crowd of people descending the wooden planks. He looked around him. The passengers all seemed to be in a hurry. No one seemed to notice him. Just what he wanted. Inside the ferry's so-called snack bar he'd inquired about transportation once he reached Sweetwater. The clerk told him unless he had someone waiting, he'd best put on his walking shoes, because Sweetwater didn't offer a taxi service, and public transportation was unheard of.

Jason didn't mind the walk. The ferry provided free maps of the island, with all the landmarks noted. He made a quick stop at a pay phone, where he thumbed through the island's forty-page telephone directory to find the addresses he needed to make his trip a success.

Jason made short work of the two miles to the Fulton estate. The place looked abandoned. White columns, three stories high with dark shutters. The word *unkempt* came to mind. There were no welcoming lights to be seen. He leaned against an electric-powered gate to catch his breath. Unless he jumped the fence, there was no way he could get to the front door. He looked around the huge expanse of lawn, hoping to see a plain gate, anything allowing him entrance.

He hadn't considered this. Obviously, Plan B needed to be activated.

Sanctuary. Bentley worked there. His house was dark as night, which probably meant he was still working.

He had to stop the son of a bitch because he couldn't even think straight anymore. He'd swallowed three Valium before leaving his hotel in Brunswick. Now, he wished he hadn't. His head felt fuzzy, and his eyes were out of focus. He shook out the map one last time and took a penlight from his hip pack. The narrow beam of light showed Sanctuary to his north. A mile at most.

Jason folded the map and tucked it inside his pocket. Taking a deep breath, he jogged about half a mile before the effects of the Valium sent him searching for a place to rest. He looked into the black night and saw the headlights of an oncoming car. The light from the vehicle's high beams blinded him as he hit the ground. The car didn't stop. It wavered from side to side, as if the driver were drunk. Jason hurled his body to the side of the road without a second to spare.

Roland Parker felt like a new man. The weight of the world had been lifted from his broad shoulders. The previous night, for the first time in years, he'd actually gone to sleep without the aid of a six-pack.

Confessing to Blake and Adam had cleared his conscience. And now, with the elder Worthington in possible danger, the good Lord had provided him with another chance to redeem himself in the eyes of the two men whose opinion of his policing skills had always been lacking. Not that it hadn't been warranted.

They'd talked long into the night. Parker's former suspicions of what really happened ten years earlier were rekindled with new sorts of possibilities after Blake and Adam left his office.

He'd always assumed Eve Worthington and Robert Bentley were involved somehow. Now it made sense why Robert had been there the night of Ronald's death. Apparently Eve had called him when she'd walked into Casey's room and caught Ronnie in action.

By the time he'd arrived Casey had wandered into the hall, positioning herself in the corner like a frightened child. Her mind had already shut down on her by then, the horror of what she'd done too much for a frightened young girl to deal with.

He thumbed through a stack of Post-its on his desk.

Vera had left a note on his desk, telling him she and Marianne searched the attic and still hadn't found the report he'd filed years ago.

Parker didn't need it. He'd kept the original in a safe place for ten years. Until the night before he hadn't told anyone of its existence. Both Blake and Adam now held copies. Just in case.

He'd never realized what it was that both-

ered him so much that night until he returned to the house on Back Bay for another
look at the crime scene. Time, too many
lookyloos, and Eve's movers had removed
most of the evidence, but the most incriminating thing of all had been left behind.
Mocking, Parker thought, *daring to be discovered.* The bloodstained mattress. Something about the blood spatters continued to
nag at him. Parker knew he'd have to consider reopening the case. A late-night call to
Walter Watts in Atlanta, head of the GBI's
Crime Analysis Unit, known as CAU, set the
wheels in motion. Parker hated to ask for
outside help, thinking it made him appear
inept, but pride was a foolish thing. A man's
life and a young woman's sanity depended
on him. While he waited to hear from his old
buddy, he recalled the scene in Casey's
bedroom, right after he'd upchucked all over
the place.

*After Robert Bentley handed him a hand-
kerchief to wipe the vomit from his face,
Parker looked back at the lifeless body on
the bed and tried to think. Remember you're
an officer of the law. Follow procedure.*

*"Mr. Bentley, I'll need to ask you some
questions," Parker said, his voice quivering.*

He took a small black notebook from his breast pocket and flipped it open to a fresh page.

Bentley walked around the bloody bedroom, stopping to stand by Eve, who'd managed to recover from her shock. "Now, now, Roland. You can see what happened here. It sure doesn't need explaining."

"I'm not . . . uh askin' you to explain, Mr. Bentley. I need to know what you were doin' here, you know, did you see anything?" God, this wasn't easy. He wished he'd gone to work at the carpet mill in Ellajay.

Bentley ushered Eve out of the room and returned seconds later.

"Now, son, I think we both know what happened here. But I'll explain it to you, for the record."

"Uh, sir, could we go downstairs?" Parker couldn't spend another minute in the blood-spattered room or he'd puke again.

"Sure, son, whatever you say."

Seated in the front parlor, Roland searched the room for Eve and didn't see her.

Bentley sat on the sofa; Parker seated himself next to him.

"Miss Eve called me. Said something ter-

rible had taken place and could I come over. 'Well, of course,' I told her. You know her being alone and all, I thought it my duty." Bentley lit a Pall Mall and blew a thick gust of smoke out of his nostrils.

"How did Mrs. Bentley feel about you bein' called out in the middle of the night? By a single woman." Parker hated to say it out loud, but knew he had to. Procedure and all.

"Well, Lord, son, Norma understands. She would've come with me, but I didn't want her traipsing all over the island at night." Bentley took another deep drag on his cigarette and walked to the front door.

Parker followed him and wondered briefly why Miss Eve had called Bentley before calling him.

The lawn was filled with the local townspeople. Vera, his dispatcher, stood on the front lawn with her sister Cora, who tried to shove the small gathering back, telling them to go home. Parker shook his head and led Bentley back to the sofa, closing the door behind him.

Thinking it might be best if he put in a call to Grady, he asked Bentley if he knew where the telephone was.

"Who are you going to call, Sheriff? The Lone Ranger? This is your town; it's up to you to protect the innocent citizens of Sweetwater. Not only from harm, but from speculation."

"What are you talking about?"

"Just think. Miss Eve. Isn't she engaged to John Worthington. The John Worthington?" Bentley asked.

"I suppose I've heard that around town a time or two. But what's that got to do with anything?"

"Everything. You know how her family suffered after Buzz died in that damned car crash. The poor woman hasn't been given a break in this lifetime. And now, Mr. John Worthington, distinguished gentleman, prominent businessman, wants to marry her." Bentley sounded envious.

"I don't get it, Mr. Bentley. What I do get is this: I've got a dead body upstairs growing colder by the minute, a young girl and her mother in shock. Miss Eve's social standing is the least of my worries."

"Then listen. A young girl kills her stepbrother after, mind you, after he's raped her. Repeatedly. I know, Sheriff, her momma knows, and I'm sure you do. What the young

girl did up there was nothing more than a favor for some other innocent girl. The state, too. And you ask just what Mr. John Worthington has to do with this." He paused long enough to reach into his immaculate white shirt pocket for another cigarette.

"Go on," Parker urged.

"If he chose, why he could have this case all over every paper in the South, and the television, too. I bet with his clout he could even get on the Today show."

"And what's that mean to me?" Parker asked.

"What it means, son, is he'd have every law enforcement agency this side of the Mason-Dixon Line up your ass. You'd be out in the cold like a snowman on Christmas in Alaska."

"Bentley, why don't you just come out and say what you want. I ain't in no mood for games. Like I said, I got a body up there." He nodded in the direction of the stairs.

"I'm just trying to protect the ladies, that's all. And you."

"Then talk fast, cause I've got to call Doc Hunter down here to view the body since he's acting coroner." Parker's hands were shaking. Hell, maybe Bentley was on to *something. But he wondered why the man was so concerned. Did he and Miss Eve . . . ? No, she was engaged.*

"Actually, what we've got here is a clear case of self-defense. Casey plunged the letter opener into her stepbrother's throat because he raped her. According to Miss Eve, they'd had a scuffle in the shed earlier. Casey attacked him with a garden spike. He must've followed her to her room. It's simple son, really. All you need to do is fill out the necessary paperwork and put this behind you. Then Miss Edwards and her daughter can go on with their lives."

Parker thought about it. Bentley had a point. Ronnie had always been an evil little son of a bitch anyway.

"What about the girl? I saw her upstairs. I might not be nothing more than a country sheriff, but I know shock when I see it, and that girl's definitely in shock."

"I thought of that, too." Bentley's voice rose in excitement.

Parker wondered if there was anything he hadn't thought of.

"As director of Sanctuary I have the authority to admit the girl. We'll have one of our staff psychiatrists evaluate her. She'd be free

to remain in the care and comfort provided by Sanctuary as long as needed. Free of charge."

"I don't know Bentley. Ain't that breaking the law or something?"

"Of course not. As I said, we'd, you'd be doing the fine state of Georgia a tremendous service, never mind the money you could save the taxpayers. Actually, Parker, you could be a true hero for this. I'm sure when Casey recovers she'd feel indebted to you. If you know what I mean." Bentley laughed.

"God, how can you laugh at a time like this? I don't know. It ain't right." Parker paced the room, sweat dampening his armpits.

"Then let me ask you this, son. Would it be right to send poor Casey to the Georgia State Women's Penitentiary? I've heard those women are worse than some of the most hardened criminals. Why they'd probably do far worse to the young girl than what crazy Ronnie ever did. I'd just hate to see the girl go to prison, that's all." Bentley stood, shoved his hands in his pockets, and went to the kitchen, where Eve waited.

Parker thought about all he said. And he

was right. Casey didn't deserve to go to prison for killing Ronnie.

He went to the kitchen in search of Bentley.

"Where do I start?" Parker asked, his voice weak and unsure.

Robert Bentley's eyes lit up, reminding him of the evil glint carved in the eye of the pumpkin he'd seen on the front porch.

He whispered to Eve before leaving the kitchen. Parker watched him. Something about the guy gave him the willies, but he'd think about that later. Now he needed his help so Casey wouldn't go to prison, and Miss Eve wouldn't die of shock.

"Listen to me, son." Bentley took a pack of cigarettes from his pocket, found it empty, and tossed the crumpled package on the coffee table before speaking.

Parker wished like hell the man would stop calling him son. He wasn't old enough to be his father.

"You write your report. You'll say something like this: Vera received a call from Miss Eve, who was in hysterics. Make sure to put that in there somewhere. Write down what you did. You went upstairs, saw Casey with the letter opener, wearing those blood-

stained clothes. Put in there Casey told you Ronnie raped her and wanted to kill her. That's important, son, get that in there. Just in case."

Parker stopped writing and looked at Bentley. "In case of what?"

"Anything. This has to look like self-defense."

"But I thought you said it was self-defense? Isn't that why I'm writing this bogus report? To save the ladies from I think the word you used was speculation."

"The report isn't bogus, son. Why you can see for yourself the girl's been ravaged. She must've snapped. Eve said something to me when I arrived. Add this to your report, too. She said something told her this isn't the first time this happened to Casey."

"Good God, Bentley! Why in the hell hasn't she reported it? Why is the bastard still in this house?" Parker shouted.

"Shhh, you'll frighten those poor women more than they are already."

"Sorry. I can't understand if her mother thought someone was messin' with her, why in hell didn't she do something about it?"

"She didn't say she knew for sure, Parker. I don't think she's in her right mind just now. I'm sure nothing like this happened to the girl before. Forget about it, don't put that in your report. Her mother wouldn't tolerate it; it has to be Eve's imagination. You know shock and all."

"I've got to get the . . . body out of here. I'll call Doc Hunter."

Bentley grabbed him by the sleeve as he stood to go to the kitchen to make the call. "Don't do that!" Robert demanded. "He's the last person we need in on this."

"He's the coroner until next month. I have to call him." Parker looked at Bentley's hand on his sleeve and pushed it away.

"All right, but listen up. Whatever you do don't call him until that body is . . . is bagged. Doc Hunter's getting too old for this. I wouldn't want him to have a heart attack. You know, seeing what's upstairs."

Parker agreed. He didn't want to be responsible for the old doctor's death. He could barely stand the sight himself, and he was supposed to be somewhat immune to it all.

Right.

"Then let's do it." Parker inhaled, bracing himself for the sight upstairs. He remembered reading about the Tate murders and all the blood and wondered if they were comparable. Casey's bedroom looked like a slaughterhouse.

"You work on the report while I"—Bentley's evil glare rolled up toward the ceiling— "get him ready."

Parker nodded, sick to his stomach. Everything he'd learned, right down the tube. He could go to jail for tampering with a crime scene. Then he remembered Casey. That poor girl hadn't made a sound in the last fifteen minutes. He tossed his notebook on the table and went to the top of the staircase. She remained huddled in the corner, only now she was shaking uncontrollably. Parker took his windbreaker off, placing it around her thin shoulders. He felt a twinge of satisfaction. The bastard deserved what he'd got.

"Casey," he whispered. Nothing. Her eyes were glassy and huge. She looked at him, and Parker knew she didn't see him.

"C'mon, hon, let's get you out of here." Parker helped Casey into a standing position, and, with his arms around her for sup-

port, they went downstairs. She paused when they reached the landing.

Knowing now wasn't the time to question her, he adjusted the large windbreaker around her shoulders and led her out the front door.

Buddy Barrenton from the Sweetwater Sentinel *greeted them with the flash of his camera.*

"Everyone stand back. And Buddy, get that camera out of here!"

Parker lifted Casey in his arms and took her to his cruiser, not caring that half of Sweetwater watched him. He refused to lock her in the backseat like a caged animal. He opened the car door and gently positioned her in the passenger seat.

"Vera! Get down to the jail. Now!" he shouted over his shoulder.

And he'd left that son of a bitch Bentley to clean up the mess. He knew now that after he left, Bentley sent for two orderlies, who came in an ambulance provided by Sanctuary. They removed Ronnie's body, taking him over to the funeral parlor. They never discussed that day again. For several weeks there'd been questions. He explained to everyone in authority the version he and Bentley agreed on. After a while the talk died down, but the suspicion remained.

Now with the help of Walter Watts and the two docs, Parker was about to stir up trouble. He knew all hell was about to break loose.

Chapter Twenty-five

Casey paced back and forth in her room. She wished she could have stayed downstairs with Julie and Flora, but Julie had to go home, and Flora wanted to go to bed early. So here she was, alone, walking up and down her bedroom, wringing her hands.

The scarlet numbers on the bedside clock glared at her. Ten o'clock. Blake promised he'd come back after his visit with Adam. Her heart raced at the thought of their planned midnight stroll.

She sat down on the bed and tried to relax, but couldn't. She felt uneasy, as if something was about to happen—something she had no control over. She wondered if her stepfather had already died. She did her best to drive the thought out of her mind.

Her mother remained a mystery to her. Her treatment of Flora was shocking. When Casey tried to apologize to Flora, Flora brushed it off by saying her momma was ill and she needed to keep that in mind. Which brought up another entire line of questions. If her mother was so ill, how could she possibly operate Worthington Enterprises? What did *ill* mean to Flora?

And Ronnie? Now, she remembered him all too clearly. When she tried to ward off the flood of memories, she was unsuccessful. They came on fast, like a movie reel and they were so very vivid and so very real . . . again, now . . .

After school or maybe after going to see Doc, she was leaving. If that didn't work out, she would leave after dark when they were all asleep. She was going to Atlanta. She had a copy of the bus schedule in her top drawer. She'd get a job, maybe as a waitress or cashier at Walmart. When she'd saved enough money she would go to college. She would take care of herself and never have to worry about being hurt again.

She'd tried to tell her mother about Ronnie, but she was always busy and didn't want to listen. Her mother never had time for

*her. She was either running over to Mr. Wor-
thington's or off with that creep Mr. Bentley.
She didn't understand how her mother
could stand the man, or why they were even
friends. He was as crazy as the patients at
the nuthouse he worked in.*

*She thought about the "other thing" as
she now referred to it. She would take care
of that, too. No one would ever have to
know. Doc Hunter would help her. No matter
what, she would keep her appointment with
him.*

*She'd miss Flora, but she would send her
letters and maybe once she found a place
and got settled in, Flora could come for a
visit. Sometimes she thought Flora knew exactly what went on in the house, especially
after her humiliating visit to Dr. Hunter's office when she was nine.*

*That had been the first time. God, she'd
wanted to die! Her mother was off on one of
her "dates." She'd been lying on her bed
reading her favorite author, Carolyn Keene. It
was hot, and she'd taken off her pants. All
she wore were her new pink panties that
read "Friday" and an oversized T-shirt with a
faded picture of Elvis across the front, a
hand-me-down from Flora.*

At first when he'd peeked in her room, she ignored him. After several minutes she'd put her book down and sat up on her bed.

"I know you're out there spyin' on me Ronnie. You jus' leave me alone, ya hear?" She shouted at the door, knowing he lurked right behind it.

He laughed at her. "Uh, no Miss Nose-in-Book I cain't hear ya." He laughed again, but this time he opened the door and peered into her room.

"Get out Ron!" Casey said. She never understood why someone his age wasn't out hangin' with the guys. He was too weird, and he made her nervous. She hadn't ever warmed up to her stepbrother the way Momma had.

"Well, now look at you." His beady eyes raked her over, and Casey wished she'd kept her jeans on. She tucked her legs beneath her, thankful for the large shirt that covered her bottom and thighs.

He kept staring at her, his eyes glassy. She suddenly felt afraid. Ronnie looked different, and his breathing was funny. He walked closer to the bed and looked down at her. Inching her way against the wall, she wanted to scream for Momma, but remembered she'd gone out.

"What's a matter, girl? You don't like Ronnie here in your room?" He sat next to her on the bed.

For the first time in her nine years, Casey knew what it was like to experience real, honest-to-goodness fear.

"Get out, Ronnie, or I'm gonna tell Momma when she gets back."

"Do you think Momma gives a crap, Casey girl? Why hell no. You know what your momma's doing about right now?" Ronnie leaned right in her face. His breath smelled like onions, and she held her breath to keep from gagging.

"Your momma's gettin' fucked by Mr. Bentley." Ronnie threw his head back and laughed. "Ever wonder what that's like, Casey girl?" He stood up and unbuckled his belt.

Hot tears rolled down her face. She squeezed her eyes shut and prayed she would disappear, prayed Ronnie would just get out of her room and leave her alone, prayed her momma would come home from her date and send Ronnie back to those people who never wanted him in the first place.

The swoosh sound of his zipper made her heart pound. She didn't need to open her eyes to know the soft thud she heard on the floor was his britches landing in a pile. She didn't need to open her eyes to know he was lying beside her. She didn't need to open her eyes to know what the hand that reached for the elastic on her new Friday panties was about to do. And she didn't need to sneak a quick peek at momma's True Story magazines to know what Ronnie was doing with his penis.

Jesus Lord! All those years ago, and she'd never told anyone about that day. And now nine years later it was finally coming to an end. Tonight. No more hiding in the closets, no more nights spent lying awake in terror while she waited for him to come to her room.

Never again.

She heard Momma come in probably from another date with Mr. Worthington. No, it was too early. Once Momma had taken her to that huge mansion and made her wait outside while she visited with Mr. Worthington. She never could understand why she wasn't allowed inside. Casey didn't think it was Mr. Worthington that didn't want her in-

side, but her mother. But who cared anyway. She was leaving tomorrow.

She heard voices downstairs and cracked open the door to hear them.

"You ain't nothin' but a whore, Eve. I know what you're up to. And it ain't gonna happen. You ain't gonna leave here to take care of that slut upstairs. No, ma'am, Miss High-and-Mighty, it ain't a gonna happen," Ronnie screeched.

"Why don't you just shut up! You're too old to be living here in the first place. I practically had to beg John to give you a job at the paper mill. I heard you left today. Why, Ronald? What more do you want from me?"

Ronnie's wicked laugh traveled up the stairs. "You know what I want. I want what you been givin' to Bentley and Worthington."

Casey heard a crash as something was hurled to the floor. "Listen," her mother's voice was dead calm, "I know what you've been doing all these years. Don't think for a minute I don't."

Suddenly Casey's heart slammed into her rib cage so hard she thought it would explode.

Her mother knew! And she'd done nothing!

Casey opened the door wider. "Yeah, old woman, I know you knew about me 'n' Casey girl. And I'm thinkin' while you laid in that there bed of yours you jus' mighta liked hearing us." Ronnie laughed again.

He was insane, Casey thought. And maybe her mother was, too.

Ronnie's next words caused her to bolt upright in her bed. She listened.

"You know she went to visit Doc Hunter today?"

"Who told you that?" her mother asked.

"I didn't have to be told. I followed her. Hell, I sat right in that dumb doctor's office and listened at the top of the stairs. She was knocked up, all right. I was thinkin' of runnin' over to Swan House, before she stabbed me. I thought ol' John might want to know what kinda woman he'd be marryin'." Another hysterical laugh from her demented brother.

"You wouldn't dare!" her mother shrieked.

"Oh, yes I would. Yes, I would. Matter a fact, I been thinkin' about limpin' over there later. Maybe tomorrow morning. After me 'n' Casey, well, you know tonight." Casey heard the back door slam and took a deep breath, hoping to calm her pounding pulse.

It couldn't possibly be true. Her mother would never let Ronnie get away with what he'd done. She was sure he'd been bluffing. He had to be bluffing because if he wasn't, it didn't bear thinking about.

Her hands trembled. Angry tears poured violently down her face. This wasn't a dream. This was real.

So many questions answered in a matter of minutes.

Her recollection of Ronnie made her sick. She ran to the bathroom and emptied her stomach until she thought she would die. Standing in front of the same mirror that only days ago revealed a woman so different frightened her. Then she'd had no conception of the misery she'd endured at the hands of her brother. She'd looked forward to resuming her relationship with her mother. Now, however, the mere thought of being in the same room with her made her want to throw up again.

All those times Ronnie came to her room, and her mother knew about it! What kind of woman was she?

And that evening, the one she thought of

as her last trip to hell. The evening Ronnie came to her room for the last time.

The shrill ringing of the telephone made her jump. She reached for the receiver next to her bed.

"Hello," she murmured.

"Casey?"

"Oh, Blake, thank God it's you! I've . . . you can't imagine . . ." She couldn't continue. How could she tell Blake about the horror she'd gone through?

"I'm pulling through the gates as we speak. I was calling to tell you to meet me in the gardens. Think you can do that?" Blake's calming voice reassured her.

She cleared her throat before speaking. "Sure."

"Hang on, sweet, I'll be there in seconds."

Casey placed the phone in the cradle and went to the bathroom to wash her face and brush her teeth.

She hurried downstairs through the kitchen and out the back door. She'd no more seated herself on the bottom step when she felt Blake pull her into his arms.

"What happened? And why are you trembling, Casey? What happened, sweetie? Come on, out with it."

"I remembered. That day. That night." Casey sobbed.

"Shhh, it's okay. You don't have to talk about it if you don't want to. Just relax." He pulled her onto his lap and rocked her as if she were a child.

Several minutes passed before she felt strong enough to get off Blake's comforting lap. Blowing her nose on the washcloth she didn't remember bringing downstairs, she turned to Blake.

She looked up into the darkened sky. Pale clouds swirled like mist around the moon, making the sky appear as if it were moving at a high rate of speed. Sort of like her life. Crickets and bullfrogs could be heard singing their throaty tunes. She remembered their gravelly calls from another time and shivered even though the humidity was thick, the temperature warm.

"I remember the evening Ronnie came to my room. When he died. And all the other nights, too. And the pregnancy. The miscarriage was a blessing." She walked to the edge of the long wooden porch, distancing herself from Blake. Right now she wanted space.

"Casey . . ."

"It's all right. I'm handling it. There are things, Blake. Oh my God! Maybe I can't go on! I'm so confused. I remember it so vividly. But then everything turns black. Blake"— she jammed a hand through her hair as she paced the length of the porch—"for the life of me I can't remember . . . killing Ronnie. I must've blacked out."

"It's in the past, Casey. Adam and I met with the sheriff this afternoon after I left the party. There's something you should know. It might explain why you can't remember killing your stepbrother." Blake sounded almost . . . sinister.

She turned to him. "Why? What is it? You sound strange."

The feeling that something was about to happen settled in her bones like a chill.

"Sit down, Casey," Blake ordered.

She did as she was told.

"Sheriff Parker has contacted a friend of his at the GBI's Criminal Analysis Unit. Seems he's got several unanswered questions about the night Ronnie died. He wants an expert's opinion."

"He does? But, why? Lilah and everyone else said he was in charge that night. Why would he question himself now?"

"He's always questioned what happened that night. If you think you're up to it, I'll tell you what the sheriff spent a good part of last night and this afternoon confessing to me and Adam."

"I'm not sure I'll ever be 'up to' anything again, but tell me anyway," she said.

"Let's take that stroll I promised you earlier."

Hand in hand they strolled through the fragrant gardens of Swan House. Honeysuckle, night-blooming jasmine, and Hank's famous roses scented the moist air. Casey wished she hadn't remembered that fateful evening ten years earlier because in gaining her memory she'd lost a mother. Blake's voice droned on, and she couldn't quite make out his words.

"Casey? Have you heard anything I've said?" Blake asked.

"No."

"I said Sheriff Parker thinks something is fishy about the . . . bloodstains on the mattress. His friend from CAU is on his way from Atlanta as we speak to analyze the spatters."

"What does it mean?"

"It means there is some doubt about your

mother and Robert Bentley's story of what actually happened that night. Enough doubt to investigate."

Casey's heart leapt at the possibility. "What kind of doubt, Blake?"

"If what Parker says is true, and I've no reason to dispute him, he thinks someone murdered Ronnie, not that you killed him in self-defense."

Casey stopped in the middle of the stone path that led to the fountain she'd viewed just days ago. The soft trickle of water sounded like a waterfall gushing in her ears.

"Then . . . I'm not . . . Oh, Blake do you know what this means? My God! It's . . . I didn't kill him!" The joy she felt couldn't be put into words. There had always been that nagging doubt. Now she was about to find out if it was justified. Then as fast as it came it left. If she wasn't responsible for taking the life of her stepbrother, who had spent nine years of his life tormenting and raping her, then that meant there was a murderer still out there somewhere. A killer who'd never paid for his or her crime.

They walked to the edge of the property, stopping once to share a kiss. Casey warmed at the direction her relationship with

Blake was taking. Among all the turmoil and confusion she felt, the one thing that remained as clear and pure as the water that flowed from the fountain was her feeling for this wonderful, kind man who'd spent the last few days bringing light and spurts of happiness into her otherwise bleak and frightening life.

They headed back in the direction of the porch, both lost in thought. Casey saw the small carriage house at the edge of the gardens and asked Blake about it.

"Hank lives there. He has ever since your mother hired him. I think it was right after she and John married."

"I don't like him. The other day when I sneaked off to my old house, the day you patched me up"—she touched the three small stitches at her temple—"he was there. Sheriff Parker told you I'd been hit by a shutter blowing in the storm, but I knew better. I didn't get hit by a shutter, Blake."

"What are you saying?"

"I'm saying someone hit me. Just as I put my hand on the screen door to open it, I heard a noise. It was raining so hard you could barely hear, but I heard someone coming up behind me. About the time I turned, I'd already been hit and he ran away, but not before I caught a glimpse of him."

"Did you tell the sheriff? Casey, there's a good possibility a murderer is still lurking on this island. You should have told us. You could have been killed!" He grabbed her and pulled her to him.

"It was him." She nodded in the direction of the carriage house.

"Hank?"

"Yes, Hank," Casey replied.

Blake released his hold on her. "I'll kill him, Casey. I swear to God I'll kill him!"

He raced toward the carriage house, leaving her staring at his retreating back. She ran after him, hoping to stop him from doing something they'd both regret. Her tainted past was enough. They didn't need another death to cloud their future.

"Blake, no!" She screamed.

He came from around the back of the small carriage house shaking his head. "The son of a bitch is gone!"

Thank God she'd caught him before he did anything he'd live to regret. "Blake, it doesn't matter. Please don't do anything when he comes back. I don't think I could bear it if something were to happen to you."

"Don't worry, Casey, I'm not likely to kill the bastard. He's packed all his things, lock, stock, and barrel. He's long gone."

"What does it mean?"

"I think it means good old Hank wanted to get out of Dodge before you recalled what you just told me."

"Blake." Anxiety coated her every word. "Is it possible Hank had something to do with Ronnie's death?"

"I don't think so. As soon as Parker's buddy rolls in, we'll know. And as soon as that happens, the sheriff will more than likely have enough evidence to make an arrest."

If he found any evidence, Casey wanted to add.

"But why would Hank want to hurt me?"

"I'm just guessing, but I'd say someone asked, or rather paid him to keep you quiet. And I think we both know who it is."

"It always comes back to the same person, doesn't it?"

"Seems old Bentley's days as a free man are numbered."

Chapter Twenty-six

Jason Dewitt stumbled onto the darkened porch and slumped into one of the white wicker chairs placed casually around a matching table. He gasped when he realized how close he'd come to getting killed by a crazed driver. The Valium he'd popped earlier had knocked him out, and he'd slept for two hours on the side of the road, in a ditch. He'd misplaced his map and wandered around the island in a frantic state, finally winding up on the front porch of Dr. Blake Hunter's house. Somewhere along the way, he'd also lost the contents of his hip pack. When he screwed up, he screwed up royally.

The drugs he knew he would find inside, the legal drugs, would be traced back to Dr. Hunter. By then he would be back on the ferry, returning to the horrid little hotel in Brunswick. Bentley would never utter a single word again. By noon he could be back in Atlanta in search of a new office.

Perfect.

He jiggled the front door handle. Locked, just as it should be. Now, all he had to do was figure out a way to get inside. He looked around the front porch, hoping to find something to jimmy the antique lock.

About to give up, and head around to the back, he stopped short when he realized he didn't need a tool to pick the lock. A giant clay pot filled with geraniums rested in the corner of the porch. People kept keys under flowerpots. That's when he felt something hard jabbed into his back.

He dropped the pot. Dirt, flowers, and chunks of clay flew in all directions.

"Who the hell are you?" He didn't move but only because he was frozen with fear.

"I said, who in the hell are you?"

Think fast, motherfucker, think fast!

Suddenly, he wanted to cry. The damn Valium slowed his thinking and his reflexes, too. Spinning around like a top off center, he lashed out at the owner of the gun. Not fast enough, he thought as he felt a fist smashing into his jaw. He slumped to the floor and moaned.

"Now," the voice above him came again, "I'm gonna give you one more chance to tell me what the hell you're doing here on the doc's porch this time of night."

"Sick . . ." He really *was* sick. He touched his cheek and knew it would be black-and-blue in a matter of minutes.

"Then why didn't you say something? Jesus Christ! C'mere." Jason felt himself being hoisted into the air.

The hulking figure dropped him in the chair.

Seated in the same wicker chair where he'd planned his break-in a few minutes before, he sat there trying to imagine a terrible illness that would bring him out to this godforsaken hole in the middle of the night. He was a doctor himself, so that didn't look too good. He'd worry about that when the time came.

"Now." The man seated himself in the chair across from him. "I can't leave you here in this condition. I'm gonna take you over to Memorial and have you checked out."

"Uh . . . no, I'm fine really." Jason struggled to his feet. "I guess it was something I ate." He patted his stomach, then doubled over for effect. "It'll pass."

"No, I'm not going to leave you here. I hit you, so that makes me responsible for your well-being. The doctors at the hospital are just as good as Dr. Blake."

Jason wobbled when he stood, and knew it was now or never. He had to make a run for it. He leapt down the porch steps as fast as he could, but he wasn't fast enough. He cursed the Valium a second time as the hulk grabbed him from behind, yanking his arms in a painful grip while he locked a pair of handcuffs securely in place.

"Let's go."

Jesus, Holy Mary, Mother of God! It was finally closing in on him.

Norma Bentley tossed the empty bottle of vodka on the floor. For the last three hours the images had continued to swim before her eyes. She sat up in bed, tugging at the skirt that inched up around her waist. She pulled it off, throwing it on the floor along-side the vodka bottle. Her panty hose were ripped to shreds. She tossed them on top of the skirt. She ripped her blouse off, sending mother-of-pearl buttons bouncing onto the floor. She still had one shoe. Somewhere along the way she'd lost the other one.

A shoe. Oh, yes. It was *her* shoe she'd found in the back of Robert's closet yesterday. The girl's. When she'd asked Robert about it tonight, he'd acted like he didn't know what she was talking about.

How much did you have to drink at the luncheon, Norma? Robert asked.

"Not nearly enough." She walked around his office, opening and closing drawers, thumbing through his files. "Where'd you put 'em?" Her voice slurred.

"Put what, Norma? I've got work to do. You need to get home. I'll have Becky drive you." He punched the small black box on his desk.

Norma stumbled over to his desk and swept her hand across its immaculate surface, sending the contraption to the floor.

"Listen to me, Robert! For fucking once I wish you would just listen!"

"I hate it when you use foul language, Norma. It's unbecoming to a lady."

"Do you really think I care what you think Robert? Really? And since when did you be-

come an authority on what constitutes a lady? Tell me, Robert." Norma plopped down in the stuffed chair across from Robert's desk and tossed her high-heeled pumps at him, just missing him by inches.

"The shoe," Norma bellowed.

"I have no idea what you're talking about. As I said, I've got work to do. Now, either you can let Becky drive you home or risk being picked up for drunkenness by Sheriff Parker. The choice is yours."

"That's what I love about you most, Robert. Your fucking compassion, consideration, and general good-fucking-hearted-ness. Most husbands would drive their wives home if they were in my condition." She released a loud burp, then smacked her lips.

"My God, Norma you sound like a rooting hog. You disgust me." Robert straightened a pile of papers she'd messed up.

"You still haven't answered my question."

"And that was?"

"Save the smart tone for someone you're trying to impress, Robert. I caught on to your game years ago."

Robert looked up from his pile of papers, hate etched all over his face. "Then why

*have you stayed, Norma? Tell me. Appar-
ently I've made you miserable."*

*"It sure as hell hasn't been for the sex.
You never had enough left over for me. That
bitch sucked you dry. Literally." She laughed
at herself. "You really don't know, do you
Robert?"*

*"This is getting very tiresome, Norma.
What is it you think I don't know?"*

"About Daddy's will."

*"You've tossed your inheritance in my
face for years, you and those stuffed shirts
your father called attorneys. You can stop
now Norma. I no longer care about your
money."*

*"Yes, I know, you have the Worthington
money, or you will as soon as the old man
dies. I heard you talking on the phone to
Eve. I heard her tell you he'd recently
changed his will, leaving his fortune to her.
Most of it anyway."*

*Robert's face turned a bright shade of
red. "Think twice before you do that again,
Norma. My business with Mrs. Worthington
has nothing to do with you."*

*"I'm well aware of that, and truly I don't
give a damn, Robert. You can have her. But I
still want to know why you have the shoe.*

The shoe I saw Marianne pick up the day that girl, uh . . . fell in the street. After the car nudged her." Norma saw Robert's intake of breath, and she knew she had him. For a minute at least.

"Marianne wanted me to give it to Eve to return to Casey."

"That's good. Chalk one up for Robbie. Remember when I used to call you that? You know what Robert? I've always secretly admired you. You've pretended for years to be something you're not and done a damned good job of it. Let me ask you this, Robert, the proverbial question: What did she have that I didn't?" Norma angrily wiped a tear from her face.

He drew in another deep breath. "Truly, you really want to know?"

"I asked, didn't I?"

"Yes, you did. And I'm about to tell you. It's really quite simple, every man's desire. She loved me. Me. Not anything I had, she didn't have anything to gain, she simply loved me."

That wasn't the answer she'd expected. Nor did she believe for one minute it was the truth, but it didn't matter. Robert's days were numbered anyway.

"Then thank her for me."

"Certainly."

"One more thing, then I'll leave. Did it ever occur to you uh . . . What did we refer to them the other day as?" She paused to think. "Oh, I remember now. Your 'indiscretions.' Did you ever consider how you and all the whores of Sweetwater were humiliating me?"

"Come off it, Norma. You could not have cared less about that. You never wanted to sleep with me. I'm a man, I have needs. Did you actually think I could live with you, knowing you were frigid? I'll admit I had an interest in your money. At first. Then I grew to care for you. Every time I would try to make love to you, you would banish me from our room for weeks. After a while I couldn't take it anymore. As I said, a man has needs."

"While we're laying our cards on the table, Robert, why don't you tell me what really happened that night you ran to her house claiming you were helping the sheriff."

"You know what happened." He walked over to his file cabinet and returned the files he'd been reorganizing.

"You're right. I do. Another case of me snooping."

"You really amaze me, Norma. Now that we've shared all our secrets, would you consider leaving so I can get this mess you've made cleaned up? Then, maybe I can finish my work. I've a hospital to run, Norma, or have you forgotten?"

It would never matter what she said. He'd always do what he wanted, to whom he wanted, when he wanted. He'd spent the last twenty years humiliating her. The household staff that once respected her now looked at her with pity. Sly glances were cast her way the few times they'd gone to The Oaks. She wondered how many of the female members he'd slept with.

She knew, she knew what they were planning. And she wasn't about to let him have the last laugh. Not in this lifetime.

It all came back to Daddy's will.

While he'd provided for her and several generations to come, there'd been a stipulation in her father's will that only she and her father's attorney's were aware of. Daddy hadn't wanted to bring shame on the Fulton name. He'd spent his entire life reminding her where they came from, how far back they could trace their ancestry. She'd been a good daughter. Her mother died when she was six, leaving her in the strict hands of her father and a houseful of help. And she'd turned out to be a good girl; she really had.

She was a virgin when she and Robert married, and she really tried to enjoy that part of her marriage, but couldn't. Robert was right. She was frigid. She could live with that. Hell, she could live with his mistresses and the humiliation.

What she couldn't live with was divorce.

She knew he and Eve Worthington planned to marry as soon as John died. She'd even thought Robert might try to kill her.

"Norma!" Robert shouted.

"Okay, okay." She stood up, searched for her shoes. Finding only one, she crammed her foot inside and reached for her handbag on Robert's desk. God, if he only knew!

"Just one more thing, Robert, and I'll drive myself home. Really, I'm fine." She couldn't wait to see the look on his face.

He was losing patience with her, she knew, but this time she had no reason to care. She had nothing to lose.

"Daddy was a fine man, Robert. You know how I respected him. Sometimes he actually reminded me of you."

"I'm honored."

"His last act of kindness, want to know what it was?"

Robert turned to face her and spoke in his usual sarcastic tone. "Enlighten me."

"Oh, I'm about to." She dug inside her purse, feeling for the small piece of paper. She held the crumpled ball in her hand, not bothering to unfold it.

"It reads something like this, I copied it from Daddy's will. Not verbatim, but close enough. If my one daughter, Norma Jean . . ." She stopped and looked at Robert before continuing, "Do you believe they actually named me that? If my one and only daughter Norma Jean Fulton-Bentley divorces, my entire estate, which I so humbly blah, blah, blah left her, is to be divided among the following charities. Blah, blah, blah."

Norma knew Robert was shocked because it took him a few minutes to recover.

"I'm sorry, Norma. I had no idea. It doesn't really matter since we're planning on keeping our marriage vows. You know, till death do us part."

"For once Robert we're in total agreement."

From inside the folded paper she re-moved a small revolver. Aiming at Robert's chest, she repeated his last words as she pulled back the hammer.

"Till death do us part."

Adam waited patiently for Blake to meet him at Parker's office. He'd made nine calls to his house and office number before he finally located him at Swan House on his cell phone. It was after midnight, and all he wanted to do was call it a night. He'd driven to Marietta and spent the morning with his father. He hadn't wanted to leave him. The look of hurt on his father's face was more than he could take. They'd talked about Eve and her possible relation-ship with Robert Bentley. His father hadn't been the fool he thought. When he asked why he'd changed his will, he'd explained that he hadn't really changed it at all. He'd only pretended, fearing Eve might find out. He was suspicious himself and had been for a number of years.

He explained how when Casey was about to return home, Eve started acting strange again, having her "spells." She'd become very secretive when she made visits to Memorial, wanting to know about the will, the business, and a host of other things.

The final straw for John had been when he learned she had fired Mort Sweeney. Adam still couldn't believe she'd done it. His father and Mort had been friends for more than fifty years.

And the icing on the cake was Mort's replacement. None other than Robert Bentley. That had been enough to persuade his father to stay at the Carriage House in Marietta until things were settled between him and Eve. He would file for divorce as soon as his lawyers could draw up the paperwork.

It was sad, Adam thought, to what lengths people would go out of greed.

Parker returned to the office carrying three mugs of freshly brewed coffee. Earlier he'd introduced Adam to Walter Watts, and now the three of them patiently waited for Blake.

"I think our prisoner is set for the night. The guy must be on drugs. I hate locking him up in a cell, but the guy has no ID on him, and I really feel bad after socking it to him. He's gonna have a helluva shiner in the morning."

"You want me to take a look at him, Parker?" Adam asked.

"It wouldn't hurt. Follow me."

"Mind if I tag along?" Walter asked.

"The more the merrier," Parker shot over his shoulder.

The cell located at the end of the hall was nothing more than a storage room with a few bars. A smart criminal would have no problem escaping, especially with the window above the cot.

Adam and Walter stood aside as Parker pulled the door open. The prisoner moaned and rolled over onto his back.

Adam stepped up to take a closer look. He gently took the man's head in his hand and prodded along his nose and beneath his eyes.

"Got a flashlight?"

Parker pulled one from his hip pocket and handed it to him. Adam lifted the man's lids and shined the light in his eyes. After several minutes, he gave the light back to the sheriff.

They went back to the front office, none of them wanting to speak in front of the man, who still remained groggy.

"What was he doing when you found him?" Adam asked.

"I thought he was about to break into the doc's house. Then I belted him a good one. He told me he was sick, looking for a doctor. Well, hell, after that I felt like a real asshole. I offered to drive him over to Memorial, that's when he jumped off the porch and tried to run. Think I hurt him?" Parker asked Adam.

"No. He'll be fine."

"You sure?"

Adam nodded, then addressed his next question to Walter. "Can you do a background check with that thing? And fingerprints?" Adam indicated the small laptop Walter placed on top of Parker's desk.

"This 'thing' as you call it can do all you mentioned and then some. Want to see?" Walter punched a button and the screen lit up with the GBI logo in bright yellow letters. He moved the mouse around a few times. Adam and Parker slid their chairs in for a closer look. "Watch this." Walter punched in a few codes, and paused while the computer searched.

"This particular program enables blood spatter analysts such as me to carry out highly sophisticated string analysis for up to fifty bloodstains on as many as twelve different surfaces at a crime scene." Walter's eyes lit up as he continued. "The data defining the strings to be attached to a blood spatter can then be entered via the keyboard or read from a file. Another program, actually one even more sophisticated, speeds up the analysis by using digital images of individual bloodstains created by a digital camera or a camcorder. This is what I plan to do with the blood splatters in question."

"Way over my head, that's for sure," Parker said.

"And mine. If I were to give you a fingerprint right now, could you run it?"

"Sure, bring it on."

"Sheriff, do you have a fingerprint kit around here?" Adam inquired.

"Somewhere, let me look." Parker got up and returned a few minutes later with the kit.

All eyes were on Adam as he made a second trip to the cell. Walter took the required prints. Their prisoner never moved a muscle.

"This will take a few minutes, guys. Parker, how about some more of that shitty coffee you just served us."

* * *

Eve stripped off her Ralph Lauren panties and bra and stood under the shower's soothing warm spray. She had wasted an entire evening waiting for Robert. Norma must've persuaded him to spend the evening with her; otherwise, Robert would've signaled for her. He knew she'd be waiting in the patient parking lot where she could see his office. The familiar flash of the lights being turned off and on three consecutive times never came.

They needed to meet to arrange their final plans. The moment they'd both been waiting for had arrived. With John out of the way, his declaration of mental incapacity just around the corner, and Robert about to share the helm with her at Worthington Enterprises, her lifelong goal was so nearly in her grasp, she could feel it.

No more begging for money. She would never have to touch John's flaccid penis again in hopes he'd lavish her with another extension on her credit card. She cringed when she thought about it. After Reed's wimpy penis and John's, Robert had been a gift from the penis fairy. And of course by the time she and John married and actually attempted to consummate their marriage he was too old to get it up, and when he did, he could hardly keep it up. Robert had spoiled her for any other man.

Then Casey had been released from the hospital. Robert explained to her how Macklin had skipped out after leaving him no other alternative than to agree to release Casey.

So far the attempts to keep her from remembering had failed. Robert wanted to take it a step further, but Eve didn't want to discuss his plans for Casey. And that pitiful excuse for an informant, Hank. She'd stopped by the carriage house before going upstairs. His truck wasn't parked in its usual spot, so Eve tapped on the door. Curious, she'd used her key to slip inside. Stunned by what she didn't see, she decided it was best that he'd packed up and left. Who knew how much more money he'd want to keep quiet. Thank God, he'd confessed to her when she questioned him about Casey's recent head injury.

She stepped out of the shower. Feeling better already, she tried to call Robert on his cell phone but there was no answer.

It would keep until tomorrow. Eve slid between the cool sheets of her king-size bed, closed her eyes, and immediately went to sleep.

She dreamed of a girl in a stained blue dress.

Chapter Twenty-seven

"You should be in bed after the traumatic day you've had," Blake said to Casey, as they traveled the quiet roads of Sweetwater.

"I've had a traumatic life. One more day doesn't seem to make much difference," Casey said.

"True. I still think you should have stayed at Swan House. Adam said he needed to talk to *me,* not us," Blake reminded her.

"I know. And I'll leave the room if he doesn't want to talk with me there. I just couldn't stay at that house. I'd wonder about Hank." And my mother, she wanted to add, but couldn't. Not yet. She needed more time to think about the crime her mother had known about all along. The crime she'd allowed to continue for nine long years.

Blake's cell phone rang. Casey hoped it wasn't the hospital. Not now.

"Dr. Hunter."

"Stop, slow down! When? Do they know who did it?" Blake pulled to the side of the road and jammed the car into park.

"What?" Casey whispered.

He held a finger to his lips.

"Hold on, I'll ask her." He placed his hand over the phone. "Casey, did you see Eve after the luncheon yesterday?"

She shook her head.

"No. We're on our way." Blake hit the end button and shifted into drive.

"What!"

"You're not going to believe this. That was Adam. Becky Trilling, Bentley's secretary, just called Sheriff Parker. Said she had to return to the office to do something, and when she stopped by his office to see if he needed anything else, she found Bentley. He'd been shot three times in the chest."

Stunned with the news, Casey could only stare ahead of her. "Is he . . . is he dead?"

"No, he's in surgery. Adam spoke with the surgeon. They're doing everything possible for him."

"Blake, I don't want to go to the hospital."

"Neither do I. We're going to Parker's."

"Do they know who . . ." Did they think her mother had shot Bentley? She might be crazy, and cruel, but Casey knew she wouldn't shoot a man.

"They're not sure. Parker called Brunswick for some extra deputies. They're sending them over on the ferry first thing in the morning."

"Blake," she paused, unsure how to word her next question, "if it were you, knowing what you know about Bentley, would you . . . you know. If you operated . . ."

"I've taken an oath, Casey. There's nothing in this world that could make me break that oath."

She released the breath she'd been holding. "Thank God!"

Blake slipped the BMW next to Adam's Jag, which was parked next to the sheriff's patrol car. Adam led them inside and introduced them to Walter. Casey knew she had a long night ahead of her when Adam passed out cups of coffee.

"What happened tonight?" Blake asked Adam.

"Bentley is just the beginning. His secretary hadn't been there, so it was lucky for him she had to go back. She thought he must've locked himself up in the office the night before because no one remembered seeing him yesterday. Parker's questioning the staff now.

"He took three shots in the chest, one of them is critical. According to the surgeon on duty, it doesn't look good."

"If anyone can patch the poor son of a bitch up, it's Byron," Blake said. "Bentley's lucky he was on tonight. He doesn't come to Memorial as often since setting up his practice in Brunswick."

Casey caught Blake's eye and nodded at Walter.

"I'm sorry," Walter said to Casey. "I don't usually stare. I'm trying to decide if you're right- or left-handed."

Relieved, Casey said, "Left."

"I knew it!" Walter jumped up and began pacing the small office.

"What are you talking about?" Casey asked.

"Roland had a few snapshots of the blood spatters. They weren't very good, some guy named Buddy took them. But they were good enough for me to scan into the system and get a readout."

"Walter's computer works miracles," Adam explained.

Casey's heartbeat accelerated, and for a minute she thought she would have a panic attack. *Is this the evidence the sheriff needed?* She forgot about Bentley while sharing Walter's excitement. "The reconstruction of the flight paths . . ."

"In laymen's terms, please," Adam interrupted.

"Keep in mind this is just professional guessing. The photographs I used aren't compatible with my system, but we're playing right now. The spatters, the width of the stain, the direction of the droplets, all indicate a right-handed person yielded the weapon. I'll know more after I take my own pictures and see the mattress."

Casey prayed he was right.

"Blake, Casey, would you both follow me for a minute? I think I've got something you might be interested in. Walter?" Adam said.

Casey looked to Blake, who just shrugged. The short walk down the hall led them to the "jail," where they observed an inmate. Casey swung around, hating the bars because they reminded her of her former room at Sanctuary.

Blake grabbed her arm and forced her to turn around and look at the inmate.

"Recognize him?"

Casey took a closer look at the man. His face was swollen and beginning to darken with purplish black bruises. "Dr. Dewitt!"

"The one and only," Adam said as he led the trio back to Parker's office.

"What is he doing here?" Casey asked.

"I wondered that myself until Walter worked his magic. At first I thought he looked familiar, but it's hard to tell with the swelling. Something about him bothered me. Walter checked his prints, and that's how we discovered who he was. He wasn't carrying any ID when Parker picked him up."

"What in the hell did Parker pick him up *for*?" Blake asked.

"This is the clincher. He found him at *your* house, trying to break in!"

"Why?" Casey and Blake said at the same time.

"We've tried to question him, but he keeps saying something about drugs. Then he mentioned the infamous Bentley, and I knew we'd better check further. Again, Walter's magic provided us with a quick answer."

Adam refilled their cups before continuing. "Blake, do you remember hearing about the young black girl over in Savannah they found hanging in that abandoned apartment fifteen or so years ago? The one who'd been released on a weekend furlough from Mercy?"

Blake rubbed his eyes, and leaned back into his chair. "Yeah, seems like I do. What's that got to do with anything?"

"According to Walter's magic box here"— Adam eyeballed Walter's laptop—"Dr. Macklin was the one who okayed the young girl's weekend furlough."

Curious, Casey sat up straight and watched the expression on Blake's face. Bewildered. Confused, maybe.

"I've been trying to call Macklin for days. His housekeeper told me he'd relocated someplace in Europe."

"She told me the same thing when I called earlier. She said she'd given Macklin your message when he called in. He said he would call you soon."

"What does this have to do with anything?" Casey asked.

"Quite possibly everything," Adam told her. "There's more. It seems her family suspected her death wasn't a suicide as the Savannah PD claimed. They begged and pleaded with the authorities to investigate her former lover, but the police never took them seriously."

"Where did you get all this information?" Blake asked.

"The magic box. Walter's GBI, don't forget. He has access to records and files all over the country.

"Amy's family finally hired a private detective, Dick Johnson, to investigate their daughter's death. And while it's never been proven in a court of law, Johnson was sure the young girl was murdered by her lover." Adam paused and looked at Casey, then at Blake. "Her lover was Jason Dewitt, grandson of the honorable Judge William Dewitt from one of Savannah's finest families. According to the autopsy report, she was pregnant.

"Not long after the girl died, Jason went away to Harvard. Macklin was fired from Mercy and termed a 'no hire.' In just a few short weeks, Macklin went to work for Bentley at Sanctuary."

"I knew I recognized that name!" Casey cried out. "He gave me the creeps the other day in his office. I remember hearing Bentley mention his name once while I waited for Dr. Macklin outside his office!"

"Are you thinking what I'm thinking?" Blake asked Adam.

"You bet. Now all we have to do is prove it."

"Prove what?" Casey said to the two men.

"Bentley blackmailed Macklin."

"That's the dumbest thing I've ever heard. Explain it," Casey said.

"I'm not talking blackmail in the traditional sense of the word, Casey. If Bentley had something to hold over Dr. Macklin's head, wouldn't Macklin be obliged to do as he ordered? To keep his job?" Adam looked at the three of them.

"But what could Bentley possibly need Dr. Macklin to do? If it's drugs, Bentley could get all he wanted from Sanctuary; he didn't need Macklin for that." Casey stood up and began pacing the small office.

Adam and Blake looked at one another, then at her. Blake spoke first. "Casey, didn't you say you spent the past ten years in a fog?"

"It was the medication. Sometimes when I remembered, I wouldn't swallow the pills they gave to me. Then when it seemed like things weren't in such a fog, one of the orderlies would give me a shot. Doctor's orders." When it came, realization was swift.

"Does this mean for the past ten years Robert Bentley blackmailed Dr. Macklin to keep me drugged?"

"You're not going to believe this!" Parker said as he burst through the door.

"Try us," Blake said.

"Norma Bentley just wrecked her car in front of the hospital. She's gonna be okay, but I wonder if she knows Robert is in surgery with a gunshot wound."

"This night is full of surprises," Adam said as he proceeded to fill Parker in on all that he'd missed.

"I'm thinking my services are of no further use, Roland. What do you say?" Walter said to all of them.

"I say we call it a night. I've got a genuine prisoner to baby-sit, and that cot in my office is starting to look good. It's 3 A.M., and I don't know about the rest of you, but I haven't seen this much excitement in Sweetwater since . . ."

Casey trudged downstairs with her eyes half-closed. The scent of freshly brewed coffee wafted up to the landing as she hurried to the kitchen. When she saw her mother seated at the long wooden table talking to Flora, she almost fainted.

"What are you doing here?" Casey knew she sounded hateful, but she didn't care.

"You're in a mood, I can see. I live here in case you forgot."

"I'm sorry. It's been a rough night. Morning, Flora." She helped herself to a cup of coffee. "I'm just surprised to see you. I figured you'd be with Robert. At the hospital." She glared at her mother, hoping to get a reaction out of her.

The woman was cold as marble. "It's been all over the radio this morning," she said. "When I woke up and heard the news, I almost died. Then to hear that poor Norma was nearly killed, why I'm not even sure if I can get through the day. First John, now Robert, and poor, poor Norma."

"Did they say anything about Bentley's condition?"

"Guarded is what the TV and radio are reporting," Flora said. "I'm sure Mr. Adam and Mr. Blake will tell us if they find anything out. Norma is in stable condition; she suffered a broken leg and three cracked ribs. Reports say she'd been drinkin'."

"That doesn't come as a surprise to me," Eve said. "Yesterday when she left the luncheon she could barely stand up.

"Now, Casey, I told you when the time came we'd see about your hair and a makeover. This is the time. We can have lunch. Spend the day doing 'girl stuff.' What do you think?"

Casey realized it was her mother who should've spent the past ten years in Sanctuary. "Are you serious? Today?"

"It'll be good for you to get away, Casey. Go with your momma and enjoy yourself." Flora smiled at her. "You need to do that girl stuff your momma's talkin' about."

"You're right, Flora. In spite of all that's happening, it's past time for Mother and me to spend some time together." She narrowed her gaze at her mother, then forced herself to smile.

Spending the day with her mother was the last thing she wanted to do. But she would go, in the hope that maybe, just maybe, Eve could offer up some kind of explanation for allowing her stepson to abuse her only child.

* * *

The Sweetwater ferry was empty because virtually everyone who lived on the island was attending a vigil in the parking lot at Memorial Hospital. Casey and her mother, along with two elderly ladies, were the only passengers making the trip to Brunswick.

Casey gazed out at the coastline, where white puffs of smoke billowed from the smokestacks, courtesy of Worthington Enterprises. Her mother stood next to her, and Casey felt her icy glare penetrating right through her.

"You know you can stop the pretense," her mother said.

Casey whirled completely around, shocked when she saw the grimace on her mother's face. Not the sweet, silly smile of a slightly deranged, one-too-many-glasses-of-bubbly-genteel-Southern-lady-from-a-fine-family she pretended to be.

Wicked came to mind, reminding her of that day in the closet when she'd found Ronnie's picture.

"I don't know what you're talking about,"

she muttered, dismayed at her mother's sudden shift of mood.

"Oh, I think you do. Tell me, something, Casey." Her mother walked toward the bow, Casey trailing behind her. Eve stopped, almost causing Casey to slam into her back. "This memory lapse of yours, just how lapsed is it?" A gust of wind lifted Eve's honey blond hair, the short strands catching her in the eye. She combed a hand through her hair, her glare never wavering. "Well?"

Casey looked around the deck, suddenly frightened. The two elderly women had gone belowdecks, and the crew was nowhere in sight.

"You know, Mother. I've recalled certain parts of my childhood." Casey paused. This was not the time or place for a confrontation. "But nothing important, at least I don't think so."

The relief on her mother's face was visible. "All those years on so many medications, if and when your memory returns, you'll probably never be able to distinguish what's real anyway. I'm sure it's for the best."

Alarms sounded in Casey's head. How could she have been so stupid? Forgetting her fear of moments ago, she was about to ask her mother a question when a gush of the past flooded her brain.

A dead calm invaded her, swam through her as assuredly as blood surged through her veins. She let its serenity possess her. She floated on a plane unattainable to her before, soaring to an otherworldly realm of consciousness.

Then she remembered. She'd been in the shed with Ronnie. They'd fought. Then she went to her room. Hours later, a shadow. An unknown presence invaded her space. A cloak of darkness blanketed her. She must have blacked out.

"Oh my God!" Casey's hand flew to her mouth. She looked at her mother, who was watching her through narrowed eyes. She inched back toward the bow, wanting to put as much distance as possible between them.

"What is it, Casey?" Her mother came toward her, forcing her to take another step back.

"You were there." Casey's hands trembled as she inched even farther toward the bow. "In my room . . . I remember the shadow!"

Her mother gave a demonic laugh. "I was right after all. You do remember!" Eve appeared to wage a silent battle with herself before centering her hard blue gaze on Casey. "Yes, I was there that evening. You should be glad, too. If I hadn't been there, there's no telling how far Ronnie would've gone."

Casey's burst of anger made her brave. "Did you know he'd been coming to my room for nine years! Nine long, horrid, miserable years!" She was screaming, and she didn't care. She wanted to slap the smirk off her mother's face.

"Oh stop it, Casey. You're just like that self-righteous, do-gooder father of yours! If you were so miserable, you should have told me. I would have done something about it sooner."

Casey clenched her fists, then shoved her hands in her pockets. She could feel her heart pounding in her rib cage. Her past clear now, she wanted answers only her mother could provide. She forced herself to take a deep breath before continuing.

"How could you, Mother! I tried several times to tell you about Ronnie. You were always with Robert Bentley or John Worthington. Why, Mother, can you just tell me, why? How could you allow that deranged psycho to rape me!" She wanted to smash her fist into her mother's face, wanted to obliterate her indignant smirk into oblivion.

For the second time Eve appeared to be in a battle with herself. Her decision made, she spoke. Her voice was sure and clear, her blue eyes glassy, almost crystal-like. Casey knew right then that her mother was truly insane. No sane woman would have allowed her child to be molested.

"Mother, how could you?" she shrieked. "Can you at least give me a goddamned reason for it? Maybe I can understand then. I need to understand!" Angry tears slid down her cheeks as she stood in front of her mother, waiting for an explanation, anything so she could begin to understand the woman who called herself mother.

Eve sighed. "Oh, I suppose I do owe you some sort of explanation. It was all so long ago." She looked over the ferry's bow, then sat on the bench on the starboard side of the vessel. Casey sat opposite her, waiting.

"You don't know what it's like to be poor, Casey. You're lucky."

"I'd rather be poor than raped!"

"It started the day I met Robert. I went to his office right after you were born. We fell in love, and it hasn't stopped. Ronnie found out about us. By then John and I planned to marry. That crazy boy threatened me. Threatened everything Robert and I had worked for." Her mother took on a faraway look as she went on.

"But what about me, Mother? What about all the horrid things Ronnie did to me?"

Chapter Twenty-eight

Eve picked up the first thing in sight and sailed it at her stepson. Too bad it was her mother-in-law's antique lamp. She was dead anyway, she'd never know.

"Listen," she said, "I know what you've been doing all these years. Don't think for a minute I don't!"

"Yeah, old woman, I know you knew about me 'n' Casey girl. And I'm thinkin' while you laid in that there bed of yours you jus' mighta liked hearing us." Ronnie laughed. "You know she went to visit Doc Hunter today?"

"Who told you that?" she asked.

"I didn't have to be told. I followed her. Hell, I sat right in that dumb doctor's office and listened at the top of the stairs. She was knocked up, all right. I was thinkin' of runnin' over to Swan House, before she stabbed

me. I thought ol' John might want to know what kinda woman he'd be marryin'." He laughed again.

"You wouldn't dare!" she screamed.

"Oh, yes I would. Yes, I would. Matter a fact, I been thinkin' about limpin' over there later. Maybe tomorrow morning. After me 'n' Casey, well, you know tonight."

Ronnie left then, thank God, because she needed to think.

Sure that Casey's child belonged to Ronnie, Eve knew she'd have to arrange for her to have an abortion. Robert would know who to call.

Think! Think! Think!

She'd suspected Ronnie was messing around with Casey, but had no idea he'd actually had intercourse with her. Casey should have told her when it first happened, but then again, Eve thought, they weren't blood-related, it could be that Casey liked Ronnie's visits. It didn't matter now, she told herself, what mattered was Ronnie keeping his big mouth shut.

Why she'd kept him after Reed's death baffled her. She really didn't like him, she had to admit, but he could be amusing at times. All those trips to his school, they'd both had a good laugh. Too bad Carolyn's family hadn't wanted him. Eve really didn't blame them. Why would they want to raise a child who'd been fathered by his grandfather? A genetic screwup. Made sense to her.

She placed a call to Robert at Sanctuary. He'd tell her what to do.

"What is it, Eve? You shouldn't be calling me here. If Worthington finds out about us, you can kiss that mansion and all those prosperous holdings of his good-bye."

"It's Ronnie. He knows about us. I told him I knew about him and Casey. He threatened to go to John. I'm scared, Robert. That little son of a bitch will do what he's threatened."

"Where is he now?" Robert asked.

"He just took off. And Robert, guess what?"

"I don't like guessing games, Eve, you know that."

"She's pregnant. Ronnie's threatened to tell John that, too. He'll never marry me if he thinks I've stood back and let this thing happen to my own daughter! God! I wish I'd given her to Gracie. I wasn't cut out for this motherhood business."

"Shut up, Eve, and listen. How often does he visit her room?"

"Almost every night, why?"

"I want you to cancel any plans you have tonight," Robert's strong voice was comforting. He'd tell her what to do.

"I don't have any."

"Good. Where's the girl right now?"

"She's upstairs in her room, why?"

"Do what you have to do to keep her there. You'll think of something; you've always had a large supply of tricks."

"Robert!"

"Oh, damn, Eve this is important. Listen: Do you want all that money? Worthington can't last much longer. If he does we'll help him out."

"Robert, what do you mean? Surely you're not planning . . ."

"No Eve, I'm not. Now listen."

Eve waited in the dark, hot closet for Casey's bedroom door to open. Casey had been asleep all day and it had been easy to slip into the closet. Something was definitely wrong with the girl. Well, she couldn't help that.

She heard the creak of the door and knew it was just a matter of time. She peered through a crack in the door and watched as Ronnie stood next to Casey's bed. Casey lay curled up in the fetal position against the wall.

For a minute she was tempted to run out of the closet and stop him, but the thought of her and Robert with all of John's holdings kept her rooted in place.

Ronnie dropped his pants on the floor and Eve watched as he piled on top of her daughter. Casey wasn't putting up a fight, so maybe she'd been right after all. Casey must enjoy Ronnie's visits.

She saw Casey's arm reach over to the nightstand and grab ahold of something shiny. The moonlight filtered in through the lace curtains, allowing Eve a shadowed picture of the couple on the bed.

Casey struggled against Ronnie, and that was when Eve made her move.

Casey held a letter opener in her hand.

Eve ran to the side of the bed and yanked the letter opener from Casey's hand.

He had to be stopped. She knew about the scene in the shed and his injuries. Though serious, they certainly weren't fatal.

That was about to change.

Without another thought Eve plunged the dull blade into Ronnie's neck, sending blood *flying everywhere. She thought she would vomit. Ronnie's body pulsed one last time, then flopped on top of Casey.*

Casey had passed out. Before she could think, Eve placed the letter opener in her daughter's hand and disappeared downstairs to call Robert to finish the job.

"And all those years you allowed Robert to instruct Dr. Macklin to drug me, so I wouldn't remember?" Shock didn't come close to the emotions racking her body and soul.

Eve looked up at her, her age suddenly visible. "And it would have worked if that Dr. Macklin hadn't been cleared. He would have continued to give you the medication as Robert ordered. John can't hang on much longer, then it's all ours."

Her mother's eyes took on that glassy look again, and this time Casey was truly frightened. "Mother, what if Robert doesn't make it? What if he dies, then what?"

"Then I'll have it all. I thought about that, too. After Norma left Robert's office last night, I followed her. I saw her toss the gun on the side of the road. Hell, she almost ran over some poor fellow."

Dewitt, Casey thought.

"Mother, you need to get help. Maybe Blake or Adam will know of a good doctor." Casey walked toward her mother, who stood at the tip of the bow.

"No, that will never happen! I'm Eve Worthington, matriarch of the family. I'm somebody now, can't you see that?" Tears flowed freely down her mother's face. They were approaching the coastline, and Casey's vision blurred from her own tears.

"I'm not that poor white trash anymore! Don't you get it! I'll never have to wear somebody's used dresses, never have to hang my head in shame! Never! I'm somebody now! I'm Eve Worthington!" Her mother's cries were pitiful.

Casey took a step toward her mother, her hand held out, reaching for her. "C'mon, Momma, let's go below. We're almost there, now."

"No! You'll never see me in a place like that!" her mother shouted, raising her fists high above her. "Never!"

Before Casey could grab on to her mother's outstretched hand, a whirl of pale pink Chanel hurled itself over the bow into the blackish green depth of the murky water below.

Epilogue

The sheer lace curtains billowed as the cool autumn breeze wafted through the partially open window. The soft tinkle of wind chimes created a mellow tune for the frogs and crickets who harmonized in the background.

A faint cry stirred the woman in bed. She rolled over and reached for the pillow next to her. Finding it empty, she came fully awake. Slipping her feet into the red slippers placed on the floor next to her bed, she went in search of the sound.

"You should be sleeping," Casey said to Blake. "Too many late nights at the hospital. Here," she said, reaching for the infant, cuddling him in her arms.

"It's hard to believe, isn't it?" She sat in the rocker next to the cradle Adam had given his godson on the day he was born. She continued to rock Jonathan Adam Blakely Hunter until his cries stopped.

Casey held her son close to her and breathed in his clean, powdery baby scent. She looked down at his sleeping face and marveled that he belonged to her. With his black curly hair and Blake's mahogany-colored eyes, her son was sure to be a heartbreaker in the years to come.

"This will be the first time I've gone out socially since John's birth. I'm looking forward to it," Casey said. "Two months already!"

"So am I. Flora and Mabel have prepared a feast, according to Julie. Said she'd never seen so much food for a little baby's christening."

"Well, I'm sure between you and that stepbrother of mine, there won't be any leftovers." Casey laughed.

"I'm glad you and Adam get along so well. I told you he was an okay kind of guy." Blake ran a hand across his son's cheek, then kissed his fingertip and dotted it on the tip of Casey's nose.

"We've really become close this last year. And John treats me like a daughter. I feel so lucky, Blake. In spite of . . . well, in spite of it all."

"Me, too, but hey, let's not let the past cloud our future."

"I'm not, but so many people's lives were hurt because of my mother and Robert Bentley's greed." Casey looked out the window, remembering Robert's attempt to run her down, the terrifying phone calls, the glass her mother put in the bottle of lotion. All those terrible "accidents" in the hope that she'd go over the edge and they could send her back to Sanctuary. Hank's feeble effort to harm her. Casey often thought of the child she'd carried, fathered by Ronnie, and knew her miscarriage had been a blessing.

She needed to remember the few good times, too. She remembered her grandmother Gracie and all the good times she'd had with her father and Flora. She even remembered Kyle, and their so-called relationship, and was thankful they'd never consummated it. And her love for Blake had been the bright light at the end of a long, dark tunnel. Had she not kept that thought close to her heart, she didn't know if she could've made it. With Adam's help she'd found a good therapist, who was amazed at

Casey's progress; she'd told her so on her last visit.

"Stop and think, honey, how lucky they were. Robert and Norma both lived, though I'm sure Robert would rather be elsewhere. I can't see him adjusting to prison life."

"I know," Casey said, "and I'm truly thankful he survived, though at the time I wanted him to die. He had his hand in everything, didn't he?"

Blake stood behind his wife as she rocked back and forth. "That he did. A shame about Dewitt, though. I guess he couldn't stand the thought of being punished for killing that poor girl. It was ironic how he hung himself in the same apartment building he killed her in."

"It is. And poor Dr. Macklin, his career almost ruined. You know"—Casey looked up into Blake's eyes as he stood above her—"I thought I would hate him for allowing Bentley to keep me drugged all those years, but I don't. I heard some people in town talking about him last week. They said he's doing quite well in Europe."

"That's what I love about you, you're forgiving, kind, decent, a loving wife and mother, not to mention, sexy as hell."

"Go on," Casey prompted.

"Do you have all day?"

"And that's why I love you so. We started off on rough ground, didn't we?"

"And it's been smooth sailing ever since. And if you don't get up and get your tush in gear, we're going to be late." Blake took baby John from her and gently placed his sleeping son in his bassinet.

"You still want to go alone?" Blake asked.

"If I'm ever to have any closure, I need to do this. I can't let this darkness taint our future. I have a son to care for, a husband to love. I'm somebody now." Casey recalled her mother's words.

"We won't get started until you get there. Get this, Parker's actually bringing a date."

Casey stood up and peered at her beautiful, perfect son. "You won't be able to start because I'm taking the merchandise with me. Who's Parker bringing anyway?"

"Brenda." Blake threw his head back and roared with laughter.

"You're not serious! An interesting couple. Blake, do you think John and Flora will ever, you know, make the connection?" Casey asked as she walked down the long hall of Adam's old beach house, now her and

Blake's temporary home while their dream home was being built.

Blake followed his wife to the bathroom and watched as she removed her clothes and stood under the shower.

"I think they made the connection a long time ago, it's just taken it a while to spark."

"I'm glad for them. I really love her, you know."

"I do, and I also know this, if you don't get dressed, you're going to be late, and then you'll have to explain to Father Troy why."

Casey stepped out of the shower into her husband's arms. Safe. He never failed to make her feel safe. She couldn't believe how good her life was.

She checked her son's car seat one last time before settling herself in the driver's seat. Blake had taught her to drive right after they were married, and in honor of receiving her license at the tender age of twenty-nine, he'd given her the bright yellow bug as a gift.

She was careful, driving slow. The light of her life rested in the backseat, and she would do whatever it took to protect him. Today was another step in protecting her son. She needed this final closure, the end, so she could finally free herself of the night-marish relationship she'd endured as a child.

She pulled the bright yellow VW into the Sanctuary parking lot. She needed to see, to make sure. She'd gone over this a million times in her head. After John's birth, she had known this day would come. It had to, if she was ever to free herself from the past.

With her son cradled in her arms, Casey stood on the steps of the dilapidated building she had called home for ten years. Casting a glance at the second floor, she spied her former room. The very room that had held her captive for ten long years now imprisoned her mother.

Casey saw the shadow at the window and headed back to her car, to her life. A thrill tingled down her spine, and her belly knotted in anticipation. For the first time in her adult life, she was free.

Truly free.